Criminal Misdeeds

A Carrie Shatner Mystery

Randee Green

coffeetownpress

Kenmore, WA

coffeetownpress

For more information go to: www.coffeetownpress.com
www.randeegreen.com

This is a work of fiction. Names, characters, places, brands, media, and incidents are either the product of the author's imagination or are used fictitiously.

Cover design by Sabrina Sun
Author photo by Paris Bretherick

Criminal Misdeeds
Copyright © 2018 by Randee Green

ISBN: 978-1-60381-709-7 (Trade Paper)
ISBN: 978-1-60381-710-3 (eBook)

Library of Congress Control Number: 2018940116

Printed in the United States of America

To my dog, Molly.
1997 – 2007
You are the love of my life and my best friend.
Sissy loves you.

Acknowledgments

---◆---

My path to publication has been a long one, and I have to thank my second grade teacher, Mrs. Patricia Ziegler, for putting me on that path when she read *Little House in the Big Woods* to my class. I also have to thank Laura Ingalls Wilder for showing me that little girls can grow up to be writers.

Thank you to Molly and Snookums for providing the support and love that only furry friends can provide.

Thank you to my mom for (mostly) not complaining every time that I've handed you a manuscript with the expectation that you find all of my grammatical and punctuation errors. And thank you to my dad for subjecting me to pro wrestling, NASCAR, The Doors, Neil Diamond, and *Star Trek: The Original Series* at a young age. That being said, I also need to thank my captain, William Shatner, simply because I said I would.

Thank you to John Bowers and Nina Solomon for providing feedback on the early drafts of *Criminal Misdeeds*.

Thank you to my wonderful agent, Jessica Alvarez, for believing in me. I knew you were the agent for me when you requested more pro wrestling in future Carrie Shatner Mysteries. You asked, and I delivered. Thank you so much, Jessica, for not giving up on me and Carrie until you found us a home at Camel Press.

And, of course, to Jennifer McCord, and everyone else at Camel Press, thank you so much for all of your hard work and support.

Last, but not least, I need to thank Carrie Shatner. Like Athena, who came kicking and screaming into the mythological world directly from Zeus's forehead, one day you sprang from my brain and demanded that I write your story.

Chapter One

———————— ◆ ————————

I come from a long line of criminals.

Moonshiners, rumrunners, and drug dealers. Horse thieves and carjackers. Bank robbers, burglars, pickpockets, and con artists. And then there has been the occasional killer. You name it, whether it's a felony or a misdemeanor, somewhere along the line a member of my family has committed it.

As far back as the Shatner family could be traced—from southern England to the mountains of western North Carolina, and now to the Piney Woods of East Texas—we had been breaking the law. And running from it, too.

It was a family tradition.

You see, the Shatners have never swum in the baby pool of life. We've always been out in the deep end, and we jumped in headfirst.

As for me, every day I fight my genetic predisposition to break the law. Some days I've been more successful than others. You see, I can't break the law when I'm the one who is supposed to be upholding it.

My name is Carrie Shatner, and for the last three-and-a-half years I have worked as a detective and crime scene technician for the Wyatt County Sheriff's Department in East Texas. That would put my Bachelor of Science in Criminal Justice from Sam Houston State University to good use except there wasn't a whole heck of a lot of serious crime in Wyatt County. I mainly sat behind my desk all day, twiddling my thumbs, playing Sudoku, and keeping up with my various social media accounts.

While my official job was to process crime scenes and deal with all parts of criminal investigations, my unofficial job was to cover up my family's illegal activities and keep them out of jail. I'd be the first to admit that what I have been doing wasn't ethical. It was probably also criminal. I tried not to think about that too much. To be honest, I tried not to think about any of it too much. Most days I felt like quitting my job. Family obligation prevented that.

I'm not saying that all of the Shatners have been hardened criminals. Sure, most of the older ones were. But at least some of the younger ones shied away from the family business and seemed to be sticking to the straight and narrow. And they were the reason why I do what I do. Yes, I clean up the crimes of the guilty. But I do it to protect the innocent.

These days, the laws my various family members break have been fairly minor ones. Okay, some were still kind of major. But it was nothing compared to what we used to engage in. I mean, I'm pretty sure we were no longer involved in contract killing or organized crime.

What I did know was that my great-uncles had a moonshine still out in the woods and a marijuana crop concealed in a bunch of old Cold War bomb shelters. Every time I caught one of my family members selling the homebrew or the pot, they would promise me it was the last time. I didn't believe them. I didn't arrest them either, because I knew it wouldn't stop them. It would also infuriate the rest of the family. And, while tempting, that wasn't a risk I was quite willing to take. At least not yet.

Occasionally, one of the younger Shatners would steal a car or deface some public property or get busted for underage drinking. The older Shatners were always getting nabbed for public indecency and public intoxication. Some of them were also heavily involved in insurance scams. And then there had been the occasional assault. But we hadn't killed anyone—accidently or on purpose—in years. Or, if someone had, I didn't know about it.

When you got down to it, the majority of the bad things that the Shatners have done were just plain dumb. And, as far as I knew, being stupid wasn't illegal. We would have been in serious trouble otherwise.

I DON'T WANT YOU TO go into this thinking that all of the Shatners were bad people. Most of them have just been a little misguided.

At least that's what I kept telling myself.

Until I found the body.

Chapter Two

———————————•———————————

W hen I was a kid, there was nothing that I loved more than when the whole extended Shatner family would get together. My various cousins and I would run wild while the adults would sit around coming up with new schemes to get away with breaking the law. Sure, most of those get-togethers would end in a near disaster, but, as a kid, it always seemed like a lot of fun.

Now that I was just on the wrong side of thirty—and working for the sheriff's department—there was nothing that scared me more than a Shatner family get-together. When the whole, or even part, of the family gathered together in one place, there was no predicting what might happen. All I know is that something bordering on the criminal would most likely happen.

Just my luck, the Shatners would have get-togethers every chance they got.

It was just after midnight on New Year's Day, and my family was welcoming in the New Year with drunken revelry and illegal fireworks. Despite the freezing temperatures, almost the entire extended Shatner family was gathered on the Wyatt County Fairgrounds midway for the unprofessional, but always entertaining, fireworks show.

Aside from the few people who had passed out from too much alcohol consumption, I was the only one who wasn't watching the fireworks that were detonating almost directly above our heads. That's because I was too busy keeping an eye on the idiots setting off the fireworks.

Mixing my family, alcohol, and fireworks was a recipe for disaster. Over the years, I'd tried to encourage my family members to think of safety first. It was more of an empty gesture considering none of them seemed inclined to take my advice. It was about like telling my family to drink responsibly. It wasn't going to happen. The Shatners might have adopted safe sex, but the idea of ensuring their own and each other's welfare while setting off fireworks had not transferred over.

Needless to say, these Shatner family get-togethers usually ended with a trip to the emergency room or with a visit from the fire department or the sheriff's department.

For the first time in at least eight years, we had managed to avoid all three. And I planned to keep it that way. Even though it was just after twelve-thirty, I was beginning to think that it was time to shut down the party. I just had to wait until the right moment to do it. If I tried to send everyone home before we ran out of fireworks, my family would mutiny against me. But if I waited too long after the last of the fireworks were set off, someone would conveniently remember that he had a few sticks of dynamite stashed in the back of his truck and wind up blowing up something or someone. It had happened before and it would happen again.

One-by-one, with no precision or timing, fifteen to twenty fireworks shot skyward and exploded into multicolored sparkles above us in the starlit Texas sky. I wouldn't call it a grand finale, but it was definitely the end of the fireworks.

The embers were still falling when I reached for the bullhorn I had stashed under my chair. Utilizing the bullhorn's siren and flashing red light, I brought my family's attention back down to ground level. The Shatners, who had been carrying on and cheering, started screaming. A few of them even dove for cover—a deep-rooted reaction when they hear sirens and see flashing lights.

"All right everybody, the party's over. You don't have to go home, but you can't stay here …." The bullhorn amplified my voice and sent it out over the fairgrounds. "On second thought, go home and stay there."

Not surprisingly, my announcement was met with a chorus of boos and accusations that I was trying to ruin everybody's good time. Beer cans and bottles, a mason jar, and a prosthetic leg whizzed through the air and just narrowly missed hitting me.

"If you want to throw things, please throw them into a trash can as you leave." Ducking to the side, I used the bullhorn to deflect a beer can that one of my cousins threw at me. "I know that was you, Dale. Don't think I didn't see you."

"Hey, Carrie! What crawled up your butt and died?" asked one of my more inebriated relatives.

"Yeah, you ain't no fun anymore!" another yelled.

"How 'bout you go home while the rest of us stay here," suggested a third, prompting a short-lived chant of "You leave! We stay!"

"There's a fine line between having fun and accidently killing ourselves," I said. "Y'all have been toeing that line all evening. Now grab your things and get out of here."

With some not-so-gentle urging, I got the Shatners rounded up and moving. I allowed them to gather up their chairs, children, and other personal belongings before I herded them towards the fairground's exit and the parking lot beyond. The week before I had drawn names from a hat to determine who would be the designated drivers following the party. Unfortunately I hadn't been able to keep an eye on all of them, and at least half of my designated drivers were the drunkest people in attendance.

After getting all of the Shatners into the parking lot, I closed the gate behind them. I then wandered back into the empty fairgrounds, ready to do one final check before I could go home. It was another downfall to being the responsible one.

The Wyatt County Fairgrounds, located a few miles west of the town of Holler, Texas, wasn't much to brag about. It was basically just a four-acre area enclosed by a seven-foot high wrought-iron fence. There were three permanent buildings on site—a block of public bathrooms to the right of the front entrance, a small, one-story building to the left of the entrance, and a large, multipurpose building at the back. There was also a row of carnival game stands and an open-air pavilion along the one side. I would have to check to make sure all of the buildings were locked and that there weren't any Shatners passed out anywhere before I could go home.

I checked the bathrooms first—going down the row of stalls and kicking open each door to make sure that no one was crouched on the toilet seats, hoping to evade my search. After clearing both the men's and the women's bathrooms, I turned off the building's interior and exterior lights, and locked the doors. With the building's exterior lights off, the only lighting that illuminated the fairgrounds, aside from the moon shine, were the overhead parking lot lights. Prior to setting off the fireworks, I had turned off the fairground's overhead lights.

Kicking spent fireworks out of the way, I trudged to the back of the fairgrounds and yanked on the door handles of the main entrance into the multipurpose building. Weeks before, while the Shatners were still in the planning stages of the party, I had deemed the multipurpose building off-limits. I knew that by the end of the night, the smaller building and the bathrooms would be trashed. I wasn't going to let my family destroy every building on the fairgrounds.

After confirming that the main entrance was still locked, I went around the left side of the building to check the side doors. I then headed for the ten-foot wide alley that ran behind the building. And that was when I hit a snag. The alley was pitch-black. The only thing I could make out was way down at the other end of the building where a shaft of light fell across the dumpster. I didn't feel like going all the way out to my car to get a flashlight, but I had no desire to wander down the darkened alley. I could have skipped checking the building's back door, but that would have meant shirking my duties.

As I attempted to tug my knit hat down to cover my ears, my long, brown curls got in the way. Thanks to my mother, I was raised to believe that the higher the hair, the closer to God. Therefore, my teased out, curly hairstyles usually come straight out of the 1980s. I heard it was a good decade—made even better because I made my appearance into this world towards the end of it.

Giving up on thawing out my frozen earlobes, I shoved my hands into my coat pockets, where my numb fingers wrapped around my cell phone. My cell phone that had a flashlight app. Behold the wonders of modern technology. The flashlight wasn't very strong, but it would get the job done.

Halfway down the alley, I came to the back door. After jiggling the door handle and confirming that the back door was still locked, I used the flashlight to light up the ground as I nearly sprinted towards the other end of the alley.

Shimmying my way through the narrow gap between the building and the dumpster, I did my best not to brush up against the disgusting dumpster. I was almost through when the heel of my right foot came down on top of a softball-sized object.

"Ouch!" My foot slid off the object, sharply jerking my ankle to the side. I lost my balance and stumbled into the corner of the grimy dumpster. "Ewww. Gross."

Shuffling my feet, I hobbled around the corner of the dumpster. I then waved the flashlight beam over the ground. Earlier that night, when I had gone around and made sure the big building was locked up, there hadn't been anything on the ground by the dumpster. Just a few hours later there were rocks of various sizes scattered around the front and side of the dumpster. The largest was the softball sized one I stepped on. The smallest were no bigger than pebbles.

"Where did you come from?" Kneeling on the ground so that I could get a better look, I realized that the rocks were part of a cinderblock that had broken apart on the ground in front of the dumpster. While I hadn't paid too much attention to the dumpster earlier, I knew that the cinderblock had been on top of the dumpster and in one piece. "What happened back here?"

A simple explanation would be that the cinderblock had either slid off or been knocked off the lid, and smashed into smaller pieces when it hit the ground. But that wouldn't explain why the dumpster lid was ajar.

Despite wanting nothing more than to go home, I knew I had to investigate what happened to the cinderblock and the dumpster. It was possible that one of my family members used the dumpster, but I had my doubts that any of the Shatners had come all the way to the back of the fairgrounds to throw something out. Not when there was another dumpster by the front gates.

Thankful that I was wearing gloves—because I wouldn't want to touch the bird crap encrusted dumpster lid without them—I took a deep breath, shoved the dumpster lid up against the fence, and jumped back. When no one popped out of the dumpster screaming "Gotcha!", I crept closer and peeked inside the putrid, stinking black hole of industrial-grade plastic.

My phone's flashlight beam illuminated a worn men's work boot. It wouldn't have been a startling find, except that the boot was attached to a leg. And the leg was attached to the rest of a body. The person's head was tucked into the far corner of the dumpster—too far away for my flashlight beam to reach.

"Oh, for God's sake, not again," I muttered.

At nearly every single Shatner family get-together, someone would have a little too much to drink and then wander off and pass out. Passing out in a dumpster was new, but it wasn't the worst. It didn't even make the top ten. Years before, at a funeral, I found my Uncle Vernon taking a nap in a casket. Thankfully he had removed his dead mother-in-law's body first. But Uncle Vernon, who was my great aunt's middle child, had always had been a special one. He was currently one of only two Shatner's in trouble with the law. Vernon was stuck on house arrest following his second DUI charge. I didn't know what he did with his ankle monitor considering he was at the New Year's Eve party, drinking and carrying on with everyone else.

"Hey!" I kicked the side of the dumpster, bruising a couple of my toes in the process. Under normal circumstances I would have left the person in the dumpster to sleep it off. But the temperatures had already dipped into the upper twenties, and I didn't want anyone freezing to death on my watch. "Come on, time to get up."

The man—I was assuming it was a man because of the footwear—didn't even budge.

"Seriously, how much have you had to drink?" I snatched up a small piece of the cinderblock and hurled it at the man, striking him in the back. No response. "All right, buddy, this is just getting annoying. I'm not crawling in there to wake you up."

Grabbing the cinderblock that was holding down the other side of the split lid, I slid it off the edge of the dumpster and set it on the ground by my feet. I then heaved that half of the lid up against the fence. Stepping up onto the intact cinderblock, I leaned over the side of the dumpster and flashed my light towards the man's head hoping that I could determine which relative he was.

My flashlight beam fell across the back of his head.

The bloody, caved-in back of his head.

"Oh shit! Oh shit! Oh shit!"

I fell off the cinderblock, twisting my other ankle, as I scrambled away from the dumpster. After putting some distance between me and the dumpster, I smacked a hand over my chest as I sucked in a deep breath and tried to slow down my heart rate.

I hadn't imbibed any alcoholic beverages throughout the evening, so I knew I wasn't having a drunken delusion. And I had kept a safe distance from anyone who was smoking pot, so it also wasn't a contact high messing with my imagination. That left two options—my family was playing an elaborate prank on me or there was a dead body in the dumpster.

After exhausting my personal dictionary of curse words, I felt calm enough to approach the dumpster again. I rubbed my hands over my blue eyes to be sure my vision was clear, and then I tentatively peered inside the dumpster to confirm that the back of the man's head was still caved-in and covered with blood.

"Definitely not a prank." Starting somewhere around my spleen, a small, kernel-sized bit of anxiety began to bounce around my body like the ball in a pinball game. The kernel shot upward and lodged in my throat where it increased in size, choking me as I tried to breathe around it. Dropping to my knees, I pressed both hands over my mouth and fought back a scream. "Oh no. This can't be happening."

Back when I lived in Nashville, and worked for the Nashville Crime Scene Investigation Section, I used to deal with dead bodies on a fairly frequent basis. And only rarely did it bother me. So I'm not saying I was freaking out over finding a dead body—though it was extremely creepy finding one in the dumpster. What had me on the verge of an anxiety attack was the fear that it was one of my family members.

I scrambled up the side of the dumpster and then swung one leg over the side. I was about to drop into the stinking abyss when my forensic science training kicked in. It hit me that, by climbing into the dumpster, I would be contaminating the crime scene.

And, let's face it, this most certainly was a crime scene. No one climbs into a dumpster and then bashes in the back of his own head. Someone had either killed the man in the dumpster, or killed him elsewhere and then disposed of him there.

Climbing down from the dumpster, I put some distance between me and the dead body. I then called my Uncle Murph. He just happened to be the Sheriff of Wyatt County. I know, I know. You're probably wondering how someone from a family of known criminals got to be elected as sheriff. It's a good question. And I wish I knew the answer. But it does explain how I got my job, doesn't it?

While I was checking the fairgrounds, Murph had taken charge of the parking lot. Since I could see cars and a few people in the parking lot, it was safe to assume that Murph was still on site. He wouldn't leave until everyone else had gone home.

"What did our family do this time?" Uncle Murph asked when he answered the phone. Murph was actually a distant cousin, but I'd always called him 'uncle'. His father was my granddaddy's younger brother. But, with the Shatners, family was family no matter how distant the connection may be.

"Are we missing anyone?" I asked.

"I don't know," Murph said. "I didn't take a headcount or anything."

"Maybe you should."

"Why? What's wrong?"

"I need you to get the family out of here and then come back to the big building. Don't touch anything on the way. There's a dead body in the dumpster."

"What? Hold on a second." Over the phone, I could hear the sound of a car door opening and closing. "Are you sure the person is dead? Did you check for a pulse?"

An image of the man's bloody head flashed through my mind. "Believe me, Uncle Murph, this guy is as dead as they get."

"Do you think he's one of ours?"

"I don't know. Just hurry up and get back here." I felt like I was keeping it together pretty well, but I wasn't sure how much longer I could do that. I hung up on Murph and turned the flashlight back on. I then returned to the dumpster and once again peeked over the side. "So ... who are you and how did you end up back here?"

The dead guy didn't respond. Not that I expected him to.

I ran the flashlight beam over the body and revealed a large "DuPont" symbol emblazoned across the back of the man's red coat, and a yellow "24" on the sleeve. Breathing out a sigh of relief, I could feel at least some of the tension ease from my body. I had no idea who the dead man was, but he wasn't a Shatner. Jeff Gordon might have retired a few years before, but it would still be a cold day in hell before a Shatner was caught—dead or alive—wearing anything that supported that particular NASCAR driver.

My moment of relief didn't last long. The dead body might not be a Shatner, but it was still a dead body at my family's party.

"I don't know what the evidence is going to tell us, but my family didn't kill you," I said to the body. "You hear that? The Shatners didn't kill you."

I was having a hard time convincing myself that the Shatners weren't involved in this. Since I knew the cinderblock had been in place on top of the dumpster just a few hours earlier, I could only come up with two possibilities on how the body wound up in the dumpster.

It was possible that the body had been stashed in the dumpster sometime before the party started. One of my family members could have wandered away from the party and, for some unknown reason, started messing around with the dumpster. But if one of them had found the body, I was almost positive he or she would have told me or Uncle Murph about it.

The only other possibility I could come up with was that the body had been tossed into the dumpster sometime during the party. And that would mean that one or more of the Shatners had probably done it. I didn't want to believe that it could be true, but I couldn't rule out the possibility.

I replayed the evening's events. Killing a man and disposing of his body had not been on the itinerary, but that's not to say it didn't happen. My family tried to hide most of their criminal activities from me, so it was entirely possible they had killed the man and stashed the body without telling me. I will admit that I turned a blind eye to a lot of what went on around me, but I'd like to think I would have noticed a man being killed—or at least evidence of it—in my general vicinity.

"Carrie?"

"I'm over here." I turned around to see Uncle Murph jogging towards me, stomping on the spent fireworks and kicking other debris out of the way. He had his coat zipped up to his double chins, and a knit hat pulled down almost to his eyes. "Stop stepping on the evidence."

"Evidence of what? Aside from the fact that our family likes illegal fireworks." Murph grabbed my shoulder and gave me the once over. "Are you all right?"

"I'm about as all right as I can be after finding a dead body." I pointed towards the dumpster. "He's in there."

Murph had brought a Maglite with him, and that illuminated the inside of the dumpster far better than my phone had been able to. I could now see bits of bone and brain matter mixed in with the dried blood and matted hair. I guessed that the man's hair was brown, but, with all the blood, it was hard to tell. I put the man's height around six feet. His winter clothing added extra bulk, but I guesstimated his weight to be around two-hundred-and-fifty pounds.

"Good Lord," Murph said. "Any idea who he is?"

"Nope. And I'm not contaminating the crime scene to climb in there to check his ID."

"One of us is going to have to. We've got to know who the son of a gun is. That way we can figure out what to do."

"There's only one thing for us to do. And that's call the Department of

Public Safety. Let them decide on how they want to handle this," I said.

Even though the fairgrounds were in the sheriff's department's jurisdiction, and we were perfectly capable of handling a homicide investigation, it would be better to alert the Texas Department of Public Safety and have them decide how they thought the investigation should be conducted. The TxDPS had statewide jurisdiction over law enforcement, and sometimes it was best to leave it up to them. Especially considering that two of the highest ranking people at the Wyatt County Sheriff's Department were at the fairgrounds all night. It wouldn't look right if we handled the investigation ourselves. Especially when Murph and I had a reputation for covering up our family's criminal activities.

"That is an option. But not the option I think we should go with considering the circumstances," Murph said. "We should ... you know ... make this disappear."

"Are you kidding me, Uncle Murph?" I asked, smacking him on the arm. Like me, Murph also helped cover up the Shatners' indiscretions. He had been doing it for a whole lot longer than me and was much better at it. I still cringed every time I got the call that one of my relatives had committed a crime. Murph would just sigh, roll his eyes, and get on with the job. But this was one mess neither Murph nor I could cover up. "That man is dead. We can't just get rid of his body and act like it never happened. What happens when someone reports him missing?"

"Maybe no one will."

"Uncle Murph!"

"I still don't think we need to call the DPS. We can handle this."

"No. We can't. And we won't. I'm calling them."

"Carrie, I think you're making a big mistake. We don't know what happened here tonight. If a Shatner is involved—"

"I said I'm calling them!" I screamed. "You're right, we don't know what happened tonight. All I do know is that I don't want to be part of it!"

Murph held up his hands and backed away a couple steps. "All right, all right. Calm down. I guess you're right. We'll let the DPS figure out what they want to do about this. But, before we start making any calls, we better let the family know about what's going on. See if any of them want to own up to this. Waiting half-an-hour to gather some information isn't going to hurt anyone."

"No! Absolutely not!"

Between Murph's gaping mouth and bugged out eyes, he resembled the largemouth bass I caught the previous spring. "But ... they ... alibis."

"Whatever alibis they have now are going to have to be enough," I said.

"Carrie—"

"Don't say it. Don't think it. This," I pointed at the dumpster, "is not our problem."

"Except it is our problem." Murph waved his arms and stomped around in a circle. "And we have to get out ahead of it."

"And that's exactly what we are doing. We're not tainting the case by messing with the crime scene or warning the suspects."

"Suspects! Jesus Christ, Carrie, they're our family."

"Would you listen to me for once? Look at the big picture. Dead body in the dumpster after our party. Of course, our family is going to make up the entire suspect list. I'm a suspect. You're a suspect. Everybody is a suspect. If we tell the family about the body, then we screw up the case. It looks like we're hiding something."

"But what if we do need to hide something?" Murph grabbed my shoulders and shook me. "You're not just throwing your family under the bus. You're running them over yourself."

I shook my head and pulled away. "No, I'm making the best out of a bad situation. And I expect you to do the same."

I dug a set of keys out of my coat pocket and handed them to Murph. The keys were for the fairground gates and for every building on the property. "Here, take these and turn on all the lights around here. I want to see what I'm looking at."

"I want it on the record that I'm against all this," Murph said as he headed for the side door of the multipurpose building. Just before he stepped inside the building, he pulled his cell phone out of his coat pocket. I had serious doubts that he was planning to call the Department of Public Safety.

"Wait." I hurried after Murph. "Give me your phone."

"Come on, my wife is still in the parking lot. I need to tell her to go home without me."

"And while telling her that, you'll let it slip that there's a dead body in the dumpster. Then Lydia will call all of her in-laws. I don't think so."

Murph glared at me for a few seconds before he slapped his cell phone into my upturned palm. While he went in search of a light switch, I placed a call to the closest DPS office.

"This is Detective Caroline Shatner with the Wyatt County Sheriff's Department. I've got what appears to be a homicide, so I'll need y'all to send down the Texas Ranger who covers my county. And probably a crime scene unit. I'd handle it myself ... but I think one or more of my family members might be involved ... "

While I waited on hold for the person who'd answered the phone to transfer me to someone else, I moved closer to the dumpster. I glanced inside one more time and shuddered—not from the cold, but from apprehension. What had my family gotten me into this time?

Just over an hour earlier, my great-uncle Houston, the patriarch of the Shatner family, had welcomed in the New Year with a prophetic toast. He'd said, "May the new year be full of nothing but smooth sailing for the Shatners."

We were sailing, all right. Straight up Shit Creek, and we didn't have a paddle.

Chapter Three

———◆———

Less than ten minutes after I called the sheriff's department for backup, the Wyatt County deputies began to converge on the fairgrounds. Those who were on duty were the first to arrive. They were soon followed by the off-duty deputies, who showed up wearing everything from their uniforms to their footed pajamas. Since this was Wyatt County's first homicide in almost a year, no one was quite sure what they should do. The deputies were either running around like chickens with their heads cut off, or they were standing around, shuffling their feet, and conjecturing over what they thought might have happened. One of them at least had the good sense to hang up some crime scene tape around the dumpster.

While Uncle Murph tried to get his deputies calmed down and organized, I kept up my vigil in front of the dumpster. I was not going anywhere until someone I could trust showed up to take over my burden. Thankfully I didn't have long to wait.

"What happened here tonight?" Chief Deputy Juan Quaranta, in his rush to get to the dumpster, ran right through the crime scene tape. The long, yellow ribbon caught around his waist for a second, before he ripped it away and let it trail off behind him. One of the deputies snatched it up and tacked the crime scene tape back in place. "What is going on?"

"Oh, you know, my family got bored, so we decided to kill somebody. The usual."

"Sounds about right." Quaranta stroked the ends of his impressive Fu Manchu mustache as he looked around the fairgrounds. "Can't your family come up with anything better to do than break the law?"

"I'm kidding, Juan. This time we didn't do it."

"Are you sure about that?" Quaranta asked.

"Yes." No. Not really. But I hoped that if I kept insisting that none of the Shatners did this that it would be true. "If one my relatives killed him, they didn't tell me about it. The only thing I did is find the body."

"Who is he?"

"I don't know."

"You telling me you didn't climb in the dumpster to figure out who the dead guy is?"

"No, but Uncle Murph wanted me to."

"I'm sure that's not the only thing the sheriff wanted you to do," Quaranta mumbled. "All right, Carrie, show me what we've got."

I led Quaranta over to the dumpster and then gestured towards it in a way that would have made Vanna White jealous.

"*Madre de Dios*," Quaranta said while crossing himself. "How do you know he isn't one of your relatives?"

"I just know he isn't a Shatner." I didn't want to explain the whole Jeff Gordon jacket theory. Quaranta doesn't watch NASCAR. He couldn't wrap his head around why a bunch of men driving in circles was entertaining. I've tried to enlighten him, but he just doesn't get it.

Quaranta pulled a notebook out of his pocket, flipped to a fresh page, and drew a rough sketch of the dumpster. He then handed me the notebook and said, "Indicate everywhere you touched."

"I was wearing gloves when I touched it. I already stuck them in an evidence bag," I said.

"But you still touched the dumpster," Quaranta said.

As I went about marking Xs on the poorly drawn dumpster, Quaranta sent one of the deputies to get a stepstool so he could look into the dumpster without having to climb up the side.

"Poor man. Killed and then tossed out like garbage," Quaranta said.

I had a hard time conjuring up much sympathy. Sure, I felt bad for the dead guy, but his death and the placement of his body were really inconveniencing me and my family. My anger should have been directed at the killer, but, not knowing his identity, my mystery victim was the only outlet I had available.

"You have any idea how this happened?" Quaranta asked.

"For all I know, he's been in there since before the party," I said. "All I did was find him, Juan. I didn't kill him. No one told me they killed him. So I have no idea what is going on. And I don't like it."

"I don't like it either." Quaranta snatched the notebook out of my hands. "It's bad enough I know about the other things your family does. Or at least some of what they do. But I don't need to get caught up in something like this."

"Neither do I. But we didn't do this," I said, hoping that, around my chattering teeth, I sounded convincing. "What are we going to do?"

"I'll be taking over the crime scene for now," Quaranta said. "I talked to someone from the Department of Public Safety. They're sending down their own forensic team to process the scene. And there are two Texas Rangers coming down to take over the investigation. I'll let them decide what they want to do about all this. For now, just don't touch anything."

"I didn't do this, Juan."

Quaranta just looked at me. He and I got along. For the most part.

Over three years earlier, Quaranta had been adamantly against the sheriff's department hiring me. While he couldn't argue with my years of experience as a crime scene technician, he did have a fairly persuasive argument over the fact that I didn't have any experience as a detective. Quaranta also didn't want to hire me since I'm related to most of the local criminals. Ultimately, the decision came down to Uncle Murph. He understood Quaranta's reluctance, but Murph also knew that the county didn't so much have a crime problem; what Wyatt County had was a Shatner problem. I was the only candidate who was qualified to deal with them. So, in the end, Uncle Murph hired me.

"You were here all night, weren't you?" Quaranta asked.

"Look, I get it. But could you lay off calling me a suspect?" I asked.

"Just tell me about what happened tonight."

I was in the process of outlining the evening when we were rudely interrupted.

"I hope you're not trying to help Detective Shatner cover this up, Chief Deputy Quaranta."

I sucked in a deep breath and then turned around to face one of my least favorite people in the world—Isaac Yates, the Chief of the Holler Police. And he wasn't alone. His son, who was also one of the Holler police officers, was on his heels. Officer Ethan Yates was a younger, skinnier, and slightly more attractive—but no less obnoxious—version of his father. They reminded me of Sheriff Buford T. Justice and his son from *Smokey and the Bandit*. Except the Yates father and son duo were far less entertaining.

There were also a number of other Holler officers mingling with the Wyatt County deputies. I cringed when I realized how many people were wandering around the fairgrounds, contaminating the crime scene and stepping all over possible evidence. Of course, if one or more of my family members killed the victim, it would be to our benefit if the deputies and officers accidently destroyed some evidence.

Holler was the largest town in Wyatt County. It was also the county seat. Just over a third of the roughly twelve thousand people who call Wyatt County home lived within the Holler city limits. Isaac Yates and his officers took care of handling all of the criminal investigations within the Holler city limits.

The Wyatt County Fairgrounds, which were outside the city limits, were located in an unincorporated part of the county. Aside from three large towns in Wyatt County—Holler, Wilder, and Mooresville—everything else in the county was unincorporated. The sheriff's department had jurisdiction over all of the unincorporated areas. Not that something as trivial as jurisdiction had ever stopped Chief Yates from sticking his nose in the sheriff's department's business. Especially when the Shatners were involved.

"One of these days, I'm going to kill Chief Yates," Quaranta whispered to me.

"That's if I don't kill him first. Now what does Yates think he's doing here?" I whispered back. Raising my voice, I said, "Hey there, Chief Yates, I don't remember inviting you to this party."

"You didn't." Yates walked over until he was standing almost on top of me. "And you should have. I have a right to know what's going on around here."

"Well, let me extend my deepest apologies then," I said.

I took a step backwards to put some distance between me, Yates, and Yates's award-winning-sized beer belly. Yates had the sagging jowls of a bloodhound, and there were coarse gray whiskers sprouting from his cheeks where he missed a spot shaving.

"Maybe I'll be seeing your pretty little face behind bars before morning," Yates tried to cross his arms over his chest, but had a hard time accomplishing it. The man was five-four, which put him at the same height as me. Unlike me, Yates weighed just south of four-hundred pounds. Tonight he was wearing one of those puffy marshmallow jackets, and it caused him to vaguely resemble a navy blue version of the Michelin Man.

I was still trying to figure out how Isaac Yates managed to rise through the ranks and become Chief of Police. The man added a whole new meaning to incompetence. The Wyatt County Sheriff's Department and the Holler Police Department were located on opposite sides of the Holler town square. Yates spent the majority of his day sitting at his second-story office window, watching the sheriff's department through his high-powered telescope. He liked to keep an eye on me and Uncle Murph. If Murph or I left the sheriff's department, Yates followed us. When he wasn't holed up in his office, Yates skulked around, hoping to catch us Shatners in some sort of illegal activity. Very few of the Shatners lived within the Holler city limits, but that didn't stop Yates from coming after us. Yates had come close to catching us a few times, but had yet to succeed. I'd never say that any of the Shatners were brain trusts, but we were smarter than Yates. For years we had managed to stay at least one step ahead of him. It didn't hurt that the Shatners didn't commit any of their crimes within the Holler city limits. Or, if they did, they hadn't been caught yet.

"What are you doing here, Yates?" Quaranta asked. "This isn't your jurisdiction."

"I just want to see the Shatners' latest crime. And make sure the sheriff and Detective Shatner ain't doing anything underhanded." Yates waddled over to the dumpster to take a look at the body. I held my breath as he mounted the flimsy, collapsible stepstool. Somehow the cheap plastic managed to hold Yates's considerable girth. "Well, shoot, that is a dead body."

"That's the general consensus, Chief Yates." Quaranta gave me a slight eye roll before he hurried over to pull Yates away from the dumpster before he toppled into it.

"Things sure are getting interesting around here," Chief Yates said as he marched towards me. After clamping his hand on my shoulder, Yates leaned in and stuck his face close to mine. The combined scents of tobacco, pork rinds, and onions on his breath grossed me out. I also got an up close look at his small teeth that had been stained brown after years of chewing tobacco. "It looks like you've finally come across a crime you can't cover up. You Shatners really screwed up this time."

"I don't cover up crimes." Mostly I shredded parking tickets and manipulated people out of pressing charges against my family. I tried to leave the heavier stuff up to Murph. He might cover up a murder, but I wouldn't. I have to draw the line somewhere. "But, come on Chief, like you've never caused some evidence to disappear or disposed of a dead body."

"Do you two mind having this conversation on the other side of the crime scene tape?" Quaranta asked as he herded us away from the dumpster.

Ducking under the crime scene tape I walked around the side of the multipurpose building and found Uncle Murph deep in conversation with Louis Groves, the Chief of the Wilder Police. Wilder, which was about fifteen miles south of Holler, was the second largest town in Wyatt County.

"Looks like everyone's turning out for the festivities," I said.

"Howdy, Detective Shatner. Heard y'all got a dead body so I thought I'd come on up to see if there's anything I can do to help out. I don't mean to be stepping on any toes. What with this not being my jurisdiction. But I've got my guys and your deputies searching the fairgrounds for evidence before it gets trampled on and destroyed," Chief Groves said as he shook my hand. "From what the sheriff tells me, if your victim was killed here, there's got to be some blood around. Maybe even the murder weapon."

"Let's look at the silver lining, Carrie. At least you won't have to come back in the morning to clean everything up," Uncle Murph said as he put his arm around my shoulders and gave me a quick hug. "I guess we can call that a good thing."

Come morning, the plan had been to round up the younger Shatners and force them to help me clean up the fairgrounds. If the children really are our future, I wanted to set a good example for those that I could. I had grandiose dreams of teaching them how to be responsible citizens that cleaned up after themselves and didn't break the law. Mainly, I didn't want them counting on me to clean up their messes. But, now that the fairgrounds were considered a crime scene, I would have to find some other way to give the kids a lesson in life.

With nothing else to do, Murph, Chief Yates, Ethan, and I lined up along the crime scene tape to watch Quaranta photograph the crime scene. I couldn't help but feel a little put out since Quaranta was technically doing my job. If I hadn't been at the wrong place at the wrong time, or related to the wrong people, I would have been in charge of documenting the crime scene. Instead it was Quaranta who got to make a video of the scene and take the crime scene photos. The only thing he wouldn't do was collect the evidence, and that was only because he was leaving it up to the crime scene investigation team that the DPS was sending.

"When is Sergeant Knapp going to get here? It should not take him this long to get here," I asked Murph after we had watched Quaranta take pictures of the dumpster for over an hour.

Sergeant Knapp was the Texas Ranger who oversaw Wyatt County. He also had two other nearby counties that he was responsible for. Knapp, who was part of the Company B division of the Texas Rangers, would be leading the investigation into how the dead body wound up in the dumpster. He lived in Tyler, Texas, and worked out of the Tyler DPS office. Tyler was about forty-five minutes to an hour northwest of Holler.

Yates, who was hovering a few feet away, started to chuckle. That chuckle turned into a full-blown belly laugh that left Yates wheezing.

I turned to Murph and asked, "Any idea what he finds so funny?"

"Knapp retired right before Christmas. He's not coming. There's a new Ranger now," Murph said.

"A new Ranger?" I stared at Murph while I tried to make sense of what he had just said. Knapp had retired? How did I not know about it? "Why didn't you tell me?"

"I thought you knew."

One bad thing about the Shatners was that none of them would ever tell me anything. I could see why the rest of them kept me in the dark about the crimes they committed, leaving me to find out about them only when the crimes were exposed. But how could Murph fail to tell me that Sergeant Knapp, who didn't like the Shatners but certainly didn't hate us either, had retired? This was not good. Not good at all.

As if I wasn't already in a bad mood, that news was enough to send me over the edge. I had enough to deal with already, I did not need some new Texas Ranger showing up—especially when I didn't know him and had no idea how he felt about my family. I could only hope that, in the few months he'd been stationed in the area, the new guy hadn't developed a deep and unwarranted hatred of the Shatners. Or looked too closely at us. One of the duties of the Texas Rangers was to suppress all organized criminal activity in their assigned counties. Not that the Shatners were all that organized.

"Who took his place?" I asked.

Murph shrugged. "I haven't met him yet."

"Hardy." Yates said. "His name is Jerrod Hardy. And, you know, Detective Shatner, Sergeant Hardy and I have become real good friends over the past couple weeks."

"That doesn't say much for the Ranger's judgment, does it?" I asked.

"I'd say the Ranger has great judgment. He hates you Shatners as much as I do." Yates spat a wad of tobacco onto the ground, just missing my boot. "I'm sure that once Sergeant Hardy gets here, he'll kick you, and everyone else from the sheriff's department, out of the crime scene, and let me and my officers help him conduct the investigation. Jurisdiction be damned. So don't be worrying your pretty little head about the new Ranger. What you should be worrying about is how many of you Shatners are going to be in jail by this time tomorrow. Sergeant Hardy and I are going to get as many of you as we can."

"You sound pretty sure of yourself there, Chief Yates."

I spun around to see who had come up behind me. As I did so, I came face-to-face with the front of a man's winter coat. The Texas Ranger badge on his chest was at my eye level.

"Sergeant Hardy, I assume," I said.

"At your service." The Ranger tipped his white Stetson in my direction. He then pointed at the man standing behind him. "And this is Sergeant Arthur Boleyn. He's also with the Texas Rangers, and works out of the Tyler office. He'll be assisting me for the time being. Could you point us towards the body, ma'am?"

"In the dumpster." I gestured over my shoulder. "We haven't touched it."

Sergeants Hardy and Boleyn ducked under the crime scene tape. When Yates tried to follow them, Hardy sent him back to the spectator side. Murph and I, along with Chief Groves, took up a position a few feet away from Chief Yates and his son.

Quaranta was still sketching the crime scene when Hardy and Boleyn walked over. They examined the contents of the dumpster for a minute or two before having an animated conversation with Quaranta. I watched, not daring to breath, as I strained to make out what they were saying. I could only pick out a few words, and none of them gave any indication as to how the conversation was going.

Hardy and Boleyn then ambled over towards where the crime scene unit was huddled together and barked out some orders. The crime scene unit gathered up their equipment and rushed the crime scene. They had officially taken over.

Yates dashed over towards Hardy and all but pounced on him. "What do you want me to do, Sergeant Hardy? Where should I start?"

"Chief, I've got a huge task for you and your son." Hardy extracted himself from Yates's clutching fingers. "I want the both of you to go home and get some rest."

"So we'll be fresh in the morning. Gotcha." Yates nudged Hardy in the ribs. "What time do you want us back?"

"That's the thing, Chief. I don't want you coming back. There's no way either of you can be objective. I understand you have an axe to grind, but you are not doing it on my watch."

Yates's jaw dropped so far that a wad of tobacco slipped out and landed on the front of his jacket. He didn't seem to notice. He just kept staring at the Ranger. After a minute, Hardy patted Yates on the back and said, "Off you go, now." When he still didn't move, Ethan finally dragged his father away.

I glanced over at Murph and shrugged. So far, so good.

Hardy and Boleyn then had a brief conversation with Chief Groves, who explained that he was overseeing the evidence collection of the fairgrounds in general. Hardy sent Boleyn off with Chief Groves to take a look around, and to go over the notes and evidence compiled by the deputies and the Wilder police officers.

That just left me and Murph to be dealt with. And I didn't expect to be around much longer. Other than providing a statement and answering some questions, my part in the investigation was over.

"You must be Sheriff Murph Shatner." The Ranger stuck out his hand. "I'm Sergeant Jerrod Hardy with the Texas Rangers. It's a shame it took a dead body for us to finally meet. Especially considering you were on site the entire night."

"Tell me about it." Murph shook Hardy's hand. "If you need anything, anything at all, you let me know. The sheriff's department is at your disposal."

"Once things are wrapped up here, I'm going to need a place to interview people. Since the crime scene is in your jurisdiction, I'd like to set up my operation at your department. I also might need to borrow some of your deputies throughout the investigation," Hardy said. He then turned his attention to me. "And I guess that makes you Detective Caroline Shatner."

"Guilty as charged, Sergeant Hardy."

Chapter Four

———◆———

"I'm going to need you to come with me," Hardy said.

"Am I under arrest?" I inched away from Hardy, ready to make a run for it if he said I was. "Because I didn't kill the guy. I just found him."

"No, you're not under arrest," Hardy said. He grasped my arm, preventing me from moving any farther away. It wasn't a firm grip, but I knew he wasn't going to let me get away from him. "Chief Deputy Quaranta told me you've been out in the cold for most of the night. I just want to take you over to that building, get you warmed up, and talk about what happened."

"I don't really have much to say about this evening. I mean, all I did was find the body. And, while that might sound exciting, it really wasn't," I said, babbling because I just knew Hardy wanted to get me alone so he could grill me about my family. And, while I appreciated that he was showing concern about my well-being, I suspected he was only doing it so that he could lull me into a false sense of security. "But I won't turn down your offer to warm up."

I allowed Hardy to lead me across the fairgrounds to the small building. Along the way, we had to weave around the Wyatt County deputies and Wilder police officers as they continued to search the fairgrounds and collect the party debris. I glanced around frantically, trying to make eye contact with my deputies. All I wanted was some sort of positive sign that they hadn't found any evidence of blood. Unfortunately, no one would look at me.

As Hardy and I stepped into the small building, a wall of marginally warmer air hit me. The building had no heating or cooling system, so my family had brought along a number of space heaters. The heaters had been off for a couple hours, but the deputies who were assigned the task of processing the building had turned them back on.

"Stay here," Hardy said, leaving me just inside the door to take a lap around the room. As he looked around, Hardy stopped and spoke to the deputies who were taking pictures and collecting evidence.

While I waited for Hardy to come back, I glanced around the room. My family had certainly made a mess of it. At our next big party—if there was a next party—not only would I have emergency crews on standby, I was going to hire a cleaning service. And security guards.

Along the right side of the room was a long row of tables holding what remained of my family's New Year's Eve dinner. At the back of the room, near the door, were a few more picnic tables. There was food and trash everywhere. In some places, the food that had been spilled on the floor was an inch thick. I noticed that one of the deputies was chipping away at the hardening glop with an ice scraper.

Having completed his lap of the room, Hardy made his way back to me. "They've cleared this corner, so we can talk over here."

Tucked away in the corner that Hardy was pointing to was a space heater. When I saw it, I rushed ahead of Hardy, shucking my coat and hat. After turning up the heat to full blast, I had a seat on the floor and all but embraced the heater as it pumped out hot air over my frozen body.

I kept my back to Hardy, hoping that he would hold off on asking any questions. I needed to not only thaw out my body, but also my brain.

Hardy gave me about two minutes worth of peace before he asked, "Why does Chief Yates hate your family so much?"

Not exactly a safe subject, but it was one I could handle at the moment.

"Years ago, my dad had an affair with Chief Yates's wife," I said. I'm still not sure when the affair started, but Yates found out about it towards the end of my sophomore year of high school. He then went public with it, embarrassing himself and my mom in the process. The last month of the school year wasn't very pleasant for me or Ethan, who was a grade ahead of me.

"That I did not know," Hardy said. "But, while it would explain why Chief Yates hates your dad, and maybe you, it doesn't explain why he hates your entire family."

I scooted back from the heater. Parts of me were still cold, but beads of sweat were breaking out along my hairline. I couldn't be sure if it was the heater or the questions that were causing me to break out in a sweat. Probably both.

From what I've learned over the years, there were multiple versions of the truth. The person you were talking to determined what version of the truth needed to be shared. Hardy, as a Texas Ranger, only warranted a boiled-down version of the truth.

"Back before he worked for the Holler Police, Chief Yates worked for the sheriff's department. He was going behind the former sheriff's back, illegally obtaining evidence against someone that he was trying to build a case against," I explained. I didn't mention that the person Yates was building a case against was one of the Shatners. I also didn't tell Hardy that, back when this happened, my granddaddy had been the sheriff. He, along with my dad and Uncle Murph, were quietly going around, cleaning up the evidence of various crimes committed by the Shatners. Yates found out, and then made it his personal mission to expose the cover-ups. Because of that, Yates didn't last very long as a Wyatt County deputy. Continuing, I said, "Chief Yates wound up getting fired over it. He then walked across the street and got a job as a Holler police officer. And the rest is history."

"Right," Hardy said. "Chief Yates has a slightly different story."

By slightly, I assumed Hardy meant drastically. "Yates has been known to exaggerate."

"Really? So the Chief's story about how you dove out of a moving car, tackled a guy, and then held him in a chokehold until a couple more deputies arrived isn't accurate?"

"Not quite." Next time I saw Yates, I was going to shoot him for embellishing stories about me. Wasn't the truth enough? "I jumped out from behind a parked car and tackled a man. He knocked himself out when he hit his head on the curb."

Hardy snickered. "It's still an impressive story."

"But you see what I mean? He makes up all kinds of stories about us."

"So, the moonshine, marijuana, and countless other crimes are just figments of Chief Yates's imagination?"

"I'm taking the fifth on that. All I can say for sure is that Yates hates us, and his sole mission in life is to see all of us behind bars."

"From what I can tell, he's just about obsessed with y'all."

"Obsessed with seeing us all in jail for crimes we didn't commit."

"So your family isn't out breaking all kinds of laws?"

"I have no idea what you are talking about." I stood up, but I continued to keep my back to Hardy. It's harder to lie to someone when you're looking them in the eye. "The Shatners are law-abiding citizens."

"So all the stories, and all the evidence Chief Yates has given me, are fabricated?"

"What stories? What evidence?" I fought the urge to turn around, afraid that the paranoia building up inside me would show on my face. Hardy asking me about Chief Yates instead of the dead body was freaking me out. "What has Yates been telling you?"

"Anything and everything," Hardy said. "Chief Yates has been coming to see me a couple times a week since I moved to Tyler to take over the Ranger job. He's been telling me all these stories about how the Shatners break the law, and how you, Detective Shatner, cover it up."

"What about the so-called evidence?" I asked.

"Let me put it this way. It's like evidence of Bigfoot. There's a lot of it, but none of it proves anything."

That argument held no sway with me since I believed in Bigfoot. But, because I didn't know Hardy's personal beliefs on the big, hairy cryptid, I had no idea if he believed in Yate's evidence or not.

I finally turned around, more to warm up my backside than to look at Hardy, but the effort was well worth it. Hardy sat slouched over at one of the tables behind me. He'd taken off his coat and hat, which finally allowed me to get a good look at him. Since there weren't many Texas Ranger job openings, and one needed to have substantial experience to even get considered, I assumed that Hardy would be in his early forties, at least. The man sitting at the table appeared to be in his mid-thirties. He was also extremely handsome.

I had to give my libido a mental scolding. No matter how attractive Hardy was, now was not the time or the place to have amorous thoughts. I had to remind myself that Hardy was my enemy—my family's enemy—during this investigation. That should have been enough of a reason to turn me off. It wasn't.

"Can I assume that all of your family members have their alibis in order for tonight?" Hardy asked. "By which I mean, have you helped them get their stories straight?"

"No. The only one of my family members who I told about the body was Uncle Murph. And I had to tell him."

"Are you telling me that your family has no idea you found a dead body in the dumpster?" Hardy asked.

"If they know about it, they didn't find out from me or Murph."

"Or because he or she or they were the ones who killed the guy and then stuffed his body in the dumpster."

Having thawed out my brain and my body, I was back on top of my game. I slid into the seat across from Hardy, leaned across the table, and stared into his brown eyes.

"Look, Hardy, my family may do a lot of asinine things. I'll even admit that we're crazy." I would say that the Shatners were doing crazy things about 97.9% of the time, but it was probably more like 99.9%. I just liked to give us the benefit of the doubt. And I'd like to think that I provided that tad bit of sanity. "But we are not that stupid. Killing a man and leaving his body at our party is just asking for trouble."

"Let's say one of your relatives did kill the man. Maybe they stuffed him in the dumpster, not expecting you to find him right after the party," Hardy said as he rubbed a faint scar that sliced across the left side of his chin, drawing my attention to his Jim Morrison-like jawline and cheekbones.

I shook my head. "If I didn't find him tonight, he would have been found on Friday. Saturday at the latest. There's an El Camino auto show at the fairgrounds this weekend, and, believe me, my family knows all about it."

"What if one of your family members was storing the body in the dumpster?"

"Are you serious?" My laugh was too high pitched and sounded forced. Hardy hit a little too close to home for my comfort. "Do you know how insane you sound?"

"Maybe—"

"You know, Sergeant," I said, interrupting. "There is no point in conjecturing. As of now, we don't know who the dead guy is. And we have no idea how long he's been dead. If you want to know what happened at the party, then ask me. If you want to play guessing games, you can play them by yourself."

"All right then. Let's get started." Hardy pulled a tape recorder out of his pocket and placed it on the table between us. He hit the record button and then went through a spiel giving the date, time, and location of the interview. After asking for my consent to record our conversation, Hardy asked, "How much have you had to drink tonight, Detective Shatner?"

"None. I don't drink." Other than the sip of homebrewed moonshine I had on my twenty-first birthday, I have never, and will never, consume any sort of alcohol. I've seen the Shatners do far too many stupid things while they were intoxicated. Plus, my mom was an alcoholic.

"A commendable choice." Hardy nodded a few times. "But I think it's safe to assume, considering all the beer bottles and mason jars I've seen, that your family members were drinking quite heavily."

"You could say that."

"I thought so." Hardy tapped the end of his pen against his cheek a few times. "What time did you arrive at the fairgrounds? And were you the first to arrive?"

"I got here just after five," I said, thinking back to the early evening. "I wasn't the first one here, but the gates were locked. I had to unlock the front gate to let everyone in."

"So nobody could have been stuffing the body in the dumpster before you got here?"

"If they had a key they could have," I said. I have a lot of relatives, but I didn't think any of them had a key. "As far as I know, I'm the only one who was here tonight who has a key. Except for maybe the sheriff. He might have one."

"How many gates are there?" Hardy asked.

"Three. The main one, and then there's one on each side except for the far end. I checked the other two gates when I got here, and they were both locked. And I checked again after I found the body. Still locked. And they don't look like they've been tampered with."

"You didn't happen to check the dumpster when you got here, did you?" Hardy asked.

"No. But I did walk past it. The cinderblock was on top of the lid then. It was when I found the cinderblock smashed on the ground after the party that I knew something was wrong."

Hardy planted his elbows on the table and stared at me. "Are you telling me that the body had to have been stashed in the dumpster sometime during the party?"

"No, I'm not saying that at all," I said. "It's possible the body was already there and one of my family members found it."

"That's one theory." Hardy pulled a notebook out of his jacket pocket, flipped to a clean page, and started writing.

I'm not an expert at reading upside down, but I could make out what Hardy had written. "5-ish—Arrives at fairgrounds. Dumpster undisturbed." He was starting to make out a timeline of the night's events.

"I should point out that the front gate was hanging open all night. It's not like I locked it once everyone was here," I said.

"So anyone could have driven in and dumped the body in the dumpster?"

"As soon as I opened the gate, my family started setting up fireworks and chairs on the midway. It would have been nearly impossible to drive in and out without running them over. There would have been a commotion if something had happened to any of the fireworks. But I guess it's possible someone could have found a path to drive around the fireworks and chairs."

"Aside from your family and guests, was there anyone else at the fairgrounds tonight that you know about?" Hardy asked.

"There were some other people who came out to watch the fireworks. They sat out in the parking lot. Maybe one of them lugged the body back there when we weren't looking," I said, thinking about how it was a legitimate possibility. "And we also had some uninvited guests show up. They could have done it."

"Anything's possible. And I want to hear all about it," Hardy said. "But, first, I'd like some more details on the fairgrounds. What else is in the area?"

"Very little. There's the dirt track across the street, but it's not like there was a race last night," I said. And, unless the track gets fixed, there won't be any races in the future. "Mainly the fairgrounds are surrounded by a lot of trees and empty fields. There are a few houses, but none are super close to the fairgrounds."

"So no close by neighbors who might have witnessed anything," Hardy said as he wrote something down in his notebook. "How many people were at the party?"

"Seventy. Maybe seventy-five." The majority of those people were Shatners either by blood or by marriage. The rest were boyfriends, girlfriends, or close family friends.

Hardy slowly shook his head. "You can't alibi over seventy people for seven hours. Not unless y'all sat in a circle, held hands, and stared at each other all night."

"You're right, I can't alibi all of them. But I can alibi some of them. And the ones I can alibi didn't leave this building long enough to kill someone."

"We don't know how long it took to kill the man" Hardy said. "Or how long it took to stuff his body in the dumpster."

"You're right. But, despite how long it took to kill him, it looked like it would have been messy. I didn't see anyone walking around covered in blood. And I didn't notice anyone randomly changing their clothes in the middle of the party."

"Tell me about the party. What all happened?" Hardy asked.

"Well, we sat down to eat around five-thirty. Dinner lasted for about an hour." I grabbed Hardy's notebook and jotted down the names of the ten people I had been sitting with—my half-brother and a few of my cousins. "They can vouch for me, and I can vouch for them. Not just for dinner, but for the entire night."

"What happened after dinner?" Hardy asked.

"We cleaned up." I waved my arm around to indicate the room. "Not that you can tell. Then, at seven, we all settled down and watched *Monday Night Raw*."

"You want me to believe that your family took three hours out of the party just to watch the WWE?"

"I really don't care what you believe. It's what happened. My one uncle brought his big screen TV along just so we could watch the show tonight."

If the Shatners took anything seriously, it was pro wrestling. We took it so seriously that we followed it with a passion usually reserved for religious cults. Most Shatners believed that the moon landing was faked. But professional wrestling? That was as real as it got. I happened to enjoy all of the hot, sweaty men in speedos. Call it a guilty pleasure.

"All right." Hardy crossed his arms and leaned back in his chair. "First segment … What happened?"

I tried not to smile. It seemed the Shatners weren't the only ones who spent New Year's Eve watching wrestling. But, if Hardy wanted to quiz me on what happened a few hours earlier on *Raw*, I would gladly oblige—in far more detail than was probably necessary. I also gave Hardy a list of who I had been sitting with during the show.

"And, before you ask, believe me when I say that none of the Shatners were killing a man and disposing of his body during wrestling. We don't even blink unless it's during the commercial break." Like I said, the Shatners took pro wrestling way too seriously.

Hardy nodded. "One more question. Who won the main event?"

"Uh, well … " I found a crack in the table to be quite interesting. "I didn't see the main event. None of us did. It was about to start when the Palmers showed up."

Hardy threw down the pen he'd been holding. "Who are the Palmers?"

"They're this other big family. Most of them live in Holler. Let's just say that the Shatners and the Palmers don't get along. At all. I guess you could call it a family feud."

Hardy perked up. "Family feud? Like the Hatfields and the McCoys?"

"Well, not quite that bad."

"I think you better tell me about this family feud."

"It's a long story."

"I've got plenty of time."

"It goes back to the War Between the States."

"I like history."

I sighed, knowing I would have to tell Hardy about the feud sooner or later. While I would have preferred to wait until later, it was probably for the best to get it out of the way now.

"Well, it all started when my many-times great granddaddy went and got himself killed fighting for the Confederacy," I said. The Shatners were dirt-poor mountain people from western North Carolina. We didn't own any slaves. We just didn't like the Yankees coming down and sticking their noses in our business. "After the war, his widow met and married a Union deserter."

"Let me guess, he was a Palmer?" Hardy asked.

"You got it." I gave Hardy a small round of applause. He rolled his eyes in response. "It was the offspring from their previous marriages that started the feud. But it wasn't until the eighteen-eighties, years after the combined family moved to Texas, that the Shatners and the Palmers began pruning the branches off of each other's family trees."

I gave Hardy the summarized and one-sided version of the Shatner-Palmer feud. There wasn't much to say other than that the two families went back-and-forth killing each other. Both families also committed a number of other crimes along the way. I didn't tell Hardy about those unless they were directly connected to the feud.

"By the time Prohibition was enacted, most of the Shatners and the

Palmers were either dead or in jail. Those that were left agreed to a truce. They then banded together to brew moonshine and run it all across East Texas and into Louisiana, Arkansas, and Oklahoma. When Prohibition was repealed, so was the truce."

"And the two families went right back to killing each other?" Hardy asked.

"Oh, no. No, the Shatners and the Palmers haven't killed each other since before Prohibition." We have tried to kill each other on multiple occasions since then. Fortunately neither side was successful. "These days, there isn't that much of an actual feud left."

"So, what, you just crash each other's parties and pick fights now?"

"More or less." Lately the feud had revolved around football, differences in religious affiliations, and anything else we could come up with to argue about—which was just about everything. There was also the fact that the Palmers made my family look like amateur criminals. We took exception to that. "We play a lot of nasty pranks on each other. It's the older generations that really carry on the feud. Us younger generations all went to school and played sports together. I'm not saying the younger Shatners and the Palmers are friends. We just aren't going around killing each other anymore."

But the hatred was still being instilled in the younger generations. The kids hated the Palmers because their parents and grandparents hated the Palmers. They were following the older generations' examples, but they had no reason for the hatred.

"Maybe someone took things a little too far tonight," Hardy said.

"It's possible." Ever since I found the Jeff Gordon jacket clad man in the dumpster, I've had a sinking suspicion that he might be a Palmer. "But I doubt it. When the Palmers showed up, they started blaring their car horns to get our attention. When we saw who it was, most of the women and kids came back in here. The men stayed outside."

"Where were you?"

"I was right in the middle of it."

The main event match had been about to start, and my family members were on the edges of their seats in anticipation, when the sound of multiple blaring car horns drew our attention outside. Momentarily forgetting about wrestling, we dashed out of the building. The men knocked the women and children out of the way in their rush to be the first outside.

In the parking lot, we found six or seven trucks doing laps around our parked cars. One of the trucks bounced off the side of my cousin Babette's boyfriend's brand new truck, tearing off the bumper. Another truck was bearing down on the fairgrounds' gates when a handful of my uncles and cousins took up a stance just inside the gates. The truck came to a screeching halt mere feet away from them. The other trucks parked behind it, and a passel of men exploded from the cabs like clowns from a tiny car.

While I didn't have time to take a head count, I estimated that there were around twenty Palmer men armed with an assortment of painful, but not exactly lethal, weapons. Regardless, blood would be shed if no one stepped up to stop the fight.

Around me, the Shatners jumped into action. The men rushed forward to meet the enemy while the women grabbed the children and retreated back into the building. I'd be remiss if I didn't say it was the men who had kept this feud alive and well. We women were smart enough to stay out of it. Sure, we didn't like the Palmer women, but we didn't feel the need to have the occasional brawl to prove our dominance either.

I set off after the men, determined to break up the fight before it really started. As I did so, one of my aunts grabbed my arm and tried to hold me back, screaming at me that it wasn't my place to get involved. I pulled free from her and dove into the fray.

All around me, the Shatners and the Palmers were facing off—exchanging insults, questioning each other's ancestry, and engaging in bouts of machismo. As the men circled each other, it was hard to determine family from foe. Between the bulky winter clothing and the overhead lights casting shadows across their faces, I couldn't tell who it was that I was shoving aside. As I fought my way through the crowd, I wished I had a Taser, a club, or both. Scramble some brains here; bash a few heads there. That might get the message through to them. Or it would just escalate the fight even further.

In the middle of it all, I found my great-uncles, Houston and Bowie, arguing with Oscar Palmer, the patriarch of the Palmer family. My granddaddy was also there, trying to talk some sense into the other old men.

"All right, boys, that's enough," I said, pushing my way between Houston and Granddaddy.

"Get out of here, Carrie!" Granddaddy said.

"What's this now? Can't keep your women in line, Crockett?" Oscar Palmer asked Granddaddy. "You might want to step aside, little lady, and tend to your knitting. There's going to be a fight."

For a liver spotted, stoop shouldered man in his mid-eighties, there was an intimidating presence about Oscar. It came from years of bossing his family around and always getting his way. Uncle Houston had the same aura about him.

"There's not going to be a fight," I said. "Not if I can help it."

"Is that so, little lady? And just what are you going to do to stop us?" Oscar asked.

That was a good question. What could one woman do in a sea of bloodthirsty men who were ready for a brawl? But I wasn't just any woman.

I was an officer of the law. And a pretty good one if I do say so myself. That meant I could throw my weight around and take charge of the situation. Even when I was off-duty, I always carried around my badge and a pair of handcuffs. I never knew when I might have to restrain one of my family members or an unruly citizen. After pulling my handcuffs out of my coat pocket, I took them out for a test drive and clamped them on Oscar's bony wrists.

"Oscar Palmer, you are under arrest."

"What do you think you're doing?" Oscar held up his hands and examined the handcuffs. "You done lost your mind."

"You're trespassing on private property, threatening lives, and inciting a riot." At first, I had to shout to be heard, but as I listed the charges, the people around me stopped fighting and fell silent. "You are also getting on my nerves."

"Hey, what are you doing?" asked one of the Palmers as he stepped forward, ready to confront me. A few of the other Palmers also moved closer, their faces screwed up in anger.

My family, meanwhile, stood around laughing. Along with the laughter came nasty comments directed at Oscar and crew. It did nothing to help the situation as the comments only riled up the Palmers even more.

One of the Palmers reached out to grab me, but I swung my arm up and pushed him away. "Step back or you're next."

I had no idea what I would do if one or more of the Palmer men tried to do something. I only had one pair of handcuffs, and, even if I had my gun on me, I wouldn't have drawn it. That would result in something similar yet larger than the Gunfight at the OK Corral. And I'm no Wyatt Earp.

The Palmers began to yell at me. The Shatners yelled at them. All around me punches were being thrown.

"Looks like you're gonna wind up in the thick of this." Oscar leered at me. "Better hope none of my boys get ahold of you."

"At least I'm not the one in handcuffs." I grasped the short chain connecting the cuffs and gave it a shake, reminding Oscar that while I might not have control of the situation, I did have control of him. And Oscar should have been used to the feel of handcuffs around his wrists. He spent nearly a third of his life in jail for various crimes. "You need to calm them down and take them home. If not, I will arrest you."

"Take the cuffs off, girlie. Seems clear this situation is too much for a little lady like you to handle." Oscar held up his hands and smirked, showing off his ill-fitting dentures. "I'll take care of mine. You call off your dogs."

I pulled the handcuff key out of my pocket and dangled it in front of Oscar. "You first."

"All right." Oscar raised his voice to a shout. Once he had everyone's attention, he said, "We best be going, boys. It seems the Shatners don't have the balls to face us, so they're hiding behind Carrie."

Both families let out a chorus of boos.

It wasn't exactly what I wanted, but I removed the cuffs from his wrists. Oscar patted me on the cheek and addressed my great-uncle Houston, "This ain't over."

"You're all hat and no cattle, and about as welcome as an outhouse breeze," Houston said. "Y'all come back anytime."

The Palmers ambled back to their trucks. After doing a few donuts in the parking lot, they peeled out and headed back to wherever they had come from. While this was going on, my family threw rocks and dared the Palmers to come back. Once the Palmers were gone, the women and children emerged from the pavilion. They, along with the men, converged in a circle around me, shaking their heads and giving me the stink eye. They didn't have to say it for me to know that they deemed my actions out of line. I'd gone and ruined their fun.

"Darn it, Carrie, when will you learn your place?" Houston asked.

"My place? Tell me, Uncle Houston, what is my place?" I moved closer to him but didn't lower my voice. I wanted them all to hear me. "Because I know what my position is. And I was just making my job easier by stopping y'all from taking a shit and stepping in it."

I shouldered past Houston and headed for the parking lot. I had every intention of going home and leaving the family to their own devices. Let them blow themselves up with the fireworks and party into oblivion.

Granddaddy caught up to me and grabbed my arm. "Hold on, Carrie. You did the right thing. Don't let them upset you. They're not mad, just embarrassed."

"I'm not upset. I'm pissed off. This feud is so stupid! Don't they realize that someday they might accidentally kill each other?" I asked.

Granddaddy had been trying to calm me down when my male family members started shouting. They broke into a run, barreling past me as they stampeded towards the parking lot. Somehow Uncle Murph got ahead of them and slid the gate closed, preventing them from getting to their cars. I was too far away to hear what he said, but Murph managed to calm them down and convince them to go back inside.

"So what happened after that?" Sergeant Hardy asked.

"Wrestling was over, so I hustled the band on stage," I said. "My family pretty much calmed down after that."

"Hold on a second. Your family hired a band?"

"Family band. You might have heard of them. The Flaming Outhouses," I said.

My half-brother and four of my cousins formed the band when we were teenagers. The band was named in honor of an incident they all participated in back when we were kids. They'd gotten their hands on some homegrown pot and then snuck into an old outhouse to smoke it. After dropping a pilfered bong down the hole, the boys rolled some lumpy joints and lit them up. They also lit up the outhouse, burning it to the ground.

Hardy made a face. "Yeah, I heard of them. Even went to one of their shows a few years ago. I wasn't impressed."

"Few people are." After having managed the Flaming Outhouses for over eight years, no one knew better than me that the only place their music was truly appreciated was among family.

"You know, you look kind of familiar. Have you ever been a blonde?" Hardy asked.

"Back when I was part of the band." Not only had I managed the band, I sang harmony on the albums and backup during live shows when they performed in Nashville and Texas. Due to my job with the Nashville Crime Scene Investigation Section, I wasn't always able to go on tour with the Flaming Outhouses.

"Well, Detective Shatner, they might have sucked, but you had potential."

"I've since quit the band."

"Probably a good decision on your part."

"That has yet to be determined." Managing the band and chasing off groupies had been far easier than cleaning up after the entire family.

"Where were you during the concert?" Hardy asked.

"On stage where everyone could see me."

The boys had talked me into performing with them—something I hadn't done since I moved home from Nashville. It was fun to get back on stage. The boys and I had some good times in Nashville. We'd gotten thrown out of almost every honky tonk in the city, received a lifetime ban from The Opry, road stolen donkeys down Honky Tonk Row, and crashed several parties, including one at Garth Brooks' house. Sometimes I missed those days.

During the short concert, we had dusted off all of our old favorites: "(That Don't Make Me) White Trash", "I'm On the Pipes (My Woman's on the Pole)", and the tearjerker "She Broke My Heart (When She Crashed My Truck)." Towards the end of the show, the Flaming Outhouses opened up a can of worms by performing "When We Were Outlaws." It was the true (at least in our perspective) story of the Shatner-Palmer Feud. The song got everyone's dander up, but the Flaming Outhouses maintained control by following up with the Shatner family's favorite song: "Family Tradition" by Hank Williams, Jr. Everyone sang along, their lighters raised towards the ceiling. A few might have been crying.

"The concert ended just before midnight. Then we all went outside and set off the fireworks. After that I found the body," I said.

"Let me make sure I have this straight." Hardy read over the notes he'd taken. "Other than when the Palmers showed up and when you set off the fireworks, y'all were inside this building?"

"Pretty much." The only times I had seen anyone go outside was to smoke, go to the bathroom, or get some fresh air.

"All right, then." Hardy snapped his notebook closed. "I'm obviously going to check your alibis for the night, but, as far as I can tell, you probably didn't kill the guy."

Chapter Five

————◆————

Hardy and I exited the semi-warm building and headed towards the back of the fairgrounds and the crime scene. As we came around the side of the multipurpose building, we could see that the body had been extracted from the dumpster. The victim lay stretched out on the ground, a white sheet between him and the asphalt to prevent further contamination.

Uncle Murph, Chief Deputy Quaranta, Chief Groves, Sergeant Boleyn, and a couple of the crime scene technicians were all crowded around the body, preventing me from getting a good look at the victim. As Hardy and I got closer, they backed away.

I tried to make eye contact with Murph, but he was too busy staring dejectedly at the body to look up at me. I noticed that the color had drained from his face, and it appeared he was on the verge of vomiting.

"Who is it?" Fearing the worst, I ran the last few steps towards the body. Even though the victim's face had been badly beaten, he was still recognizable. "Oh, fuck."

"He one of yours?" Hardy asked.

"No. He's not a Shatner," I said, wanting to breathe a sigh of relief and scream at the same time. "He's Kyle Vance. An in-law of the Palmer family."

"So maybe more than punches were thrown," Hardy said.

"Maybe." I nudged Murph in the arm and said, "I didn't see Kyle tonight. Did you?"

Murph shrugged. "Between the coats and the hats, I wasn't sure who any of them were exactly. I could barely tell the Shatners from the Palmers. Vance could have been here."

I cursed under my breath. Yes, the Shatners were definitely traveling down

Shit Creek, and we were entering the rapids.

"What do we know about the victim?" Hardy asked.

Since I had a very strong, thoroughly negative opinion of Kyle, I opted to keep my mouth closed for the time being.

Chief Groves cleared his throat. "Kyle Vance is—was—an all-around bad guy. In the two-and-a-half years Vance lived in Wilder, my officers arrested him a bunch of times for drunk and disorderly, public intoxication, driving under the influence, drug possession, assault, and a few other things. Vance also had a lengthy record before he came to town."

"Look on the plus side, Lou," Murph said. "Now you won't have to deal with him anymore ... Sorry, that was inappropriate."

But totally understandable.

"Well, despite what kind of man he was, he's now dead. Personal feelings aside, we need to figure out who killed him," Hardy said. "So, what have we got?"

"What we don't have is any blood," Groves said.

"None?" Hardy asked, sounding surprised.

Groves shook his head. "My officers and the Wyatt County deputies went over every inch of the fairgrounds, and they didn't find any blood spatter."

"I'll have the crime scene technicians go over the fairgrounds again once the sun is up. It doesn't hurt to look twice. But the way people seem to have been trampling all over the fairgrounds, I'm not sure we'll be able to find any traces of blood." Hardy looked around at all of us gathered around him and then addressed Sergeant Boleyn. "What about the dumpster, Sergeant?"

"The crime scene people went over the outside and the inside with Luminol. Aside from some skin, a bit of tissue, and a little blood on a sharp edge, they didn't find anything," Sergeant Boleyn said. He then held up a clear evidence bag. Inside the evidence bag was a tire iron. "But this was under the body."

I snatched the tire iron out of Boleyn's hand and gave it the once over. There was a smear of blood on the curved end, but there was no tissue or hairs. If the tire iron had been used to bash in the victim's head, I would have expected some sort of trace evidence aside from a small blood smear. Since it was possible the killer had wiped off the tire iron, I didn't voice my suspicions that this was not the murder weapon.

"Any idea on time of death?" I asked.

"How should I know?" I'm a Texas Ranger, not the medical examiner. But I don't think he's been dead all that long. Rigor hasn't started setting in yet. What I can tell you is that the killer redressed him," Boleyn said, giving me a disdainful look. He and I have had a few run-ins over the past couple years when Boleyn was helping out the former Ranger covering Wyatt County.

Boleyn had always made it very clear that he didn't like me.

"How do you know the killer redressed the victim?" Hardy asked.

Boleyn and Quaranta knelt beside Kyle's body. Together they rolled him over on his side.

"There is no blood on the back of the victim's coat." Boleyn tugged the coat away from Kyle's neck and upper back. "But the back of the victim's shirt is covered in blood."

Even though Boleyn only exposed the very top of Kyle's shirt, I could see what he meant. There was dried blood all around the collar of the shirt, but there didn't appear to be any on the collar of the coat. If Kyle had been wearing the coat when he had his head bashed in, there would be blood on it.

"There's also this," Sergeant Boleyn said. He and Quaranta settled Kyle down onto his back. Boleyn then opened up the front of Kyle's coat and pulled up the front of his Hooter's t-shirt to reveal a laceration that bisected Kyle's stomach. Whatever had done it had left a jagged gash, deeper in some sections than in others.

"Since there's no bleeding or reaction to the cut, I'm guessing this happened after the victim was dead. His shirt also has a long tear in it," Boleyn said as he pulled Kyle's shirt back down and showed how the ragged tear in the t-shirt matched up with the cut on his stomach. "It's possible his stomach is what got caught on the sharp edge of the dumpster."

"What evidence did the crime scene technicians find on the body?" Hardy asked.

"Aside from the bits of trash and rotten food?" Boleyn held up a few evidence bags. "Since the dumpster contaminated the victim's clothing, it's hard to say what was already on him and what came from the bottom of the dumpster. The crime scene people found some brown hairs on the coat that are probably the victim's. The color and length appear to match up. There was also a long blonde hair on his sleeve."

"Kyle's wife is a blonde." I yanked the evidence bag out of Boleyn's hand and held it up to the light so that I could get a better look at the blonde hair. "Could be hers."

"Gimmie that!" Boleyn snatched the evidence back from me. "There are what look like either dog or cat hairs on his coat and pants as well. I also found a used lollipop, a piece of wax paper, and seventeen popcorn kernels stuck to the victim's clothes. There's probably more evidence on him, but that'll be up to the medical examiner to collect."

"Did they find anything else?" Hardy asked. "Any evidence that points to the killer, or at least to the primary crime scene?"

"They found a short red hair stuck between two of the victim's teeth." Boleyn held up an evidence bag containing a short, auburn colored hair.

"Do any of your relatives have red hair?" Hardy asked.

"A few. But none of them have hair that shade of red," I said, pointing at the evidence bag that Boleyn was holding.

"It's possible that hair belongs to the killer. It could have wound up getting stuck in the victim's mouth during the altercation," Hardy said.

"I'd like to know how this wound up in the victim's mouth," Boleyn said as he held up a small evidence bag that contained a scrap of dark blue fabric. The edges were jagged and frayed as if it had been torn from a larger piece of cloth.

"Maybe the red hair was stuck to this," Hardy said. When he flipped the bag over, revealing a generic white name patch with red stitching forming the name 'Dale', I groaned. Hardy looked down at me and said, "You don't sound happy, Detective Shatner. Does this means something to you?"

"It means this nightmare is getting worse," I said.

"My oldest boy. His name is Dale," Murph said. "He's a mechanic at a local garage."

"Well then, this certainly is interesting," Hardy said.

I didn't think Hardy was gloating, but I certainly didn't like the smile on his face.

"Dale don't have red hair, though. He's got blonde hair," Murph said.

"And I'm sure my cousin isn't the only Dale in the area who wears a dark blue work uniform with a name patch." I didn't like what the name patch and the tire iron were implying though. Dale wasn't the brightest crayon in the box. I couldn't imagine him killing anyone. But, if he had, it was entirely believable he would leave behind such incriminating pieces of evidence.

"No, but I'm assuming he's the only Dale who was here tonight," Hardy said.

"Dale wasn't here tonight." Murph ripped off his hat and ran his hands through what little blonde hair remained. "I mean, he was here. But he only showed up around eleven-thirty. The Palmers were long gone by the time Dale got here. He couldn't have done this."

Hardy shook his head. "We have no evidence that the victim was killed here. And, since we don't know where or when he was killed, I will be looking into your son's alibi for the evening."

"If—and I'm saying if—Dale killed Kyle elsewhere, he certainly wouldn't have loaded up Kyle's body in his car, and driven him over here to stash him in the dumpster. Not when his entire family was having a party here. Dale may be dumb. But he is not that dumb," I said.

Hardy turned his back to me and addressed Chief Groves. "There's too much going on for me to be able to handle everything myself. I'm going to need you to inform the victim's wife of his death. I would do it myself, but I think it's more important for me to stick around here. I also want you to take your officers, and as many of the Wyatt County deputies that you think you'll need, and go round up the Palmers. You're in charge of interviewing the Palmers about what happened during the past few hours. I want to know where the victim was last night, and why the Palmers felt the need to crash the Shatners' party."

I was trying to eavesdrop on what else Hardy had to say to Groves when Murph grabbed me by the arm and hauled me a few feet away.

"What are you doing, Murph?"

"Do you still have my phone?" Murph tried to stick his hand into my zippered coat pockets. "I need my phone! I need to call Dale!"

"You can't call Dale!" I slapped Murph's grasping hands away from where he was trying to yank open the zippers to get into my coat pockets. "Think of how it would look."

"I don't care how it looks! I need to protect my boy!" Murph grasped my wrist and wrenched it behind my back so that he could unzip my right coat pocket. I didn't bother pointing out that his phone was in the left pocket. "I'm never going to forgive you if Dale did this!"

I tried to squirm away from Murph, but he kept hanging onto my arm and tugging at my coat. With my free arm I swatted at his head and shoulders, but I couldn't get in any solid blows.

"Let go of me, old man!" I yelled, startling Murph and attracting unwanted attention.

"Everything okay over here, Detective Shatner?" Hardy asked from somewhere behind me. "Or is this some kind of weird Shatner family ritual I don't know about?"

"No, this is called Murph's desperate attempt to get his phone back from me." I shoved Murph away and then sidled closer to Hardy.

"Any particular reason the sheriff wants his phone?" Hardy asked. "And why do you have it?"

"I took it from him earlier so that he couldn't tell anyone about the body," I said.

"Shut up, Carrie. I wasn't going to tell anyone," Murph said.

"I think I should take a look at both of your phones." Hardy held out his hands. "Give them to me."

"Don't do it, Carrie," Murph said. "He can't make you."

"The sheriff is right, I can't make you do anything," Hardy said. "But I can arrest you for obstruction."

Since I didn't have anything to hide—at least about the body in the dumpster—I unzipped my coat pocket and pulled out both cell phones. I then slapped the phones into Hardy's hands. If someone called or texted to confess, that was their own fault.

"You did the right thing, Detective Shatner," Hardy said.

"No, she didn't," Murph mumbled.

"Looks like you both have quite a few texts and missed calls." Hardy tossed my cell phone back to me. "Let's see them. Now."

"Carrie, don't you do it … " Murph said.

I unlocked my phone screen and brought up the text messages. The most recent one was from my cousin Cletus. The message, which was partially made up of emojis, wasn't entirely coherent. But neither was Cletus.

"Which one of you let the cat out of the bag?" Hardy asked.

"I didn't. How could I when Carrie had my phone?" Murph asked, backing away.

"I didn't say anything to anyone," I said.

"Well someone said something," Hardy said.

"Look around and take your pick." I gestured towards all of the deputies and police officers lurking around the fairground. "Any one of them could have called or texted a Shatner. After that, the word would have gone around faster than a hot knife through butter."

"You're right. Anyone could have spread the word. But I still want to read all those texts and listen to the voicemails. Now," Hardy said.

Between the two of us, Murph and I had been contacted by every Shatner over the age of twelve. And every single one of them wanted to know the same two things—did we really find a body at the fairgrounds and, if we did, who was it? None of them admitted to killing someone and hiding the body. No one asked for help in disposing of the body and covering up the crime. None of them even admitted to having found the body in the dumpster. The texts Murph and I were most interested in came from Dale. He had sent the same one to each of us asking what was going on. Murph relaxed after reading his son's text.

The majority of the most recent texts and calls were from family members telling us that a large group of them were headed over to Uncle Houston's house. It sounded like his stock of canned rations and toilet paper would be in use since everyone was planning to hang out there for the time being. It warmed my heart knowing that my great-uncles would get to play with all of the security cameras they had installed. That would keep them entertained for a while.

When Uncle Houston had the security cameras installed intermittently around the five thousand acres that some of the Shatners jointly own, I told him that he was being paranoid. I still thought he was being paranoid but, for that day at least, he had a legitimate reason to be. I could picture Houston and Bowie seated in front of the security camera monitors, watching for any sign of movement in the woods and outside the houses. Meanwhile, I just knew that the women and children were huddled in Houston's living room while the rest of the men took turns pointing their guns out the windows. Collectively, my family had enough weapons to invade a third world country. Whether we could successfully take over or not was another question.

Houston and Bowie had also set up multiple booby traps around the perimeter of the property, making the area a minefield of destruction should any unknowing or unsuspecting persons wander into areas where they were not welcome. I wasn't sure who they expected to make an unwanted visit— the Palmer family, federal agents, or little green men from outer space—but my family was ready for whenever they did come. So far, the only living creatures they'd managed to capture were a few possums and skunks, a white tail deer, and Chief Yates. Yates was trying to locate the moonshine still when he stumbled into a ten-foot deep pit that was camouflaged by leaves and fallen limbs. He was stuck in there for two days before anyone bothered to go haul him out. The security footage of Yates trying to get out of the pit was hilarious.

"I think I'll hang onto your phones for a while," Hardy said, tucking the two cell phones into his coat pocket. "Now that your family knows about the dead body in the dumpster I'm going to have to approach this far differently than I had been planning to. I just need to figure out exactly how to go about doing this."

Murph and I exchanged another look.

"Uh, Sergeant Hardy, I know my niece and I are probably the last people you want to take advice from—"

Interrupting Uncle Murph, I said, "But we have years of experience dealing with the Shatners. And you don't. So we're going to give you some advice anyway."

"Oh yeah?" Hardy took off his cowboy hat and slapped it against his leg.

"Yeah. The Shatners … well, I know you've heard plenty about us, so I'm sure you know we don't work well with the authorities," I said.

"I've heard some rumors," Hardy said.

"Even if they haven't done anything wrong, most of them still aren't going to cooperate," Murph said.

"Then how do you suggest I get something useful out of them?" Hardy asked.

"Right now you just need to get them out of Houston's house," I said. "And you can't just send my deputies or, well, anyone short of a SWAT team to go get them. I don't know how they'll react, but I do know that it won't be pretty."

"Some of the Shatners would rather be taken in dead than alive," Murph added.

"I think the best way to get them out of the house, and into the sheriff's department, would be to send my grandfather over to Uncle Houston's house to talk some sense into everyone. He's probably the only person who can talk his brothers into coming in. And if he can get Houston and Bowie to come in, then the rest of them will follow."

"I really hate taking advice from y'all, but in this case I think I'm going to have to," Hardy said. "And, I assume you'll want to help with all this, Detective Shatner?"

I rocked back and forth on my heels as I thought about the best way to phrase my answer. Of course, I wanted to help out as much as possible on the investigation. My family's collective butt was on the line. But I had my doubts that Hardy would even consider letting me or Uncle Murph help, which was why I have to make it sound like he needed our input.

"This is your investigation, I get that," I said. "But you're dealing with people who are used to running from the law. Not helping the authorities. I'm just saying your investigation might go a little easier if you let me and Uncle Murph smooth things over with our family. If you let me talk to them before you start interviewing them, I can convince them to answer your questions."

"Is this some elaborate ploy?" Hardy asked. "Are you two actually trying to help me or are you doing this to undermine my investigation."

"We're trying to help you help our family," I said.

"I'd be crazy to even consider letting you two help." Hardy walked off a few feet before spinning around and coming back. "But I'll play along. Though I already have a bad feeling that I'm going to regret this."

Chapter Six

---◆---

Hardy wanted me to go straight to the Wyatt County Sheriff's Department with him, but I convinced him that I needed to go home and check on my dog first. Before I left the crime scene, Hardy threatened to throw me in jail for obstruction if I contacted any of my family members about what was going on. I swore up and down that I would keep my mouth shut and not leak any information about the case to anyone for any reason. Hardy must have known I had my fingers crossed behind my back because, at the last second, he shoved a deputy into the passenger seat of my Jeep and instructed him to not let me out of his sight.

"What do you think is going on?" Deputy Timmy Grant asked. "Who do you think killed that guy?"

"It was probably a contract killing," I said.

"Oh, my goodness, do you really think so?"

"Sure, Timmy, anything is possible," I said, rolling my eyes at his gullible excitement.

Timmy was the youngest deputy in the department. I'm pretty sure that Uncle Murph hired him out of pity and kept him around for the same reason. In the past year, Timmy had pepper sprayed himself three times, wrecked two of the sheriff's department's cruisers, accidently discharged his weapon five times, and almost set the squad room on fire.

The drive east through the gently rolling hills and heavily wooded areas to my small neighborhood on the east side of Holler might have passed in silence were it not for Timmy's inability to shut up. He always had to be talking—even if it was to himself. Timmy managed to remain silent for nearly two minutes before he launched into a story about the last professional wrestling event that he went to. At least he had a hobby.

I didn't pass too many cars during the half hour drive across the county. At five in the morning, most people were still in bed, sleeping off hangovers before spending the day watching college football. I had intended to do something similar, but, thanks to Kyle Vance getting himself killed, my plans had changed.

Reaching my darkened neighborhood, I pulled into my driveway and killed the engine. I then climbed out of my Jeep and trudged up the sidewalk to the front door. Timmy scurried along at my heels.

My house was the same one that I grew up in. It might not hold the best memories, but it was home for the first sixteen years of my life. My earliest memories involved my mom with a drink in her hand. I'm not sure when she went from casual drinker to full-blown alcoholic, but one day it happened—leaving me and my two sisters to hide the full bottles and clean up the empties. My dad, who did holier-than-thou better than anyone I knew, was always getting on Mom about the drinking. Meanwhile, Dad was out running around with other women. That's how I wound up with two younger half-brothers. I had no doubt that there may be more. Either way, the more Dad cheated, the more Mom drank. And the more Mom drank, the more Dad cheated. It got to the point where Dad would stay away for days at a time, and we had no idea where he was. When Dad was at home, my parents' favorite pastime was to scream at each other. It was like being trapped in a room full of landmines, powder kegs, and dynamite. Anything and everything could cause an explosion. I lost count of the number of times I locked myself in my room, pillows pressed against my ears to block out the sounds of their fighting. When things got really bad, I would climb out my bedroom window and ride my bike to my friend's house.

Reminding myself that my parents and sisters were long gone from this house, I shoved the key in the lock and took a deep breath before unlocking the front door. It has been almost fifteen years since both of my parents checked out of my life—Dad died when I was sixteen and Mom moved to Dallas not long afterwards—but, sometimes, I still expect to walk in the front door to find bottles shattered on the floor and holes punched through the walls.

I swung open my front door and was about to step into the house when a hundred pounds of dog hit me square in the chest. I stumbled back into Timmy, which helped me retain my balance. Timmy went crashing over backwards and landed in my flowerbed.

"I'm okay!" Timmy said, spitting mulch out of his mouth.

"Hi, Molly!" I wrapped my arms around my dog and then lowered her to the ground, forcing her backwards into the house. "I see that you missed me. I missed you too."

After getting Molly back into the house, I had a seat in the middle of the foyer so that she could go through her ritual greeting. Molly's fluffy tail whipped back and forth, making a racket as it banged against the wall. She also stepped on me multiple times as she danced around me, sniffing my clothes, slobbering kisses all over my face, and jabbing her cold nose into my eyes.

I got Molly just after I moved back from Nashville. I needed some sort of company, but I was going through a phase where I didn't want any sort of human companionship. Since my parents refused to let me have a dog when I was a kid, I decided a dog was exactly what I wanted. When I first saw her, Molly was a little golden ball of fluff. These days, she was a much larger golden ball of fluff. For the most part, she resembled a golden retriever. She was what kept me sane while the Shatners were doing their best to drive me crazy.

"Does she bite?" Timmy asked.

I glanced back at Timmy, and found him cowering in the doorway. His usually pale face was drained ghost white, causing his freckles and crimson hair to stand out in stark contrast.

"No, she doesn't bite. Now get in here," I said. Molly was too excited to see me to even pay attention to Timmy. "Kitchen is straight back the hall. Don't bother searching for food, because I haven't been to the grocery store in a few days. Living room is to the right. You can just hang out and watch TV while I take a shower and change clothes."

"The Texas Ranger said I am not to let you out of my sight."

"Timmy, let me make this clear … If you try to follow me into the bathroom, I will shoot you. If you try lurking in the hallway while I'm in the bathroom, I will shoot you. But if it makes you feel better, I will leave my house phone, laptop, tablet, and all other devices on which I could possibly contact someone with you."

"I guess that's okay," Timmy said.

Herding Molly ahead of me into the living room, I flipped the switch to turn on the room's lights.

"Holy Pat Green!" I screamed, taking my favorite Texas singer and songwriter's name in vain when I spotted a man casually sitting on my leather cowhide couch. He had a beer in hand, and his feet were propped up on my rustic wagon wheel coffee table. I think I handled finding the dead body better. Of course, this was my house. That was a dumpster. "What are you doing?"

"Waiting for you." The man slammed his beer bottle down on the coffee table.

"I can see that, Andrew," I said, addressing my cousin. Andrew Bohannon is my dad's sister's youngest kid. He lived with me when he wasn't in Nashville. I shouldn't have been surprised to find him in the house, but it about scared the crap out of me to come across him lurking around in the dark. "Mind putting that bottle on a coaster?"

"So, we heard you found a body," Andrew said.

"Oh yeah? Who says?" I asked.

"Aunt Lydia was waiting around in the fairgrounds' parking lot for Uncle Murph when the deputies started rolling in. They told her what was going on. When she couldn't get in touch with Murph, and no one would let her into the fairgrounds to find him, she went to Uncle Houston's house," Andrew said. "It would have been nice if you or Murph had let us know what's going on. I called you, like, three times. And sent you a bunch of texts. Why didn't you call me?"

"I've been a tad bit busy, Andrew."

"Whatever. So … who's dead?"

I threw myself down onto the couch beside Andrew. Molly jumped up and stretched out beside me, and Timmy had a seat on the floor.

Andrew was a little more than two months older than me. He was more of a brother than a cousin. Since we were old enough to talk, he and I had told each other everything. And I do mean everything. This would be the first time in a long time where I couldn't confide in him.

"You know I can't tell you anything about what happened," I said.

"Can you at least tell me if it's a Shatner?"

"No, it's not one of us." I shouldn't have even said that much, but I wanted to assuage his fears at least a little bit. "But I'm going to need you to come in to the sheriff's department with me to answer some questions."

"No thanks. I didn't kill anyone," Andrew said. "And I don't know anyone who did."

"I know. I know. But right now I just need you to cooperate with me." Standing up, I made my way towards the kitchen. "And don't bother asking Timmy about the dead person. He doesn't know anything."

After filling up Molly's food and water bowls, I scrounged around the kitchen and managed to find enough edible food to make a sandwich. It had been hours since I last ate, and I didn't know how long it would be until I got another chance at a meal. After inhaling the sandwich, I ran back the hall and jumped in the shower. I knew I should hurry up and get to the sheriff's department as soon as I could, but I stayed under the hot water until I felt human again. I then put on clean clothes and redid my hair and makeup. I used up all of my concealer trying to hide the purple bags that had appeared under my eyes during the long, sleepless night.

After putting myself together, I returned to the living room. I found Timmy tentatively petting Molly while Andrew watched an infomercial for a weed whacker. Andrew had changed out of his pajamas and into ratty street clothes for his upcoming visit to the sheriff's department.

When he felt like it, Andrew could clean up quite well. He hardly ever felt like it though. Years ago, Andrew grew out his brown hair and someone mistook him for me without makeup. Andrew was humiliated. And I was still a little disturbed that someone mistook Andrew for me. Sure, we looked a lot alike, but I wanted to believe that I was prettier than him.

"All right, let's do this," I said.

"Yeah, let's get it over with," Andrew said.

THE TOWN OF HOLLER GOT its start in the mid-eighteen hundreds. When the Shatners and Palmers arrived just after the Civil War, Holler wasn't much more than a general store, a post office, a livery stable, a couple churches, and a few other businesses. There were also a couple dozen houses. It wasn't until the very beginning of the nineteen hundreds that the town began to flourish. The old, wooden buildings were razed, a town square was plotted out, and new, brick buildings started going up.

The Wyatt County Sheriff's Department took up the entire block on the western side of the town square. The old, red brick building used to be the general store, but, in the fifties, the store closed down. After some renovations, the sheriff's department staff moved in. The outside of the building had definitely seen better days, but the inside was still in fairly good shape. The rest of the buildings located around the town square were also the original ones that were built in the early nineteen hundreds. Wandering around the Holler town square was like taking a trip back in time. But, once you left the town square area, the homes and businesses became more modern looking. Aside from a couple apartment buildings and hotels, none of the buildings in the small town were over two stories.

I opted to park out front as opposed to driving around back and parking in the sheriff's department's lot. I assumed that the officers and the deputies would bring my family in through the back. And I wanted to put off seeing them for as long as I could.

Sneaking through the lobby, I waved at the night receptionist/dispatcher. I then passed through the doorway into the actual sheriff's department. Finding no one lurking in the hallway, I dashed across the hall, and ducked into Uncle Murph's office. I then almost tripped over a chair that was lying on the floor. Murph's office could be mistaken for a disaster zone. Papers were strewn across the massive desk, and the other guest chairs were overturned. It looked like someone had ransacked the place, but I wasn't concerned since this was Murph's usual controlled chaos. What had me concerned was that Murph wasn't in his office.

Tiptoeing down the department's main hallway, I finally spotted Murph's balding head peeking out around the side of the breakroom doorway. He waved at me and then ducked back into the breakroom.

Scurrying down the hall, I rushed into the breakroom and found Murph slumped at the small table in the middle of the room. There were two empty bags of pork rinks on the table, and Murph was scooping the contents of the third into his mouth.

"You know that stuff will kill you, right?" I asked.

"I've got more important things to worry about," Murph said.

"Right, like the dead body."

"And the fact that the crime scene investigation team found evidence linking my boy to the dead body."

"That too." I leaned against the wall and closed my eyes. If not for Murph's heavy and frantic breathing, I probably would have fallen asleep. "How'd your interview go with the Texas Ranger?"

"All right. I gave him an account of the night's events and a list of the people I was with throughout the night." Murph drummed his greasy fingers on the edge of the table. "Despite the fact that he knows I have an alibi for the entire evening, he's making me sit in here. It's the only room without a phone aside from the jail cell, bathrooms, and evidence lockup room. He doesn't trust me near any electronics."

"I wouldn't either," I said.

"But what do you think? Can we trust Sergeant Hardy to investigate this properly? Or is he going to railroad us?" Murph asked.

"So far Sergeant Hardy seems okay. Not only didn't he arrest us on suspicion, he even listened to our advice. But, how do we know he is qualified for the job?"

"Now, Carrie, I'm sure he's a highly trained officer." Murph stopped drumming his fingers long enough to pop an antacid in his mouth. "And, if it makes you feel any better, I had Quaranta run a background check on Hardy as soon as he got back here. Quaranta didn't get much yet, but it's enough to get an idea." Murph picked up a sheaf of papers and flipped through them. "Let's see, Jerrod Patrick Hardy … He applied to the State Trooper trainee program when he was twenty-one. He's started out working in and around Waco. He was on the highway patrol for a couple years and then got transferred to the Criminal Investigations Division. Over the years he's worked everywhere in the state except around here." Murph flipped through a few more pages. "Sergeant Hardy has an outstanding record. He's been involved in a bunch of drug busts and been part of some big investigations. This guy is good, and he plays by the rules."

On one hand, I was glad Hardy excelled at his job. On the other, I was worried that Hardy only saw things as black or white. That would be bad for my family considering we preferred to live in the grey areas.

Murph and I were discussing how we should handle Hardy, when Chief Deputy Quaranta slipped into the room.

"The deputies have your family down in the conference room. As usual, they are demanding lawyers and are claiming police brutality and false arrest," Quaranta said as he stroked his Fu Manchu mustache. "Otherwise, they're mostly behaving. Good idea sending your granddaddy over to Houston's to talk them into coming here willingly. He managed to talk some sense into most of them. From what I've heard, only one of them tried to make a run for it. But three of them did assault the deputies."

"Yeah, that's not bad at all," I said. Of course, it was only six in the morning, and most of the Shatners were either still drunk or battling a hangover.

"They might have come in semi-willingly, but they're not happy," Quaranta said. "They're demanding to see both of you."

"I'm not going in there," Murph said. "Not until Sergeant Hardy says I can. And, even then, I don't want to go in there. You can deal with them, Carrie."

"Oh no. We're going to determine who talks to them the same way we decided on everything else around here. A Rock Paper Scissors tournament." Turning my back to Murph, I addressed Quaranta. "Has Sergeant Hardy been in to talk to them yet?"

"He peeked in at them, but he wants to let them to calm down some before he sends in the deputies to start questioning them."

"I hope you told Sergeant Hardy that they won't be calming down," I said. The Shatners were not calm, rational people. The longer they were kept in the conference room, the more agitated and uncooperative they would get.

"I tried to tell him," Quaranta said. "He didn't listen."

"If Sergeant Hardy doesn't get things started soon, he'll probably have a riot on his hands," I said. "Where is Sergeant Hardy now?"

"In your office," Quaranta said.

"Unsupervised?" I panicked thinking that I might have left a piece of incriminating evidence about my family's illegal activities on my desk. There was so much of that kind of stuff lying around that I couldn't remember if I locked it up in the evidence lockup room or not. I forced myself to take a deep breath and relax.

"Like I said, he's looking for you."

Chapter Seven

━━━━━━━◆━━━━━━━

I found Sergeant Hardy kicked back in my only guest chair as he flipped through his notebook. His boots, which were propped up on the edge of my desk, were mere inches away from the large, bright blue bong that I had confiscated from some underage family members the previous week.

"Glad you could join me, Detective Shatner. I saw you darting by earlier." Hardy swung his feet off my desk, knocking the bong into the trashcan and breaking off the top half. "Whoops. That wasn't yours, was it?"

"Don't worry, I have a bunch more."

"I'm sure you do." Hardy closed his notebook and tossed it onto the table. "Did you learn anything interesting or do something I wouldn't approve of while you were at home?"

"That depends on what you do and do not approve of." Having a seat, I propped my elbows on the edge of the desk and smiled at Hardy to convey that I was being friendly. "What about you? What have you been up to while I was gone?"

"I'm sure you already know I spoke with the sheriff," Hardy said. "And I just got off the phone with Chief Groves."

"Oh, yeah? What has he found out so far?" I asked as my smile faded.

"Chief Groves tried talking to Whitney Vance, but she couldn't stop crying long enough to answer his questions. About the only useful thing he got out of her was that the last time she saw her husband was sometime yesterday afternoon. She claims he went in to work, which is at the Dancing Cowgirl. Whatever that is."

"It's a strip club on the south side of town. Oscar Palmer owns the building. One of the other Palmers runs the strip club out of it," I said.

"Interesting … According to Oscar Palmer, who Chief Groves also spoke with, the Palmer family held their New Year's Eve party there."

"Did Whitney or Oscar say if Kyle was at the party?" I asked.

"It doesn't sound like Mrs. Vance was in attendance at the party. Chief Groves got the impression that none of the Palmer women were there. But Oscar insists that Kyle was there," Hardy said. "He claims that Kyle went along with the rest of the men to crash your family's party. It wasn't until they got back to the Dancing Cowgirl that they noticed Kyle was missing, but they didn't seem too worried that he was missing."

"Why did the Palmers crash our party?" I asked.

"Chief Groves asked Oscar, but all he got was some rambling answer about family pride and perceived insults. Groves thinks it might have been revenge for what happened on the Fourth of July. I'm curious to know about what happened back in July."

"More stupidity," I said. "The Shatners have been putting on a big fireworks show every year on the Fourth of the July. It's turned into quite an event. So last summer a handful of the Palmers spent the spring and early summer making their own illegal fireworks. They're lucky they didn't blow themselves up in the process. No one knew what they were up to until late June. That's when they went around telling everyone about their homemade fireworks and how they were going to have a better fireworks show than us."

"I think I see where this is going," Hardy said.

"No, you probably don't," I said. "Somehow one of my cousins found out where the Palmers were making and storing their fireworks. In the early hours of the fourth, a bunch of my cousins and uncles commandeered one of the Holler Fire Department trucks and drove over to the building where the Palmers were storing the fireworks. I was later told that the plan was to douse the fireworks in water to ruin them. Instead, some idiot threw a lighter into the building and basically blew it up."

Since a number of Shatners were volunteer firefighters, they just rolled out the hose on the firetruck and put out the flames. The fire was out by the time I arrived on scene.

"Were any charges filed?" Hardy asked.

"Of course not," I said. "That's one thing you've got to learn, Hardy. No matter what the Shatners may have done, there is never going to be any evidence of it."

"And that's at least partially because of you, right?" Hardy asked.

Deciding to move on from the subject, I stood up and moved towards the door. "I think you've kept my family waiting long enough. You better get the interviews started before they start revolting. I'm telling you, things could get ugly."

"Your family can wait for a few more minutes." Hardy picked up a paper bag and plopped it down on my desk, squashing a big bag of marijuana that I had confiscated along with the bong. "I still want to go through the evidence that Sergeant Boleyn removed from Kyle's body before he packaged him up and sent him off to the medical examiner. Care for a look?"

"You're going to let me near the evidence?" I asked, automatically assuming that Hardy was up to something.

"For the moment." Hardy reached in the paper bag and pulled out a handful of clear evidence bags. Inside the evidence bags were all of the items that Boleyn had found in Kyle's pockets. "Let's see, we've got a wallet, some change, receipts, keys, and a Swiss Army knife."

"No cell phone?" I asked.

Hardy read over a sheet of paper that had been tucked into the bag. "There isn't one listed on the evidence log."

"That's weird. You think he lost it?" I asked. "Or maybe the killer took it."

"Both are possible. I can get a warrant for his phone records. And, if his phone is on, maybe we can track its location." Hardy removed Kyle's wallet from the evidence bag. "Driver's license. A couple credit cards. Wad of cash … And a naked picture of some woman."

I looked at the picture and cringed. The woman in the photo probably would have looked better clothed. She'd tried for sexy, but she'd achieved awkward.

"That's his wife, Whitney," I said.

Hardy stuck the picture back in the wallet, and then returned the wallet to the evidence bag. He then picked up the bag containing the car keys. "I'll have to find out what kind of car Kyle drives and put out a BOLO."

"I can tell you one place the car isn't, and that's the fairgrounds parking lot," I said.

"No, there weren't any random cars in the parking lot," Hardy said. "I haven't had a chance to send anyone else out to check the fields and woods around the fairgrounds yet. Kyle's car could be hidden somewhere."

Hardy opened up the evidence bag containing the receipts and flipped through them. All three receipts were from last night. The first was for gas from the Exxon on the north side of Wilder. Kyle had been there in the afternoon. The other two receipts were from early evening. One put Kyle at Walmart around five. The other put him at one of the local Dairy Queens, fifteen minutes later. Kyle's last meal was a burger, fries, and a sundae. The receipts gave us a timeline of Kyle's final hours. We didn't know when or where he died, but we now knew he was still alive and eating around six o'clock on New Year's Eve. And if Kyle was alive and well around six o'clock that meant his dead body was not discarded in the fairgrounds' dumpster prior to the party getting started. He had to have been killed and stuffed in the dumpster sometime during the party. Along with that knowledge went my last shred of hope that none of the Shatners had killed Kyle.

"I'll get a warrant for the security footage from these three places," Hardy said. "And once we have all the evidence in order, I'll ship it off to the lab."

"Do you have to send everything?" I asked. When Hardy raised an eyebrow, I sighed and then said, "The fireworks my family had last night were illegal. I know the remains of the fireworks were collected as evidence, but I'm pretty sure they had nothing to do with how or why Kyle wound up dead. He was most likely dead before we started setting the fireworks off."

Hardy shook his head. "Did you know the fireworks were illegal?"

"Yes. And don't ask me why I didn't confiscate them."

Hardy patted my shoulder. "Sorry, Detective Shatner, but the fireworks were collected as evidence. Just because I'm sending them to the lab doesn't mean that anyone will look at them. And, even if anyone does, you've got more important things to worry about than illegal fireworks."

"I know," I said. Hardy was right; the fireworks were the least of my problems at the moment. "What do you think?"

"There is a lot we still need to find out about the victim's final hours. I also want to hear what your family has to say. But, more importantly, there is one thing I need to know from you," Hardy said.

I had a good idea what he was going to ask me. "The answer is no. If one or more of my family members killed Kyle, I don't know about it. I'm not trying to cover for anyone. I know you have no reason to believe me, but I'm telling you the truth."

"I don't know if I believe you, but I want to." Taking me by the arm, Hardy steered me out of my office. "Come on, I think your family has been waiting long enough. Let's get the questioning started."

Hardy and I headed down the hallway towards the other side of the building. The closer we got to the conference room, the louder the voices from inside sounded. When Hardy opened the conference room door, roughly seventy Shatners turned to face us. There weren't many chairs in the conference room, so the majority of my family was left standing. Some of the kids had brought toys along, and they were playing under the table. For a few seconds, my family members fell silent. Then the bevy of questioning began.

"What the hell is going on?"

"Who's dead?"

"Do you have any idea what time it is?"

"I'm not talking, and you can't make me."

"Who's that guy?"

"We've got nothing to do with this."

When my family started directing their questions Hardy's way, he pulled me back into the hallway.

"Are they usually this uncooperative?" Hardy asked.

"Oh no, they're actually on their best behavior right now."

Hardy rolled his eyes. "Can you get them under control?"

"Yeah, sure. Nothing easier than that." I stepped back into the room and screamed, "Everybody shut up!"

A few people listened to my directive, but others started getting on my case about how disrespectful I was being by talking to them that way. Despite my best efforts, the Shatners actually got worse. With no other alternative, I opened my mouth and let loose with a primal scream. That finally shut them up. And the screaming certainly calmed me down, downgrading me from borderline homicidal to mildly annoyed.

"Everyone, this is Sergeant Jerrod Hardy of the Texas Rangers. He's here because I found a dead body in the dumpster after our party. Did any of you know about that prior to me finding it? Let's see a show of hands." No one raised a hand. "I'm guessing no one wants to admit to killing anyone and stowing the body in the dumpster either?"

"Screw you, Carrie," mumbled someone towards the back of the room.

"The deputies are going to ask all of you some questions about what happened last night," Hardy said. "They will be asking you about the party, so just tell them what you were doing and who you were with."

When the protests commenced, I held up my hands for silence. "I know none of you want to talk to the law, but it's in your best interest to do so. If you haven't done anything wrong, then there is no reason for you to not answer some questions."

"I ain't answering nothing!" one of my uncles or male cousins yelled.

"How 'bout you tell us who's dead? Maybe then we'll answer your questions," Uncle Houston said. "Hard to answer 'em if we don't know what happened."

"We will tell you the identity of the victim," Hardy said. "But only after y'all are done answering the questions. Now, if you'll excuse us, Sergeant Boleyn will be with you in a few minutes."

Hardy and I stepped out of the conference room, shutting the door behind us.

"They're all going to refuse to answer anything and then demand lawyers, aren't they?" Hardy asked.

"I'm sure some will. And they might have already talked the rest into not cooperating. But there are a lot of people in there who know they didn't do anything wrong. They aren't the killers. And they might just talk to save their own butts," I said.

"Let's hope that they do." Hardy spun around and headed back the hall towards my office. "Come on, Detective. I've still got some more questions for you."

Back in my office, I found a file folder containing Kyle's criminal record sitting in the middle of my desk. I wasn't sure who brought it in, but I was thankful for it simply because the criminal record distracted Hardy and kept him from asking me any more questions.

I leaned back in my chair and watched as Hardy quickly flipped through the record. He had been handed a novel when, for the time being, he wanted the cliff notes.

"I see our victim definitely wasn't up for the Citizen of the Year Award," Hardy said.

"He wouldn't have had a chance at Boyfriend of the Year, either," I said.

"Is that so?" Hardy tossed the file onto my desk where it landed with a thud. "I guess you better start talking."

"It was two-and-a-half years ago," I said, hoping Hardy would decide that it wasn't really relevant. "It was nothing."

"Everything is something, Detective Shatner. Let's hear it."

"It was about a year after I moved home from Nashville. I was hanging out at the lake with my friends when someone introduced me to Kyle. He had just moved to Wilder and a friend of a friend was going around introducing him to people."

"Let me guess, it was love at first sight?"

I scowled at Hardy. "No. It definitely was not. Well, at least not on my part. When we met, Kyle couldn't stop staring at my boobs long enough to look me in the eye. I saw him around a few times after that, but it's not like I was going out of my way to hang out with him. It wasn't until about a month later that I really talked to him. We were both invited to the same Fourth of July party out on the lake. A few of those double decker pontoon boats were roped together to have a party on them. I didn't stay too long. There was a lot of drinking and I have only so much tolerance for drunken people who aren't related to me. I got sick of it and had one of my uncles come out on his fishing boat and rescue me."

"Was Kyle one of those drunken people that got on your nerves?"

"He was one of the worst. Which is why, when he started texting me later that night about how much he wanted to be with me, I ignored him. I figured it was just drunken ramblings. Except, once he sobered up, he kept pursuing me."

"So you two started dating?"

"No, I wouldn't say what we were doing was dating."

"Then it was just sex?"

"Oh, God, no! I never had sex with Kyle. Ever." I wanted to make sure I was clear about that. "Never ever."

"Okay, we've established that you never had sex with the victim. What did happen?"

"Like I said, Kyle came after me. And he was really persistent about it. He would text me from the moment he got up until he finally fell asleep. And if I didn't answer within five or ten minutes, he would send me another text. And another. And so on until I finally responded. It was a real pain in the butt."

"You want to summarize these texts for me?" Hardy asked.

"Oh, it was nothing that interesting." There were things Kyle said to me that I didn't want anyone to ever know about. Things too offensive or personal to share with anyone else. "Mainly, the texts were about how much he wanted to be with me and that he couldn't live without me. Kyle was the kind of guy who always wanted things to go his way. He thought he owned me and could tell me what to do."

"Yet you still dated him?" The left side of Hardy's mouth twisted up in a disgusted sneer. I wasn't sure if it was directed at me or Kyle.

"I wouldn't say I dated him. I just talked to him. And I still can't figure out why I did that. I really didn't like him. And the more I got to know him, the less I wanted to do with him. Especially after I ran a background check and found out about his criminal record."

Hardy scribbled something into his notebook. When he caught me trying to read it, he drew the notebook closer to him and then used his arm to block my view.

"How did this so-called relationship end?" Hardy asked.

"I caught him getting a hole-in-one with Whitney Palmer."

"You caught them in the act?" Hardy asked. "How'd you manage to do that?"

"I was on duty, helping cover part of the night shift about five or six weeks after Kyle started coming after me. Chief Deputy Quaranta and I were driving around when we got a call about a disturbance at the one mini-golf place." Wyatt County had two mini-golf courses. The nicer of the two was in Holler. It was across the parking lot from the bowling alley. The one we got called out to was the Christian-themed golf course down in the southern end of the county. "When we got there, Quaranta and I split up and wandered around the course. We assumed that it was just teenagers defacing the religious statues again. Instead, I found two people having sex at the feet of Jesus on the eighteenth hole."

"How did that make you feel?" Hardy asked.

"What are you? A therapist? How do you think I felt?" I asked. "At first, before I realized who it was, I was ready to jerk them both bald for doing the nasty at the feet of Jesus. Just because he's made out of concrete doesn't mean he couldn't see what they were doing. Then I saw who it was, and I was mainly relieved that Kyle had found someone else to bug."

"Were you mad enough to kill Kyle?" Hardy asked.

"Don't you think if I was that upset about it I would have killed him back then? I had my gun in my hands. I could have shot him. Why would I wait two-and-a-half years for payback? Especially when I didn't even really like him?"

"Didn't Kyle wind up marrying Whitney?" Hardy asked.

"Yeah, he married her about a year after the mini-golf incident. Turns out he was dating Whitney the same time he was trying to hook up with me."

"So that's it? Kyle married Whitney, and you went on your merry way?" Hardy asked.

"No, that wasn't the end of it. Despite telling Kyle that I wanted absolutely nothing to do with him, he had the nerve to tell me that, considering what had happened, he wasn't sure that he wanted to be with me anymore. But he expected me to wait around until he figured it out. Can you believe that? Three months later, Kyle called me. He claimed that he had finally figured out what he wanted and that was to be with me. I laughed so hard that I literally hurt myself."

The corner of Hardy's mouth tilted up in a smile. I noticed that his eyes were laughing. Whether he was laughing with me or at me I wasn't sure. "Are you saying that you're still mad at him?"

"Again with the shrink stuff. No, I just can't believe Kyle could be that stupid."

"How did Kyle react to all this?" Hardy asked.

"When I told Kyle that we were done, and reiterated I wanted nothing to do with him, he threw a fit. Apparently what I wanted didn't matter. He started screaming at me, demanding to know why I didn't wait for him. After that, I changed my phone number and put the whole Kyle incident in the past."

"So that's it?" Hardy flipped his notebook closed.

"Not quite. Last summer, about a year after he married Whitney, Kyle showed up at my house. He stood on my front lawn, screaming at me for ruining his life. Just like it was my fault again that he had hooked up with Whitney, it was my fault that he married her. Apparently everything that has gone wrong in his life in the past two-and-a-half years has been my fault."

"Is it your fault he's dead?"

"How should I know?" I asked. "But I really doubt it. Not after all this time."

But what if it was my fault Kyle was dead? I might not have been the one to kill him, but someone might have killed him on my behalf. I didn't want Kyle's blood on my hands. Sure, I disliked him. And I might even be secretly relieved that he was dead because that meant I no longer had to worry about him bothering me anymore. Kyle's random appearances into my life—especially when he was harassing me and blaming me for somehow ruining his life—had caused me way too much stress. But I didn't want to be the reason someone killed Kyle. I had enough on my conscience; I didn't need Kyle thrown on top of everything else.

Hardy shook his head. "What else happened that day?"

"Kyle left, but then he came back a few days later and stumbled around my front yard in a half-drunken stupor, serenading me with a slurred and off-key rendition of 'Sweet Caroline.'" I'd been slightly appalled at the time, but now I could look back on that day and laugh. It had been quite hilarious. Kyle couldn't remember the words—if he even knew them—so he was trying to make them up as he went along.

"I guess that's fitting."

"Too fitting. I'm named after that song. My full name is Caroline Diamond Shatner."

Hardy stared at me for a few seconds. "Are you serious?"

I nodded. "Let me tell you something Hardy. There are two types of people in this world—those that love Neil Diamond and those that don't. My Dad was obsessed."

"So obsessed that he named you in honor of the man?"

"I have two older sisters. Their names are Holly and Rosie." My parents hadn't planned on having a third child, but that didn't stop me from showing up. Mom, who was not as die-hard of a Neil Diamond fan as Dad, said he could name me Caroline if I turned out to be a girl. For some reason she hated "Sweet Caroline." I think it was because Dad played it all the time. I don't think Mom has ever forgiven me for not being the son she so desperately wanted. "And my half-brothers are named Lucas Neil and Elijah Song."

"Good Lord." After a moment, Hardy added, "I guess it could be worse. Your dad could have named you after 'Carmalita's Eyes' or 'Cherry Cherry.'"

I grimaced. Personally, I had nothing against Neil Diamond. I spent the majority of my childhood being subjected to his music.

"So, what did you do about Kyle and his performance?" Hardy asked

"I thought about shooting Kyle to put him out of his misery." I made it sound like I was joking, but I really had considered it that day. "Instead I called Chief Deputy Quaranta and had him arrest Kyle. Then I got a restraining order against him."

Hardy shoved his notebook aside, and snatched up Kyle's police record. Somewhere, in that thick stack of paperwork, would be the arrest report and the restraining order I had filed. Hardy was still searching for it when my office door was flung open and crashed into the wall. Hardy and I leaped out of our seats as three elderly men barged into my tiny office.

"What is really going on?" Uncle Houston demanded, his gray, grizzled beard shaking with suppressed anger.

"Couldn't one of you have knocked?" I asked the three men.

"I tried to stop these two pea brains from rushing in here, but it's been a long time since they've listened to me," Granddaddy said.

"That's because it's been a coon's age since you had anything of importance to say," Uncle Bowie said.

"No, the problem is you've been listening to Houston since you were knee high to a grasshopper. And he's made you stupid," Granddaddy said.

"Sergeant Hardy, meet my Granddaddy Crockett. He's the former sheriff of Wyatt County," I said. "And these are my great-uncles, Houston and Bowie."

"I won't say it's a pleasure to meet you," Hardy said, holding his hand out.

My great-uncles, Houston and Bowie, eyed up Hardy's hand as if it were an armadillo decaying on the side of the road. Only Granddaddy had the decency to shake the hand of a Texas Ranger. As the middle brother, Granddaddy may be a carbon copy of Houston and Bowie when it came to looks, but, personality and temperament wise, Granddaddy came out the winner. Houston was a crotchety old man who expected his every word to be obeyed. Bowie was Houston's lackey. I don't think he did anything besides go to the bathroom without Houston's permission. Granddaddy was the fun loving and sweet tempered brother. He was much easier to get along with than Houston and Bowie, but that didn't mean he couldn't put the fear of God into someone.

My great-grandfather named his five children after some of the most notable heroes of the Texas War of Independence—Samuel Houston, Emily Morgan, David Crockett, James Bowie, and Benjamin Milam. Ben died when he was nineteen. No one talked about it, but I gather it was in some sort of criminal endeavor. Emily Morgan, who was a terrifying woman, was the brains of the whole Shatner operation until she died just over a year earlier. After his sister died, Houston took over and things slowly started going downhill. Not that we were ever really uphill of anything.

"Could one of y'all tell me what is going on? All I wanna know is how Kyle Vance wound up dead at my party," Houston said.

"Today is your lucky day," Hardy said. "Because I'm here to figure all that out."

"I'll consider it my lucky day when you get out of my business," Houston said. He then turned to me and asked, "What were you thinking calling in the Texas Ranger?"

"I don't have to explain myself to you," I said.

"Everything okay in here?" Uncle Murph asked as he joined the already crowded party going on in my office.

"Where have you been hiding?" Houston asked. "And why can't someone just tell me what's going on?"

"It's pretty simple," I said. "I found Kyle Vance's body in the dumpster after the party."

"You found the body!" Granddaddy said. "That darn deputy who interviewed me never said a word about you being the one that found the body."

Granddaddy, who was now under the impression that I was scarred for life, set to comforting me. Bowie berated his son for not warning the family of what had happened. Murph, who apparently wasn't man enough to take the blame, claimed I was the one who didn't want to tell the family. Of course, I had been the one who insisted we couldn't, but that didn't mean Murph couldn't back me up on my decision. Houston turned his wrath on both me and Murph. He cursed us out and threatened to tan both of our hides.

During the melee, Hardy slipped out the door. I was about to follow his example, when Houston pushed me into a chair, and then leaned over me. After scolding me for not warning the family about Kyle's dead body in the dumpster, he said, "You better get rid of any evidence that makes us look guilty."

"If none of us killed Kyle, there won't be any evidence against us. Besides, making evidence disappear is Murph's responsibility."

"Oh no, don't drag me any further into this," Murph said.

"I don't want my baby girl dirtying her hands in this business," Granddaddy said.

"Her hands are already filthy," Houston said.

"And that's your fault," Granddaddy said. "All the dirt and blood on Carrie's hands is because of you."

"I just want to know why you're asking me to cover up evidence when you claim we had nothing to do with this," I said.

"I ain't saying there's any evidence." Houston's left eye twitched twice. At his advanced age of nearly ninety, Houston had learned how to control himself and his reactions. The only one he couldn't hide was that eye twitch. He was nervous about something, and I was curious to know what it was. "What I'm saying is that once a dog starts digging, you never know what he'll turn up."

"How am I supposed to get near the evidence?" I asked. "I'm sure that once the family is done being questioned, Sergeant Hardy won't let me or Uncle Murph have anything to do with his investigation. He only agreed to let us help during the questioning."

"Then you'll just have to get friendly with the Ranger, Carrie," Houston said. "Convince him that he needs your help investigating."

"And how would you propose I do that?" I leaned back in my chair and crossed my arms over my chest. "Especially when I'm one of the last people Sergeant Hardy would want helping him."

Houston winked at me. "You're a pretty, young woman. You'll figure out a way to distract him."

Pretty. Not smart. For some reason, Uncle Houston seemed to think that I was dimwitted. I wasn't sure what it was about me that made him think that the only thing holding up my rather impressive head of naturally curly brown hair was hot air; but once he got that idea in this head, I have been unable to convince him otherwise.

"You better not be suggesting what I think you are." Granddaddy's gnarled hands curled up into fists. Since my dad was such a lousy father, Granddaddy was the one to step up and be the main man in my life. Unfortunately Granddaddy still thought that I was a child and that I needed him to come to my rescue. "Because that's my little girl you're talking to."

"Now, now, Crockett, I'm just suggesting that Carrie flirt with the Ranger." Houston patted me on the head. "A cute little thing like Carrie should be able to distract him. What else does she got to do around here?"

"A lot actually. Do you have any idea what my job is?" I asked Houston.

"Cleaning up after your family, like a good girl," Houston said.

"Now, Uncle Houston, you know Carrie does a lot more than that around here," Murph said. "She's a real good detective despite her not having any experience when she started. And her crime scene investigating skills … well, let me tell you, Carrie knows what she's doing. Couple times now she's found evidence that the rest of us would have missed. She's even solved some of our cold cases. You should show her the respect that she deserves."

"See Uncle Houston … all this beauty. And brains, too," I said.

"I don't care about any of that," Houston said. "The only thing I care about is you protecting your family. That's why I had Murph hire you. So that you can help him clean up after the rest of us. I didn't have him hire you to solve all these other cases that ain't got nothing to do with us."

"I actually hired her for both. She's the best thing that's happened to this department in years," Murph said.

Houston sighed. "Right now, the only thing you've got to do, missy, is keep the Ranger from looking too closely at the family."

"Keep him more interested in you than in the case," Bowie added.

"Think you can handle that?" Houston asked.

"You know, you two really are horrible people," I said. I stood up and stared Houston in the eye. "I know you, Uncle Houston, and I know you're suggesting I do more than flirt with the Ranger. Anything to keep the Shatners out of trouble, right?"

"That's my girl." Houston patted me on the cheek. "I always knew I could count on you."

"Carrie … " Granddaddy said.

"It's all right, Granddaddy. Just because I know what Houston is asking me to do doesn't mean I'm going to do it." The collective moral compass of the Shatners had never pointed north, but I prided myself on the fact that mine at least pointed northwest. I wasn't sure where sleeping with a Texas Ranger to keep my family out of trouble was located, but it was not in the direction I was headed.

"You'll do the right thing, Carrie," Houston said. "The family is counting on you."

It wasn't a question of whether I would do the right thing or not. There wasn't even a question of what the right thing to do was. My job was to make sure that none of the Shatners were arrested on homicide charges. Or anything else, for that matter. That would be easier to do once I knew, beyond a shadow of a doubt, that they were all innocent.

Houston and I were still engaged in a stare-down when Quaranta entered the room. "Hey, Sheriff, the Ranger is about to question Dale."

Chapter Eight

———◆———

"**I** understand you weren't at your family's party last night, Dale," Hardy said.

Sergeant Hardy and Uncle Murph's oldest son were seated in the sheriff's department's only interrogation room. Hardy had his back to the one-way mirror through which Murph and I observed the interview.

"I was at the party. Just not the whole time," Dale said. "I don't know nothing about what happened last night. All I know is that Carrie found a dead body. But it ain't a Shatner, so why should I care?"

"We'll get to that. But first I need you to answer some questions," Hardy said.

"Do I have to? I mean, I'm a little hungover here," Dale said, belching loudly. "Okay, I'm a lot hungover. And I already told you that I don't know jack about that dead body."

"I don't care if you know anything about the dead body or not. I'm going to ask you some questions and you're going to answer them," Hardy said.

"But I don't wanna. Is my dad in the other room? I wanna talk to him."

"I'm sorry, Dale, but I can't allow that."

"Why not?" Dale leaned to the side and looked directly at the one-way mirror. "What's going on, Dad? I didn't do nothing."

Hardy turned around to face the mirror. He raised his eyebrows and gestured over his shoulder at Dale. I could sympathize with him. There were times when talking to Dale was about as productive as beating a dead horse.

"My son is an idiot." Murph banged his head into the wall.

"You're only now realizing that?" I asked. Dale should have been two grades behind me in school. He finished four behind because he failed eighth grade twice. Actually, I think he failed it three times, but the teacher felt bad so she passed him. Or maybe she just wanted to get rid of him. Either way, Dale was never that sharp.

"You think I should call a lawyer?" Murph asked me, sounding like a worried father. "That's my boy in there. If I can't protect him, I need to bring in someone else who can."

"I don't think Dale needs a lawyer. At least not yet." I inched along the glass, trying to find a spot where I could at least see the side of Hardy's face. "But I still think I should be in there to make sure Dale doesn't say or do something stupid."

"I want to be in there, too. But there's no way Sergeant Hardy would agree to that," Murph said. "I'm surprised he's even letting us watch the interrogation."

"It's only because we agreed not to interfere," I said.

Murph pushed away from the glass and paced back-and-forth across the small, dark room. Over the years, the observation room had been converted into a storage room. There were three floor-to-ceiling filing cabinets against the one wall. What was in the cabinets, I didn't know. To my right, the sheriff's department's shabby holiday decorations took up an entire corner of the room. There was also an old bookcase full of odds-and-ends that should have been thrown away back when the first President Bush was still in office.

"Tell me, Dale, where do you work?" Hardy asked.

"Huh? What's that got to do with anything?" Dale asked.

"It's just a question. Could you answer it?"

"Well, yeah, I can answer it. I work at You Wreck 'Em, We Fix 'Em Paint and Body Shop." Dale looked around the room before pointing at the one wall. "It's, like, right next door."

"What kind of clothes do you wear for work?"

"We all have to wear this blue shirt and matching pants."

"You have a lot of those shirts?"

"I guess. What does this have to do with last night?"

"I didn't say it does," Hardy said. "Why didn't you go to the party with everyone else?"

Dale leaned back in the chair and stared up at the ceiling. "Well ... I went to see my girlfriend. We were supposed to have a date."

"Supposed to?" Hardy said.

"She broke up with me." There was a flicker of emotion across Dale's washed out face, but he hid whatever it was he was feeling.

"Why did she break up with you?"

"That ain't your business!" Dale's eyes narrowed and his neck muscles bunched together. "Ain't your business at all."

Breaking his vow not to interfere, Murph flipped the switch on the intercom system and said, "Answer the questions, Dale!"

Dale came around the interrogation table and approached the mirror. "Come on, Dad. I'm not telling this guy about my personal life. And you can't make me."

"Dale, if you don't sit your butt back down and tell the Ranger what he wants to know, I'm gonna come in there and cancel your birth certificate," Murph said.

"But Dad ... "

"Dale!" I slammed my hand against the glass in frustration. "NOW!"

"Uhh ... Fine." Dale shuffled around to the other side of the table and collapsed into the chair. He then laid his head down on the table. "I'm still not telling you all the personal stuff."

"You will tell me what I want to know," Hardy said. "Let's try this again. Why did your girlfriend break up with you?"

"She gave me the old 'it's not you, it's me' line. But then she pretty much told me it was me."

"What time did you get to her place?" Hardy asked. "How long were you there?"

"I don't know. I think I might have got there around five. I went to her place right after work. My boss was a jerk and made us work till five, but I snuck out a little early." Dale traced circles on the tabletop. "I was only at her place about twenty minutes."

"Where does your ex-girlfriend live?"

"Whispering Pines. It's a trailer park on the west side of Wyatt Lake," Dale said. Wyatt Lake was a few miles southwest of Holler. It was a man-made lake with a handful of beaches and boat ramps scattered along the edges. At least a thousand people live along the lake shore year-round, and there are another thousand or so who have summer homes.

Hardy shoved a notebook across the table towards Dale. "I'm going to need her name, phone number, and address."

"No! I don't want you dragging her into this crap. She's got nothing to do with whatever happened at the fairgrounds," Dale said.

"Dale, let me make something clear to you. I am not asking you these questions for my own personal entertainment. I am trying to establish your alibi for last night."

"Why do I need an alibi? I got nothing to do with that body."

"Dale, from what little we know, the victim died sometime during your family's party. I still don't know where the victim died, but the body was found in the fairgrounds' dumpster after the party. I am trying to figure out what happened. Right now, I need to know where you were, what you were doing, and who you were with last night. Just give me your ex-girlfriend's name and contact information so that I can verify you were at her house at the time you said."

Dale sighed, but he did as Hardy instructed. After scribbling something onto the page, Dale tossed the notebook back to Hardy. "There's her name, address, and phone number."

"After you left … " Hardy glanced down at the notebook. "Amanda's house, did you go straight to the fairgrounds?"

"No, I swung by the bar for a little bit. Everyone was partying, so I left."

"Can anyone verify you were at the bar?" Hardy asked.

"The bartender. He's a friend of the family."

"I'll need his name and the name of the bar." Hardy handed the notebook back to Dale. "Where did you go after you left the bar?"

"I bought a bottle of Jack Daniels, went to a playground, and got wasted."

"Which playground?" Hardy asked.

There were half a dozen playgrounds in and around Holler, so Dale had his pick. I just wanted to know what Dale was thinking by going to a children's playground and getting drunk. Not only was it a bad idea, it was also somewhat disconcerting.

"The one by Wyatt Lake," Dale said.

Hardy turned around and looked at the one-way mirror. I turned on the intercom and said, "There's a recreational area along part of the northern shore of Wyatt Lake. There's a small playground with swings, a sandbox, and a couple jungle gym-type things."

Hardy nodded, and then turned back to Dale. "I have to ask, but what kind of man buys a bottle of whiskey and then drinks it at a playground?"

"A pissed off one. Besides, it's not like any kids were there." Dale pushed one of his sweatshirt sleeves up, revealing a forearm that was covered in various abrasions.

Hardy reached across the table and grabbed Dale's wrist. "Where did all these bruises and scratches come from? Did you get in a fight or assault anyone?"

"I'm a mechanic. Most of these are from the job." Dale tugged his sleeve back down and lowered his hands to his lap. "The rest are from the playground. I was drunk and I fell a lot."

That I could believe. Even when he was sober, Dale wasn't that coordinated.

"All right. All right," Hardy said, backing off. "Did anyone see you at the playground?"

"I was the only one there. Well, except for the teenagers trying to get it on in the backseat of a car. But they wouldn't have seen me," Dale said. "And there were some people out on the water setting off fireworks on their boat."

"So no one saw you?"

"Well, a deputy showed up and interrupted the teenagers. They freaked out. It was pretty funny. The deputy heard me laughing and asked what I was doing there."

"Hold on, one of the Wyatt County deputies saw you?"

"Yep." Dale nodded. "I talked to him."

"When did this happen?"

Dale shrugged. "I don't know. Can't you ask him?"

"I'm asking you."

"Uh … probably around ten-thirty. It was right before I left and went to the party."

"I will be talking to this deputy." Hardy scribbled a few lines into his notebook.

"Are we done then? I'm really tired and I have no idea what happened last night," Dale said, standing up. "This whole conversation is kinda pointless."

"I have just a few more questions," Hardy said, motioning for Dale to sit back down. "What was going on when you got to the party?"

"I got there, like, halfway through the concert. When that ended we set off the fireworks. Then Carrie made us all go home."

"So you weren't there when the Palmer family tried crashing the party?"

"Nope. I missed that. But I heard all about it."

"What do you think of the Palmers?" Hardy asked.

"Uh, well, I guess I hate 'em because everyone else does. But I've never had a personal problem with any of them. To be honest, I think the whole feud is pretty stupid." Dale sniffed his armpit. "Hey … it's not a Palmer that got killed last night, is it?"

"Do you know Kyle Vance?" Hardy asked.

"Not very well, I guess. I know who he is. It's not like I hang out with him." Dale looked around the room for a minute before he asked. "He's the one that got himself killed, ain't he?"

"Yes, Kyle Vance died sometime last night. What do you know about that?"

"Nothing! I told you I wasn't there when the Palmers crashed the party. How could I have killed Kyle when I wasn't there?"

"I know you weren't there when that happened, Dale." Hardy ran his hands through his hair and sighed. "We're still not sure if Kyle was killed at the fairgrounds or not."

Dale scrunched up his nose. "Why do you think I would know where he was killed?"

"Oh, I don't know," Hardy said. "Maybe because you killed him and then dumped his body at the fairgrounds when you got to the party."

The vacant look in Dale's eyes slipped away. He was finally beginning to catch on. "What the hell, man? You think I killed Kyle? Why would I do that?"

"I don't know, Dale. But, so far, the evidence is pointing at you."

"What evidence?" Dale jumped up from the table. "What is this guy talking about, Dad? What's going on? Why don't you stop this, Carrie?"

"Do these look familiar?" Hardy laid the evidence bag containing the scrap of fabric and the name patch on the table along with the bag holding the tire iron.

Dale snatched up the two bags, and studied both of them. "This looks like it came from one of my work shirts. But I've never seen this tire iron before. I don't use this kind. Where did you get these?"

"Let's just say they were found close enough to the victim's body to be considered evidence." Hardy pried the two evidence bags out of Dale's hands. "I was wondering if you know how they got there."

"How should I know? I didn't put them there." Dale rushed around the table and threw himself at the one-way mirror. "Dad! Carrie! What's going on? I didn't kill Kyle! Get in here and help me!"

"That's enough, Dale! Sit back down." Hardy slammed his fists down on the table, and Dale reluctantly returned to his seat. "Let me make something clear to you, Dale. Believe it or not, I am trying to help you. As far as I know, you are the only member of your family that wasn't at the party for the entire evening. That either puts you at the very top or the very bottom of my suspect list. I am trying to remove you from said suspect list because, at least up until we started having this delightful conversation, I assumed you weren't stupid enough to kill Kyle and then dump his body at your family's party. Now, I'm beginning to think otherwise." Hardy had a seat on the edge of the table and leaned over Dale. "Now, I have just one more question for you. Will you give me permission to search your car?"

Dale tilted his head back and stared up at the ceiling. He seemed to be giving the request some serious thought. I wanted Dale to say no. Hardy didn't have a warrant and his so-called evidence wasn't enough to get him one. Not unless he proved the name patch and tire iron definitely belonged to Dale.

"Yeah, all right. If it'll make you leave me alone," Dale said. "But I want Carrie there when you do it. I don't trust you not to plant evidence against me."

"That's funny because I don't trust her not to conceal evidence," Hardy said.

In the observation room, Murph and I let loose a string of curse words.

"What's wrong with your son?" I asked Murph. "Is his New Year's Resolution to cooperate with law enforcement officials?"

"I take it back," Murph said. "My son is not an idiot. He's a moron."

AFTER CAREFUL CONSIDERATION AND COFFEE, Dale came to the conclusion that he wanted to be there while Hardy and I processed his car for evidence.

That was how he came to be hanging out in the sally port with me and Hardy when his blue 1977 Pontiac Firebird was brought in on the back of a tow truck.

"Anything we need to know before we search your car?" Hardy asked Dale.

Dale shrugged. "Just don't mess it up. You've got no idea how much money I put into it."

Without waiting for Hardy's permission, I swung open the driver's door and caused the most overpowering stench imaginable to waft out of the car. The foul air burned the inside of my nostrils and caused my eyes to water. It was so bad that I could taste it.

"What died in here?" I asked once I was done gagging.

"Don't know what you're talking about." Dale leaned over my shoulder and sniffed. "Smells fine to me."

After putting on a face mask and gloves, Hardy pulled out all of the trash littering the front and back seats, and the floorboards. Under the front passenger seat, he found the moldy remains of a bean and egg breakfast burrito.

"I'm going to assume that is what's smelling up the car," I said.

"And now it's evidence," Hardy said.

During the search, Hardy also found two grease-stained work shirts wadded up on the floor of the backseat. While ragged, both had their name patches intact.

Once the car was free of trash, and Hardy finished searching the car for visible signs of blood, he grabbed a bottle of Luminol out of his crime scene kit and handed it to me. He didn't have to tell me what he wanted me to do. Luminol reacts to the hemoglobin in blood, which causes a latent bloodstain to luminesce. Just because we couldn't see any blood didn't mean that there wasn't any blood there.

I snatched the bottle out of Hardy's hands and spritzed the interior of the car. After turning off the overhead lights, Hardy grabbed an ultraviolet light and began shining it on the areas I had already sprayed down.

"Looks like we have a stain." Hardy held up a camera and snapped a picture of the right side of the tiny backseat.

The stain seemed too small considering the size of Kyle's head wound. I also couldn't fathom Dale driving around with a dead body stretched out in the backseat.

"I think we both know what that stain is," I said.

Hardy coughed, but I suspected he was trying to cover up the fact that he was laughing. "We'll have to test it."

Shoving Hardy out of the way, I flipped on the lights and then went over to my crime scene kit. I pulled a handful of cotton swabs out of my kit and then returned to the car.

I used three of the cotton swabs to take samples from the stain. Then, with my cotton swabs in hand, I fished a small bottle of phenolphthalin reagent out of my kit. I added a drop of the regent to each swab. I then followed up with a drop of hydrogen peroxide. If there was blood, the hemoglobin would catalyze the oxidation of phenolphthalin into phenolphthalein and the swabs would immediately turn a bright pink color.

When the swabs didn't immediately turn pink, I breathed a sigh of relief. "You want me to confirm its semen? Because I can do that test, too."

"No, I think that's all right." Hardy rubbed a hand over his mouth, but he couldn't hide the smile around his eyes. Hardy then turned to confront Dale. "Hey, Dale, when was the last time you had sex in the backseat?"

"Just after Thanksgiving," Dale said. "It was her idea."

"She sounds like a classy lady, Dale. Too bad things didn't work out."

"You're telling me, man. Hey, how many days do you think I should wait before I start begging her to take me back?" Dale asked Hardy.

"Why not start now?" Hardy asked. He then turned to me and said, "All right, Detective Shatner, let's move on to the trunk."

Using the key, I popped the trunk of Dale's car. I took one look inside and slammed the trunk closed. "I am not searching that."

Hardy pried the keys out of my hands and reopened the trunk. I'm sure he was expecting a massive bloodstain. Instead he found the trunk filled to capacity with all kinds of junk. There were three milk crates full of car parts, a half-inflated basketball, an inside-out umbrella, a bag of rocks, a snow shovel, a mounted deer head, and a four-foot-tall doll wearing a cheerleader's uniform. It was the doll that really had me concerned.

Hardy helped me take everything out of the trunk. One-by-one I sprayed Luminol over anything that could have been used to bash in Kyle's head. That included the creepy cheerleader doll. Hardy then went over everything with the ultraviolet light. Once the trunk was empty, I used up what Luminol I had left and sprayed the trunk's interior.

"No sign of blood. If Dale did it, he didn't transport the body in his car," I said.

"Lack of blood does not mean Dale couldn't have transported the body in his car," Hardy said. "He could have had Kyle wrapped up in a tarp."

"He could have, but we didn't find any evidence of that. As far as I can tell, you've got nothing that proves Dale is the killer," I said.

"I don't have anything that disproves it either," Hardy said.

Dale had fallen asleep while Hardy and I were processing the contents of the trunk. We woke him up to tell him that we hadn't found anything incriminating in his car and that he was free to go.

"But I didn't kill Kyle," Dale said. "That's what I've been trying to tell you."

Chapter Nine

———————◆———————

"**W**here's Dale?" Murph asked, knocking off the thunderous, fake snoring that had been blasting from his nose for no other reason than to annoy Sergeant Boleyn. "What have you done with my boy?"

"Dale's gone home. We didn't find any evidence in his car," I said.

"Thank God!" Murph said. "Told you my boy didn't do nothing wrong. Dale may be an idiot, but he's not stupid."

"That makes no sense," Hardy said. "But, like I told Detective Shatner, just because we didn't find any evidence doesn't mean that your son's not guilty."

"The only thing Dale's guilty of is being stupid. But his stupidity has nothing to do with what happened to Kyle Vance," Murph said.

"You just said Dale's not stupid," Hardy said.

"Dale's my boy, and I love him just the way he is, but he's so dumb he couldn't find his butt with two hands and a search warrant. And that's putting it nicely," Murph said.

Hoping to prevent Hardy from inquiring any further into Dale's mental prowess, I nudged Sergeant Arthur Boleyn in the arm and asked, "What about the rest of my family? What did they have to say for themselves?"

Boleyn glanced up from his notebook long enough to reward me with an icy glare.

"Boleyn, play nice," Hardy said. "What have the rest of the Shatners had to say?"

"The officers and deputies just finished questioning all of the men over the age of fourteen. They've also been collecting coats, gloves, and clothing that the Shatners wore last night," Boleyn said, pointing at the mountain of evidence bags behind him. "None of them confessed to killing the victim or disposing of the body in the dumpster. Of course, I'd expect them to deny their involvement. These aren't the kind of people who admit to any wrongdoing."

"Arthur … " Hardy said, sounding exasperated.

Ignoring Boleyn's barb, I asked, "Did any of them admit to finding the body in the dumpster?"

"No, none of them admitted to that either," Boleyn replied. "But you wouldn't really expect them to, do you? Not when they're covering for each other."

"That's enough, Arthur," Hardy said. "Did any of the Shatners admit to seeing Kyle Vance at the fairgrounds at all?"

"No. None of the Shatners that we've interviewed so far have mentioned seeing the victim at the fairgrounds." Boleyn held up his notebook, showing me and Hardy a list of names. All but one of the names had at least two checkmarks beside it. "This is a list of the Palmer family members that Oscar Palmer claims went with him to crash the Shatners' party. Chief Groves faxed it over as soon as he got the list from Oscar. Of the twenty-two men on this list, all but one of them was seen by at least two Shatners last night. The only one who wasn't seen by any of the Shatners is Kyle Vance."

"Interesting. Oscar Palmer claims the victim was at the fairgrounds, yet none of the Shatners saw him," Hardy said.

"Or admitted to seeing him," Boleyn said, interrupting Hardy. "It's possible they're all claiming Kyle wasn't there because they know he really was there and that one of their family members killed him."

"It's possible," Hardy said. "What do you think, Detective Shatner?"

"I honestly don't know what to think. But I know what I want to believe."

I wanted to believe that Kyle Vance never set foot on the fairgrounds on New Year's Eve. But, if that was the case, how did his body wind up in the dumpster? Did Kyle storm the fairgrounds with the rest of the Palmers and then somehow get himself killed without anyone other than the killer seeing him? Did the killer then stick the body in the dumpster in an attempt to cover up the crime? Did Murph know more about what happened than he was letting on?

I spent the next two hours cooped up in Murph's office along with him and Sergeant Boleyn. Boleyn wasn't much for conversation, and Murph and I were afraid to speak about anything in front of him. As far as I could tell, the only benefit to being babysat by Boleyn was that, once the deputies were done with their interviews, they had to report the results to him. One-by-one the women and children were questioned. And every single one of them denied seeing Kyle Vance at the fairgrounds.

Hardy was in and out of Murph's office during those two hours. One time he came back with some much appreciated pizzas. The next time he returned with Chief Groves in tow.

"How's it going, Lou," Murph asked. He'd given up on the fake snoring and switched over to singing Shania Twain songs in a high-pitched falsetto that had Boleyn—and me—cringing. "Want some pizza?"

"Right now, all I want is a nap." Groves sank into the chair next to me and groaned. "Only three or four of the Palmers live in the Wilder city limits, and they give me enough headaches. I don't know how Chief Yates puts up with the dozen or more Palmers who live in Holler. Sergeant Hardy, if you need those Palmers interviewed again, do it yourself. Or get Chief Yates and his officers to do it. Most of them are his problem after all."

"I do appreciate that you stepped in and helped me out, Chief Groves. I needed to get the Palmers interviewed right away, and you were the only person I could trust to oversee that. Now, did you get anything useful from the Palmers?" Hardy asked.

"Not from the widow. Poor gal is shattered," Groves said. "But the rest of them had plenty to say. My officers and the deputies interviewed all twenty-one of the men who tried crashing the Shatners' party. All of them claim that Kyle was at the strip club with them for the family's party. He then allegedly went with them to the fairgrounds. They never saw Kyle after that."

"And none of them were concerned that Kyle just went missing?" I asked.

Groves shrugged. "I got the impression that, aside from the wife, none of them really give a darn that Kyle's dead. A few of them even seem happy about it."

"Now that is suspicious," I said.

"The whole situation is suspicious. Regardless of what anybody says, Kyle Vance wound up dead in that dumpster. I need to figure out how that happened and who's responsible for it." Standing up, Hardy moved towards the office door. "Detective Shatner, I'd like a private word with you."

Donning our coats, Hardy and I slipped out the front door of the sheriff's department and then walked across the street to the town square. Hardy wandered through the barren flower beds in silent contemplation while I scampered along behind him. I was beginning to think that Hardy had forgotten about his request for a private word when he abruptly stopped walking and spun around to face me.

"Detective Shatner, did you or Sheriff Shatner do anything at the crime scene to tamper with the body or the evidence?"

"No! I admit I touched the dumpster in a few places. But, as soon as I realized that I had a dead body on my hands, I backed off. That's it. I mean, that's it aside from walking around the fairgrounds while closing up. But I can't be held accountable for any evidence I might have contaminated or destroyed before I knew there was a dead body on site."

"And I'm not holding you accountable for that. I'm more concerned about what happened after you found the body," Hardy said. "Did you or the sheriff plant any evidence or destroy anything after you found the body? Did you move the body?"

"If Uncle Murph or I had done anything, don't you think we would have completely disposed of the body and the evidence? Why would we destroy some evidence, but leave the body?" I asked.

"The reason I'm asking is because it's common knowledge that you and the sheriff cover up your family member's crimes."

"It's a common misconception." When I accepted the job at the sheriff's department, it was with the understanding that I would not cover up any horrible crimes. Like murder or rape. Unfortunately I don't think there's any crime that Murph wouldn't cover up.

"No, it's not a misconception. It's a known fact." Hardy led me over to a bench and gestured for me to sit down. "You're just lucky that you haven't been caught sweeping evidence under the rug. But let me tell you this—one day the shit is going to hit the fan, and you'll be in as much trouble as the rest of them. What I don't understand is why you do it."

"Ever heard of the saying 'like rats abandoning a sinking ship'?"

"Yeah, sure."

"Well, if this ship is going down, it's with all hands on deck."

"Is the ship sinking?"

"The ship is always threatening to go down. While the rest of the family is up partying on deck, Murph and I are down below pumping out the water." Standing up, I paced back and forth in front of the bench. "Let me make this clear, in the past, the Shatners have hit bigger icebergs than this and we've stayed afloat."

"It's not your responsibility to take care of all of them," Hardy said. "Most of them are adults. Shouldn't they be responsible for their own decisions and criminal activities?"

"They're all I've got, Hardy. And, whether I like it or not, I'm on that ship. And it's up to me to make sure it stays afloat."

"Do me a favor, Detective Shatner ... If this turns out to be the iceberg that sinks your family's ship, don't try to keep it afloat. Just grab a life vest and try to save yourself. You should do that despite how this case turns out. Don't let something one of your family members does ruin the rest of your life."

"I wish I could, Sergeant Hardy. But there are a bunch of innocent Shatners that I need to protect. I can't abandon ship and leave them to sink with the guilty ones. Besides, I'm not the one steering the ship."

"I'm pretty sure no one is steering the Shatners' ship." Hardy rubbed his hands over his face and groaned. "But let's say one of them did kill Kyle. What would you do? Would you tell me? Or would you try to cover it up? And what about the sheriff?"

"Murph would cover it up in a heartbeat. I would tell you."

"I actually believe you would" Hardy said. "But you and the sheriff aren't going to stay out of this, are you?"

"We can't leave it up to you clear our family's tarnished, but still somewhat good, name."

"What did I just say about taking care of yourself? You and the sheriff can't just run around and try to investigate this on your own. What if you do something that jeopardizes my case? Is that what you want?"

"No. It's not." Unless a Shatner turned out to be the murderer, I did not want to screw up Hardy's investigation. "Besides, I know some people are going to be more comfortable talking to me than they will be talking to you."

"Obviously, your family members would rather talk to you than to me. And I'm sure they'll tell you all sorts of things they would never tell me," Hardy said, sounding a little defeated. "But what are you going to do if someone doesn't want to talk to you?"

"You'd be surprised how willing people are to talk after you've got them strung up to some kind of medieval torture device. They'll tell you pretty much everything you want to know. Just last month, Uncle Murph and I had a burglary suspect who didn't want to answer our questions. We had him in the rack and, well, let's just say he 'fessed up pretty quick."

"Are you serious?" At first, Hardy looked horrified. Then he started to laugh. "Very funny, Detective Shatner. Regardless, I forbid you from running around and doing crazy stuff, and then claiming it's all part of the investigation."

"You can forbid me, but how are you really going to stop me?" I asked. "The way I see it, we should be working together to solve this case."

"How am I supposed to trust you when I can't be sure if you'd be working with me or against me?"

"I've been working with you so far."

"Well, today must be your lucky day, Detective Shatner. Earlier, I called my lieutenant to fill him in on what's been going on down here. I told him about how you've been trying to help me when it comes to dealing with your family. My lieutenant wasn't overly impressed with your helpfulness, but I convinced him that you might be useful throughout this investigation. Despite the fact that he doesn't trust you at all, my lieutenant has agreed to let you to assist me for the rest of the day."

"Do you trust me, Sergeant Hardy?" I asked.

"Not at all," Hardy said. "But I'm willing to take a chance on you. Just don't cross me or stab me in the back."

I held out my hand, pinky extended. "I promise that I will do everything I can to help your case more that I hurt it."

"That's reassuring." While rolling his eyes, Hardy linked his pinky with mine. "Now, let's get this partnership off to the right start. I'd appreciate it if you answered some questions."

"What else do you want to know about me or my family?"

"For now, nothing," Hardy said. "I want to know about Whitney Vance."

"I'm not sure how much I can tell you. I don't exactly associate with her."

"I understand that. But whatever you can tell me will help."

"Well, Whitney and I went to the same high school. But she was a year or two behind me so we didn't have any classes together. We were both on the cheerleading squad though."

"Hold on." Hardy held up his hands in the universal signal for 'time out.' "You were on the cheerleading squad?"

"Why is that surprising?"

"I don't know. I kind of figured you had detention at least a couple times a week."

I huffed in annoyance. "For your information, I never once had detention."

"Really? I had detention all the time." Hardy paused for a few seconds, possibly waiting for me to ask about his rebellious teenage years. When I didn't, he asked, "Have you seen Whitney much since high school?"

I had to think about that one. Obviously, I saw her the night I caught her and Kyle having sex at the mini-golf course. Quaranta and I arrested both of them for public indecency. I was the one who put Whitney in handcuffs. On the drive back to the sheriff's department, Quaranta sensed that something was wrong and had the good sense to send me home. Since then I had seen Whitney a handful of times, and those were all times when our paths crossed accidentally.

"I see Whitney around every once in a while, but I certainly don't go out of my way to talk to her," I said. "What I can tell you is that she's crazy."

"You have any proof of her mental state? Or is this your opinion?"

"No, I don't have any proof. But I'm telling you that Whitney's elevator doesn't go all the way to the top. Ask anyone."

"I'm asking you," Hardy said.

"Okay, fine, Whitney is nuts. Or, at least, she used to be. You're going to have to take my word on it. When we were on the cheerleading squad together, we all called her Whiney Whitney. She was vindictive and had major jealousy issues. She also stirred up a lot of drama. And she was always faking an injury so she didn't have to practice. Why are you asking?"

"Because I'm about to head down to Wilder to talk to her. I'm hoping she's calmed down enough to give me something useful."

"Have fun with that," I said.

"You're coming with me, partner," Hardy said. "Just leave your thumb screws at home."

"We're going to need more than thumb screws to deal with the Palmers."

Chapter Ten

———————◆———————

"That doesn't look like the grieving widow to me," Hardy said, pointing at the man who had whipped open the front door and stepped out onto the porch of Whitney Vance's house.

"That's her grandfather, Oscar Palmer," I said.

As the elderly man maneuvered down the front steps and then shuffled out into the yard, I noticed that, while he was wearing both a belt and suspenders, his pants were still sagging. Oscar took up a stance by the old tractor tire that held a place of honor in the front yard. In the middle of the tire sat a cracked and discolored toilet. Sticking out of the toilet bowl was a colony of faded, plastic flamingos. The overall effect was tragic.

"He doesn't look all that intimidating," Hardy said.

"That's because you haven't met him yet."

Two young men emerged from the house and wandered out into the yard. The taller of the two had a shaved head and was decked out in tattered Army fatigues. The shorter one was wearing jean shorts and a wife beater under his knee-length winter coat.

"Are those Mrs. Vance's brothers?" Hardy asked.

"That they are. Toby is in the fatigues. The other one is Russ."

"What do you know about them?"

"I don't really know them." Russell and Toby were both younger than Whitney. I would have been out of high school by the time they started. "Russell's been in and out of prison since he was a juvie. As far as I know, it was all minor stuff. And Toby joined the Army right out of high school. I think he's been deployed three times. Either way, he got hurt pretty badly during the last one and now he has PTSD. Back in October, when Toby's girlfriend came out of the bathroom with a towel wrapped around her head, he mistook her for a member of a terrorist group and lost it. She was in the hospital for a couple days because of what he did to her."

"So this is going to be a tough crowd." Hardy unlatched his seatbelt and opened the driver's side door. "You ready for this?"

"Just give me a bandana and a cigarette," I said.

"Remember, Detective Shatner, you're the one who wanted to help with the investigation."

Hardy climbed out of the truck and exchanged a few words with the men gathered on the lawn. He then came around the front of the truck and opened the passenger side door, revealing that I was the shadowy figure in the passenger seat. As soon as Russell and Toby saw me, they both reached under their coats and pulled out handguns.

"What is she doing here?" Oscar grabbed one of the plastic flamingos and used it to point at me. "Why didn't Chief Groves come back with you? And where is Chief Yates?"

"Put the guns down, boys." Hardy waited until Russell and Toby lowered their guns before speaking again. "Chief Groves was only briefly helping me out by speaking with y'all. And Chief Yates is not assisting me on this case. Because the body was found in her jurisdiction, Detective Shatner is assisting me."

"Detective?" Oscar moved closer and jabbed Hardy in the chest with the flamingo. "She ain't no detective. Glorified janitor is more like it."

"She's got a badge. She's a—"

Interrupting Hardy, Oscar said, "You better check where that badge came from. I don't think them ones that come in cereal boxes are the real deal."

"Detective Shatner's badge is just as real as mine. So if you threaten her, or try to hurt her, I will arrest you." Hardy pushed the flamingo away. "Now let's all behave like civilized human beings and try to figure out what happened to Kyle."

"I know what happened to Kyle." Oscar pointed the flamingo at me. "Her family killed him."

I opened my mouth to protest, but Hardy cut me off with a slight elbow jab to the ribs. During the twenty minute drive to Whitney's house on the east side of Wilder, we had discussed our approach to interviewing her. Hardy wanted to see what she knew about her husband's whereabouts on New Year's Eve and what she thought happened to him before we shared any of what we knew. It seemed Hardy wanted to stick to the plan even though there were going to be a few more people in on the interview. Since Oscar, Russell, and Toby had all insisted that Kyle was with them up until they crashed my family's party, it would be interesting to hear what they had to say.

"All right, Carrie can come in. But she leaves her gun out here," Oscar said. When Hardy agreed, Oscar rounded up his grandsons and retreated into the house.

"You know, this might actually work to our advantage," Hardy said.

"Yeah." I pulled my handgun out of the holster on my hip. "It might also get me killed."

"The Palmers aren't going to kill you." Hardy took my gun and stashed it in his truck. "Then they would have to kill me, and I doubt they'll want to risk killing a Texas Ranger."

"I wouldn't put anything past these people." I handed Hardy the rest of the weapons that were hanging on my belt—handcuffs, an extra-large can of pepper spray, a stun gun, and a police baton. I also had a backup handgun in an ankle holster. Without my array of protection, I no longer felt safe. Not that I had ever felt safe about this endeavor. For a second, I regretted asking Hardy to let me help out.

Hardy led the way to the front door of the house, and, since it was hanging open, we let ourselves in. We'd just stepped into the living room, and were allowing our eyes to adjust to the dim light, when a picture frame whizzed by my head. The frame clipped my teased out brown curls as it went by. The frame then slammed into the wall, shattering the glass.

"You home-wrecking whore!"

Hardy stepped in front of me while I picked up the frame. "Are you Whitney Vance? I'm sorry about what happened to your husband and I understand that you're upset; but, like I told your family, if you threaten or harm Detective Shatner I will arrest you."

"Arrest me?" Whitney said. "You should arrest her! It's her fault Kyle's dead!"

I glanced up from the picture to look at Whitney. She was waving around her clenched fists and calling me ugly names while being physically restrained by her mother.

I hadn't seen Whitney in a while, and wouldn't have recognized her if I had. Her nose and eyes were red from crying, and her blonde hair was hanging in limp, greasy clumps about her face. There was a big stain on the front of her sweatshirt, and her jeans looked like they should have been thrown out at least a year ago. I couldn't be sure if it was being married to Kyle or his death that was causing her to look so haggard.

"Told you she was crazy," I whispered to Hardy. Some of that had to do with being a Palmer. I blamed Kyle for the rest. My theory was that Whitney had been hitchhiking on the road to crazy when Kyle picked her up and drove her the rest of the way there.

I handed Hardy the frame holding Whitney's and Kyle's wedding photo.

Whitney's smile was so big it could have been seen way over in West Texas. Kyle looked miserable. And drunk. I was fairly certain there was a shotgun barrel jabbing him in the back.

Hardy drew me away from the relative safety of the doorway and into the living room that was cluttered with floral-patterned furniture and cheap knickknacks. There weren't many places to sit in the living room and Whitney's brothers had to surrender the loveseat so that Hardy and I could sit down. Toby and Russell took up a stance on either side of the recliner where Oscar sat lording over the room.

"How's it my fault that Kyle's dead?" I asked Whitney.

"Because you were sleeping with him!" Whitney said.

"That's so absurd it's funny," I said.

No surprise that I was the only one who found it funny. Even Hardy looked a bit suspicious. It was Oscar's reaction that had me worried. He scooted forward in the recliner, his hands grasping the arms of the chair so tightly that I was waiting for his fingernails to pierce the fabric. His chest rose and fell in rapid succession as his breathing rate increased. I was afraid he was either having a heart attack or preparing to kill me.

"Oh, for God's sake … I was not sleeping with Kyle," I said.

"You're lying!" Whitney turned to Hardy. "She's lying. Tell her she's lying."

"There's no evidence that Detective Shatner was having an affair with your husband." Hardy gave me a look that said I'd better speak up if I had been. "Why do you think she was?"

"Because Kyle said they were." Whitney's voice was so soft that I could barely hear her. "And I know he still had feelings for her."

I didn't know how much of Whitney's story I believed. I knew Kyle still had some sort of obsession with me since he stalked me on occasion. But I had to assume Kyle would have kept those feelings a secret from his wife and in-laws. And at no point during the two months Kyle harassed me, or in the two-and-a-half years since, did I think that Kyle ever actually cared about me. I think he was just looking for a good time and, when he didn't get it, he continued to harass me because I had bruised his ego.

"Remember, Whitney, you're the one Kyle married." I couldn't help myself. I may not have wanted Kyle, but stumbling upon him and Whitney fornicating still irked me. "Though he clearly had to settle for second best."

Whitney jumped off the couch and would have vaulted over the coffee table had her mother not grabbed her by the shirt tail and yanked her back down.

"Wasn't Kyle good enough for you?" Whitney asked. "Is that it?"

I was about to say that Kyle wasn't good enough for the human race, when Hardy cut me off. He gave me a quick headshake and then turned back to Whitney. "Mrs. Vance, Detective Shatner and I are here to ask you a few questions about last night."

"I already talked to Chief Groves," Whitney said.

"What is this about, Sergeant Hardy? Whitney don't know what happened to her husband. You're barking up the wrong tree here. If you want to know what happened to Kyle, ask *her*," Oscar said while pointing at me with the flamingo.

Everyone turned to look at me.

"How many times do I have to tell you that I don't know what happened to Kyle? All I did was find his body," I said.

Oscar worked his dentures around in his mouth. "If you believe her, Sergeant Hardy, then you're 'bout as sharp as mashed taters. Them Shatners killed my grandson-in-law. You're wasting your time here."

Hardy looked at Oscar for a few seconds before turning to face Whitney. "When was the last time you saw your husband, Mrs. Vance?"

"Early yesterday afternoon. He said he was going over to the strip club to help get set up for the party. He's been working there the past few months. Ever since he got fired from the construction company he'd been working for," Whitney said.

"Did you hear from him after he left for work?" Hardy asked.

Whitney shook her head.

"Where were you last night?" I asked.

"I was here all night. Waiting for my husband to come home." Whitney started to cry. "Instead, Chief Groves came to tell me he's dead."

"Look at what you've done," said Whitney's plump and thoroughly unpleasant looking mother. "You've gone and upset the poor girl. As if she wasn't upset enough."

"Where were you on New Year's Eve, Mrs. Palmer?" I asked.

"I was at home." Whitney's mother grabbed a handful of tissues and handed them to her daughter. Mrs. Palmer glared at me as if she wanted to blame me for everything that had happened in the previous twenty-four hours. "And no, I can't prove it, because I was alone."

"Was your husband at the party?" Hardy asked.

"No ... my husband is ... on an extended vacation."

"What she means is that her husband is in jail. And he's going to be there for at least ten more years," I said.

Hardy gave me a sideways look before inquiring about Kyle's family.

"His mom died from cancer last year," Whitney said. "And his dad and siblings live in Kansas. Kyle didn't have much to do with them. But his dad told me that he's gonna come down for the funeral."

I had tried to keep my mouth shut and leave the questioning up to Hardy, but I couldn't take it anymore. I was sick of dancing around the subject of what happened on New Year's Eve. I doubted that Whitney knew anything, so I really didn't care what she had to say. The person I wanted to talk to was Oscar.

"So, Oscar," I said, "we understand that you told Chief Groves you were with Kyle in the hours before he died."

"We were at the strip club. Russ and Toby were there, too, weren't you, boys?"

Russell and Toby both nodded. Toby said, "From around six until we left to crash your party, we were there. So was Kyle."

"So Kyle was there around six when you arrived?" Hardy asked. "And he was there the entire time up until you left to crash the Shatners' party? By the way, why did you do that?"

"Houston called me. Said some mean things," Oscar said.

I rolled my eyes. "You and Uncle Houston exchange at least half a dozen nasty phone calls a day. What was so insulting about the one last night?"

Oscar inched forward in his seat and asked, "So Houston hasn't told you yet?"

"Told me what?" I said.

"He bought that empty building across the street from *my* strip club. Told me he's gonna open up a strip club of his own. Also said he's gonna make it better than mine and hire all my dancers away."

The story didn't sound all that farfetched. Opening a rival strip club across the street from the Dancing Cowgirl was something that Houston would do. I didn't think any of the female Shatners would be too happy about it though. "So that's why you crashed the party?"

"I wanted to make sure Houston knows I'm not going to roll over and play dead," Oscar said. "He can try to run me out, but I ain't going nowhere."

Hardy cleared his throat. "But you're sure Kyle went to the fairgrounds with y'all?"

"Of course he went with us," Russell said. "How else would he have gotten to the fairgrounds?"

"When did you notice he was missing?" Hardy asked.

"Sometime after we got back to the club," Toby said. "When we left the fairgrounds, we jumped in different cars. No one realized he wasn't there until after we got back to the club."

"Our families had a near brawl, but none of you were concerned that something bad might have happened to him during the confrontation?" I asked. Had the roles been reversed, an alarm would have gone up had my family returned with less people than we had set out with.

"Like the boy said, we didn't realize he was missing right away. But no one thought he might've gotten left behind at the fairgrounds" Oscar said.

"Then where did you think he was?" I asked.

Oscar sank back into the recliner and shrugged. "Don't matter where I thought he was."

"Toby? Russell? Where did you think he was?" Hardy asked.

The brothers exchanged a look over Oscar's head. "In the front room."

"Why are you being so evasive, boys?" Hardy asked. "What did you think Kyle might have been doing that you don't want to say in front of your sister?"

"They probably thought Kyle left to be with one of his girlfriends," Whitney said.

"He had more than one?" I asked.

Whitney, who'd been quietly crying for the past couple of minutes, suddenly burst out laughing. "Kyle had so many girlfriends that he couldn't keep track of them. If it was young and female, he wanted to screw it. And, given the opportunity, he did."

"You knew about this? And you stayed with him?"

"Of course, I stayed with him. I loved him." All at once, Whitney stopped laughing and crying. "Well, I loved him up until a few months ago. That's when he … he gave me … he gave me a STD."

Whitney's mother jumped up from the couch. "Kyle gave you what? Why didn't you tell me? I'd have skinned him alive."

"Shut up, Mom. You wouldn't have done anything. None of you ever did anything, and all of you knew about what he was doing to me."

"We might have done something had you asked," Russell said.

Toby leaned over the back of the recliner and cuffed Russell on the side of the head. "What my brother means is that we would have beat him up and run him off. We wouldn't have killed him or nothing. Man like that ain't worth going to jail for."

Whitney snorted. "Anyway, that's when I had all that I could take. I could forgive the cheating because clearly I wasn't giving him what he wanted. But I couldn't forgive the STD."

"You have any idea who these women are?" I asked.

Whitney shook her head. "I don't know. Maybe the girls at the club. But probably any willing woman he could find. Check out his phone. He took naked pictures of all of his girlfriends."

"It's true," Toby said. "Kyle would show them to me and Russ."

"Unfortunately we have not been able to located Kyle's cell phone. But we will go through his photos once we have access to the phone." Hardy rubbed at the scar on his chin. "But let me get this straight … what y'all are telling me is that Kyle was at the party with you and that he went with everyone to the fairgrounds? And the last time you saw him was at the fairgrounds?"

"Yep," Oscar said. "Them Shatners killed Kyle and stuffed him in that dumpster. You best be talking to them again. They're the ones that killed the boy. Now I think it's time for you two to get going."

"I would like to look around the house and go through Kyle's belongings," Hardy said.

"Ever since the … the STD … Kyle hasn't been living here," Whitney said. "I kicked him out. He's been living in a trailer out back."

"Then I would like to search the trailer."

"THERE IS ONE THING I have to know," Hardy said as he led me across Whitney's front yard and over to where his truck was parked in the driveway. "Were you having an affair with the victim or not?"

"Are you serious? I can't believe you would listen to Whitney's ramblings above me." I kicked the right front tire of Hardy's truck in agitation. "Okay, I can believe it. It's not like you really have any reason to believe me. But I was not sleeping with Kyle! I have never slept with him. I didn't want anything to do with him!"

"Cool it, Detective Shatner!" Hardy swung open one of truck's doors and grabbed his crime scene kit out of the backseat. "I don't think anyone has told me the complete truth since I got here. And that includes you. The Palmers clearly weren't telling me everything about Kyle back there. And your family seems to be hiding something as well. How do I know you aren't lying to me?"

"You don't," I said, forcing myself to calm down. "But I'm not. I might not have told you the whole truth, but I haven't lied to you."

Hardy rubbed his hands over his face, smoothing out the deep furrows on his forehead. "Detective Shatner, just answer my question. And tell me the truth this time. I'm not judging you, but I need to know how far your relationship with Kyle went."

"It didn't go anywhere," I said. "I definitely told you the whole truth about Kyle."

"You didn't kill him?"

"Two-and-a-half-years is a long time to wait."

"And you're not covering for any family members that might have killed him?"

"I told you, we had no reason to kill Kyle. Or at least no reason that I know about."

"None of them would have killed Kyle because of any past wrongdoing towards you?"

"No. I keep telling you, it's all in the past. I'm a big girl, Sergeant Hardy. I don't need a man to take care of my problems. I can take care of myself."

"Noted," Hardy said as he brushed past me. "Let's go check out the victim's trailer."

A dilapidated single-wide trailer sat towards the far end of Whitney's large backyard. Taking into account the overgrowth of weeds and ivy, along with the run-down exterior of the small building, it appeared that the trailer had been in its current location for quite some time. I couldn't help but wonder why Kyle didn't go any farther than the backyard when Whitney kicked him out. Maybe he had nowhere else to go.

Stepping into the trailer, I started to gag when I smelled the combined scent of cheap cologne, rotten food, and stale sweat. Clothes, food, and all sorts of other junk lay scattered across the small living room. The only furniture in the room was a camouflage print recliner, a big screen TV, and a few milk crates Kyle had been using as tables and for storage. There was also a hutch in the corner that overflowed with Jeff Gordon memorabilia.

"Try not to disturb too much for the time being. I plan to have the crime scene unit come down to collect evidence later. The less we tamper with the better," Hardy said.

"I'm not sure I want to touch anything in here." After tugging on a pair of latex gloves, I swung open the glass door on the hutch and picked up a little doll that was dressed in a Jeff Gordon jacket and hat. The doll's lifeless eyes stared up at me under its shaggy hairstyle. The doll sat in front of a piece of sheet metal that might have once been part of a race car. "Maybe someone killed Kyle for his vast collection of Jeff Gordon memorabilia."

"People have killed for weirder things," Hardy said.

After poking around in the living room and coming up with nothing that appeared to be related to Kyle's death, Hardy and I split up. He went to check out the bathroom while I wandered into the kitchen and discovered that the cupboards were crammed full of boxes of Mac-and-Cheese, cans of soup, and enough SPAM to feed a small army. The refrigerator was full of beer, moldy lunch meat, and cheese, and the freezer was packed with frozen dinners. On the kitchen counter I found a suspicious white powder. I had Hardy come in the kitchen to get a look at the white powder.

"Part of me thinks Kyle wasn't a baker," Hardy said, inspecting the powder.

"Depends on what your definition of a baker is. Everyone thinks my family is horrible because we grow pot. At least we're not manufacturing and selling cocaine," I said.

"The Palmers are drug dealers? What else are they into?" Hardy asked.

"Let me put it this way, everything you've heard about the Shatners ... times it by three and you've got the Palmers."

"Why haven't I heard of this? And how do they get away with it?" Hardy asked.

"That's something I would also like to know. Because, as far as I know, they don't have any family members in law enforcement who are covering up their crimes."

"Maybe they're just better at being criminals than your family."

"No, they just keep getting lucky and wind up getting busted for the small stuff," I said, feeling a brief shot of rage towards the collective Palmer family and their combined ability to get away with major crimes. The Shatners needed me and Uncle Murph to keep them out of jail. The Palmers apparently only needed dumb luck to save them. "Did you find anything?"

"Just towels and sheets in the hall closet." Hardy collected a sample of the white powder and tucked it into his crime scene kit. "And I found what you'd expect to find in a bathroom. Toothbrush and toothpaste. Soap and shampoo. A tube of prescription-strength hemorrhoid ointment. And a bulk box of generic condoms that are neither lubed nor ribbed for her pleasure. And there are three used condoms in the trash can."

"Funny Kyle had condoms in here when it sounds like he and Whitney haven't had sex in a while."

"Maybe Kyle brought his girlfriends here."

"That would be low. Super low. Whitney can see the trailer from her back windows." I pointed at the dirty window over the kitchen sink. Through the bare branches of two oak trees, Whitney's house was clearly visible at the other end of the yard. "Unless that was the point. Knowing Kyle, he probably would have gotten a sick joy out of knowing she could see him bringing his girlfriends here."

"Come on, let's take a look at the bedroom," Hardy said as he walked out of the kitchen.

I followed Hardy into Kyle's cramped bedroom. Like the living room, there wasn't a whole lot of furniture in there, but what little there was took up the majority of the small space. Aside from the queen bed, there was only a bedside table, a dresser with a broken drawer, and a card table on which Kyle had set up his laptop. On the wall above the bed hung a poster of Johnny Cash.

"Let's see if Kyle was bringing his girlfriends here or not." Hardy got an ultraviolet light out of his crime scene kit and shone it around the room. The bed sheets lit up with countless white sex stains. Hardy and I groaned in disgust. "That's a yes."

"Here's evidence of one." I picked up a hot pink thong that lay on top of one of the pillows and waved it around for Hardy to see.

"That looks a little too small to be the wife's." Hardy knelt on the floor and then stuck his head under the bed. "Nothing under the bed but dust bunnies, a shoe, and another thong."

"Uh huh," I said as I admired the view of Hardy's backside.

"This one is a large." Hardy held up the red lace thong. "Two different sizes. Two different women?"

"Three different sizes." I stepped over a pile of Kyle's dirty clothes and plucked a pair of polka dot boy shorts off of the card table and twirled it around my gloved finger. "These are a two-XL."

"Whitney is right, her husband had a lot of girlfriends." Hardy walked over to the dresser and yanked open the top drawer. "Four! Medium-sized, ruffled, baby blue panties."

"What a scumbag." I tugged open the top drawer of Kyle's beat-up nightstand and screeched in surprise and disgust. Hardy rushed to my side, demanding to know what I had found. Using two fingers, I gingerly held up the monster-sized dildo I found in the drawer. "You think Whitney would have kept this."

"Maybe it's not hers. Kyle could have gotten it for his girlfriends. Or for his own use."

I cocked an eyebrow at Hardy.

"Don't look at me," Hardy said. "Actually, don't bother looking around here anymore either. The crime scene technicians can handle it from here. Whatever we are looking for, I have a feeling we're not going to find it here."

Chapter Eleven

———◆———

Hardy didn't stick around too long after we returned from Wilder. Speaking to Whitney and company, and then searching Kyle's trailer, had taken up the majority of the afternoon. Even though there was a lot left to be done in the investigation, Hardy decided to call it a day. After thanking me for my help, and leaving me with little hope that he would further require my assistance, Hardy packed up all of the notes and evidence and then hit the road.

I wandered around the sheriff's department for a while, hoping to find someone who could fill me in on any new developments. But the crime scene technicians were long gone, and my deputies didn't have any new information. I was fairly certain that Quaranta knew something, but he wasn't sharing it with me.

As for Uncle Murph, he, too, was long gone and no one had any idea where he was or what he was doing. I assumed that Murph has gone off to conduct his own investigation into Kyle's death. I was just glad he hadn't requested my assistance.

Accepting that there was nothing for me to do at the sheriff's department, I headed out to Uncle Houston's place to see what my family was up to and to confirm that they hadn't all fled the country.

Taking the main road out of Holler, I headed north towards the old Shatner farm. The town quickly gave way to scattered neighborhoods broken up by fields and woods. Passing the Shady Grove Baptist cemetery, I entered Shatner Country. My family didn't do any actual farming anymore—unless you count the marijuana—but a number of Shatners still lived on the five thousand acres of land. Various companies and real estate agencies have offered generous sums to get my family to move off the land, but the Shatners have held fast. It has been our land for over one hundred and fifty years, and it will still be ours one hundred and fifty years from now. There were too many dead bodies and illegal activities spread across the land for us to risk giving up any acreage.

On the left side of the two lane highway was Shatner's Alpaca Farm and Wild West Town. The Wild West town—Wyatt County's top tourist attraction—was comprised of weathered-looking buildings that my family claim are authentic. I wasn't sure how truthful that statement was. The buildings were definitely older than I was, but I had my doubts that they dated back to the 1800's. During the spring and summer, the family staged fake gunfights in the town and had can-can shows in the dancehall. In the fall, the town and other parts of the ranch were turned into a Halloween attraction with a hayride and haunted barn.

On the right side of the highway, a half dozen gravel driveways snaked back into the woods, marking the homes of some of my relatives. I turned into Houston's half-mile long driveway, passing the billboard-sized "NO TRESPASSING" sign. At first, the road was gravel, but, as soon as I hit the tree line, the gravel faded away into packed dirt. I drove slowly, scanning the darkening woods for booby traps and security cameras. All I could see were rusted out cars, and towering piles of lumber, metal, and old tires scattered among the trees. The closer I got to the house, the nicer the cars got.

I was just about to the clearing where Houston's farmhouse was located when two camouflage-clad individuals stepped out of the shadows and took up a stance across the road.

I hit the brakes and stopped just short of hitting them. After putting my Jeep into park, I lowered my window and stuck my head out. "What are you doing?"

"Protecting the homestead." Andrew came around to the driver's side and grabbed the door handle. He tugged the handle a few times before I decided to be nice and unlock the doors. He then whipped open the door and leaned inside. "We're going to have to check your car."

"Am I the enemy now?" I asked.

Andrew shrugged. "You've got that Ranger looking into the family, so you tell me. As of this morning, I don't know if I can trust you anymore."

"You know I couldn't tell you about Kyle." Andrew might be mad at me at the moment, but I had my doubts he would remain mad for too long. "Get over it."

While Andrew scanned the front seats, my half-brother, Luke, opened the rear hatch and crawled into the cargo area. Luke was my daddy's love child—or at least he was one of them. Or should I say, Luke was one of my two half-siblings that I knew about. Given Dad's tendency to cheat on Mom,

I was sure there were more out there. It wasn't until I was in my early twenties that I learned the truth about Luke. Up until then, he was the boy that Uncle Houston's oldest son had adopted. I looked at Luke as just another one of my cousins. Since Dad was dead by the time Luke found out the truth about his birth parents, and Luke's birthmother wanted nothing to do with him, we were still sketchy about the details surrounding his conception.

"Uncle Houston knew you would show up sooner or later, so he sent me and Luke out here to intercept you. He wants to be sure you ain't bringing some uninvited guests along," Andrew said.

"You mean the Ranger?" I asked, shoving Andrew away as he leaned over me to look in the center consol. "Believe me, the last place I would ever bring him would be here."

After confirming that I wasn't hiding anyone in my Jeep, Andrew slammed the door shut. "She's good."

I didn't give Luke a chance to get out of my car. I just put my Jeep into drive and took off with him still in the back.

"Hey, Carrie."

"Yeah, Luke?"

"Everyone is real mad at you."

"I kind of expected they would be."

Weaving around cars, people, Houston's fifteen hunting dogs, and a potbellied pig named Mr. Giggles, I found a parking spot for myself beside the old Soviet tank sitting in the yard. I had no idea where Houston acquired the tank nor did I want to. For years he swore to us that the tank was disabled and that nothing in it worked. My doubts were confirmed two years ago when Houston had too much to drink and decided it would be a good idea to take the tank out for a test drive. He caused over twenty thousand dollars' worth of damage before Murph was finally able to get him to stop the tank.

I climbed out of my Jeep and went around to the other side of the tank. There I found Granddaddy standing under a ragged tent that had been erected over an oversized grill. Houston and Bowie were over by the dilapidated barn housing Houston's collection of priceless junk. Behind the barn was one of the bomb shelters in which my family grew the marijuana plants. Even farther back in the woods, at a location unknown to me, were the rest of the bomb shelters and the moonshine still.

"Hi Granddaddy."

"There's my favorite girl." Granddaddy took the time out of rotating hotdogs to give me a hug. "How you holding up?"

"I'm all right." I looked over at Houston, who was whacking away at the ground with a gardening hoe. "What's Uncle Houston doing? And don't even tell me he's digging a grave."

"Too late for that. Though my brothers both think you should've buried Kyle out in the woods over calling the Ranger," Granddaddy said. "No, Houston's planting a garden. He wants to enter the largest pumpkin contest at the county fair in September."

"What, having the biggest ego in the county isn't enough?"

"Carrie!" Houston tossed the hoe on the ground and marched over to the grill. A number of other Shatners who had been lurking around the yard also wandered over. "Is the dog still sniffing around or has he started to dig someplace else?"

"You know I can't tell you anything." I made a circular motion with my index finger. "Ongoing investigation and all that."

"We're your family. We have a right to know what's going on," Houston said.

"Eh." I shrugged. "Not really."

"Murph is off doing me a favor, so it's up to you to keep us informed," Houston said, moving closer and backing me up against the tank. "We know the Ranger took you off somewhere for most of the afternoon. Where did he take you? Tell me everything."

I looked back-and-forth between Granddaddy, Houston, and Bowie. All three of them had nearly identical expressions on their wrinkled faces. They were hiding their fear under a thin layer of frustration. I couldn't help but take pity on them since I knew how worried they were about the whole situation. I was worried, too. But no amount of pity could convince me to share details of the investigation with any of them. Except for Granddaddy.

"All I can tell you is that the Ranger is still looking at the family," I said.

Houston and Bowie were still badgering me for details when their wives, Mabel and Imogen, came out of the house and pushed their way into the crowd. Mabel shoved a package of cheese slices into Houston's hands before turning to me.

"Don't tell me you showed up empty-handed, Carrie," Mabel said, when she noticed that I hadn't brought a homemade dish to contribute to the night's feast.

"I was busy all day trying to prove this family didn't kill someone. I didn't have time, Aunt Mabel."

"Didn't have time? Did you hear that, Imogen?" Mabel's beehive hair-do shook in righteous indignation. Her eyes, almost hidden behind thick glasses, narrowed into slits. "Carrie didn't have time to make something. She didn't even have time to go to the store."

"She should be ashamed of herself." Imogen shook her arthritic finger under my nose.

I wasn't ashamed. And I wasn't about to let my great-aunts send me on a guilt trip. Nevertheless, I would be hearing about my lack of etiquette until the next major party, and probably for some time after.

"Leave the poor girl alone." Grandma Thelma pushed her way in between Mabel and Imogen, using her large chest to make way for her slight frame. "Carrie's been through enough today. She doesn't need you two old biddies harassing her."

Mabel and Imogen grumbled under their breath, but they backed down. Grandma might be a small woman, but she was very strong willed. She didn't take crap from anyone. Not even from her sister-in-law, Emily Morgan, when she was alive.

"Come with me, sweetheart." Grandma looped her arm through mine and pulled me towards Houston's old farmhouse. The house started out as a one room cabin back in the eighteen hundreds. Over the years, various generations of Shatners have added on to the cabin and turned it into the sprawling, ramshackle farmhouse.

When Grandma and I got to the enclosed back porch of the house, she guided me over to the porch swing. "You look like you've been rode hard and put up wet."

I knew I wasn't looking my best, but I didn't think I looked *that* bad. "It's been a long day."

Grandma made some sympathetic noises and gave me a hug. "Now where is that nice looking Ranger? Is he married?"

I tried not to groan. As her last unmarried granddaughter, Grandma was determined to help me find a good man so that I could settle down. She claimed she wasn't looking for any more great-grandchildren. She just wanted me to be happy. What she didn't understand was that I was just fine on my own. I tried the relationship thing, and it didn't work. I kept telling Grandma that I wasn't ready to try it again, but she didn't listen. She just couldn't understand why any woman would willingly be single. I kept it simple and explained to her that I just hadn't found the right man yet. She said it's because I was too picky. And, who knows, maybe I was. These days, when I was talking to a man, or dating one, and he did or said something that sets off Red Flag Warnings in my head, his chances of being around much longer were about the same as those of a nameless, red shirt wearing ensign surviving past the first commercial break on *Star Trek*—between slim and none.

"I'll admit that Sergeant Hardy is good looking." I didn't comment on the married part since I wasn't sure. At the moment, I didn't want to know. I had enough to think about besides Hardy's relationship status. "But I don't think a criminal investigation is the right place to go husband hunting."

"You might not believe this, considering the wrinkles and the lack of hair, but your Granddaddy used to be very good looking. He was quite a catch.

And he's such a good man." Grandma patted me on the leg. "Then again, your daddy was rather handsome, but he was nothing but trouble."

I shifted and accidently set the porch swing into motion. My grandparents hardly ever mentioned my dad. They claim it was because they didn't like to speak ill of the dead. I don't think they liked talking about Dad because it forced them to think about all of the upsetting things he did while he was alive.

Dad died when I was sixteen. He was out riding his motorcycle when a sudden, violent thunderstorm broke out. Dad wound up wrecking his motorcycle when he skidded out crossing a bridge that spanned the Neches River. The next morning, a passerby noticed various broken bike parts on the bridge. Looking over the side, he spotted the mangled bike on the riverbank. Divers searched the river for a week, but they never found Dad's body. We assumed his body got swept downriver and wound up in one of the swampy areas farther south of us.

"Your daddy just had too much of the devil in him. He was too smart and charming for his own good. The only thing he loved more than getting into trouble was getting out of it."

"That's the only thing Elliott was ever good at," Granddaddy said as he stepped up onto the porch. "Boy had a talent for making trouble and then covering it up. I blame myself. If I hadn't started bringing him along to help cover up what my brothers were doing, Elliott might never have got caught up in it."

"Don't blame yourself, Crockett. Elliott was attracted to trouble like a duck to water. He would have found his way to it with or without your help," Grandma said.

"You're right, Elliott didn't have much of a chance. None of these poor kids do. But I didn't raise my son to be an adulterer."

"Your poor mother never knew what hit her." Grandma squeezed my hand. "Elliott just swept her off her feet with all that charm."

While I had never been told the whole story, I knew that my parents had a whirlwind romance. My parents met while Dad was attending a law enforcement seminar in Dallas. Two weeks later, they were married. Over the years, I tried to get more details out of Mom, but she refused to talk about it.

"I don't know what lies he told her, but this was not what Frances expected." Granddaddy waved his hand around, indicating Wyatt County and the Shatners. "She was tough, though. She tried to stick it out."

"She just needed the entire liquor store to do it," I said, causing Grandma to give me a sharp look. With Dad dead and my two older sisters off at college, Mom dumped me with Grandma and Granddaddy, and then she moved back to Dallas to live with her parents. They sent her to a private rehab facility to get her off the sauce. I didn't know if it was the healing powers of the center or the absence of Dad, but Mom cut back on her alcohol consumption. She still drinks though, quietly and in private. She was clinging to the side of the wagon, but every once in a while she fell off. When Mom wasn't sneaking a drink, she spent the majority of her days playing tennis at the country club and attending charity fundraisers.

"Your parents might have been lacking, but you, Holly, and Rosie managed to turn out okay," Grandma said. "We're so proud of you."

"You are nothing like your father," Granddaddy said as he crushed me in a hug that I desperately needed. "You have a conscience. And you know the difference between right and wrong. I know your Uncle Murph wanted to get rid of the body and cover things up. And I know you're the one who insisted on calling the Department of Public Safety. That was the right thing to do, and Thelma and I are proud of you for doing it. But, now tell me the truth. Is that Ranger really looking for other suspects?"

I waited until Houston, Bowie, and their wives had all crossed the porch and entered the house before I answered. "So far, no one has been able to find any evidence that Kyle was killed at the fairgrounds. And there is no solid evidence that any of us killed him. None of us admitted to seeing Kyle at the fairgrounds. But there are twenty-one Palmers claiming he was there."

"And considering you found Kyle in the dumpster, everyone is more likely to believe the Palmers," Granddaddy said. "Did y'all find anything connecting the family to the murder?"

"We found a tire iron under the body, but we're not sure if it's the murder weapon or not. What we do know is that Kyle was still alive when the party started."

"Damn it," Granddaddy said.

"David Crockett! Watch your language," Grandma said.

"Don't nag me now, woman," Granddaddy said. "Carrie, what else?"

"Sergeant Hardy knows that the gate was unlocked all night, so he can't rule out that we were the only people who had access to the dumpster. We might be the best suspects, but he can't say that we're the only ones." Standing up, I moved towards the back door. "Now, I am about starved, so I am going inside and getting something to eat."

"No." Grandma pushed me back on to the swing. "You've had a rough day. Just sit here and rest. I'll go get you something to eat."

Granddaddy waited until Grandma went inside before he said, "Carrie, about what Houston said this morning ... "

"Don't worry, Granddaddy. I'll only do so much for this family. And I won't do that."

"You're a good girl. The family shouldn't take advantage of you the way they do."

I couldn't agree more. "Granddaddy, if you'd found the body in the dumpster, what would you have done?"

"Doesn't matter what I would have done, Carrie. All that matters is what you did. Just don't do anything you might wind up regretting." Granddaddy squeezed my hand. "You're real good at what you do, Carrie. The sheriff's department never really had their own crime scene investigator before you came along. I made sure my deputies had the basic training. But I never had anyone with a degree and years of on-the-job experience. You're also turning into a top notch detective. Focus on that, Carrie. Not on saving the family. Most of them aren't worth saving."

"Granddaddy, I don't do this to protect the ones who aren't worth saving. I'm doing it to protect the ones who are."

"That's the opposite of why your dad and I did it. And why Murph is still doing it. But, despite our reasons, we're all doing the same thing," Granddaddy said.

After reviving myself with food, I made it inside just in time for the opening kick-off of the Sugar Bowl. About twenty Shatners were crowded around the big screen in Houston's living room, rabidly cheering on the University of Texas. I didn't know where the rest of my family members were hanging out, and I didn't bother to ask.

During commercial breaks, I went around the room, asking my family members if there was anything they hadn't told the deputies that morning—including if they had seen anyone else at the fairgrounds. Since everyone was caught up in the game, I couldn't get much out of them. They all wanted to know about the progress of the case, but none of them wanted to contribute to the progress. Instead, they chastised me for calling in the Department of Public Safety over what they considered to be a trivial matter.

By halftime, my family came to the unanimous decision that they'd put up with me long enough. Houston guided me over to the door and basically threw me out.

"Carrie, how 'bout you stop hassling us," Houston said. "You being here is about as useless as tits on a bull."

"Well, what do you want me to do?" I asked.

"How should I know?" Houston asked. "Go plant some evidence. Or get rid of some. Just get one step ahead of the Ranger and stay there."

"Uncle Houston, do you know something I don't? Because if you've got information that you're not sharing—"

"What? You'll do what?" Houston asked. "Just get out of here and go do something useful. Or go home and get some sleep. You've got to get back to investigating in the morning."

"What's the point? I doubt Sergeant Hardy is going to let me help him anymore."

"No, he probably won't," Houston said. "But that shouldn't stop you from making friends with the Ranger. Remember what I said, Carrie … "

"You know what, Uncle Houston. I think I'm going to call in sick tomorrow."

"Why would you do that?"

"Because you're making me sick."

Chapter Twelve

— ◆ —

I spent a sleepless night running through my family tree and trying to shoehorn each of my relatives into a scenario where they killed Kyle and then stuffed his body into the dumpster. I came up with a lot of good theories, but I didn't want to believe that any of them were correct.

After hitting the snooze button four times, I dragged myself out of bed with just enough time to throw on some clothes and shove a breakfast bar in my mouth. I was running out to my Jeep when my phone rang. I dug it out of my coat pocket and checked the caller ID.

"Why are you calling me?" I asked myself when I saw Catfish Devereux's name.

Catfish was one of Uncle Houston's partners in crime. And I meant that literally. They've been best friends almost since they were born. Together, they've broken multiple laws and raised some serious hell. Catfish may not be related to the Shatners by blood, but he was family. I answered the phone with caution. Catfish wasn't the type of man to just call someone up to chitchat. And, even if he was, I wasn't on the short list of people he would call.

"Hey, Catfish. What's going on?" I asked after answering the phone.

"One of your cousins is at my place raising hell."

"The bar or the store?" Catfish owned a bar and a massive beverage distribution store, both of which shared the same parking lot.

"The bar."

Catfish hung up before I could ask him which one of my cousins was disturbing the peace. Or what exactly he or she was doing.

Realizing that I wasn't up for dealing with a drunken Shatner by myself, I retreated back inside my house and went looking for help.

Andrew was still asleep in my guest room, curled up under the covers and loudly snoring. Sneaking across the small room that my older sisters used to share, I licked my finger and stuck it in Andrew's ear. He woke up pretty fast.

"What are you doing?" Andrew grabbed his pillow and took a wild swing at me. "I was having that sexy dream about Miranda Lambert again."

"Good for you." I jerked the pillow out of his hands and smacked him over the head with it. "But I need your help."

After explaining the situation to him, Andrew reluctantly crawled out of bed, but he refused to change out of his pajamas. He then promptly fell back to sleep before I even backed the Jeep out of the driveway.

Catfish's Cantina, which was about a fifteen minute drive west from my neighborhood, was on the main road heading south out of Holler. The Cantina was not the place to go if you wanted to socialize. It was a place to go to get drunk. The large structure housing Catfish's Beer and Fine Liquor Emporium was located behind the bar. While Catfish still owned the bar and the store, he didn't have much to do with the daily operation of either of them.

Catfish, who was waiting for me on the front steps of the bar, was puffing on a cigar and patting out a tune on his beer belly. It sounded like he was trying to play along to the music that was playing inside the bar. The thick wood walls muffled the music, but the song sounded very familiar.

"I didn't know the bar was open this early," I said.

"It ain't. This lunacy has been goin' on since last night," Catfish said in a voice made raspy from years of chain smoking. "Howdy, Andrew."

"How's it hanging?" Andrew asked.

"Low and to the right."

Interrupting Andrew's and Catfish's complicated handshake, I asked, "How come no one called me about this last night?"

Catfish tilted his head back and blew out a perfect smoke ring. "That's what I'm still tryin' to figure out. The kid probably wouldn't have caused all this trouble if someone had given him a ride home."

"Which one of my cousins is it?" I asked.

"The one with the broken heart." Catfish kicked open the bar's heavy wood door and led the way inside.

With the door open, I could finally make out the music playing inside. It was the greatest song of all time—Billy Ray Cyrus's "Achy Breaky Heart."

Stepping into the bar, I gave my eyes a few moments to adjust to the shadowy interior. The walls were covered in dark wood paneling, and the lights were kept intentionally dim. The room was sparsely decorated with mangy-looking animal heads and old metal beer signs. A bar ran the length of the back wall, and there were a number of mismatched tables and chairs scattered about the cramped floor area. The three forms of entertainment were an old jukebox, a dart board, and a pool table.

My cousin Dale was slumped over a table next to the jukebox. The table and nearby floor were littered with empty beer bottles. There was also a nearly empty bottle of Jack Daniels in one of Dale's hands.

"Why didn't you call Uncle Murph? That's his boy," I said to Catfish.

"You know I can't keep track of all you Shatners," Catfish said. "Y'all need to hand out a family tree to people."

"Speak for yourself. You're the one who's got eleven children by six different women." And all eleven of those kids were named Leslie after their father. Though, like Catfish, none of them willingly went by their given name.

"You're right, I can barely keep my own kids straight. And don't even ask about the grandkids and great-grandkids." Catfish blew another puff of cigar smoke in my face and then wandered towards the door "I'll be back. I gotta get Kinky from the store."

"Hey, Dale!" I yelled. "You alive over there?"

Dale lifted his head from the table and gave me a weary look before finishing off what was left of the whiskey. He then let his head fall back down to the table.

Leaving Dale where he was, I danced my way across the room and had a seat at the bar. Andrew had beat me to the bar, and was drinking a beer for breakfast. Behind the bar, the youngest of Catfish's nine sons was restocking the shelves.

"How's it going, Red? You wrestling anywhere this weekend?" I asked Red Devereux. He wrestled at small, independent wrestling shows across eastern Texas and Louisiana. His ring name was The Ravishing Redneck. Sometimes I valeted for him.

Red brushed back his long, blonde hair, and then propped his elbows on the bar and leaned towards me. "Got an event down in Huntsville on Saturday night. You gonna come? I could always use a beautiful valet."

"That'll depend on how the case is going. But I'm sure some of the Shatners will make it down for the show."

"I'll be there," Andrew said.

As "Achy Breaky Heart" came to an end, I turned around and watched Dale painstakingly feed another quarter into the jukebox. The same song began to play.

"Twenty-seven! That's the twenty-seventh time he's played that song since I got here!" Catfish's third son stomped into the bar and hurled a breakfast burrito in Dale's general direction.

"For God's sake, man, who throws a burrito?" Red asked.

"One who is losing his mind!" Kinky tried yanking off his cowboy boot, but Catfish dragged him towards the bar. Red quickly poured a shot of tequila and slid it across the bar to his half-brother. After downing the shot, Kinky slammed the glass down on the table and said, "I'm gonna kill someone if you don't turn that damn song off."

"Don't be insulting my favorite song," I said to my uncle-by marriage. Kinky was one of five Devereuxs to have married into the Shatner family. He was married to Uncle Murph's older sister, Margaret. Kinky was one of the various Devereuxs caught up in the Shatner's criminal misdeeds. He had a bad habit of selling the Shatner family's moonshine out of the back room of Catfish's liquor store. I kept telling Uncle Kinky to knock it off. The liquor store was within the Holler city limits, and there was nothing Murph or I could do if Chief Yates or any of the Holler police arrested him. Kinky, who assumed he was a lot smarter than he was, claimed had had a whole system in place and swore there was no way he would get caught.

"You and Andrew were barely out of diapers when this song came out," Kinky said.

"We were four," Andrew said. "Listening to this song over and over again is one of my earliest memories. And some of my fondest."

"Mine, too." Turning to Kinky, I asked, "Where's Dale getting all the quarters from? And why didn't you just unplug the jukebox?"

"Dale broke into the jukebox. He's using the quarters that were already in there." Kinky swallowed the second shot. "And I tried to unplug the jukebox, but that maniac came at me with a broken bottle."

Add vandalism and assault with a deadly weapon to the drunk and disorderly charge. Not that Dale would be charged with anything.

"You want to tell me what happened?" I asked.

Kinky shook his head and pointed across the bar at Red. "Let Red tell you how he got the boy drunk."

I should have known that Red was involved with Dale's drunken state. Wrestling was Red's hobby. It was the bartending that paid the bills. Red may take everyone's keys as they came in the door, but he lacked the restraint to cut anyone off when they had too much.

"What?" Red gave me a sheepish smile. "The guy was upset. I wanted to help him drink away his sorrows."

"Looks like you did a pretty good job." I gestured over my shoulder when the song ended. Within seconds, Dale had it playing again.

"Twenty-eight! I'm seriously about to kill him." Kinky turned towards Dale and yelled, "There are other she done-me-wrong, stole-my-dog-and-my-truck, and broke-my heart country songs on that damn jukebox. Play one of those!"

"Dale was a mess when he came in last night. Now he's just a drunk mess." Red walked over to the cash register and then came back with a credit card and a two-foot-long piece of receipt paper. "Here's his tab."

Andrew leaned over my shoulder as I skimmed the receipt. Between last night and this morning, Dale had consumed twenty beers, eight shots of tequila, and an entire bottle of whiskey. I wasn't sure how Dale was still alive, much less semi-awake.

"He drank all that?" Andrew asked.

Red nodded. "I pity his liver."

"The problem is not that Dale drank all this. It's that you gave him all this alcohol." I leaned over the bar and hit Red on his over-developed arm. He was wearing a sleeveless shirt so that he could better show off his tattoos and muscles. On his right bicep was a pinup girl that looked a little too much like me for comfort. Even though he named the pinup girl Diamond, he continued to deny that I inspired the tattoo.

"It was busy last night." Red sidled down the bar until he was out of arm's reach from me. "I lost track of how many I served Dale."

"Gimmie 'nother beer!" Dale yelled from across the room.

"You've had enough. I'm cutting you off." Red pointed over at Dale and said, "He was like that all last night. What was I supposed to do?"

"Oh, I can think of about ten things off the top of my head that you should have done."

Red shrugged. "Look, Carrie, baby, you didn't see Dale last night. He came in here crying 'bout his ex-old lady and how she won't take him back. It was pitiful. So, yeah, maybe I over-served Dale. But I did it with the best of intentions."

I grabbed an empty beer bottle and smashed it on the bar. I then leaned across the bar and waved the broken bottle in Red's face. We both knew that the broken bottle was nothing more than an empty gesture. Red was one of my closest friends and I would never do something to physically scar him.

"First of all, don't ever call me 'baby' again. Second, what exactly were those best intentions?"

"To help him drink away his pain. I mean, he showed me pictures of the chick. She is fine. And the stories ... When Dale sobers up, can you try to find out who she is? She sounds like my type." Red winked at me.

From what I'd seen, Red had never needed help when it came to finding female companionship. He had a flock of female groupies following him around the independent wrestling circuit. Yet, despite all of the women throwing themselves at him, Red was still trying to get me into bed. After fifteen years of rejection, you'd think he would give up. He hadn't.

"What happened after you got Dale drunk?" I asked.

"After a while Dale had to go praise the porcelain god. He made an epic mess in the men's room. Which I had to clean up." Red grimaced. "When

I came out of the bathroom, I found Dale passed out on the pool table. I decided to just leave him there to sleep it off."

"Hold on, you got Dale dangerously drunk and then you just abandoned him?" I asked.

Catfish reached over the bar and smacked Red on the side of the head. "Ya dumb idiot, the kid coulda died or somethin'."

"Look, I'm sorry. But Dale's fine." As Red tried to convince us that Dale was fine, Dale leaned over the side of the table and puked. "Okay, maybe he's not fine. But he's still alive, right? That's gotta count for something."

"Uncle Kinky, you want to tell me about what happened this morning?" I asked.

"Yeah, so, like, this morning I woke up and I had a text from Red telling me that Dale was sleeping in the bar." Kinky shoved his phone in my face so that I could see the text. "I had to come in early anyway 'cause of a delivery. That's when I found Dale. He wasn't passed out no more. He was drinking and playing that song."

"What did you do?" I asked.

"Like I said, there was the delivery. I had to take care of that first." Kinky jumped up from the bar stool and waved his arms around in exasperation. "Then I came back in here and tried to deal with Dale. When he came at me with the broken bottle, I called Red."

"And Red called Catfish, and then Catfish called me. Got it." I turned around in time to watch Dale fall out of the chair and crash into the side of the jukebox. In the process, he knocked a number of bottles off the table. The bottles shattered on the floor.

Catfish, who had been sitting quietly the past few minutes, stomped across the room and pulled Dale away from the jukebox. "Now, Carrie, we ain't gonna press charges or nothin'—"

"Well, that's good. Because if you pressed charges against Dale, I would have to press charges against Red for reckless endangerment."

"Like I said, I ain't pressing charges. I just want you to get the boy's sorry butt out of here. And keep him out. He got himself a lifetime ban."

I had my doubts that the lifetime ban would last the month. Despite that, it was a good idea to get Dale out of the bar and take him someplace to recover.

I went over and knelt on the floor by Dale's prone body. He didn't look too good, and he smelled even worse—a combined scent of vomit, alcohol, and sweat. I peeled back his eyelids and examined his bloodshot eyes. I also checked his pulse. From what I could tell, his heartbeat was slow and regular.

"Andrew, I'm going to take Dale to his mom's house. I'll drive his car. Follow me in the Jeep." I jabbed Dale in the side and said, "Time to get up, princess."

Dale groaned, but he managed to open one bloodshot eye enough to look up at me. "She dumped me."

"I know. It sucks. But getting drunk only made you feel worse, right?"

"I wanna die." Dale closed his eyes and turned his face away from me. "Leave me 'lone."

"Want me to haul him out of here?" Red asked.

"I think it's the only way we'll get him out to his car." I stood up and put some distance between me and Dale.

Red grabbed Dale and swung him up over his shoulder into a fireman's carry. Andrew held the front door open while I helped guide Red outside.

"And what is this?"

Stepping out from behind Red, I found Isaac Yates leaning against the side of my Jeep. After cursing under my breath, I said, "Nothing you need to be concerned with, Chief Yates."

"Oh, but I do need to be concerned." Yates pushed away from the car and stepped in front of Red, blocking his path to Dale's car. "This is my jurisdiction, after all. You do remember that, don't you Detective Shatner? The Holler police department has jurisdiction a couple hundred more feet south of this place."

"I'm aware of what the Holler city limits are," I said.

"Don't know what you're doing here, Chief Yates. Ain't no crime been committed," Catfish said.

"Still, I want to know why Detective Shatner was tearing through my town while greatly exceeding the speed limit." Yates cocked his head to the side and glared at me.

"Carrie always exceeds the speed limit," Dale mumbled.

"Shut up, Dale!" Covering Dale's mouth with my hand, I asked, "If I was going that fast, why didn't one of your fine officers pull me over?"

"He would have, but he decided it would be a better idea to follow and try to figure out what you were up to. Once you got here, my officer called me." Yates pried my hand away from Dale's mouth and then eyed him up. "What's his problem?"

Before I could respond, Dale lifted his head and threw up. The vomit splashed over Yates's shoes and the bottom of his pants. Gagging, Yates took a step backwards.

"His girlfriend broke up with him." Red pushed past Yates and headed for Dale's car. Andrew hurried after him to open the passenger side door. "I sat up with him all night, talking him through it."

I appreciated Red's insistence that he had been with Dale all night. I just hoped Yates believed it. Not that it really mattered. Before Yates got over being grossed out and could continue asking questions, I shoved Andrew towards my Jeep. I then slipped into the driver's side of Dale's car and peeled out of the parking lot. Normally, I would have hung around until Yates left, but I had more pressing matters to deal with.

Uncle Murph and his wife live in one of the more expensive neighborhoods on the western side of Holler. Murph chose the location, and the house, specifically because the Holler city limit line ran right along the small creek that marked the eastern edge of the neighborhood. Murph thought it was funny that he lived a few yards away from Chief Yates's jurisdiction. On the ten-minute drive to Aunt Lydia's house, I learned more about Dale's sex life than I ever wanted to know.

As soon as I pulled into Aunt Lydia's driveway, Dale clambered out of the car and collapsed into the front yard. He proceeded to empty his stomach in his mom's flowerbed. When Dale was done, Andrew and I hauled him inside and stuck him in the downstairs bathroom.

Before leaving, I advised Dale not to tell his mom about his sexual escapades. I could only hope he was sober enough to take my advice.

During the drive back to my house to drop off Andrew, my cousin turned to me and asked, "Is that the typical stuff you have to deal with?"

"Every day."

"That's really sad."

"Tell me about it."

UNCLE MURPH WAS PACING AROUND the sheriff's department's parking lot, muttering to himself and gnawing on a toothpick, when I finally arrived at work. I was glad to see he survived performing whatever favor Uncle Houston had asked.

"What were you up to last night?" I asked.

"It's better if you don't know." Murph pulled me towards the back door of the department. "You're late. Where have you been all morning? And why didn't you answer your phone?"

"Why didn't you answer your phone last night," I asked, yanking my arm away from Murph. Last night, after Uncle Houston gave me the boot, I tried calling and texting Murph a few times. He never answered.

"I had my phone turned off," Murph said. "What's your excuse?"

"I was dealing with your idiotic son."

"Which one?"

"The one who tried to drown his sorrows over getting dumped, and wound up almost destroying Catfish's bar."

"So not Dickie."

"That would be correct. Now what's got you sweating like a virgin at the prison rodeo?"

"That nosy bastard has been lurking around my department since before eight o'clock. You should have been here over an hour ago to deal with him."

"What nosy bastard?" I asked, knowing that Chief Yates couldn't have been lurking at the sheriff's department for the past two hours. Not when he was hassling me at the Cantina.

"It's that Texas Ranger. He's back. And he won't tell anyone why he's back." Murph shoved me through the back door and into the building. "All the Ranger will say to anyone is that he needs to talk to you. He's been sitting in your office since he got here. You've got to get in there and find out what he wants."

At the far end of the hall, down near Murph's office, Deputy Timmy Grant bounced on his toes while staring at his watch. Glancing up, he spotted me and Murph, and scurried our way.

"I've walked by seven times since you went outside, Sheriff Shatner," Timmy said. "The Ranger is still just sitting in Detective Shatner's office."

"That man is up to something," Murph muttered.

"Maybe he's here to arrest Detective Shatner," Timmy said.

"Shut up, Deputy Grant." Murph put his arm around my shoulders and prevented me from heading down the hall to my office. "Now, Carrie, you have to sweet talk the Ranger and convince him that he still needs your help. I need you on the inside, gathering as much information as you can. And while you're dealing with the Ranger, I'm going to … well, you don't need to know what I'm going to do."

"Nor do I want to know. Just try not to get yourself killed. I'd hate to have to break the news to Aunt Lydia."

I pushed away from Murph and crept towards my office, hoping to sneak up on Sergeant Hardy. Murph and Timmy tiptoed along behind me. Poking my head around the doorframe, I eyed up Hardy. Not only did he have the nerve to take over my desk, he was also using my computer. Spread out on the desk were various folders and crime scene photos. I didn't appreciate that he was making himself at home in my office.

"Don't just stand there, Detective Shatner. Come on in." After I stepped through the doorway, Hardy rolled the desk chair across the small room and slammed the door in Murph's face. "Were you off sticking your nose in my investigation this morning?"

"No. I had a little family emergency to take care of."

Hardy's shoulders sagged. "What kind of crime did they commit now?"

"Don't worry, Sergeant Hardy. No one is going to press charges."

I tried to move around Hardy, but he wheeled the desk chair in front of me and cut me off. "When a tree falls in a forest, does is make a sound if no one is there to hear it?"

"Yes."

"Then, despite the fact that no one is pressing charges, someone in your family still committed a crime."

"Oh, Sergeant Hardy." I patted him on the shoulder. "You still need to learn how things work around here."

"No, things seriously need to change around here." Hardy rolled the chair back over to the desk. "While you were off having fun—"

"I never said I was having fun." I reached out to pick up one of the folders that was on my desk and Hardy swatted my hand away. "I have a right to know why you've commandeered my office."

"All in good time, Detective Shatner," Hardy said. "Right now I'd like to know if you've learned any new information regarding my case."

"Not really. Last night I went over to Uncle Houston's house to watch the game for a while. No one would really talk to me and I wound up leaving before halftime. And, before you ask, no, none of them admitted to killing Kyle."

"Too bad. That would have made my job a lot easier."

"What were you up to last night?" I asked.

"I read over all of the notes and transcripts from the interviews. And there were a lot of them. The one thing I noticed is that there are no inconsistencies on either side. All twenty-one Palmer men swear Kyle went with them to the fairgrounds and never returned. And every single one of your family members claim they never saw Kyle. Given, most of the women and children didn't witness the fight. But I honestly do not know what to make of this."

"So what's next?" I asked.

"The autopsy is taking place right now. Hopefully we will learn something from that and can move forward with the case. And I've got some DPS agents tracking down information," Hardy said. "For the moment, I would like to speak with you about your involvement with the case."

"Aside from talking to some of my family members, I haven't gone behind your back or tried to investigate on my own."

"And I appreciate that," Hardy said. "I also appreciate that you were so cooperative and helpful yesterday. I spoke with my lieutenant about the case last night. Sergeant Boleyn won't be available to assist me much over the next few days. He has a couple cases of his own that he needs to get back to. Because of that, I told my lieutenant that I think you might be an asset to my investigation and asked him if it would be okay to have you continue to help me. My lieutenant questioned my sanity."

"It is a crazy move on your part. I even think you're nuts for letting me help," I said.

"Yesterday it was worth the risk. It annoyed Oscar Palmer to no end. Both he and Whitney complained to my lieutenant about you being there yesterday. They both demanded that you no longer be allowed to assist me. As did Chief Yates. I think that, more than anything I had to say, convinced my lieutenant that your continued presence may be useful to the investigation. I'm not sure how well my lieutenant knows Chief Yates, but I get the impression that he isn't a big fan of the man. My lieutenant also wants me to keep you where I can see you, just in case you are covering something up."

"What about Uncle Murph?" I asked. "What if he's covering something up?"

"The sheriff has years of experience and no conscience. If either one of you is going to slip up, I'm betting it will be you."

"Guess it's a good thing that I have nothing to hide," I said. Okay, I had a lot to hide, but none of it was connected to what happened to Kyle. "What do you have planned for us today?"

"I believe a visit to the Dancing Cowgirl is in order."

Chapter Thirteen

———————◆———————

The Dancing Cowgirl, which happened to be Wyatt County's only strip club, was located just down the road from Catfish's Cantina. Considering the outside appearance of the Dancing Cowgirl, I was terrified to see the inside, much less the talent working at noon on a Wednesday. The club was housed in a long, low bunker-style building made of concrete blocks. The neon "open" sign on the roof was the only thing that classed up the joint.

Hardy led the way across the parking lot and opened the strip club's door with a flourish. Stepping inside, we found ourselves in a cramped area walled off by old pieces of plywood. Duct taped to the plywood were pictures of what I assumed were the better looking talent. Hardy and I paused for a moment to look them over.

"At least two of these women are Palmers," I said, pointing to the pictures of the two Palmer women. I recognized a couple of the other women as well.

Hardy shoved aside the faux-velvet curtain and waited for me to step around him and into the club. "Let's get this over with."

As my eyes adjusted to the dim light, I glanced around the room—horrified of what I might see, but curious enough to want to see it. On the left side of the room was the stage, and the only real lighting in the place. On stage, swinging around the pole, without much enthusiasm or talent, was a woman dressed in nothing more than a G-string and a bottle of baby oil.

Seated on the mismatched plastic lawn furniture closest to the stage were the club's five lone patrons. Considering the age range, they were dipping into their Social Security funds to pay for the lap dances. I couldn't help but wonder if they were on some sort of nursing home outing.

One of the geriatric customers got up and approached the stage, dragging his oxygen tank behind him. With shaking hands, he reached out and tried to grasp the dancer's G-string so that he could tuck a dollar bill under the waistband. The man struggled for a few seconds before the dancer finally took the bill from him and did it herself. Watching the travesty play out, I didn't know whether I should laugh, cry, or throw up.

"Come on, if anyone in this hellhole will be able to give us some information, it'll be the bartender," I said. While the dance floor and the seating took up the majority of the room, there was enough space left over for a small bar in the back corner. "Though he probably won't want to talk to me considering he's a Palmer."

Hardy and I were halfway to the bar when one of the strippers intercepted us, planting her six-inch high, clear plastic shoes right in our path. Like the woman on stage, this stripper was also wearing a G-string. Thankfully, this one had included the matching bra. Not that the bra covered anything beyond her nipples. The woman's teased out, bleached hair resembled a rat's nest. The obvious facelift sucked her eyebrows up to the middle of her forehead and left her with a perpetual startled expression. She could have been anywhere between twenty and fifty.

"Hi there, handsome. What do you say to a lap dance from Sparkles?"

"I don't think so, honey," I said, laying on the southern drawl thicker than the shimmering layer of glitter that covered every square inch of Sparkles' exposed skin. I wondered how many men had gotten in trouble after going home covered in her glitter. "The amount of glitter that would fall of you would probably turn him gay."

"A lap dance from me could turn a gay man straight," Sparkles said.

"That's enough, ladies." Hardy tapped his badge. "I'm Sergeant Hardy with the Texas Rangers. And this is Detective Shatner with the Wyatt County Sheriff's Department. We're here about Kyle Vance."

"Oh. Too bad about him getting killed and all." Sparkles readjusted her G-string. "You know, I saw him a few hours before he died. Creepy."

"So Kyle was here on New Year's Eve?" I asked, disappointed that someone other than a Palmer could verify Kyle's whereabouts before he was killed.

"Yeah, Kyle was here. He's been working here the past few months. And he was real friendly with most of the girls, if you know what I mean." Sparkles nudged me in the side with her elbow and winked. "Guess he wasn't getting enough at home, so he got it from us."

"Did you wash off the glitter before having sex with Kyle or did you leave it on?" I asked. Sparkles opened her mouth to answer, but I cut her off. "On second thought, I don't want to know."

"What time was Kyle here on New Year's Eve?" Hardy asked.

Sparkles shrugged. "Sometime in the afternoon. We weren't open yet. A bunch of us girls came in early to decorate the place. Kyle helped out."

Glancing around the room, I noticed the lackluster decorations. There was a "Happy New Year!" banner hanging on the wall behind the stage, and some streamers and partially deflated balloons tacked up to the ceiling and walls. The decorations were more depressing than festive.

"What happened after you had all the decorations up?" Hardy asked.

"Me and most of the girls left. There's not much of a changing room here so some of us went home to get ready. Kyle left too. I don't know where he went."

"About what time was that?" Hardy asked.

"Before five, I guess. I had to be back here before seven. That's when the club opened for the New Year's Eve bash."

"Did you see Kyle after you came back?" I asked, hoping she would say no.

"Nope. But he would have been in the back. I was working out here." Sparkles stuck out her lower lip. "I didn't get invited to the private party."

"What a shame. You probably would have been the life of the party," I said.

Sparkles, who failed to realize I was being sarcastic, said, "I know, right? The Palmers, like, totally missed out by not inviting me."

"Is there anything else you can tell us about the victim?" Hardy asked.

"I'm tired of talking about Kyle. I want to talk about you." Sparkles latched onto Hardy's arm and sucked it into the black hole between her breasts. Her teeny, tiny bra shifted, revealing one of her glitter coated nipples. She proceeded to rub her nipple against Hardy's chest, leaving a streak of multi-colored glitter on the front of his coat. I knew I should do something to help Hardy, but the appalled look on his face was just too amusing.

"Uh, ma'am ... would you mind letting go?" Hardy asked as he attempted to remove his arm from between Sparkles' sagging breasts.

"You know, we have a special deal just for law enforcement officers." Sparkles pressed her knee against Hardy's leg and rubbed it against his inner thigh. "Anything you want, on the house. And I do mean *anything*."

"Sparkles!" shouted the bartender. "How 'bout you go find some paying customers."

Sparkles made a pouty face at Hardy, before freeing his arm and wandering away.

"I'm pretty sure I was just propositioned for sex," Hardy mumbled as he inspected the damage to his coat. Thanks to Sparkles the majority of the one sleeve was coated in glitter and baby oil. She had also left a trail of glitter on Hardy's jeans. "You think that'll wash out?"

"I don't know. That looks like syphilis-by-contact to me," I said before walking over to the bartender who had saved Hardy from Sparkles. Between the dim light and the shadows cast by the overhead racks of glasses, it wasn't until I was almost to the bar that I figured out which Palmer was pouring drinks. "Hey, Zeke. Long time, no see."

"Wish I could have gone even longer without see you." Beneath his low, protruding Neanderthal-like brow, Whitney's cousin glared at me. "You ever think of changing professions, Carrie? I think you'd do real good here. The bigger the tits, the bigger the tips. With them puppies you could make a fortune."

"Bite me, Zeke. We're here about Kyle."

"I don't know nothing." Zeke set down the glass he'd been polishing and leaned across the bar. "Wasn't my responsibility to keep tabs on him."

"That doesn't mean you didn't notice anything," I said.

"Look, I don't know anything. I didn't see anything. And even if I had any information—and I'm not saying I do—I certainly wouldn't tell you." Pushing away from the bar, Zeke grabbed a bottle of beer and took a swig. "But I'm gonna be honest with you about one thing … I hated Kyle. I didn't kill him, or nothing. But I'm not sorry he's dead."

"Should you be drinking on the job?" I asked.

"If you worked at a place like this, you'd want to be half in the bag too. Besides, my usual daytime bartender called in sick and I couldn't get anyone to cover. I'm going to be stuck here until closing." Zeke leaned across the bar towards me and said, "But thank whichever one of your relatives killed Kyle. I'll make a donation to his defense fund."

"We won't need it, but we'll gladly take your money," I said

"Detective Shatner." Hardy put his hand on my shoulder. "That's enough, Palmer. Now is there any particular reason why you hated Kyle?"

"Look, the guy was a major douchebag. When Kyle wasn't cheating on my cousin, he was smacking her around," Zeke said.

This was the first we had heard that Kyle was physically abusing Whitney. There weren't any domestic abuse charges in Kyle's file, but Whitney might not have gone to the police.

"You know for sure he was physically abusing her?" Hardy asked.

Zeke shrugged. "Come on, how many times are we supposed to believe that she accidently walked into a door? Whoever killed Kyle did Whitney a favor."

"I'm not sure Whitney feels that way. She seemed pretty upset," I said.

"Yeah, well, give her some time. She'll realize that she's better off without him."

"Sparkles told us that Kyle was working here the past few months. What was his job exactly?" Hardy asked.

"He was supposed to be a bouncer. Occasionally, he did his job, but he usually just got drunk and harassed the girls. You know, I never once had to pay him since he spent his paycheck as he was earning it."

"Maybe I should bring you and the dancers in for questioning," Hardy said. "Sounds like y'all might have had a good motive for getting rid of Kyle."

"I'm not the only Palmer with motive," Zeke said before chugging the rest of his beer.

"You know, Zeke, I don't think this place is up to code. What do you say I call the health inspectors and have them come down to take a look?" I turned around and found Sparkles seated on one of the tables. She rubbed a chicken wing over her cleavage and inner thighs before handing it to an elderly gentleman. He inhaled the glitter coated wing. "Now that can't be healthy."

"Hey, no one is forcing that man to eat those wings," Zeke said. "In fact, he's probably paying Sparkles good money to rub that food on her. Certainly ain't the weirdest thing I've seen some of these men pay for."

"Does that include sex? Because I've heard some rumors about this place. Wouldn't be hard to set up an undercover operation," I said.

"Now that's a lie!" Zeke ran a hand through his thinning blonde hair and groaned. "Let's talk in the back."

Leaving the bar unattended, Zeke led me and Hardy out of the main room and then back a narrow hallway to a small office. An old metal desk took up the majority of the space, leaving just enough room for the three of us to have a seat on old lawn chairs.

"First off, where were you on New Year's Eve?" Hardy asked.

"I was here. From early-afternoon until closing time. Plenty of people saw me."

"You didn't happen to leave for a while to help crash my family's party?" I asked.

Zeke let out a harsh laugh. "I had nothing to do with that. My family was partying in the back room while I was out in the main room tending bar. I went back every once in a while to check on them and make sure they weren't running low on alcohol. To be honest, I didn't even know they'd left until I went back to check on them and found them all gone. And I had no idea where they had charged off to until they came back."

"What can you tell us about New Year's Eve?" Hardy asked. "Was Kyle supposed to work that night?"

"Nope. Kyle wanted off that night because he had a party to go to. I assumed it was my family's party. I made him come in during the afternoon to help us get set up, but he left around four-thirty or five. That's the last I saw of him. Whether he came back for the party or not, I don't know. But if Pop-Pop says Kyle was here and that he went with everyone else to crash your party, then I guess that's what Kyle did."

"You don't really question anything Oscar says or does, do you?" I asked.

"Oh, I used to question things. Then I started working here. Lost all my curiosity."

"Did anything notable happen while Kyle was here?" Hardy asked.

"Not really. But he had a bruise on his cheek when he came in. I asked him about it, but he wouldn't tell me what happened." Zeke slid open the bottom desk drawer and pulled out a bottle of expensive whiskey. He splashed some whiskey into a dirty glass and then gulped it down. "After that, I hardly talked to him. He was helping the girls put up decorations while I restocked the bar. At some point he left. I don't know what happened to him after that."

"Stop being difficult." I scooted closer to the desk and pried the whiskey bottle out of Zeke's hand. "I think you know something about what happened that night. Either you can tell us now, or Sergeant Hardy and I can bring you in for questioning. Your choice."

"Look, I don't know who killed Kyle. All I know is that he was here during the afternoon. That was the last time I saw him. I have no idea how or why he ended up dead at the fairgrounds. And I have no idea why my family crashed your family's party. I can't help you."

"Oh, I think you can help us, Zeke," Hardy said. "I just don't think you want to."

"Hey, I have no problem helping out the Texas Rangers. I don't even mind helping the sheriff's department. I just don't want to help Detective Shatner." Zeke scowled at me. "Now, I've told you everything I know. I need to get back to work, and you two need to leave."

"One more thing, Zeke, and we'll get out of here," Hardy said. "I want to see the security footage from New Year's Eve."

"We don't have any security cameras."

"Then what was that thing I smiled for in the lobby?"

"Shoot … " Zeke spun around in his chair. Behind him was a small cabinet, which he opened to reveal two ancient looking VCRs. He grabbed two tapes out of the cabinet before turning back to us. "We only have two cameras. One just inside the front door and one over the back door."

Hardy held out his hand for the tapes, but Zeke clutched them to his chest.

"Oh no, Pop-Pop told me not to help you out. You want these tapes, you get a warrant." Zeke shoved the tapes back into the cabinet, which he locked.

"Thanks for your time, Zeke." Hardy tucked his notebook in his jacket pocket and stood up. "We'll be back with a warrant for those tapes."

Chapter Fourteen

───────────◆───────────

Stepping out of the Dancing Cowgirl, I sucked in a deep breath of cold, fresh air to cleanse my lungs. "Let's get out of here."

"Soon. I want to get a look at the security camera above the back door before we leave." Hardy pulled his cell phone out of his coat pocket and glanced at the screen. "I missed a call from the medical examiner. I guess he's done with the autopsy."

"Quick, call him back," I said, anxious to find out the autopsy results.

"Worried about what the ME might have found, Detective?" Hardy asked as he placed the call. The medical examiner answered almost immediately. "Hey, Doc, it's Sergeant Hardy. I've got Detective Carrie Shatner with me, and we're both wondering if you learned anything from the autopsy".

"I learned plenty, actually," the medical examiner said. "During the external exam I found what appears to four red pubic hairs mixed in with the victim's pubic hairs. These red hairs are similar in color to the hair that was found between the victim's teeth. There are also vaginal secretions around the victim's mouth, and on and around his genitals."

"So we can safely say that the victim engaged in relations with a redheaded woman sometime before he died," Hardy said. "Doc, can you make a request for the lab to put a rush on running the DNA from those pubic hairs? From what we've learned, the victim had multiple girlfriends. We need to figure out which one he was with before he died."

"I'll do what I can, but I can't make any promises. Either way, it will takes weeks to get results from the lab," the medical examiner said. "Also, concerning the wound on the victim's stomach ... It is a postmortem injury. The wound started out as a scratch and then progressively got deeper, piercing nearly half an inch into the victim's body. Inside the wound I found what I can almost confidently say is bird excrement."

"The dumpster was covered in bird crap," Hardy mumbled to himself. "What did you learn from the autopsy?"

"The victim suffered extensive internal and external damage," the medical examiner said. "He had multiple bruises covering his body. Most of the bruises were faint, indicating the victim acquired them perimortem. I did find one bruise on the victim's jaw that did have time to form."

"So someone socked the victim in the jaw hours before he was killed," Hardy said.

"And then someone gave him a beat down just before he died," I added.

"I worded it a little differently in my report, Detective Shatner," the medical examiner said. "As for the internal damage, the victim has three fractured ribs. Two other ribs are cracked. The victim's left orbital socket is shattered, as is his nose. He also has a couple broken fingers, and one of his ulnas had a hairline fracture. It is probable that he received the injuries to his hands and arm while attempting to defend or protect himself."

"What about cause of death?" Hardy asked.

"Blunt force trauma. The victim received multiple blows to the back of his head, fracturing the skull and causing bleeding around the brain. I cannot say with any certainty if the tire iron you found near the body is the murder weapon or not."

"Is there anything else we need to know about?" Hardy asked.

"There are fresh scratch marks on the inside of the victim's forearms. They could be defensive wounds, or the victim could have received the scratches while engaging in relations with the redheaded woman. I will email you photos of the scratches, as well as photos of the victim's other injuries."

"What about time of death?" I asked, far more concerned about when Kyle was killed than how he was killed.

"I found large pieces of mainly undigested food in the victim's stomach," the medical examiner said. "It usually takes between four and six hours after a meal for the food to be digested and the stomach to empty. Since the victim's stomach is full of undigested food, he must have died an hour or two after he ate."

"According to the Dairy Queen receipt, Kyle ate dinner before six last night. Can we safely say he died between seven and nine?" My family would have been watching *Monday Night Raw* when someone was beating Kyle to death. Bad for Kyle; good for my family. "Then Kyle would have been dead before the Palmers crashed my family's party."

"Hold on," Hardy said. "We don't know that the food in Kyle's stomach is his meal from Dairy Queen. He could have eaten something else later. All the

Dairy Queen receipt proves is that Kyle was still alive around six. You didn't find him until twelve-thirty."

"But he was dead for at least a little while before I found him. The blood in the head wound had time to clot," I said.

"Between six and midnight gives us six hours," Hardy said. "That's a wide time frame."

"I would say it's more like eight to eleven," the medical examiner said. "There are too many unknown factors and outside variables for me to narrow it down anymore."

Better, but the time of death still didn't rule out any or all of the Shatners.

Hardy finished up his conversation with the medical examiner and then led the way around the side of the Dancing Cowgirl. Behind the building, we found a nearly empty parking lot. The security camera mounted on the corner of the building was directed at the back door.

While Hardy tried to determine the exact angle that the security camera picked up, I wandered around the parking lot. At the far end of the lot sat a large dumpster. I spotted the front end of a blue vehicle sticking out from behind the dumpster. It seemed like an odd place to park considering the dumpster sat on the back edge of the parking lot. I wasn't sure why anyone would park in the knee-high dead grass and weeds behind the dumpster when there were perfectly good spots closer to the door. Unless the driver didn't want his or her car spotted at the strip club. I walked around the side of the dumpster and saw that the vehicle was a truck.

"Sergeant Hardy ... what kind of car did Kyle drive?" I asked.

Hardy, who was still standing by the back door of the strip club, pulled a notebook out of his jacket pocket and flipped through the pages. "Blue Ford F-150. Why?"

"I think I just found it," I said as I pointed at the blue truck parked behind the dumpster.

Hardy jogged across the parking lot to join me. "Make, model, and color are all right. Let's see if the license plate matches."

Hardy and I picked our way through the dead weeds to the back of the truck. Below the license plate hung a pair of chrome testicles.

"Now that is classy," I said.

Hardy rolled his eyes. "License plate is the same. This is the victim's truck."

"Shit." Finding Kyle's truck parked behind the strip club could be one more nail in the Shatner coffin. "But this doesn't prove he was here. It just proves that his truck was here."

"I'll go back inside and get Zeke," Hardy said as he headed for the front of the club. "Call Chief Deputy Quaranta and ask him to come down here and help us process the truck. Then call for a tow truck."

I finished up with the two phone calls before Hardy came back with Zeke. Figuring it wouldn't hurt, I moved closer to the truck and peeked in the windows. The floorboards were covered in discarded fast food wrappers, and there was a plastic bag with the Walmart logo printed on it lying on the backseat.

I was eyeing up the pile of junk in the truck's bed when Hardy and Zeke walked up.

"Yeah, that's Kyle's truck," Zeke said. "Why is it parked back here?"

"That's what I was going to ask you," I said.

Zeke sighed. "Look, I already told you everything I know. Kyle was here during the afternoon on New Year's Eve. And, when he left, he drove off in his truck. This truck right here. How it wound up parked back here, I don't know. I guess he came back to the party like everyone says."

"How much of the parking lot does the security camera cover?" Hardy asked.

"Unless Kyle drove over the back steps, the camera would not have gotten this." Zeke walked off, but then turned around and came back. "Not to do your job or anything, but I might know why the truck is parked back here. Two months ago, I caught Kyle and one of the strippers getting it on in the bed of his truck. And they were parked around front that time. You said Kyle had sex before he died. Could be they did it back here. There aren't many private places in the club, especially when we have a full house."

"Has he done it here before?" I asked. "Aside from the time you caught him out front?"

"I've caught him at it four times. Four times! As far as I know, he slept with most of our dancers. It was his personal mission," Zeke said.

"Do you have any redheaded strippers working here?" Hardy asked.

"She a natural redhead, or does she dye it?" Zeke asked.

"Natural." I thought about the long blonde hair that Sergeant Boleyn had found on Kyle's coat. "But the carpet might not necessarily match the drapes."

"Let me think about this. We're not licensed for full nudity and a lot of the girls dye their hair or wear wigs, so I'm not quite sure what anyone's natural hair color is." Zeke leaned against the dumpster and studied the clouds. "Let's see, Bubbles is a strawberry blonde."

"No, too light," I said. "And could you use their real names?"

"Sorry, I don't know their real names. My job is to tend bar and deal with the customers. My older brother is the one who hires the strippers and basically runs the place. You could talk to him, but he's in the hospital. Emergency tonsillectomy." Zeke hummed to himself for a few seconds before he said, "Juicy dyes her hair a purplish red, but I think she's a natural redhead. Chas-Titty has red hair. So does Scarlett. I think Champagne and Busty Betty have red hair, but they both dye it, so I can't be sure."

"Do you know if Kyle slept with any of them?" Hardy asked.

"Rumor is that he had sex with all of them. Except for maybe Juicy. She's married."

I looked over at Hardy, who had been jotting down the names in his notebook. He was staring at Zeke, his eyes wide with disbelief. Kyle could have been with any one of those women before he died. We were going to have to track them all down so we could question them.

"Thanks Zeke. We'll let you know if we have any more questions." Hardy waved Zeke off before turning back to me. "What do you think?"

"I think there are more romantic spots to have sex than in a truck that's parked behind a dumpster. Other than that, I'm trying not to think anything. What are you thinking?"

Hardy was saved from answering when Quaranta and Deputy Timmy Grant pulled up nearby. Quaranta dragged a crime scene kit out of the trunk of the cruiser before coming over to join us by Kyle's truck.

"You want to dust the passenger side for fingerprints?" Hardy asked Quaranta. "I'll take the driver's side."

"What about me? I'm the crime scene technician," I said.

"Be patient, Detective Shatner. I'll find something for you to do," Hardy said.

Quaranta was lifting a partial fingerprint from the passenger side door when the tow truck pulled up. An older man whose name patch read "Bruce" climbed out of the front seat and wandered over. Seeing that we wouldn't be needing him for a while, Bruce disappeared in to the strip club.

Once Hardy and Quaranta were finished going over the outside of the truck for fingerprints and other evidence, Quaranta pulled an evidence bag out of his crime scene kit. Inside the bag were the set of keys that the crime scene technicians found in Kyle's pants pocket at the crime scene. Quaranta unlocked the driver's side door and swung it open. A combined scent of wet dog and cheeseburgers wafted out.

While Hardy bagged and tagged all of the loose items in the cab, Quaranta dusted the steering wheel and dashboard for fingerprints. He even used a small vacuum cleaner to go over the seats and the floor of the truck. Meanwhile, I picked my way through the truck box that was packed full of rusting tools, a tackle box, a smashed box of condoms, and various other odds and ends. I bagged and tagged all of them.

I was picking through the other debris in the truck bed when I heard a car pull up. A few seconds later, Chief Yates came around the side of the dumpster.

"What are you doing, Detective Shatner?" Yates planted his meaty fists on his hips and scowled at me.

"My job," I said. "What are you doing?"

"Heard over the police scanner that you were here. The strip club is in my jurisdiction. That means this is my crime scene." Yates walked over to Hardy and jabbed him in the chest with his index finger. "I'll be taking over now."

"No, you won't." Hardy swatted Yates's hand away. "This truck belongs to my homicide victim. I don't care whose jurisdiction the truck is parked in. I'm in charge of the investigation, so that makes this my crime scene."

"Well … you should have called me in to help you search. Detective Shatner and Chief Deputy Quaranta shouldn't be allowed to process a crime scene that's in my jurisdiction." Yates spat a wad of tobacco onto the ground. "And Detective Shatner shouldn't be here at all. She's probably planting evidence as we speak."

"No, I'm not," I said. "Besides I'm done back here."

Hardy gave me a hand, helping me out of the truck. "Find anything?"

"Nope. Did you?"

Hardy shrugged. "Chief Deputy Quaranta and I found some stuff. Don't know if any of it means anything yet."

Since we were finished processing the truck for the time being, Hardy sent Timmy in search of the tow truck driver. After five minutes had passed, Hardy and I trooped inside and found Timmy and Bruce sitting front-and-center for the mid-afternoon show. Sparkles, who had removed her bra, crawled all over Timmy while in the process of giving him a lap dance. Timmy's eyes were wide, and sweat was literally pouring down his face. His uniform was coated in glitter—a lot of which was concentrated around his crotch.

I tore the Happy New Year banner off the wall, wrapped it around Sparkles, and hauled her away from Timmy. "For God's sake, woman, look what you did to his uniform. How's he going to explain all that glitter to his mama?"

"You're not gonna tell Mama about this, are you?" Timmy asked me. "She'd tan my hide if she found out I was visiting such a sinful place."

"Cutie, there ain't nothing sinful about what I do," Sparkles said. She grabbed Timmy's crotch and gave him a squeeze. "You come back later and I'll show you how heavenly I can be."

"Stop that!" I swatted Sparkles' hand away from Timmy.

Once Timmy was free of Sparkles, he hightailed it out of the club. The tow truck driver was much more reluctant to leave. He was so enthralled with the nearly naked, petite blonde who was strutting her stuff that Hardy and I practically had to drag him out of the Dancing Cowgirl.

A few minutes after we dragged the tow truck driver outside, he drove off with Kyle's truck. Timmy rode along with him to keep an eye on the evidence.

"Now what?" I asked.

"Now Sergeant Hardy goes and arrests whichever Shatner you've been protecting," Chief Yates said.

"Knock it off, Chief Yates," Hardy said. "There's no solid evidence that any of the Shatners killed Kyle. And I still don't have any evidence that Kyle was killed at the fairgrounds. I don't even have proof that Kyle was at the fairgrounds at all on New Year's Eve."

"Oh, there's evidence," Yates said. "The question is where Detective Shatner has been hiding it."

"She's not hiding anything," Hardy said.

"Get your butt off your shoulders, Sergeant Hardy. Detective Shatner is up to her pretty little nose in this crap," Yates said, pointing at me. "The Palmers all claim Kyle was at the club with them on New Year's Eve. Finding his truck back here goes towards confirming that."

"No it doesn't," I said. "Someone else could have parked his truck back here to make it look like Kyle was at the club that night. What we need is indisputable evidence he was here. And that he went with the rest of the Palmers to the fairgrounds."

"I'll get us a warrant for the security camera footage," Hardy said.

"I want more than security footage." In frustration, I kicked the dumpster. What was up between Kyle and dumpsters? I found his body in one and his truck parked behind another. "We need to check the dumpster. If it hasn't been emptied yet, we might find something from New Year's Eve."

"Like what?" Yates asked. "A cup with Kyle's fingerprints on it? What's that gonna prove? Other than that he was here?"

"It's a good idea," Hardy said. "I'm going to ask Zeke when the dumpster last got emptied."

"Ask me, it's a waste of time," Yates said.

"That's why no one asked you," I said.

While we waited for Hardy to come back, Yates rambled on about how he knew one or more of my family members killed Kyle, and that Murph and I were covering up the crime. I didn't bother arguing with him. I just let him rant until Hardy returned a few minutes later.

"Zeke said the dumpster gets emptied twice a week," Hardy said. "It hasn't been emptied since the party. Let's get to it."

Hardy, Quaranta, and I wiggled into ratty, oversized coveralls that we found in the trunk of the sheriff's department cruiser. Quaranta then crawled into the dumpster to haul out the bags. Hardy remained outside the dumpster, ready to take the bags of trash from Quaranta. I perched on the edge of the dumpster, a camera in hand. My job was to photograph the process and keep my eyes peeled for anything suspicious. Yates paced around the dumpster, grumbling about how we were wasting our time. He also incessantly reminded us that this was his jurisdiction, and that the sheriff's department had no right to be collecting evidence when his men should be doing it.

The first few bags that Quaranta dug out of the dumpster were large, clear bags. Inside the bags were the remains of food, SOLO cups, and streamers and other party decorations.

"Hey, what's that?" I asked, pointing at a piece of pipe that was eight or nine feet long. It laid on the bottom of the dumpster, tucked against the back edge. While I didn't really want to get into the rank smelling dumpster, I slid into it anyway. I then waded over the remaining bags to get to the pipe. Quaranta came to stand beside me while Hardy leaned over the edge of the dumpster and peered inside.

"Looks like a curtain rod," Quaranta said.

"This isn't just one length of pipe. It's three smaller pipes that are slotted together," I said.

"Could be a collapsible shower rod. I've got one of those at my house," Hardy said.

"It looks like there is blood on it. I think this might be the murder weapon," I said as I knelt down to get a closer look at the piece of pipe. At both ends were brackets to attach the pipe to the wall. One of the brackets, along with a section of pipe, was covered in a dried, dark reddish-brown substance. And stuck to the substance were what appeared to be matted, brown hairs. I tried to conjure up a mental picture of someone using the length of pipe as a murder weapon. It would be unwieldy, but still possible. "But can you imagine swinging that thing around to beat someone to death?"

"How could that be the murder weapon?" Yates asked as he leaned over the side of the dumpster to get a closer look. "The victim was killed at the fairgrounds."

"No, his body was found at the fairgrounds," Hardy said. "We still don't know where he was killed."

"You might not be sure, but I am," Yates said.

"Would you stop accusing us, Chief Yates? You're starting to sound like a broken record," I said. "We're not sure if this is the murder weapon or not. Right now it's just a suspicious item that appears to be covered in blood and hair."

I finished taking pictures of the pipe. I then grabbed it in the middle and picked it up. The pipe turned out to be heavier than I thought. It was also coated in a slippery substance, causing it to slide out of my gloved hand and crash against the side of the dumpster.

"Jesus, Carrie!" Quaranta said. "Be careful with that thing."

"Sorry, it slipped." I grabbed a cotton swab out of the crime scene kit and ran it over the pipe. "There's either grease or oil on the pipe. Maybe something from the trash leaked on it."

Taking extra precautions, we removed the pipe from the dumpster and transferred it into an extra-long evidence bag that we had fashioned out of smaller evidence bags and duct tape.

Quaranta then climbed back into the dumpster to sort through the remaining trash bags.

"That one's different." I pointed at a black trash bag. It was the only black trash bag in the dumpster. "Let's see what's inside."

After I took pictures of the trash bag, Quaranta opened the top. "It's full of towels."

Quaranta removed the three dark purple bath towels one-by-one and dropped them into individual evidence bags that I held up for him.

"What do you think?" Hardy asked when I handed him the evidence bags full of towels.

"It's possible one of the dancers just dumped her personal garbage back here," I said. But why would someone throw out three towels in the dumpster behind the club? From what I could tell, there was nothing wrong with the towels. "But it could also have something to do with Kyle."

"I'll get a warrant to search the club," Hardy said.

"Another waste of your time," Yates said.

"I found something else," Quaranta said, pointing at the wadded up piece of vinyl that was jammed into the one corner of the dumpster. "Looks like a shower curtain."

Quaranta and I climbed out of the dumpster so that we could carefully spread out the vinyl shower curtain. Once we got it stretched out, we could see that the shower curtain had a brown and black leopard print pattern. One of the top corners of the shower curtain had been torn away, and every hole at the top was ripped.

"Looks like someone tore this down," Hardy said.

"Is that blood?" I pointed to a large, brownish smear that was near one of the bottom corners of the shower curtain.

Quaranta and I continued to hold the shower curtain while Hardy grabbed a swab out of the crime scene kit. After wetting the swab with distilled water, Hardy rubbed the swab over the reddish blotch. Hardy then added the phenolphthalin reagent to the swab. He followed that up with a couple drops of hydrogen peroxide. The swab turned bright pink.

"It's blood," Hardy said.

Hardy took numerous other samples from the blood stain before we folded up the curtain and slid it into an evidence bag.

"What do you think? Kyle was killed with a shower curtain rod, and then wrapped up in the shower curtain?" Hardy said.

"Maybe Kyle was killed in the strip club," I said. "The Palmers keep claiming that he was here that night."

"If that was the case, someone would have seen something," Yates said. "And if Kyle was killed here, how did his body end up at the fairgrounds?"

"Obviously someone stuck him there to frame my family," I said, finally voicing the theory that had been plaguing me since I discovered Kyle's body. From what I had heard, most of the Shatners believed we were being framed. They'd spent the past day arguing over who they thought was trying to frame us. The majority thought it was the government.

Yates laughed. "Now that is just crazy talk."

Chapter Fifteen

———◆———

Leaving it up to Quaranta to transport the evidence back to the sheriff's department, Hardy and I headed over to Whitney Vance's house.

"As long as none of her family members are lurking around, I want you to go in there by yourself," Hardy said.

"You want me to talk to Whitney alone? Why?" I asked.

"Because she hates you and sees you as a threat. I'm stuck playing the role of sympathetic cop. 'I'm so sorry for your loss, ma'am. I'm going to do everything in my power to find your husband's killer and bring that person to justice.' Meanwhile, you can go in there with the attitude of 'Screw you and your husband. I don't care who killed him as long as it's not one of my family members.' I need you to piss her off and get her talking."

"You might not believe this, but I am an expert at pissing people off."

"No ... you don't say." Hardy pulled into Whitney's driveway and killed the engine. "If there is anyone else inside, come right back out."

"Will do."

Jumping out of the truck, I hustled up to the front door and rang the bell. I had to ring it two more times before Whitney wrenched open the door.

"What do you want?" Whitney opened the screen door and stuck her head out so that she could eye up Hardy's truck in the driveway. "What's the Ranger doing sitting in his truck? And why are you still working with him?"

"Because he asked me to." I held up a cotton swab. "Open up. I need a DNA sample."

"No way." Whitney yanked the screen door shut. "I'm not giving you anything."

"Just give me the sample." I grabbed the screen door's handle and pulled on it until Whitney let go. She then stepped backward and started closing her front door. Propping my shoulder against the front door to prevent her from closing it completely, I said, "Come on, Whitney … Otherwise I have to get a warrant."

"What do you need my DNA for?" Whitney asked.

"We found some hairs on Kyle's clothes. I need a sample of your DNA to figure out if the hairs are yours. I'll also need your fingerprints to compare to the ones we found in Kyle's trailer and in his truck."

"What else are you people going to want from me? My husband was murdered. Go harass whichever one of your family members killed him and leave me alone."

"All of this might help us find his killer," I said, pushing my way into her house. "The more you fight us, the longer it will take us to find the person responsible."

"Fine … " Whitney spun on her heel and then stomped into her living room.

A black and white English springer spaniel slunk past me as I followed Whitney into the living room. I snagged a hunk of loose fur from the dog's back and tucked it into a plastic evidence bag. The crime scene technicians had found animal hair on Kyle's clothing. The lab could compare Whitney's dog's hair to the hairs found on Kyle's clothes.

"What's she doing here?" asked Russell Palmer. He was on his knees in front of the entertainment center while he replaced Whitney's small TV with a large, flat screen TV. The flat screen looked exactly like the one that had been hanging on the wall in Kyle's trailer. I wouldn't have put it past Russell to break into his dead brother-in-law's trailer to steal the TV. He probably helped himself to a lot of other stuff as well.

"Annoying me," Whitney said. "Though probably not as much as you and Toby."

"We're trying to cheer you up and keep you company," Toby said as he walked into the room with a sandwich in his hands.

"Yeah, well, you're doing a pretty bad job at it," Whitney said.

"You boys ready to tell me the truth about what really happened on New Year's Eve," I asked. Despite Sergeant Hardy telling me to come back outside if any of Whitney's relatives were in the house, I decided to stick around. I had a gut feeling that Toby and Russell knew something about Kyle that they hadn't shared with me and Hardy. I wanted to know what that was.

"We already told you the truth," Toby said. "We was at our family's party at the Dancing Cowgirl. Then we left to crash your party at the fairgrounds. We don't know how Kyle wound up in that dumpster."

"How 'bout you tell us what you know," Russell said.

"I know that Kyle wasn't killed at the fairgrounds. And I know that none of my family members killed him." Or, at least, I hoped that was the case.

"Yeah, yeah, keep telling yourself that." Toby stepped closer to me and then jabbed me in the chest with his forefinger. "You wanna tell us about what you found in Kyle's truck? Our cousin, Zeke, called us a couple hours ago and told us that you found it behind the club. He also said you were digging around in the dumpster."

"I can't tell you about what we found. But I can tell you that it was very interesting." I held up the cotton swab. "You boys want to give me a sample of your DNA and your fingerprints. That way I can rule out that you didn't have anything to do with Kyle getting killed."

"You'd probably use it to frame me!" Russell shoved past me and then stomped upstairs.

"That's okay, Russ. Your DNA and fingerprints are already on file since you've been arrested so many times," I shouted after him.

Russell yelled an unflattering comment down the stairs at me.

"Can we please get this over with?" Whitney asked. "I've got a lot of paperwork I need to finish up so I can get Kyle's affairs taken care of."

"Open up." After using a cotton swab to take a DNA sample from the inside of Whitney's mouth, I pulled out a few of her blonde hairs. I may have pulled harder than necessary, and Whitney flinched. We then sat down at her dining room table so that I could get her fingerprints. As I pressed Whitney's right thumb into an ink pad, I asked, "Why'd you stay with Kyle when you knew he was cheating on you?"

Whitney flicked her wedding ring with her left thumbnail a couple times. "Because I loved him. Kyle may have strayed a lot, but he always came home."

I could tell that I wasn't going to get anywhere with Whitney by bringing up Kyle's infidelities. She was so used to it that it didn't really affect her anymore. I decided to change tactics. "Why didn't you tell us that Kyle abused you?"

"Who says that he did?" Whitney asked.

"A reliable source." Since Zeke helped us out in the investigation—albeit reluctantly—I didn't want to reveal him as my source.

"So what if Kyle smacked me around every once in a while?" Whitney said.

"Seriously, Whit? Kyle hit you?" Toby asked.

"Oh, please, like you didn't know," Whitney snapped at her brother.

"I knew he was cheating you. And I knew he wasn't treating you right. But I didn't know he was hitting you," Toby said.

"Like you would have done anything about it. Besides, it was no big deal," Whitney said.

I had never been able to understand women who downplayed abuse, and pretended like it was nothing or claimed they deserved it. Whether it was physical, verbal, or emotional, it was abuse. And it wasn't right.

"My source said Kyle did more than smack you around," I said.

"Only when he was drunk. It's not like he made a habit out of it," Whitney said.

"Being drunk is no excuse. He was physically abusing you," I said.

"Haven't you ever had a man smack you around?"

"If a man ever tried to lay a hand on me, I'd make sure he regretted it."

"That's why you're still single." Finished with the fingerprinting, Whitney headed into her kitchen to wash the ink off of her fingertips.

I took a deep breath and then I followed her into the kitchen. "Whitney, hold on. I'm trying to figure out who killed Kyle."

"Why? You probably don't even care that's he's dead."

"You're right. I don't care that he's dead. But I can see that you do."

"Of course, I care! I loved him!"

It felt like our conversation was going in circles. "Do you have any idea who Kyle might have been with the night he was killed?"

"No. Just because I knew that Kyle was cheating on me doesn't mean I know who he was cheating on me with."

"Okay." Had I been in the same situation, I would have wanted to know who the other woman was. "Any idea who might have killed him?"

"How would I know that? It was your family that killed him!" Whitney picked up a packet of tavern ham lunchmeat that Toby had left on the counter. As she hurled the ham at me, she yelled, "Get out of here, Carrie! I'm done talking to you!"

Accepting that my conversation with Whitney was over, I trudged outside and climbed into Hardy's truck.

"Did you piss her off?" Hardy asked.

"I did. But I'm not sure I got anything useful out of her."

"THE REST OF THE WARRANTS just came in." Hardy tossed a handful of papers onto the table in front of me. "We may as well pick up all of the security camera footage before we head over to the strip club to help Sergeant Boleyn and Chief Deputy Quaranta."

"I think we should also get something to eat," I said. "Mainly because I'm starving. But I also don't really feel like helping them search the club for evidence."

"I like the way you think." Hardy cracked a smile. "Though I am curious about what they will find. Especially since the towels and the shower curtain rod were all covered in blood that matches Kyle's blood type."

"Oh, I'm sure they are going to find plenty of body fluids in the club. But the majority of it probably won't be blood."

"But, if they find Kyle's blood in the strip club, we might finally have the crime scene."

"In that case, I really hope they find Kyle's blood."

After leaving the Dancing Cowgirl earlier in the day, Quaranta had taken the blood samples to Wyatt County General Hospital. While the hospital didn't have the technology needed to run a full DNA test to compare Kyle's blood to the blood found on the rod and curtain, the technicians did have the equipment to determine blood type. Kyle had A-Positive blood. The test confirmed that the blood on the rod was also A-Positive. While we couldn't yet say the rod was the murder weapon, chances were good that we were finally on the right track.

Upon returning to the sheriff's department, Hardy and I went over the shower curtain, towels, and the rod for additional evidence. We confirmed that the towels had traces of blood on them. Quaranta made a return trip to the hospital, and it was determined that the blood on the towels was also A-Positive.

Hardy and I also went over the rod and shower curtain for fingerprints, but were unable to come up with even a crummy partial fingerprint on either item. As for the fingerprints from Kyle's truck, they hadn't panned out either. The majority of the prints belonged to Kyle, and a few on the passenger side matched Whitney's.

Leaving the sheriff's department, Hardy and I headed towards the southwest side of Holler. Overall, the Holler city limits encompassed an area that was a little less than five square miles—the older businesses and homes were in the center of the small city. The farther you got from the center of town, the newer the homes and businesses were.

Hardy and I stopped by Walmart to pick up their security footage first. The Walmart that Kyle shopped at on New Year's Eve was in a relatively new shopping center that was on the southwestern edge of Holler. Also in the Lone Star Strip Mall was a furniture store, a bank, a gas station, and a couple other small stores. The Dairy Queen that Kyle ate dinner at was also in the same shopping center.

We then drove down to Wilder, stopping first at the Exxon on the north side of town. The gas station was only a couple miles from Whitney's house.

"Where should we eat?" Hardy asked me after we collected the security footage from the gas station.

"Head towards the lake. Baby Doll's Tavern is along the east side of Wyatt Lake. It's one of my favorites. Though it's better in the summer because the back patio overlooks a really pretty section of the lake." I said before giving Hardy directions. The tavern was a little out of the way, but it was still one of the most popular restaurants in the county.

As Hardy and I followed another couple through the front door of the one story, log cabin style restaurant, I caught sight of my sometimes best friend behind the hostess stand. Either Veda Houser got laid off from the beauty parlor or she had to get a second job to help pay the bills. I was betting on the second. Veda had to pay for the boob job somehow. Since the last time I had seen her about two month earlier, Veda had gone from mosquito bumps to double-D boobs that were almost as big and perky as mine.

"Carrie! Look at you!" Ignoring the other couple, Veda skirted around the hostess stand and threw her arms around me. While the other hostess was dressed in her uniform of jeans and a gray shirt, Veda was dressed like she belonged at Hooters.

"No, look at you!" I gave Veda a hug back.

"You look great!"

"Oh no, you look great!"

Releasing me, Veda used her hand to flip her natural blonde hair over her shoulders. "Oh, I know I look great."

Typical Veda. As my Grandma would say, she was so stuck up she would drown in a rainstorm.

Veda and I go so far back that I think a few dinosaurs might have still been roaming the earth when we met back in preschool. We had been best friends up through high school when Veda started dating my cousin, Bubba. After that neither of them had time for anybody else, and Veda and I began to drift apart. Veda stayed in Holler while I went off to college. And then I moved to Nashville. Even though I'd been home for over three years, Veda and I had never quite gotten back to where we once were.

"Well, my stars." Veda grabbed the menus and guided us towards a table. I had to steer the way since she was too busy glancing over her shoulder at Hardy to pay attention to where she was walking. "That man is hotter than hell's door hinges."

"That's Sergeant Jerrod Hardy. He's a Texas Ranger. We're working together to figure out who killed Kyle Vance."

"God, I hated that jerk. But if I were you, I'd help Sergeant Hardy right out of his pants." Veda tossed the menus on the table and turned to Hardy. He was trying to slide into the booth, but Veda wrapped her arms around his and forced him back onto his feet. "Hi, Jerrod."

"Seriously, Veda?" It was the second time that day that a woman latched on to Hardy, and it was getting disturbing. Did Hardy have to fend off women with a stick? Of the two, it was Veda that upset me the most. I knew why Veda was hitting on Hardy, and I wasn't about to play her little game. Back in July, Veda and I drove up to Nashville to spend a week with Bubba and the rest of the Flaming Outhouses. I still don't know exactly what happened, but Veda and Bubba had a big fight and broke up. I wasn't too worried about it at the time. They broke up and made up so many times over the last thirteen years that I'd lost count. What had me worried was that Veda and Bubba still hadn't patched things up. In all the years they'd been together, this was the longest one of their many breakups had gone. The reason Veda and Bubba were usually off-again had nothing to do with their feelings for each other. I was almost positive that what they had was true love. Their problem—other than that Bubba spent most of the year in Nashville and Veda refused to move there to be with him—was that Bubba's mother did not approve of Veda, and, therefore, the majority of the Shatners did not approve of her. It wasn't that there was anything wrong with Veda; Aunt Loretta didn't think any woman would ever be good enough for her precious baby boy. No, the reason Veda was hitting on Hardy was because she wanted me to intervene and help her get back together with her man. I didn't care enough about her sex life to do that. Besides, I'd always thought it should be up to Bubba to grow a set and stand up to his controlling mother.

"Yeah, howdy there, ma'am." Hardy disengaged himself from Veda's grasp and slid to the far end of the booth. "Nice meeting you."

Veda leaned over in front of Hardy and put her chest at eye level with his face. "So how long will you be in the area?"

"Until we figure out who killed Kyle Vance," Hardy said as he looked over the menu. He had some unnaturally perky boobs all but shoved in his face and he wasn't even looking. "So what's good here?"

Veda seductively recited the daily specials. Fried chicken had never sounded sexier. "If you need anyone to show you around and give you a good time, I can give you my number."

I considered giving Veda a polite kick under the table, but I knew that would either make her try harder to annoy me or cause her to make a big scene about me kicking her.

"If I need someone to show me around, I'm sure Detective Shatner will," Hardy said.

"Well, if you change your mind, I'm not that hard to find." Veda's hand closed around my wrist in an iron grip; her acrylic nails digging into the fleshy underside of my forearm. "If you'll excuse us, Carrie needs to use the little girl's room."

Hardy didn't bother to look up from the menu as Veda dragged me towards the women's bathroom. I didn't put up much of a fight since I wanted to talk to her anyway.

"You could have just told me you wanted to talk. You didn't have to drag me back here." After checking to make sure there wasn't anyone else in the bathroom, I locked the door. "Since when did you go up three cup sizes?"

"'Bout five weeks ago." Veda yanked up her shirt, revealing that she wasn't wearing a bra. "Awesome, right?"

"They look really nice." Her breasts would look even better once the incisions fully healed and the scars faded. "I'm sure Bubba will love them."

"Considering the way things are going, Bubba will never see them. But you should tell him about it and mention how amazing they look."

"I'll be sure to tell him. Now how about you pull your shirt back down so we can talk?" I waited until Veda covered herself before I asked, "So was Kyle Vance harassing you too?"

"He did for a while last summer. Doesn't matter since he's dead." Veda inspected her makeup in the mirror. "I ran into him at the bar right after I flew home from Nashville. I was mad at Bubba and, well, Kyle kind of swooped in for the kill."

"Oh my God, are you telling me you had sex with Kyle?" I angled myself so that I could see Veda's reflection. As far as I knew, Veda and Bubba lost their virginity to each other back in high school, and neither had been with anyone else. It was possible that whatever Bubba did to Veda upset her enough to send her into the arms of another man.

"Don't get your panties in a wad. Bubba and I might be broken up, but I'm not that desperate for sex to be having it with that scumbag." Veda added another layer of hot pink lipstick. "Kyle just got a little obsessed with me. That's all. I thought about getting a restraining order, but it seemed like too much of a hassle."

I decided not to press Veda for the details. Knowing the way Kyle was with women, I doubted Veda's story would be much different from mine. "Did you happen to tell Bubba about all the unwanted attention Kyle was giving you?"

"Of course, I did." Veda turned away from me, but I noticed that she swiped an index fingers under each eye. "Not that he did anything about it."

Behind me, someone pounded on the door and demanded to know what was taking so long. I yelled back at the woman that if she was desperate she could use the men's room.

"You all right, Veda?" I asked.

"Yeah, go on. Get back to the Ranger."

I'd just flipped the lock on the door and was about to leave the bathroom when I decided to turn back.

"You sure you're all right?" I asked, wanting to say or do something that would make things go back to the way they had been when we were younger.

"Well, about Bubba ... I haven't really heard from him that much since we broke up." Veda looked everywhere but at me. She lacked the shame to hit on my dinner date, but it was painfully embarrassing for her to ask me about

Bubba. "How is he?"

"You know you could call him." With that I exited the bathroom, having made my minimal effort in helping the lovebirds. If Veda and Bubba were destined to be together, then they had to get there on their own. I was not going to intervene.

When I got back to the table, a waitress was taking Hardy's order.

"Does the hostess flirt with all the male diners, or am I just special?" Hardy asked once the waitress scurried back to the kitchen.

"The only reason she was flirting with you is because she knows I'll say something to her boyfriend. He has commitment issues, and she's always trying to make him jealous." And it worked, though never in the way Veda wanted it to.

"Probably not her smartest move. But, believe me, I'm not interested. She isn't my type."

"Oh yeah?" I'd noticed that Hardy hadn't checked Veda out, and that seemed strange to me. Men always checked Veda out. It was hard not to when she wore tight fitting, skimpy clothes that left little to the imagination. "You have a girlfriend or something?"

"Nope. My life is complicated enough at the moment."

"Oh." I fiddled with my silverware a bit and then asked, "You got any family?"

"They're dead. I just accidently adopted a stray cat though." Hardy dug his cell phone out of his jacket pocket, played with it for a moment, and then handed it to me. "That's Manny."

"Oh my God, he's so cute." I flipped through Hardy's picture gallery, looking at all of the pictures of his fluffy, orange cat. "How did you accidently adopt him?"

"He kept hanging out around the house I'm renting. I felt bad for the little guy, so I put out some food for him. Next thing I know, he's shoving his way inside. Turns out Manny belonged to the people who used to live in the house. They left him behind when they moved out. I didn't exactly want him, but my only other choice was to take him to a shelter. So now I have a cat."

Accidently hitting a button on Hardy's phone, I found myself looking at a picture of two teenagers in football uniforms. One of the boys appeared to be a younger Hardy. It was hard to tell which one since the teenagers looked exactly alike.

"Hey, who's this?" I asked, turning the phone towards Hardy.

Hardy snatched the phone back, scratching my hand in the process. He had his phone tucked away in his jacket pocket before I had a chance to blink. Before I could ask Hardy what his problem was, the waitress swooped in with our food.

Ignoring me, Hardy dug into his cheeseburger. Not sure what else to do, I followed suit. I was so absorbed with trying to figure out who had been in the picture with Hardy that I barely tasted my taco salad. The two men had been wearing football uniforms—one with the number 12, the other with a 21. The identical features left me with only one answer.

"You have a twin?"

Hardy grunted, but didn't look up. Instead, he stabbed his fork into a French fry.

"Had a twin?" Hardy said that his family was dead. But there was dead-dead, and there was never-going-to-speak-to-him-again dead.

"Had," Hardy said around a mouthful of food. "I don't want to talk about it."

Hardy polished off his food in record time. I glanced up at him and our eyes met for a moment. Hardy broke the eye contact when he reached for his drink and proceeded to chug it. He didn't say anything until the waitress came to take our plates and ask if we wanted dessert. Hardy asked for the check.

"What was his name?" I asked.

"Josh. His name was Josh." Hardy pulled his phone out of his pocket and brought up the picture of the two young men in football uniforms. He then handed me the phone. "Since I know you won't drop it … That was taken our senior year of high school. I'm on the left. Number twelve. Josh was the quarterback, and I was the wide receiver." Hardy reached over and brought up another picture of him and Josh, this time in street clothes. "We both had a full ride to the University of Texas."

The Shatners were avid University of Texas fans, so I think I would remember either a Jerrod or a Josh Hardy. I didn't. "What happened?"

"Our team won State during our senior year of high school." Hardy picked up a straw wrapper and shredded it, dropping bits of paper onto the table.

"But that's a good thing."

"Oh, don't get me wrong, winning State was amazing. It's what happened the next day that ruined everything." Hardy wadded up what was left of the straw wrapper and tossed it on the table. He then took a couple of deep breaths before continuing. "Josh and I went out partying with some of the other guys. I was driving. Josh was in the passenger seat. We were driving through an intersection in downtown Waco when a drunk driver blew through the red light and slammed into the passenger side of the car. Josh was killed instantly."

"I'm so sorry." I reached across the table and squeezed Hardy's hand. I couldn't imagine what it was like to lose a sibling, much less a twin. I only knew what it was like to gain unsuspected siblings from Dad's indiscretions. "What about you and the other guys?"

"We all got pretty banged up. A lot of lacerations and a couple broken bones." Hardy rubbed the scar on his chin. He then pushed his black hair back from his forehead, revealing a scar along his hairline. "I was … I was out of it for a while. I suffered a minor head injury, and that caused some memory loss. I didn't even know Josh was gone until after his funeral. Once I was coherent, my mother finally came to visit me in the hospital. She said the whole thing was my fault, and then she said she never wanted to see me again."

"Oh my God, your mom not only blamed you for the accident, but she kicked you out of the house. What kind of woman does that?"

"The kind who never wanted to have kids in the first place."

"What did you do after she kicked you out?"

"I moved in with my football coach for a few months. I was in really bad shape, but he kept me going. He's the one who went over to Mom's house and got all my stuff and some of Josh's," Hardy said. "In the fall, Coach sent me off to the University of Texas. He said I had to do it for Josh. I still had my scholarship, but I blew it. I never went to class. I just showed up for practice and that was it. After a couple months, my scholarship was pulled, so I left. My coach came up to get me and then basically forced me to go to community college."

"How did you wind up as a State Trooper?" I asked.

"I saw a lot of ugly things when I was growing up and I wanted to try to put a stop to it."

The waitress interrupted Hardy's confession when she returned with our check. On the way out, Hardy and I passed Veda at the hostess stand. She snagged the receipt out of Hardy's hand and scribbled something on the back.

"My number. In case you change your mind." Veda smirked at me.

I was leaning towards having a conversation with Bubba. And, if that didn't work, I was going to hold a gun to his head and force him to fix whatever he broke.

Chapter Sixteen

———————◆———————

"**S**ergeant Hardy, did you come back to take me up on my offer?" Fully clothed, and sans glitter and makeup, I almost didn't recognize Sparkles. Earlier her makeup must have been an inch thick to cover all of the lines around her mouth and eyes.

"I'm still on duty," Hardy said, taking a step back from Sparkles.

"Maybe when you get off duty." Sparkles took a step closer to Hardy.

"Lady, whether I am on duty or off, there is no way I'm going to take you up on anything you're offering."

"What are you? Gay?" Shoving me out of the way, Sparkles tottered off in her six-inch heels. "You have no idea what you're missing."

"I'm sure it ain't much," Hardy mumbled to me as he swung open the front door of the Dancing Cowgirl. He then had to raise his voice to be heard over the deafening level of what passed for music. "Stay close to me until we figure out what kind of crowd is in here. I don't want some drunken idiot to mistake you for a stripper."

"Do I look like a stripper?"

"You're certainly not dressed like one, but let's not take any chances." Hardy pushed the faded red velvet curtains aside, and we entered the club. "My mom used to work at a place like this when I was growing up. Sometimes she would take me and Josh to the club with her, and the dancers would take turns babysitting us. I've seen things that I will never be able to forget."

The club was much more active than it had been that afternoon. I spotted at least six half-naked women strutting around, and the age-range of the patrons had dropped considerably. The old coots must have had to be back at the nursing home for the early bird dinner. Their table was taken over by a group of men who didn't look old enough to shave.

And the lackluster blonde from the afternoon was replaced by a busty brunette in a cowgirl costume. In the few seconds I watched her swing around the pole, she shucked her cowboy hat, chaps, and the skimpy, fringed vest.

"Come on." Hardy tightened his grip around my shoulders and pulled me towards the bar. "Let's get this over with and get out of here."

We were halfway to the bar when Zeke Palmer glanced up and saw us. He grimaced, but then pointed towards the doorway that led to the back rooms. Hardy waved to show that he got the message. We then weaved our way around the scattered tables and chairs, making it across the room with only one incident. A toothless, old man grabbed my butt. I confiscated his beer and poured it over his lap.

"You all right?" Hardy asked.

I leaned against the wall beside the office door and closed my eyes. "I will be once I get out of here."

"I should have taken you home and then come here. This is no place for a lady."

Before I could say anything, Zeke appeared at my side. He looked exhausted.

"She's no lady." Zeke held out his hand to Hardy. "Got your warrant?"

Hardy handed Zeke a folded piece of paper. Zeke read it over twice before unlocking the office door. The three of us crammed into the office and shut the door behind us. It didn't do much to block out the music, but at least we didn't have to shout to hear each other anymore.

"Your guys are in the back," Zeke said. "Don't know why they had to do this while we're open, but at least they aren't messing with the business."

"Yeah, I would hate to hinder the exploitation of women," Hardy said.

Zeke went around the desk and unlocked one of the drawers. He pulled out two videotapes and held them out to Hardy. "All yours."

Hardy pushed the tapes back towards Zeke. "We want to watch them here. With you."

"Oh, come on." Zeke slammed the tapes onto the desk. "Can't you see how busy we are? I've got to get back out there."

"I saw another bartender. He can handle it for a while without you."

Zeke shook his head, and glared at us. "This is harassment."

"No, it's not," Hardy said. "We need you to identify your family members for us."

Zeke sighed. "All right. Give me a minute to tell my guys I'm taking a break."

While Zeke was out of the room, Hardy and I set up two lawn chairs in front of the small television mounted on the wall. "You know, we really don't need him to ID his family. I can probably do that."

"I know. I just like busting his balls," Hardy said. "Besides, I think he might know something that he isn't telling us."

"About how Kyle wound up dead?"

Hardy shook his head. "Not necessarily."

Zeke reentered the room and drew up a chair for himself. He then stuck one of the video tapes in the VCR and hit play. The footage was from the camera mounted over the back door. The time code on the bottom of the screen showed that it was just after one-thirty in the afternoon on New Year's Eve.

"I put this tape in right after I came in for work that day," Zeke said.

Since there wasn't much action at the back door, we fast-forwarded through the footage, slowing it down only when someone entered the picture. Kyle arrived at the Dancing Cowgirl just after two in the afternoon. A few of the strippers arrived around the same time.

Zeke fast-forwarded a little more and then hit the play button when Kyle emerged from the back door just after four-thirty. That went along with what we already knew, since we had evidence Kyle was in Walmart around five. The strippers left right after him.

Around six-thirty, there was a flurry of activity by the back door when a number of the strippers returned. They were followed by the Palmers, who straggled in between six-fifteen and seven-thirty.

The only other real moment of interest was when the Palmers left en masse just before nine-thirty. They were back by ten-thirty, and none of them left the building—at least by the back door—until just before two in the morning. Kyle didn't show up in any of the footage.

"Do we have to go through the footage from the front door?" Zeke asked. "My family wouldn't have gone in or out that way."

"We still want to go over it with you," Hardy said. "We need to see if Kyle came in or left through the front door."

"It also wouldn't hurt to see who else was here that night," I said.

The footage from the security camera just inside the front entrance started just before seven. Zeke had turned the camera on just before he unlocked the doors. There was a lot more action at the front door than there had been at the back. Later, when we had time, someone could watch the footage at regular speed and note the comings and goings. At the moment, we really just wanted to see if Kyle returned to the strip club. And, if Kyle did come back, did he walk out or was he hauled out wrapped in a shower curtain. Though, if Kyle had been killed at the strip club, I couldn't imagine anyone carrying his body through the main room and out the front door. Too many people would have witnessed it.

"Look, it's Chief Yates and his son," I said.

"I guess they weren't on duty." Hardy turned to Zeke. "Do Chief Yates and his son come in here often?"

Zeke scratched his head as he thought about it. "The chief, no. I don't see him much. But Ethan Yates has been coming in a couple times a week during the past few weeks. He sits in the back and gets plastered. Pays for a few lap dances. Chief Yates or one of his other officers always comes by to pick Ethan up before closing time."

We went back to the tape. I recognized a few other people on the footage, but none of them were interesting enough to actually watch. I noted that Chief Yates left the club between eight and eight-thirty. He then came back around eleven-thirty. The next time he left was around one in the morning. He had Ethan in tow. Since they were at the fairgrounds less than twenty minutes later, I assume that they had just found out about the body and were headed over to check it out.

"I didn't see Kyle," I said.

"Neither did I, but it's not like we could see everyone's face." Zeke shoved the tapes into a plastic bag and handed it to Hardy. "Are we done? I really need to get back to work."

"Just a few more questions," Hardy said.

"Whatever." Zeke glanced at me and scowled. "Does she still have to be here?"

"Yes. I'm not sending Detective Shatner out where the patrons are. One guy already grabbed her. I should have arrested him for sexual assault."

"No. It's all right." I leaned closer to Hardy. "I can check on Quaranta's and Sergeant Boleyn's progress. And maybe I can find some of the strippers and ask them about Kyle."

I let myself out of the office, and into the hallway. The question was where were Quaranta and Sergeant Boleyn?

I took a few steps down the hallway, and opened the first door that I came to. Quaranta and Sergeant Boleyn looked up from where they were dusting a stripper pole for fingerprints.

"When did you get here?" Quaranta asked.

"Over an hour ago," I said. "Sergeant Hardy and I have been in the office with Zeke Palmer. We went over the security footage from the other night. We didn't see Kyle."

"Interesting," Quaranta said. "We've finished processing the other rooms. Saved this one for last since this is where the Palmers allegedly were most of the night."

"You're already done with the main room?" I asked.

"Nope." Quaranta finished taking a picture of a fingerprint on the stripper pole. "The judge refused to sign the warrant until we took the main room off it."

"What? Why?"

"Said too many people would have been in the main room that night. If Kyle had been killed in there, someone would have seen it and reported it. Including him. From what the judge said, he's been spending a lot of time at this fine establishment ever since his wife died. He claims he was here all night on New Year's Eve."

"Gotcha. What about the other rooms? Anything?" I asked.

"Plenty of body fluids. Not enough of it was blood," Quaranta said.

"Well I hope you find something in here."

I backed out of the room and shut the door behind me. The next door I came to was already open, so I stepped inside and looked around. The small room reminded me of a fitting room at the mall. Using plywood and shower curtains, the room had been broken down into five smaller spaces. It took me a second, but then I realized that this must be the special back room where the paying customers could get a more private show.

Since we found the shower curtain and rod in the dumpster, I examined the ones in the room. No match. The shower curtains in the back room were all plain black fabric. And the curtains were strung up on pieces of thick dowel rod.

Kneeling, I checked under the curtains. The small booth to my right was occupied by two people—one in heels and the other in men's boots. There was also a bra, a skirt, and wads of crumpled up tissues on the floor. I made a mental note to disinfect the bottoms of my shoes when I got home.

The booth to my left was unoccupied as far as I could tell. I brushed the curtain aside and peeked in. There was nothing in the cramped area other than a chair bolted to the floor and a small table with a box of tissues and giant-sized bottle of hand sanitizer on it.

Returning to the hallway, I continued on my search. I skipped over the men's bathroom, but I did check the women's.

The final door I came across had a sign declaring "Staff Only" on it. I didn't let that stop me. I shoved the door open and stepped into the strippers' tiny changing room. A table ran along the length of the one wall. Spread out on the table were makeup compacts and wigs. On the wall across from the table was a wall of cubbies. The cubbies overflowed with thongs, boas, and other costume necessities. Also in the room were a couch and a couple chairs.

"Are you new here?" asked one of the two strippers occupying the room. She was wearing nothing but a thong and tassels. "Where's your stuff?"

"She's not a stripper." The woman on the couch pushed herself up into a sitting position. "She's a cop. Unless she's contemplating a career change. How you doing, Carrie?"

"Nikki?" I blinked a few times to make sure that I wasn't seeing things. "I didn't know you worked here."

Nikki had been the head cheerleader during my freshman year of high school. We hadn't been close, but we'd been friendly. After graduating, I knew she went to college. The last I had heard was that she'd moved to California, gotten married and popped out a few kids.

"They call me Scarlett these days." Nikki pointed at her natural red hair. "I guess you're here about Kyle."

Kyle could wait. "I didn't know you moved back to Wyatt County."

"Had to. My husband got into drugs and snorted all our money up his nose. Left me and the kids with nothing. So I moved back in with my parents. This was the only job I could find. But it could be worse. So, what do you want to know about Kyle?"

"I … well, I heard that Kyle was cheating on his wife."

Tassels snorted. "Honey, that man couldn't keep it in his pants."

"So, you, uh, you slept with him."

"I wouldn't call what we did sleeping. But, yeah, I had sex with him a few times."

"Why?"

"I may not like my job, but it's all I've got."

I looked over at Nikki for an explanation.

"Kyle pretty much said that if we didn't sleep with him, he'd get the Palmers to fire us," Nikki said.

"So all of you slept with him?" I asked.

"Not all of us," Tassels applied a final coat of baby oil to her stomach and then turned to face me. "But most of us."

"Why didn't any of you go to Oscar or Zeke and tell them what was going on?"

"Oh, please, like Zeke would do anything," Tassels said.

"And one girl did go to Oscar," Nikki added. "He fired her for complaining about Kyle."

The more I learned about Kyle, the less I wanted to catch his killer. I had to remind myself that, until Kyle's was caught, a cloud of doubt still hung over my family. It was also my job to find out who murdered Kyle.

"Was there anyone in particular who Kyle was having sex with? Maybe a redhead?"

Tassels looked over at Nikki and opened her mouth. Before she could say anything, Nikki said, "Once. I slept with him once, and that was months ago."

Tassels nodded. "If Kyle was having more than a one or two night stand with any of us, then both of them kept it a secret."

"We have evidence that Kyle was with a redhead not long before he died. Zeke said a number of natural redheads work here. Do you know which ones were working that night?"

Tassels and Nikki both shrugged.

"It was busy that night," Nikki said. "No one was really scheduled. If you wanted to come in and work that night, you could. But I'd say almost everyone was here. The men usually give us bigger tips on holidays."

Behind me, the door swung open and two nearly naked women entered the room. Tassels and Nikki both jumped up and rushed for the door. Nikki explained that their break was over and they had to get back to work.

I tried to talk to the two strippers who were now on break, but neither of them had any more information than Nikki and Tassels did. Both had worked on New Year's Eve, but neither of them could remember seeing Kyle that night.

I made my way back out into the hallway. With no other doors to check out, I wandered into the rest of the club. Nikki hustled around the room with a tray of drinks, and Tassels was on stage. I scanned the crowd, looking for familiar faces. I spotted one towards the back of the room, but it wasn't anyone I wanted to talk to. I made my way over to his table anyway.

"What are you doing here?"

Ethan Yates glanced up from his beer. "I could ask you the same thing."

I pulled up a chair and had a seat. I tried not to think about who might have sat in the chair before me or what they might have done in it. I was going to burn my entire outfit as soon as I got home. Then I was going to take seventeen showers.

"Your wife okay with you spending so much time here?"

"She left me." Ethan slammed his beer on the table.

"And this is your way of winning her back?"

"She left me for another man. She doesn't want me back."

"Oh. Sorry." I wasn't really sorry. I didn't know who the other man was, but it would be hard for him not to be an improvement over Ethan. "What were you doing here on New Year's Eve?"

Ethan shrugged. "I wasn't working, and I didn't feel like being at home."

"So you came here with your dad?"

Ethan leered at me. "I needed someone to pay for my drinks and lap dances."

I returned the smile, but, on the inside, I cringed. It was not my idea of father and son bonding. "How come he left you here by yourself?"

"He said I was too depressing since I wouldn't stop talking about my wife. So he left. He wanted to go home and watch the bowl games. He came back after a while."

"You see any of the Palmers while you were here that night?"

"Just the one behind the bar." Ethan took a swig from his bottle. "And Oscar came out to say hi to me and Dad. He bought us drinks and paid for a lap dance in the back room for me."

"That was nice of him."

Ethan nodded. He then leaned across the table, putting his face so close to mine that I could smell the beer on his breath. "You still single, Carrie?"

A hand clamped down on my shoulder, but it wasn't Ethan's. I looked up to see that Hardy had joined us. Quaranta and Sergeant Boleyn were with him.

"Time to leave. Now," Hardy said as he propelled me across the room and out into the parking lot.

"Please tell me you found the crime scene," I said to Quaranta.

Quaranta just shook his head. "Like I said, there were plenty of body fluids in this place. Blood wasn't the main one. If Kyle was killed somewhere in there, we didn't find any evidence of it."

"Damn!" I turned to Hardy. "Did you find out anything from Zeke?"

Hardy nodded. "Not sure how much of it has to do with Kyle getting killed. From the way Zeke tells it, Kyle was practically forcing the strippers to have sex with him."

"I think we found a new motive as to why someone might have killed Kyle," I said. "And we have a whole new set of suspects. Starting with the mystery redhead."

"We'll find her, Detective. We'll find her."

Chapter Seventeen

———◆———

"**W**ere you expecting company?" Hardy asked, parking his truck in front of my next-door neighbor's house since there were already two trucks parked at the curb in front of my house. At least my Jeep was in the driveway, meaning Andrew had the decency to return it after he carjacked it from the sheriff's department's parking lot earlier in the day. "Or do you need me to come inside with you to make sure everything's okay?"

"It's fine. My cousin, Andrew, just assumes he can have the guys over whenever he wants." No matter how many times I'd told Andrew to stop inviting people over without asking me first, he continued to do it. Every time he did it, my house wound up getting trashed. And Andrew would make no effort to clean it up. "You're welcome to come in though."

"I don't think that would be a good idea," Hardy said.

"Okay, I get it." I opened the passenger side door and climbed out of the truck. "I guess I'll see you tomorrow, Sergeant Hardy."

"Carrie, wait!" Hardy said before I slammed the door shut. He then got out of the truck and walked around to join me on the passenger side. Placing his hands on my shoulders, Hardy pressed me against the side of the truck. He then propped one arm above my head and leaned in close to me. "First of all, you can stop calling me Sergeant Hardy. It's Jerrod."

"I think I can handle that." I leaned back against the truck and looked up at Hardy's shadowy face. My neighborhood didn't have any streetlights, but the moon was providing enough light for me to make out most of his features. "Jerrod."

"Second, it's not that I don't want to come in. It's that I can't come in. If my lieutenant or anyone else found out, I could get in a lot of trouble. I'm already taking a risk by letting you help me with the case. It's a risk I'm willing to take because I believe you're an asset. But going inside your house, regardless of who else is inside, probably won't look good for me."

"I understand."

"No. You don't understand." Hardy stepped closer to me, pressing his body against mine. "I'm trying to be professional. But it's hard, darling … "

Hardy's lips were just brushing mine when we were interrupted.

"Hey! What's going on over there? Get away from her!"

Hardy jumped backwards, putting a good two feet between us.

"Seriously, Floyd?" I walked around the front of Hardy's truck to confront my overly nosy neighbor who lived across the street from where Hardy was parked. Floyd, who rushed outside wearing only a bathrobe and winter boots, was retired and had nothing better to do than spy on the neighbors. He'd probably been sitting at his front window, acting out his duties as the self-appointed neighborhood watch, when Hardy and I caught his attention. He then rushed outside to defend my honor. "Can't you mind your own business for once, Floyd?"

"You all right, Carrie?" Floyd yelled. "Or is that boy harassing you?"

"Everything is fine, Floyd. Go back inside."

"You sure you're all right, Carrie? I can go in the house and get my gun."

"I told you everything is fine. Please go back inside."

"All right, but I'm going to keep an eye on you two."

I waited until Floyd closed his front door before turning to face Hardy. Whatever momentary spell we had been under was broken. I wasn't sure how to feel about that. I was excited that Hardy was attracted to me, but I had to pull up on the reins before I wound up diving in headfirst only to realize the water was shallow. Floyd might have been a godsend.

"I better let you go. I don't want to give the neighbors something to gossip about." I could just make out two silhouettes hovering in Floyd's front window. Either his wife, Margie, had been spying on the neighbors with him, or he woke her up to join him. "Or get you fired."

"I guess I'll be seeing you in the morning." Hardy hurried around to the driver's side of the truck. "Good work today, Carrie."

"Yeah … See you, Jerrod."

Dejected by Hardy's abrupt departure, I trudged up the sidewalk to my house. Swinging open the front door, I encountered my dog, Molly, lying just inside. If a dog could look livid, she did. It was understandable since an awful noise was coming from the back of my house.

Last summer I had a small sunroom put on the back of the house. Andrew, who happened to visit right after the sunroom was built, took it upon himself to have a bar and sound system installed. From the sound of it, he and his guests were taking advantage of both.

Passing through my living room and then the rarely used dining room, I stepped into the doorway of the sunroom and surveyed the scene before me. Andrew had invited the other four members of the Flaming Outhouses over to my house. My half-brother, Luke, and cousins Bubba and Skeeter were sprawled out on the patio furniture. Another cousin, Junior, was sitting at the bar. Bubba and Junior were brothers, and their mother was Uncle Houston's only daughter. Skeeter was another of Houston's grandchildren. His father was the one who adopted Luke after my father begged him to. The six of us were close in age, and we hung out all the time when we were growing up. Skeeter was the same age as me and Andrew, while Junior was older and Bubba and Luke were younger.

"So, Carrie, how was your date?" Andrew asked, setting his beer on the glass table.

"It wasn't a date, Andrew." I walked farther into the room and had a seat at the bar. Junior leaned over the bar and extracted a diet soda from the mini-refrigerator for me.

"Then how come you and the Ranger were making out?" Luke asked, causing the other four to snicker.

"Bow chicka wow wow!" Bubba laughed so hard that beer shot out of his nose.

"We were not making out," I said. "And the five of you are as bad as Floyd."

"Not quite. None of us ran outside in our bathrobes," Andrew said.

"You were still spying on me from the front windows," I said.

"But Carrie's dating the fuzz," Luke said, picking on me. "Carrie and the Ranger sitting in a tree. K-I-S-S-I-N-G!"

I debated smacking Luke for being childish, but that would require more of an effort than I was willing to make.

"I never thought I'd see the day that my own sweet Carrie would turn her back on the family and associate with the lawmen. What would all the outlaws in our family say?" Skeeter said, trying not to laugh. It seemed he'd forgotten that I worked for the sheriff's department. Of course, my job was to keep my family out of trouble, which was family business, not police business.

"You guys really need to grow up." I took another sip of soda before launching into a conversation I didn't want to have, but knew I needed to. "So, Bubba, I saw Veda."

Bubba's entire two hundred and fifty pound body tensed. "How is she?"

"Well, she's gone up three cup sizes," I said. "And she hit on Sergeant Hardy."

"Son of a bitch." Bubba's hand curled into a fist, crushing the beer can he was holding. A stream of beer shot out of the can, splashing onto Bubba's hand and my no-longer-clean tile floor. "I'm gonna kill him."

When I decided to tell Bubba about the encounter with Veda, I knew it would make him mad. I didn't expect him to direct his anger towards Hardy.

"Hey, I said Veda hit on Hardy, not the other way around. To be honest, Hardy didn't show any interest in Veda."

Bubba chucked his beer can across the room and jumped out of his chair. "I'm still gonna kick his ass."

Bubba was not the kind of guy you'd want to mess with. He was big, he was bad, and he would beat up a person with little provocation. But, aside from a couple assault charges that were dropped, Bubba had never committed a crime. To battle his sexual frustration when he was away from Veda, Bubba spent hours a day in the gym. He had muscles on top of muscles.

Bubba stalked back and forth across the small room, slamming his fist into the palm of his other hand. The other guys weren't helping to diffuse the situation. They started referring to Veda as Yoko Ono, and saying things about how Bubba could do better than her. I still couldn't figure out what it was that made the guys dislike Veda so much—we were all the best of friends growing up. But, over the past couple years, friendship turned into animosity. Their comments directed Bubba's anger away from Hardy, but focused it on them.

"Everybody shut up. You're making this worse instead of better." Since I didn't want my sunroom destroyed, I grabbed Bubba by the ear and directed him back to his chair. "Bubba, we both know that Veda hit on Hardy because I was there. She knew I would tell you about it. All she wants is some attention. You need to call her."

"She can call me." Bubba slumped back in the chair and crossed his arms over his broad chest. "I'm not playing her childish games."

"You both need to stop playing games. Call her. Now, if you'll excuse me, I'm going to bed," I said as I headed for the door into the house.

"Wait, there's something you need to know," Bubba said as he grabbed the back of my shirt and yanked me down onto the arm of his chair. Beads of sweat popped out on his forehead, and his dark eyebrows were drawn so close together that it looked like he had a unibrow. The last time I saw Bubba that freaked out was four years ago when Veda had a pregnancy scare.

"This about Veda?" I asked.

"No. Well, yeah. Kinda." Bubba raised his head and briefly made eye contact with me. "You ain't gonna like it."

"What did you do?"

Before Bubba could respond, Junior said, "Hey, Bub, I thought we agreed that we aren't going to tell Carrie about that."

"What is going on?" I shook Bubba's arm. "What did you do?"

Andrew, Luke, and Skeeter added their voices to the questioning, demanding to know what Junior and Bubba had done to get them that worked up over the confession.

"Bubba, you need to tell me," I said.

"Carrie, the other day—"

"We may have lost our record contract." Junior said, interrupting his younger brother. Junior, who was thinner and slightly taller than Bubba, had sweat stains forming in the armpits of his t-shirt. "We didn't want to tell you in case everything works out."

"You what?" I screamed. "What did you do?"

All five guys shot each other wary glances. None of them would even look in my direction. Whatever they had done, it had to be bad.

Eight years ago, when the six of us packed up and headed north to Nashville, the Flaming Outhouses had nothing but a few thousand bucks, some second-hand musical instruments, a couple original songs, and a dream. They wore out the soles of their shoes trudging the sidewalks from honky tonk to honky tonk, and record company to record company. Meanwhile, I tried to manage the band while working for the Nashville Crime Scene Investigation Section.

Admittedly, the Flaming Outhouses got off to a slow start. The boys didn't have much musical talent, and I had no idea what it took to be a manager. But, thanks to some honky tonk proprietors who were either desperate or believed in us, the band started getting their music out there. A small, but loyal, group of followers began to build up. After we'd been in Nashville for a year, a small record company approached the Flaming Outhouses about recording an album. A year later, the self-titled debut album hit the stores with little to no fanfare. A year later, the Flaming Outhouses released their second album called "White Trash." The title song "(That Don't Make Me) White Trash" got some local radio play, and, almost overnight, became a nationwide sensation. The Flaming Outhouses had arrived.

Following the one-hit wonder, a larger record company snatched up the Flaming Outhouses. By then, we'd been in Nashville for just about five years. Not long after the boys went into the studio to record their third album, I packed up and moved home to Texas.

"What happened?" I asked.

It was Andrew who finally spoke. "We screwed up, all right. We screwed up big time. But I came up with this brilliant idea on how we can fix it. It's going to blow y'alls mind."

"Andrew, the last time you had a brilliant idea, we all ended up in the infield jail at Talladega Superspeedway," I said.

"Seriously, Carrie, this one is legitimately brilliant," Andrew said.

"Show of hands for who has no desire to hear Andrew's brilliant idea because he already knows it will end horribly?" I asked. Luke, Bubba, Junior, and Skeeter all raised their hands. "You've been out voted, Andrew."

"Y'all suck," Andrew said.

"Hey, Carrie, you ever think about moving back to Nashville and managing the band again?" Junior asked.

Just every day for the last three years. Managing the Flaming Outhouses had been fun, but it was also a nonstop headache. Still, it had been easier to deal with the five of them than the entire Shatner family.

"Yeah, maybe you can move back and fix this," Luke added.

"Oh no. You got yourselves into this, you get yourselves out. I'm not your babysitter. Not any more, at least." I stood up and moved towards the door. "Now I want to thank all of you for ruining my evening. I'm going to bed."

Chapter Eighteen

———————◆———————

Neither Hardy nor Uncle Murph was at the sheriff's department when I got to work in the morning. Worried that Murph was up to no good—and possibly in need of rescue—I called him from my car. As I suspected, Murph was on another secret mission for Uncle Houston. But he assured me that he was fine and demanded that I leave him alone for the rest of the morning.

I waited until eight-thirty before I gave Hardy a call. When I was sent straight to voicemail, I left a message asking him to give me a call when he had a chance. I then sat around my office for an hour and played games on my computer. I would have gone over the information and evidence gathered in Kyle's case, but Hardy had taken it all with him.

By nine-thirty I was starting to get a little antsy, worried that Hardy wasn't coming. For all I knew, he'd solved the case and was off arresting someone. I was about to text Hardy when Murph wandered into my office to let me know he was back.

"What favor did Uncle Houston have you doing this morning?" I asked.

"Nothing you need to be concerned about."

"Come on, Murph … What were you up to?"

"I'm telling you it's best if you don't know," Murph said. "While you're working with the Ranger and doing things the legal way, I'm using some more creative means to find Kyle's killer."

"All right, all right." Actually, it wasn't all right at all. But if Murph wanted to keep his activities a secret, I wasn't going to pry. The less I knew was probably for the best. "Did you learn anything new from our family?"

"No. They're all still claiming they never saw Kyle that night." Murph waved as he backed out of my office. "And even if I had a full confession from one of them, I wouldn't tell you about it. Ain't nobody going to trust you after you called in the Texas Ranger and got him looking into the family."

"I did what I had to do!" I yelled after Murph.

Deciding I should wait a little longer before texting Hardy, I set aside my phone and resumed playing computer games. Lost in the mindless repetition of the game, I ran through a list of all of my family members. If one of them killed Kyle—even by accident—they probably would have done something afterwards that was suspicious or out of character. Unfortunately, with having joined the Flaming Outhouses on stage, I hadn't been focusing on my family directly after the fight. In the end, I couldn't come up with anything that stood out.

By noon, I finally gave up on seeing or hearing from Hardy. Whatever was going on with the investigation, it seemed I was no longer a part of it. I was getting ready to run home to check on Molly when I spotted Hardy's black truck driving past my office window. Taking off my coat and shoving my purse back into my desk drawer, I had just enough time to grab a random file and settle in at my desk before Hardy came strolling into my office.

"Good to see you and Sheriff Shatner hard at work on something that isn't my case." Hardy had a seat in my guest chair. "What are you reading there?"

"Just a report." I glanced down at the paperwork and realized it was an old case file from last year. Three teenagers broke into a restaurant to steal a few cases of beer. Within an hour of getting the call, I found the kids passed out drunk two blocks down the street from the restaurant. "What have you been up to all morning?"

"Worried you were missing out on all the fun?"

"Were you having fun?"

"Sadly, no I was not. I've been at my office up in Tyler all morning. I had to go over everything with my lieutenant and get him up-to-date with the investigation."

"And? ... "

"My lieutenant admitted that allowing you to help hasn't been an epic mistake," Hardy said. "We also came to the conclusion that I have nothing. I'm no closer to solving this case than I was when I arrived at the fairgrounds."

"That's not true. When you showed up you had no idea who the victim was or how he wound up dead in a dumpster."

"Okay, I have slightly more information. But none of it has helped me figure out who killed Kyle and where. Or why."

"What about all of the clothing that was collected when you brought my family in for questioning? Has the lab tested it for blood yet?"

"All of the clothes have been tested. No blood."

Sighing in relief, I leaned back in my chair and allowed myself to relax. While the lack of bloody clothing didn't prove none of my family members killed Kyle—it was possible one of them killed Kyle and disposed of the bloody clothes before he was brought into the sheriff's department—it continued to leave open the possibility that Kyle was killed elsewhere.

"What about the rest of the evidence?" I asked.

"The lab hasn't had a chance to run the DNA for the red hairs or vaginal secretions that were collected from Kyle's body, or the blood samples from the shower curtain, rod, and towels. I talked to one of the lab technicians this morning and she promised to get started processing the evidence this afternoon. If I could just get some lab results, I could move forward. But I don't need to explain to you that lab results can take weeks."

"That's it for the evidence? You really do have nothing."

"Well, not quite nothing. Someone did go through Kyle's laptop and found a file folder of naked pictures of various women."

"How many is various?"

"Over fifty."

"Gross," I said.

"I absolutely agree with you. Especially if he had relations will all of them. Right now we aren't sure if Kyle took all of the photos or if he got them off the internet." Hardy pulled his laptop out of his bag and set it down on my desk. "I've got all of the pictures on here. They're saved in chronologic order. None of the women in the recent photos have red hair."

"Hard to tell what color hair some of these women have considering Kyle only took pictures of their body parts." I concentrated on the four photos from December. A brunette, a bottle blonde, a natural blonde, and a woman with jet black hair. "The brunette looks familiar. It's possible we saw her at the strip club. And there's something about the bottle blonde that seems familiar, but it's hard to tell since part of her face is hidden by her hair. As for the other two, I don't think I've ever seen them before."

"Once we confirm that Kyle took the pictures of these women, we can work on tracking them down," Hardy said.

"Then what is our next step? What can we do to solve this?"

"Aside from wait on the lab to get me some evidence?" Hardy held up a handful of papers. "I finally got a hold of Kyle's phone records. I went through and highlighted all of the numbers that Kyle called on a frequent basis during the past couple months. We need to track down who Kyle was calling so much. We've also got the all security footage to go over."

"Then we may as well work on the security footage. We need to confirm Kyle was at all those places that the receipts place him at," I said.

Hardy brought up another folder on his laptop, and started clicking on files. "I have all of the security footage uploaded onto here. I started looking through the Walmart footage last night, but I kept losing Kyle in the aisles."

Hardy opened up a video file and we watched the footage of Kyle driving through the Walmart parking lot. We then followed him across the lot and into the store. Hardy then switched to an interior camera, picking up Kyle as he walked through the doors. It went on like that for a half-an-hour—jumping from file to file as we followed Kyle around the store. None of the footage was overly entertaining, though I did enjoy the part where he wandered into the women's clothing section and examined the ladies' panties. That was followed by the anticlimactic footage of Kyle leaving Walmart.

"What about the security footage from Dairy Queen?" I asked.

Hardy opened up another folder and clicked on a file named 'DQPL.' We had to fast forward through hours of useless footage from earlier in the day before we finally spotted Kyle's truck pull into the Dairy Queen's parking lot. Parking in a spot that wasn't quite big enough for his truck, Kyle banged his driver's side door into the SUV next to him. Even after Kyle walked out of frame, Hardy and I continued watching the parking lot footage. Finally, about ten minutes after Kyle went inside, the owner of the SUV came out. If Kyle did any damage to the petite woman's car, she never noticed it. Hardy made a note to track down the woman just in case.

Moving inside, we found Kyle flirting with the young woman working behind the cash register. The girl barely looked eighteen. She also didn't look interested in Kyle. Giving up on impressing the girl, Kyle grabbed his tray full of food and had a seat. After stuffing his face, Kyle disappeared into the bathroom for almost ten minutes.

"Well, this certainly isn't getting us anywhere," I said.

"No, but at least we've determined that Kyle was still alive at this time," Hardy said.

"That just leaves us with the footage from Exxon," Hardy said.

"But that was from earlier in the day. We already know Kyle was still alive then," I said.

"Doesn't matter. We need to confirm that he was there." Hardy had just started up the security footage from the Exxon's parking lot when his phone rang. "It's my lieutenant. I gotta take this. Just keep watching the footage without me."

While Hardy slipped out into the hallway, I watched Kyle pull up to one of the gas pumps and fill up the tank. He then headed inside the store and disappeared from the frame for about five minutes. When Kyle reentered the frame, he was drinking a soda and munching on a snack cake. He was headed for his truck when something drew his attention to the other end of the parking lot. From the angle I was watching, I couldn't see what it was that distracted Kyle. And, since the security footage had no sound, I couldn't hear it either.

Whatever it was that Kyle had seen or heard freaked him out. He dropped what was left of his snack cake and tried to shove the car key into the lock. Kyle was still struggling to unlock the driver's side door when my cousins, Bubba and Junior, entered the frame.

"No." I straightened up in the chair. "Oh no. No. No. No. Shit!"

I watched as Bubba and Kyle exchanged words. I was no lip reader, but I could make out some of the words being said. And none of them were good. The two were about nose to nose when Bubba socked Kyle in the jaw. The blow sent Kyle staggering into Junior, who drove Kyle to his knees after a punch to the gut. Bubba also slammed Kyle's head into the side of the truck. Once Kyle was on the ground, Bubba and Junior walked away as if nothing had happened.

"How long have you known about this?"

Unbeknownst to me, Hardy had reentered the room. I spun around in my chair to face him. "I just found out. I had no idea Junior and Bubba beat up Kyle. But I know why they did."

"Yeah, sure," Hardy said. "Seriously, how long have you known?"

"I'm telling you, I just found out."

"I'm not talking about the fight." Hardy let out a half-strangled scream. "How long have you known that Bubba and Junior killed Kyle?"

"What? Are you kidding me? They didn't kill Kyle. I was with them that night."

"Yes, you were. You were trying to clean up the mess they made." Hardy took a few steps into the room, crowding the already tight space. "After the altercation in the parking lot, your cousins wanted to beat up on Kyle some more. It was probably an accident that they killed him. So they called you, who, of course, had to clean up the mess they made."

"That's not what happened." I tried to stand up, but Hardy pushed me back into the chair. "They didn't kill Kyle."

Hardy shook his head. "That's not what this new evidence is telling me."

"Your so-called evidence is from hours before Kyle was killed, and you have no idea what was going on. You're taking the fight out of context and shaping it to fit your theory. Bubba and Junior were at the fairgrounds all night. They were with me. They did not kill Kyle, and I am most certainly not covering up for anybody that did."

"Your cousins still withheld information during a police investigation. Why didn't they tell the deputies about this when they were questioned?"

"Seriously, you can't come up with a reason why Bubba and Junior wouldn't want to admit to the fight? Aside from not wanting to get charged for assault?"

"All right, I can understand why they didn't want to tell me or the deputies about the fight. Especially if they knew Kyle was dead and had already agreed to not mention the fight." Hardy paced back and forth across the small room. "But why didn't they tell you?"

"They probably didn't think we would find out about it," I said, assuming that was the reason. Bubba and Junior probably didn't know that the fight had been captured by the security cameras, and even if they did know that, they wouldn't have known we were going to be looking at the security footage.

"Doesn't matter, because now it looks like they're hiding something. Get up. You're coming with me, Detective Shatner."

Now it was back to Detective Shatner? What happened to calling me Carrie? "Where are we going? To talk to Bubba and Junior?"

"That's where I'm going," Hardy said. "You're going into the jail cell until I'm done dealing with them. I am not going to have you interfering."

Hardy yanked me out of the chair, but I was ready for him. As soon as he said he was going to lock me up in the jail cell, I slipped my handcuffs off my belt. I had one end clapped around Hardy's right wrist before he knew what hit him. I wrapped the other end around one of the desk's drawer handles. The drawer only opened about halfway before it got stuck. I'd spent the past three years trying to get the drawer fixed, but it seemed to be jammed in there for good.

"Detective Shatner!" Hardy yelled, his voice a mixture of anger and confusion. "Carrie!"

"I'm sorry, Jerrod. I really am. But interfering is what I do." I grabbed my car keys and cell phone, and then fled the room. As I sprinted to my Jeep, I called Junior. He answered after the second ring. Skipping the preamble, I asked, "Where are you and Bubba at right now?"

"We're at Mom and Pop's place. Why? What's going on?" Junior asked.

Hanging up, I dropped the phone into the center console cup holder. I then pulled out of the parking lot with squealing tires. I did my best to obey the speed limit driving north through town; but once I got to the edges of the Holler city limits, I flipped on the emergency light on the dashboard and floored it.

Not long after I passed under the 'Welcome to the Shatner's Alpaca Farm and Wild West Town' sign, the road split into three branches. The left branch headed to the Wild West town, the middle road went to the multiple animal barns, and the right branch led to my Aunt Loretta's and Uncle Elvin's ranch house. As I bounced over the rough road and potholes, I apologized to my Jeep's suspension for the abuse.

Slamming on my brakes while swerving to avoid crashing into the covered porch that ran along the front of the one-story rancher, I narrowly missed taking out some of Aunt Loretta's rose bushes. I did clip one of the three-foot tall, plastic Nutcrackers that Uncle Elvin had lined up across the front lawn. The Nutcracker somersaulted through the air until it landed in the bare branches of the oak tree next to the house.

"Whoops! Could have been worse. I could have run over one of the people in the Nativity scene," I said to myself as I parked next to the life-size manger that Uncle Elvin built to house the Nativity. Running across the yard, I dodged around and jumped over the plethora of tacky outdoor Christmas decorations that Uncle Elvin had yet to put away. I didn't know why he put out so many holiday decorations considering the house sat half a mile back from the road.

After almost tripping over a mannequin dressed as Mrs. Claus, I let myself into the house through the unlocked front door. I immediately spotted Bubba sitting on the leather couch in the spacious living room. He had his back to me and was wearing headphones, so he didn't see or hear me come in.

Sneaking up behind Bubba, I whacked him upside the head. "You son of a bitch."

On most days, I was a very calm and rational person. But we all had our breaking points. My breaking point was named Bubba. Over the years, Bubba had pushed all of my buttons. He was the only person who could send me into a full-on tail-spinning, nosedive of fury. We've had some knockout, drag-down brawls over the years. Of course, in all of them, Bubba never laid a hand on me. He might get rough in trying to throw me off him or pin me down, but he usually just let me take out my rage on him. He did so because he knew that he deserved it. Today was different.

"What are you doing here, Carrie?" Bubba tossed the headphones on to the coffee table. "You got a problem or something?"

"You lowdown, lying, idiot." I grabbed a magazine off of the end table next to the couch, rolled it up, and then beat Bubba around the head with it. "You know what you did!"

"Calm down, woman." Twisting around, Bubba tried grabbing at my arms. He managed to snatch the magazine out of my hand and chuck it across the room. "If this is about Veda, I swear I'm going to call her today."

"You still haven't called her?" Jumping over the back of the couch, I landed on top of Bubba and pounded my fists onto his chest. "What is wrong with you?"

"What's wrong with me? I was just sitting here minding my own business when you went all crazy on me." Bubba squirmed around onto his stomach and buried his head under a cowhide-print throw pillow to ward off my blows. "I wanna know what's wrong with you."

"You're what's wrong with me." Shoving the pillow aside, I locked my arms around Bubba's thick neck, and fastened on a headlock. Beneath me, Bubba tried to push himself up onto his knees and elbows. I drove my knees into his back and forced him back down. "I swear to God, one of these days I am going to kill you."

"Great … now what?" Junior asked as he ran into the spacious living room. He wrenched my arms away from Bubba's neck. He then pulled me—kicking and screaming—off Bubba.

Bubba took the momentary reprieve to escape to the bathroom. It was the only room in the house without a window. The only way out was the same way he had gone in. Bubba couldn't stay in there forever, and I would be waiting for him when he came out.

"What are you waling on Bubba for now?" Junior asked as he held my squirming body in the air. I landed a solid kick on his shin, but he didn't loosen his grip. "Ouch! Is this about us losing the recording contract?"

"No, it's about you two beating up Kyle Vance in the Exxon parking lot."

Junior let go and dropped me onto the couch. "How did you find out about that?"

"Security footage."

"We figured you didn't need to know about that. You know we didn't kill Kyle."

"You still should have told me." I sagged against the couch cushions and tried to catch my breath. Beating up Bubba took a lot out of me. I was out of practice.

"What's going on out there?" Bubba yelled through the door.

"Carrie found out that we saw Kyle at the gas station," Junior yelled back.

The bathroom door cracked open, and Bubba peered out. "I told you Carrie would find out. I tried to 'fess up last night, but you had to open your big mouth and tell Carrie about screwing up our contract."

"Look, Carrie, I get we should have told you earlier," Junior said.

"But we can explain," Bubba added.

"That's good, because I'm looking for an explanation." Hardy said as he stomped inside with my handcuffs dangling from his right wrist. I could only imagine what kind of shape my desk was in. Hopefully, he fixed the broken drawer instead of making it worse. Uncle Murph, Chief Deputy Quaranta, and Deputy Timmy Grant crowded through the front door behind Hardy.

"Oh, crap!" Bubba stuck his head out of the bathroom long enough to identify the speaker. He then pulled his head back in, slammed the door shut, and then locked it.

"Get out of there, Buford McCarty," Hardy yelled at Bubba. "Otherwise, I will kick down that door and come in there after you!"

"Go ahead and try, lawman! You don't scare me!" Bubba yelled.

"No, but you are scared of me, right, Bubba?" I asked.

"That's only because you're crazy!" Bubba swung open the bathroom door and trudged out to join his brother. "And because you'll say something to Veda and get me into even more trouble with her."

"Caroline Shatner, Buford McCarty, and Elvin McCarty Jr., all three of you are under arrest for interfering with a police investigation." Hardy strode across the room to where Junior, Bubba, and I were clustered together.

"I didn't interfere with nothing," Bubba said as the muscles in his body tensed up. He wasn't about to go down without a fight. I'd seen Bubba in enough brawls to know he fights dirty and that his opponents rarely walked away in one piece. It didn't help that Junior usually jumped into the fray to watch his brother's back. "Just try and arrest me."

"I've taken down meatheads with bigger muscles than you." Hardy undid his gun belt and then dropped it onto the floor. "Come at me, Bubba."

"Jerrod, don't." I stepped in front of Hardy and planted my hands on his chest. "For God's sake, don't."

"Don't what, Miss Shatner? Arrest y'all when I have every right to?"

I let my hands fall away from Hardy's chest and took a step back. While I had done my best to work with Hardy to solve the case, I had also worked against him while trying to protect my family. When I handcuffed him to the drawer handle and raced off to confront Junior and Bubba, I had crossed the line. Considering the angry and hurt look on Hardy's face, I wasn't sure if there was any going back.

I took another step back and bumped into Junior and Bubba. Against my shoulder, I could feel the rise and fall of Bubba's chest as he sucked in deep breaths and fought to control himself. While his brother was a ticking time bomb, Junior was standing completely still. He was no less dangerous. I held my arms out to hold them back, but my gaze remained locked with Hardy's.

"Sergeant Hardy, hey, how about we all take a deep breath and calm down," Murph said. "You know Bubba and Junior didn't kill Kyle."

"No, Sheriff Shatner, I don't know that," Hardy said. "For all I know, they did kill him, and Detective Shatner has been trying to cover for them the whole time."

"But—"

"Shut up, Carrie," Murph said. "You three just shut up. Sergeant Hardy, I've known these three since they were babies. None of them are capable of what you're accusing them of doing."

"I'm still arresting them," Hardy said.

"Then you're making a huge mistake," Murph said. Quaranta and Timmy spoke up in agreement.

It could have been five seconds or it could have been five minutes, but Hardy broke eye contact with me to glance first at Bubba and then at Junior.

When his stare returned to me, I could sense that a shift has taken place in his brain. He put the handcuffs away.

"I still have to take them in." Hardy looked over his shoulder to address Timmy and Quaranta. "Put them in different cars, but leave off the handcuffs."

Quaranta and Timmy came forward and gestured for Junior and Bubba to come with them. Instead of obeying, Bubba and Junior looked to me.

"Go. Just tell the truth," I said.

Hardy waited until they left the room before he spoke again.

"What were you thinking?" Hardy's jabbed me in the chest with his finger. I backed away from him until I bumped into an armchair and sat down hard. Hardy leaned over, sticking his face close to mine. I scrunched back as far as I could in the chair to get away from him. "What were you thinking?"

"I wasn't."

"You weren't thinking? Well, it seems to me like you knew exactly what you were doing, little lady. Did you come out here to help them make up a story? To cover up what they did? That's what you do, isn't it? Make things go away?"

I opened my mouth to answer but what was there to say? He had me pegged dead to rights. For the most part, at least. I hadn't rushed to Junior's and Bubba's aid to cover up anything they did. I came looking for answers. But I knew that regardless of what they did, they didn't kill Kyle. It just wasn't possible. I'd been hanging out with Junior and Bubba all that night.

"That's it; you're off the case. Why I even let you on the case, I don't know."

"You knew I could help you."

"Oh yeah, you've been a big help. Maybe Chief Yates was right about you all along." Hardy yanked me out of the chair. "I'm taking your badge."

Hardy snatched the badge off my belt and then turned on his heel. He stomped across the room and knocked Murph out of the way to leave by the front door.

I waited until after the sounds of tires crunching over gravel faded away before I ventured to speak to Uncle Murph.

"I messed up, didn't I?"

Chapter Nineteen

———◆———

Murph and I arrived at the sheriff's department just in time to see Bubba and Junior get escorted inside. Neither of them put up much of a protest—even when Quaranta stuck Bubba in the interrogation room and Timmy locked up Junior in the holding cell.

Hardy, who was waiting for me in my office, was seated in my chair with his feet propped up on my desk. I peeked around the side of the desk to see that the drawer was no longer stuck. It was lying on the floor, and the handle was long gone.

"I want your ass in that chair. Now."

"I guess this is where I should say I'm sorry." I sank into one of the guest chairs, leaned back, and crossed my legs. I put up a false front of calm because I didn't want Hardy to know that he rattled me back at the ranch. "I'm sorry."

"No explanation?" Hardy's chest heaved, each breath coming out raspy.

I'd just apologized. What else was I supposed to say? I didn't want to anger Hardy further. Nor did I want to cower before him. I shrugged, not sure how to explain my actions. I'd acted rashly and caused more problems than I solved. Hardy had to at least somewhat understand the motivations behind what I did.

"Well, I guess it doesn't really matter anymore. I should have known you'd do something like that sooner or later. Anything to protect your family, right? You've been using me for your own gain since you manipulated me into letting you help me on the case. I've been a pawn in your game from the beginning, and you played me for a fool," Hardy said.

"What game have I been playing?" I asked.

Hardy laughed. "Oh, Carrie, the sweet and innocent act isn't going to cut it this time. You handcuffed me to a drawer."

"I panicked."

"Of course, you did." Hardy ran his hands through his hair, messing it up. He then stared at me across the desk for a few seconds before mumbling, "What have I gotten myself in to? Better yet, what did I do to deserve this?"

"Why have you been letting me help?"I leaned forward, wondering about the answer to that question myself. Aside from the very beginning of the investigation, Hardy didn't really needed my assistance. Sure, I had been helpful, but Quaranta could have basically done the same things that I had.

Hardy laughed. It wasn't a jolly kind of laugh. It was more like the 'I'm losing my mind' maniacal laughter. "Because, despite all the bad things I heard about you, I wanted to believe that you have some integrity. I couldn't believe you were as bad as Chief Yates and other people said. Or, at least I didn't want to believe it. I guess I just didn't want it to be true."

"But most of what Chief Yates says about me isn't true."

"No, Carrie, it is. Chief Yates was right about you."

"So that's why you let me help you? You wanted me to prove that I'm not a horrible person? Wow, that's pretty low of you."

"Yeah, well maybe it is. And, I'll admit when I first saw you at the crime scene, looking sexier than you had any right to, I started thinking with my little head and not the big one. Here I am in the middle of a dry spell that would make West Texas look like an oasis, and I find myself working with the funniest, smartest, sexiest—" Hardy kicked the trashcan. "I'm trying to solve a homicide and all I can think about is getting in your pants. I must be out of my mind."

"Are you all right?" I asked. Hardy was starting to get a crazed look in his eyes. I was worried about him and for myself.

"No, I'm not all right! I thought we might have something, and here you are just using me so that I would let you help on the investigation."

"I'm not using you."

"Oh, yeah? Then why did you want to help out on the investigation so badly?"

"To, you know, prove that no one in my family killed Kyle." And to make sure you didn't look into them too closely, I thought. "I also want to help you figure out what really happened and find the killer. Just like I would do for any other murder in Wyatt County. Despite … well, despite what you've heard, I do take my job seriously. I didn't get a degree in criminal justice to better help my family break the law. Not when I don't exactly approve of what they're doing. I just … I'm stuck in a bad situation and I'm trying to make the best of it."

"Doesn't matter anyway." Hardy tossed my badge onto my lap. In the excitement I forgot he'd taken it from me back at the ranch. "I'm giving back your badge, but only because I have no right to take it. At least not at the moment. I think it would be best if you don't have anything further to do with my case. And don't try to solve it on your own, or I will arrest you. This time it's not just an idle threat. Leave the investigation to me."

"Can we at least talk about this like two rational people?"

"No. I don't want to talk to you at all." Hardy headed for the door. "Now get out of here and go home."

"Where are you going?"

Hardy braced his arms against the door and then banged his head into it, causing a dull thud. He spat out a couple swear words before turning to face me. "If you must know, which you don't because you are off the case, I'm going to talk to your cousins. Would you like to get them a lawyer, or should I let them do that?"

"They don't need a lawyer. If you would just let me explain—"

Hardy walked over to where I was sitting and hauled me out of the chair. "What did I just tell you? You are no longer part of my investigation. And why should I take your word anyway? You've lied to me from the moment I got here."

I pulled away from him. "I know why Bubba confronted Kyle. And if you would just let me explain, your chat with Bubba and Junior may go a lot smoother."

"Humor me." Hardy stepped back and indicated that I should continue.

"While Bubba may enjoy a good fight, he doesn't go around attacking people in parking lots without reason or provocation. I know it was stupid of him, but he did have a good motive."

"Carrie, there is never a good reason to attack a man in a parking lot."

"This time there was. You remember the other night when Veda hit on you and I said it was because her boyfriend has commitment issues?"

Hardy nodded. "Let me guess. Bubba is her boyfriend."

"For the past thirteen years. He loves her, but he's too afraid to marry her because his mom can't stand Veda. And because … well, you don't need all the details."

Hardy shrugged. "Still doesn't explain why Bubba beat up Kyle. Or what Junior's involvement was."

"I can't explain Junior." Other than he probably didn't want to miss out on his brother's action. "But Veda claims Kyle was harassing her the past five or six months."

I passed along what Veda told me the other night in the bathroom at Baby Doll's Tavern.

"I think I still have Veda's number," Hardy said as he pulled out his wallet.

"Oh my God, you kept it?"

Hardy froze, his wallet in one hand and a scrap of paper in the other. "She wrote her number on the back of the receipt. I kept the receipt."

"With her number on it."

"It's not like I was planning to call her." Hardy grabbed some papers and flipped through them. "Just as I thought. Check this out."

Hardy handed me the receipt and a stack of papers that he had grabbed off of my desk. The papers were the printouts of Kyle's phone records for the previous three months. There were three numbers highlighted in different colors.

"The wife's number is highlighted in yellow." Hardy jabbed the paper with his index finger. "The number highlighted in pink is Veda's. Looks like he called her quite a few times starting in July."

"And then stopped around Thanksgiving. That's when Kyle started placing a lot of calls to this number." The last three pages were almost entirely highlighted in green. "Do we know who he was calling?"

"Nope." Hardy took the phone records back. "I called the number a couple times, but no one answers. Other than the voice belonging to a woman, the voicemail isn't very informative. The woman doesn't even say what her name is. She just says to leave a message. Which I have. I've been trying to track her down, but every time I do, I get distracted by you."

"What if she's the woman Kyle was with before he died? We have to find her."

"We? There's no 'we' anymore. This partnership is over." Hardy herded me towards the door. "Now I'm going to talk to Junior and Bubba. You are leaving."

"You do know Junior and Bubba won't talk to you, right?"

Hardy sighed. "But they'll tell you everything? Nice try, but I don't think so. Now get!"

"Jeez, you don't have to be so rude about it."

I was pulling the door open when Hardy slammed his hand against the door and pushed it shut. He braced his arms on either side of my head, trapping me between him and the door. I turned to face him, the door handle jabbing me in the back.

"Maybe I was born rude," Hardy said. "Or maybe you acting like a spoiled brat has brought out the worst in me."

"Hey. There's no need to call me names."

"Carrie, at this point I could call you a lot worse." Hardy grasped my chin in his hand and tilted my head back against the door. He then stared down at me. His brown eyes were lit up with anger. "Listen up, Carrie. I liked you. A lot. And I don't appreciate the way you used me. A man doesn't like having his heart and his ego trampled on."

"But—"

Hardy pressed his thumb over my lips. "Not another word. I've had all I can take."

I had no idea what would have happened next because Timmy pounded on the door and yelled, "Bubba's real angry. He's bashing a chair into the table and hollering something fierce."

"Tell him I'm coming. And get Junior." Hardy released me and stepped back so that I could open the door. "Get out of here, Carrie. I don't want to see you again."

"Don't you want to keep Bubba and Junior separate?" I asked. "Make sure they both give you the same story?"

"I don't have time for this." Hardy stepped around me and headed down the hall towards the interrogation room. Despite his request that I leave, I followed him. "And I really don't need you telling me how to do my job. Now, get out of here."

"Hey, Texas Ranger, get in here and face me like a man," Bubba yelled. Every other word was punctuated by the sound of metal striking metal. "I'll tear this wall down if you don't get in here."

Hardy came to an abrupt halt in the middle of the hallway. Not expecting that, I crashed into his back. Whirling around to face me, Hardy said, "I thought I told you to go home."

"I will. After you release my cousins."

Hardy sighed. "You know what, I'm going to let you handle this. If you're so convinced you know why they beat up Kyle, then you can get them to confess. Just remember, I'll be watching from the other side of the glass. You try anything funny, and all three of you can share a jail cell."

Bubba stopped bashing the folding chair on the table when the door swung open. He was raising it over his head, his face red and contorted by rage, when he realized it was me.

"You're buying the department a new chair," I said.

Bubba examined what was left of the chair before tossing it into the corner as Junior walked into the room.

"All yours, Detective Shatner," Hardy said.

I didn't get a chance to respond before Hardy shut the door, leaving me in the interrogation room with Bubba and Junior.

"Y'all want to tell me about what happened with Kyle?" I leaned against the one-way mirror even though I could feel Hardy's eyes boring a hole into my back through the glass.

"You ain't going to like it," Bubba said.

"I don't expect to. I'm just going to assume it's your fault. Or should I blame Veda?"

"Hey, it's not Veda's fault that jerk was after her. She did nothing to lead him on. I was just letting Kyle know that Veda's my woman and he better stay away from her."

Junior shot Bubba a sideways look full of disdain. Even after thirteen years, Junior does not approve of his brother's choice in women. Personally, I think Bubba could do a lot worse. Veda and I might not always get along anymore, but she was devoted to Bubba.

"Something you want to say, Junior?" I asked.

"Just that Veda probably did lead Kyle on."

Bubba grabbed Junior around the neck in a headlock. To break the hold, Junior launched his weight backwards and slammed Bubba into the wall. They were on the floor scrapping in a matter of seconds. I watched them duke it out until I realized that no one was coming from the other room to break them up. I grabbed the chair that Bubba had dismantled and brought it down on both of them. It was not the first time I'd done something along those lines. I didn't hit them hard enough to hurt them. I just wanted to remind them who was in charge.

Junior scrambled up. "She's all wrong for you, Bubba. When you gonna realize that?"

"Veda is the only thing in my life that's ever been right!" Bubba yelled as he punched Junior square in the face.

"Ouch!" Junior screamed as a trickle of blood ran out of his nose. He used his sleeve to wipe it away. "I think you broke my nose!"

"If you don't shut up, he'll do worse." I forced Junior into a chair and then scurried down the hallway to my office. After grabbing two tampons out of my desk, I ran back to the interrogation room and inserted the tampons up Junior's bloody nostrils. "There. That should stop the bleeding. Now talk."

The tampons distorted Junior's nose, and the strings kept getting caught in his mouth as he tried to talk. It would have been comical, but I'd had all I could take of him and Bubba.

"Veda told me about Kyle harassing her a few months ago. We weren't really talking, you know; but, when we did, I knew something was wrong," Bubba said. "I made her forward me the voicemails and some of the texts he sent her. You should have heard some of the crap he said to her. It was disgusting."

Chances were I'd heard some of the same things. "But Veda said Kyle stopped harassing her almost two months ago. Why did you attack him?"

"He was hassling my woman. Didn't matter to me that he'd stopped," Bubba said.

"Did Veda ask you to beat up Kyle?" I asked.

"Nope. That was my idea." Bubba beamed with pride.

"Spur-of-the-moment idea," Junior added, nudging his brother in the ribs. "We ran into Kyle by accident. And you know how Bubba is."

"You didn't try to stop him?" I asked.

"I would have, but there's no stopping Bubba when he's about to open a can of Whoop-Ass. I just tagged along to make sure things didn't get out of hand."

"You punched him, too," I pointed out. Standing up, I said, "Next time y'all do something stupid, just tell me, okay? Make all of our lives easier."

Leaving Junior and Bubba in the interrogation room, I joined Hardy in the hallway.

"I guess you were right," Hardy said.

"I told you so. I guess we better call her though. Just to make sure she didn't put Bubba up to it."

When Veda didn't answer her cell phone, I called the beauty parlor she worked at and asked the receptionist if I could speak to her. After a couple minutes wait, Veda came on the line.

"To what do I owe the pleasure?" Veda asked.

"Did you know that Bubba beat up Kyle Vance hours before he died?"

"So what? Bubba beats up a lot of people."

"Let me rephrase that. Did you know Bubba beat up Kyle to defend your honor?" My question was met with the sound of dial tone. Hanging up, I turned to Hardy and asked, "Are you done with my cousins, Sergeant Hardy? Because Junior probably needs to get his nose looked at. And Veda is on her way to see Bubba. You do not want to get in her way."

"No, I probably don't. I also never want to get in your way again," Hardy said. "And, yes, I'm done with your cousins. They can go."

I stuck my head into the interrogation room and told Junior and Bubba that they were free to go. I then had one of the deputies take Junior to the hospital while Bubba and I waited for Veda to show up. Five minutes after hanging up on me, Veda flew into the sheriff's department's small lobby. The receptionist buzzed her through the locked doors.

"Carrie told me you beat up Kyle for me," Veda said to Bubba, who was still hanging out in the interrogation room.

"Yeah, well … you know." Bubba shoved his hands into his pockets and shuffled his feet around. "It happens."

Veda, who looked so elated a minute before, deflated like a slow-leaking balloon.

"Would you two just kiss and make up?" I asked, shoving Veda towards Bubba.

Taking my advice, Veda grabbed the front of Bubba's sweatshirt and yanked his head down so she could kiss him. Backing out of the interrogation room, I shut the door behind me to give Veda and Bubba some privacy. I then turned around and bumped into Hardy.

"So … what do we do now?" I asked.

"There is no 'we,' remember? You are going home, where you will stay out of trouble and let me conduct my investigation. Now get out of here. I don't want to see you again."

Chapter Twenty

———————◆———————

"Carrie, I am fit to be tied. Are you trying to get us arrested? Or have you forgotten about family loyalty?"

I closed my eyes, leaned back in the armchair, and sighed. I should have known that Uncle Houston wasn't summoning me out to his farmhouse for anything good. He'd started calling me not long after I left the sheriff's department. Uncle Murph must have informed Houston that Sergeant Hardy had given me the boot.

I ignored Houston's first five or six calls, but, once he started alternately calling my landline and my cell phone, I finally answered. I cursed myself for having obeyed the order to report immediately to his house.

"What did I do this time?" I asked.

"You let that Ranger arrest my grandsons!" Houston shouted.

I glanced over to where Junior and Bubba were sitting side-by-side on Houston's couch. Bubba refused to make eye contact. And I couldn't see much of Junior's face around the bag of frozen corn that he held to his nose in an attempt to keep down the swelling.

Granddaddy and Uncle Bowie sat on the other side of the room. Bowie didn't look as angry as Houston, but I didn't have much hope he would come to my defense. Bowie, like the rest of the family, usually did whatever Houston told him to do. I knew—or at least hoped—Granddaddy would take my side. I didn't know what I would do if he turned against me when I was almost at rock bottom.

The six of us were holed up in Houston's Man-Cave on the second floor of the farmhouse. The men sat in a semi-circle around me, blocking my path to the door. And the glass eyes of numerous mounted animal heads looked down on me in silent judgment.

"Sergeant Hardy didn't arrest them," I said. "He brought them in for questioning."

"You still let it happen." Houston shook the finger of shame at me.

Since Houston blamed me for what happened, I figured I should deflect the blame to the actual guilty parties. "Perhaps if Junior and Bubba had told me about their encounter with Kyle at Exxon, it wouldn't have happened."

Houston opened and closed his mouth a few times. I assumed it was hard to come up with a response to my logic. I wasn't positive, but I didn't think Houston knew about the assault at the gas station prior to Junior and Bubba's trip to the sheriff's department.

"I tried to tell you, Carrie," Bubba said.

"You clearly didn't try hard enough." I turned to Junior and Bubba, and asked, "You two are aware that beating up someone is known as assault? It's against the law."

"Is it an assault if the jerk deserved it?" Bubba asked.

"Yes, Bubba."

"So you assaulted me earlier today when you beat me up?"

"Bubba, I wouldn't go around claiming that Carrie beat me up if I were you," Bowie said. "Makes you sound like a sissy."

Bubba hunkered down in the chair, his face bright red. "She didn't actually beat me up. She just got the drop on me, is all."

"Was it an assault when Bubba broke my nose?" Junior asked.

"That wasn't an assault." Bubba punched Junior in the arm. "I was defending my woman's honor."

Houston and Bowie both snorted.

"Leave the boy alone," Granddaddy said to his brothers. "You were trying to do the right thing, Bubba. You just went about it the wrong way."

Bubba nodded. "Damn straight."

"What about me? I may need to have surgery to fix my nose," Junior said.

Bubba shrugged. "Once the swelling goes down, you won't be any uglier than you were before."

Junior punched Bubba in the arm and then returned the frozen bag to his face.

"So, Uncle Houston, are the rumors about you opening a strip club true?" I asked. With everything else that had been going on, I'd forgotten to ask Houston whether or not what Oscar Palmer had told me was true.

"Strip club? How low are you going to sink, brother?" Granddaddy asked.

"Where'd you hear that, Carrie?" Houston asked.

"I heard it from a few people." Okay, the only person I heard it from was Oscar Palmer. "I looked into the records, Uncle Houston. I know you bought that empty building across the street from the Dancing Cowgirl."

"Yeah, I bought it. But I never said I'm going to open up a strip club in there. All I said is that I'm going to provide Wyatt County with another form of adult entertainment," Houston said.

"If it's not a strip club, what is it?" I asked.

"I'm opening an adult store," Houston said.

"Next time, don't pull the cloak-and-dagger crap," I said, debating whether I should laugh, cry, or kill Uncle Houston. I couldn't say I was thrilled that Houston was planning to open an adult store, but it was much better than a strip club. "Oscar Palmer thought you were going to cut into his territory. That's why he brought his family over to crash our party."

"That old coot is lucky I don't open up my own strip club. Maybe I can have a strip club in the adult store. That'd be a hoot!" Houston smirked at the idea. He then ordered Junior and Bubba to leave the room. Once they were gone, Houston turned to me and said, "I gave you two tasks, Carrie. And you've managed to fail at both of them."

"What are you talking about? What have I failed at?" I asked.

"One, I told you to get rid of the evidence connecting us to Kyle's murder."

"You also insisted that none of us killed Kyle, so why did you think there would even be any evidence? And how am I supposed to get rid of evidence when I didn't know if there was any? The evidence that implicated Dale was in the dumpster, concealed by Kyle's body. What was I supposed to do about that? Climb in the dumpster and check for evidence before I called the Department of Public Safety?"

"You shouldn't have called the DPS at all," Houston said. "What you and Murph should have done was get rid of the body. Then we wouldn't be having this problem."

"What were we supposed to do? Take Kyle out to the middle of the woods and bury him in a shallow grave? Then what? Obviously someone would have filed a missing person's report. The Palmers would have been looking for him. Besides, don't you want to know how Kyle wound up in the dumpster?"

Houston snorted. "You still could have looked into that without letting the whole world know that Kyle was dead."

"How was Carrie supposed to do that when she's covering up the fact that he was murdered?" Granddaddy asked.

"You could have pulled it off, Crockett," Houston said. "You covered up all sorts of crimes when you were the sheriff."

"None of which I'm proud of. And the only reason I did it was because our sister asked me to help keep you two pea brains out of jail," Granddaddy said.

Ignoring his brother, Houston berated me on how I allowed Hardy to see the security footage of Junior and Bubba beating up Kyle. Houston wasn't blaming me for not knowing about the fight, but he still thought I should have somehow prevented Hardy from seeing the footage. Houston couldn't wrap his head around why Hardy needed to see the security footage of Kyle in the first place. I tried to explain that we were still trying to determine when Kyle was killed, but Houston cut me off to lecture me about how I was supposed to be helping the family, not helping the Ranger figure out who killed Kyle.

"I was helping the family by helping Sergeant Hardy. Until we figure out who killed Kyle, where they killed him, and how he wound up in the dumpster, the Palmers, and other people, are going to think that we're the ones that killed him. It won't matter to them that the evidence says otherwise," I said.

Granddaddy and Uncle Bowie tried to back me up, but Houston didn't want to listen to them either.

"Your other task was getting friendly with the Ranger, but you messed that up too, didn't you? Murph called earlier and told me about the fight you had with the Ranger. From what I hear, the Ranger doesn't want anything to do with you." Houston pounded his fists onto the arms of his recliner. "All you had to do was get the Ranger into your bed, but you couldn't even do that."

"Are you kidding me?" I asked. "You told me to flirt with him."

"What I meant was that you should sleep with him. We need that man on our side. Not just now, but period. You were supposed to take care of that," Houston said.

"I … I … " I sputtered, too shocked and enraged to form words.

"That's my granddaughter you're talking to." Granddaddy pushed himself out of the recliner, leaned over, and punched Houston across the face. "How dare you say that to her?"

Houston kicked out at Granddaddy, almost knocking him over. Jumping up, Bowie tried to break up his older brothers. Junior and Bubba, who must have been lurking outside the door, ran in and dragged Houston and Granddaddy to opposite corners of the room.

"You know what, I'm sick of this. I'm out of here," I said.

I was halfway to the door when Houston said, "You need to fix this, Carrie. And if that means going to bed with the Ranger, then you damn well better do it. Because, if you don't, I'll find one of your cousins who will."

I could only take so much. I turned around and yelled, "You know what, Uncle Houston? I am so sick and tired of all this shit! Do you even consider that you're breaking the law? Or do you think that the laws don't apply to you? You make moonshine, grow pot, and do God knows what else, but do you even think about it? And have you ever considered how I feel about covering it up?"

"It's your job to cover it up," Houston said.

"Not because I have to, or even want to. I do it because your sister asked me." Three-and-a-half-years ago, right after she found out she had cancer, Aunt Emily Morgan begged me to come home from Nashville and try to help Uncle Murph keep the Shatner family's criminal misdeeds under wraps. Aunt Emily Morgan had reigned over the family for years—keeping everyone in line because they were afraid of her. With her soon to be out of the picture, she knew that her older brother, Houston, would take control and loosen the reigns. She knew that things were about to get ugly for the family, and she needed me to help keep things under control. Emily Morgan then manipulated Houston into thinking it was all his idea. But, had I known what my job would entail, I would have thought long and hard before I accepted it. "Aunt Emily Morgan begged me to come home and go to work at the sheriff's department because she knew you aren't half as smart as she was. She knew you would run this family into the ground and wind up getting everyone sent to jail. My job is to keep you from doing that. And I'm done."

"What are you saying?" Houston asked.

"I'm saying that I don't take orders from you. You want to break the law, fine, go ahead. But don't drag me into it any more. Good luck finding someone to replace me." I made my way to the door. I needed to get out of the room and away from Houston before I really snapped. "But you'll have plenty of time to think about that while sitting in a jail cell."

"You've gone back on your raising, Carrie."

"It's my life, Houston. Stay out of it."

"Carrie, where are you going?" Granddaddy asked.

"To find someone I can trust."

THE QUESTION WAS WHO COULD I trust?

As I sped away from Houston's house, I blew past the Shady Grove Baptist cemetery and then pulled into the nearly empty parking lot of the Roadhouse Motel. The motel was rundown, and no one stayed there if they could help it. It used to be a hot-sheets motel. And, I suspected, that for the right price, it still was. The only times I'd graced the Roadhouse with my presence was when one of my male family members was caught with his pants down—literally and figuratively—and needed me to bail him out.

I parked sideways next to a black truck. It took me a minute or two of deep breathing before it hit me that the truck was Hardy's. Instead of heading back to his place in Tyler like he had the past few nights, it appeared Hardy had decided to spend the night in Wyatt County.

Despite the fact that I already apologized to Hardy back at the sheriff's department, I felt like I should apologize again. But what were my reasons for apologizing? Did I just want Hardy to know that I was sorry for the way I had acted? Or did my reasons go deeper than that? Did I want to fix things between us? Was there anything between us?

There was only one way to find out.

Inside the motel's front office, I woke up the night clerk. I had to flash my badge before he would give me Hardy's room number.

Back outside, I ran up the steps to the second floor. I was just about to knock on Hardy's room door, but stopped just short of doing it. I let my arm fall and then pressed my forehead against the door. I was worried that, if I went inside Hardy's room and confront him, I might tell him things about myself and my family that he did not need to know about. If the Shatners' ship was sinking, I didn't want to be the one to torpedo it.

Despite serious misgivings, I pounded on the motel room door. Seconds later, the lights flashed on and the curtains were whipped aside. When Hardy glanced out the window, I gave him a little wave. Hardy let the curtains fall back into place, and then he opened the door.

Hardy stood before me barefoot and shirtless. For a few seconds, all I could do was stare at him. The man was ripped. Hardy's arms were muscular, but not overly so. And his upper right arm, from shoulder to elbow, was covered in a tattoo. The tattoo was in the shape of Texas, and filled in with the state flag. Around the state, there were bluebonnets and yellow roses, an armadillo, cowboy boots, a longhorn, and The Alamo. And that's just what I could see. I'll admit that I had a weakness for men with tattoos, and Hardy had some very nice ink.

Hardy also had abs—eight of them. I took the time to count. Dragging my eyes away from the strip of dark hair that disappeared into the top of Hardy's low-slung plaid pajama bottoms, I tried to ignore the carnal thoughts running through my mind and forced myself to look Hardy in the eye.

"I know you said you never wanted to see me again, but—"

"You want to come in?"

Lead me not into temptation. "Yes."

I stepped inside and glanced around the room. Strips of wallpaper were missing from the walls, the furniture was held together by duct tape, and the bedspread was so faded it was hard to tell what color it had originally been.

I plopped down on the edge of the queen-sized bed while Hardy shut the door. With his back to me, I could see that he also had a tattoo on his upper back—a lion's head. The lion had a football in its mouth. The numbers 12 and 21 were tattooed on either side of the lion's head. I wondered if he got the tattoo before or after Josh died.

"You got any more tattoos?" I asked.

"I'll show you mine if you show me yours."

If Hardy had any more tattoos, I was willing to search for them. Even if he didn't have any more, I was still willing to look at the rest of his body.

"I'd have to take my clothes off to show you where mine are," I said.

"Go right ahead. I don't mind." Hardy smiled at me. He then grabbed a t-shirt out of his duffle bag and put it on. "Depending on where this situation is going, I'm either not wearing enough or you are wearing too much. What are you doing here anyway?"

"I don't know." I wanted to breakdown and cry, but I didn't want to do that in front of Hardy. "I can't do this anymore, Jerrod."

"Do what?" Hardy sat down beside me and pulled my hands away from my face.

"Any of this. I don't think I can deal with my family anymore. I love them, but ... I don't know. I just can't be part of this any longer."

"Are you trying to tell me something?"

"No. I'm not confessing to anything." I pressed my forehead against Hardy's shoulder and fought back tears. "I just had a fight with Uncle Houston and we both said some nasty things. I then told him I was going to find someone I could trust and ran out of his house. I was driving home and I pulled in here to calm down. That's when I saw your truck and ... I don't know what I was thinking. I should leave."

"No, you should stay."

I tried to move away from him, but Hardy put his arms around me and pulled me against him. Hardy's lips were brushing against mine when a knock on the door drove us apart. Hardy got up and yanked the door open without checking to see who was on the other side. I just barely caught a glimpse of Chief Isaac Yates before Hardy tried to close the door.

"What is she doing here?" Yates asked. Kicking the door open, Yates shoved Hardy aside and rushed into the room. "What are you doing here, you little slut?"

"Don't talk to her like that," Hardy said.

"And don't you defend her." Yates smacked Hardy on the chest. "Don't you see what she's doing? She's here to seduce you. Houston probably told her to sleep with you to keep you distracted while the sheriff cleans up after whichever Shatner killed Kyle."

"You have no idea what you're talking about, Chief Yates," I said. The saying was that great minds think alike. But, in the case of Uncle Houston and Chief Yates, it was more like small minds think alike. "I was just leaving."

Hardy tried to stop me, but I pulled away from him and walked out of the motel room. After slamming the door shut behind me, I ran down the steps to my Jeep and then tore out of the parking lot on two wheels. On the drive home, I wondered what Yates was doing at the motel. How had Yates known Hardy was at the Roadhouse? Had Hardy changed his mind and invited Yates to help with the investigation? Or was Yates only there to annoy Hardy?

When I got home, I turned on an episode of pro wrestling from earlier that evening. Molly and I curled up on opposite ends of the couch to watch all of the hot, sweaty men in speedos.

"You know, Molly, no matter how hard my days are. No matter what unethical and immoral things I've had to do. No matter how confused or angry I am. There is almost always pro wrestling to come home to each night."

I was going to be okay.

Chapter Twenty-One

———◆———

I'm ashamed to admit it, but I fell asleep watching wrestling. A deep, dreamless sleep that would have made up for the past few sleepless nights had someone not rudely awoken me by grasping my shoulder and instructing me not to scream.

I screamed.

With my heart racing like a jackrabbit on speed, I thrashed around blindly and took a swing at the intruder.

"Ouch!" The person grunted when my fist connected with his stomach. "Would you calm down?"

"Uncle Murph?" Shoving him away from the couch, I pushed myself up into a sitting position. "Haven't you ever heard of knocking?"

"I did knock. You didn't answer."

"So you just broke in?" Turning on the floor lamp next to the couch, I bathed my living room in a blinding, bright light. Squinting, I eyed up Molly. She lay curled up at the other end of the couch. Her wagging tail thumped against the cushions. "Some guard dog you are. I could be getting murdered in my sleep and you wouldn't even bark."

"Maybe you should try turning on your alarm system," Murph said.

"Shut up." With my eyes finally adjusted to the light, I glanced around the room and took in the muddy footprints all over my wood floor and area rug. Murph's boots and the cuffs of his jeans were also coated in a thick layer of drying mud. "Look what you did to my floor! You're cleaning that up."

"No time." Murph pulled me off the couch. "We're having a family emergency."

"Every day is an emergency when you have a family like ours," I said.

"What did they do this time? Or is this related to Kyle getting killed?"

"I don't know if it has to do with Kyle or not." Murph practically picked me up and carried me towards the front door. "Wes and Waylon done got themselves stabbed. We need to get to the ER."

"What? Put me down. Before we go running out of here, I need shoes and an explanation." Wes and Waylon were two of Uncle Bowie's grandsons. They were also two of the biggest troublemakers in the younger generation of Shatners. Neither of them seemed to have any desire to be upstanding, contributing members of society.

At twenty-one, Wes already had three children by two different women. Lately I'd been hearing rumors that he'd gotten another girl pregnant. As for Waylon, last year when he was a senior in high school, he got caught smoking a joint in the school's parking lot. He wound up getting expelled less than two months before graduation.

"Grab some shoes. I'll explain in the car." Murph dropped me next to the front door. "We ain't got time to waste."

I kept a pair of old shoes next to the front door. While shoving my feet into them, I reached into the hall closet and grabbed the first coat I laid my hands on. It was one of Andrew's. I tried to swap it for one of mine, but Murph scooped me up and carried me out the front door.

"What happened to Wes and Waylon? How bad are they hurt? Who assaulted them?"

"I honestly don't know," Murph said. "A nurse called me and said the boys were admitted to the ER with stab wounds. She didn't tell me what condition they're in. She did say that Waylon drove them there. So he can't be too bad."

Going twice the speed limit, and blowing through stop lights and signs, we made it to the hospital in just under twenty minutes. Not wasting time to park in one of the many empty spots in the hospital parking lot, Murph parked his car on the sidewalk outside the Emergency Room.

Racing inside, we found that the Emergency Room had been taken over by Shatners. Uncle Bowie and his youngest son, Woodrow, were at the nurse's station, yelling over each other as they demanded answers from the frazzled looking nurse. Murph rushed over and joined his father and brother. With a third person screaming at her, the poor nurse broke down in tears.

Great-Aunt Imogen, who was wearing a voluminous plaid nightgown and had curlers the size of Coke cans in her gray hair, was on her knees in the middle of the waiting room. She was loudly bargaining with God, and praying that He spare her grandchildren and take her instead. Woody's wife, Deidra, lay on the floor near her mother-in-law. She was screaming incoherently and yanking at her cinnamon-colored hair. From what I could make out, she was convinced that her two oldest children were near death. Sitting on either side of Deidra were her two youngest children. Twelve-year-old Wade was engrossed in a video game while ten-year-old Willow was studying her mother as if she was a science fair project. I was almost as concerned about those two as I was about their older brothers.

I wandered around the waiting room, searching for someone sane who I could talk to, when Uncle Woody's middle child, Wynonna, popped up next to me. At sixteen, Wynonna was my shining hope for the younger generation of Shatners. She had never been in trouble and had done an excellent job of distancing herself from the family's crimes. Wynonna was also the only one of Woody's and Deidra's children not to genetically inherit her mother's red hair. Instead, Wynonna got her father's ash brown hair.

"Ohmigod, am I glad to see you." Wynonna gave me a quick hug. "Everybody is losing their freaking mind."

"You have any idea what's going on?" I asked.

"Nope. I've been trying to stay out of it."

Forcing our way to the nurse's station, I commanded Murph, Bowie, and Woody to calm down. While Wynonna led her dad and grandpa away from the desk, I yanked Murph's sheriff's badge off of his coat and held it in front of the nurse's tearstained face.

"We're here to see Wesley and Waylon Shatner. Just point the way."

The nurse raised a shaking arm and pointed towards the double doors into the Emergency Room. "They're back that way. But you can't just go back there. Even if you are with the sheriff's department."

"Lady, do you have any idea who you're talking to?" Wynonna asked, rejoining me at the desk. "This is Detective Carrie Shatner. You don't tell her what to do. She does what she wants."

"Thank you, Wynonna." Leaning across the desk, I whispered, "I know I can't just go barging back there. But that's exactly what I'm going to do. And neither you nor anyone else in this place is going to stop me. Got it."

The nurse removed her hand from under the desk. "I already pushed the security alarm. The guards should be here any second."

"There's plenty for them to deal with," I said, pointing over my shoulder at the circus behind me. Uncle Bowie was on the phone, screaming at whoever was on the other end. Aunt Imogen gave up on praying to God and was trying to make a deal with the Devil. And Uncle Woody had joined Aunt Deidra in hysterically crying while rolling around on the floor. "Just don't send them after me."

Ordering the rest of the family to remain in the waiting room, I grabbed Murph and Wynonna, and shoved them through the double doors. "How are the two of you related to those nutcases? Not that either of you are exactly normal."

"Woody always was a bit touched in the head," Murph said.

"You're related to them, too, Carrie," Wynonna pointed out. "And you aren't all that normal either."

At one in the morning, the Emergency Room was a ghost town. There was only one other person besides my cousins being treated.

"So, yeah, this huge, tatted up dude was going at my brother with a hunting knife. So I threw myself in front of Waylon. That's how I got stabbed in the shoulder," Wes said.

"No it's not," Waylon said.

"Shut up, Waylon."

Poking my head around the privacy curtain, I found Wes and Waylon sitting side-by-side on an exam table. Wes, who was shirtless, flexed his scrawny muscles for the pretty, young nurse. She didn't appear to be interested in him. Wes had a bandage wrapped around his shoulder, and there were other bandages on his arms and a large Band-Aid stuck to his stomach. Waylon, who was wearing boxers and a grimy tank top, had a bandage on his arm and another around his left hand.

"How are they, doctor?" I asked the middle-aged doctor who was busy stitching up a small cut on Waylon's thigh. "Will they live?"

"They're fine." The doctor put the last stitch in Waylon's leg and then wrapped it with a bandage. "Everything is superficial except the stab wound to Wesley's shoulder."

"I could have died," Wes said.

"No, you would not have died," the doctor said. "Even if you hadn't sought treatment, you would have been fine. The knife didn't hit anything vital, and you hardly lost any blood."

"It was a huge freaking knife." Wes held his hands a foot apart to show us how large the knife supposedly was. "Tell 'em, Waylon."

"It was a tiny pocket knife," Waylon said. "It barely scratched us."

"Can you give him something, doc? He's out of his mind with pain," Wes said.

"No I'm not," Waylon said.

The doctor finished bandaging Waylon's leg, instructed the boys to keep their wounds clean, and then strode off.

"Either of you want to tell me what happened?" Murph asked.

"Like I was saying, some huge dude with a hunting knife came at us for no reason. It was a total assault," Wes said.

"It was an average sized guy with a pocket knife," Waylon said. "But it was an assault."

"Would you let me tell the story?" Wes smacked Waylon on the leg, bringing his hand down directly onto his brother's stab wound.

"I would if you would tell it right." Waylon punched Wes in the arm, hitting him in the middle of a bandage.

"OW! You little brat!"

Wes and Waylon went after each other, prompting Murph to jump between them to push them apart. While Murph handled Wes, Wynonna and I grabbed Waylon and pulled him away from the exam table that the brothers had been seated on.

"One of you better tell me what happened. And I want the truth," I said.

Wes and Waylon settled down and exchanged a look.

"It was nothing, Carrie," Wes said. "Nothing for anyone to be concerned about. Not even worth mentioning. Right, Waylon?"

"Yeah. Totally," Waylon said.

"We'll just be heading home now," Wes said.

"You ain't going anywhere," Murph said. "Not until you tell us what happened."

"Like I said, it was nothing," Wes said.

"Just a misunderstanding," Waylon added.

"What are you boys hiding," I asked. "Oh, wait, let me guess. You're selling pot for Uncle Houston and your grandpa again. After you swore you'd never do it again after the last time I busted you for it."

"I swore I'd stop selling it at the bowling alley," Wes said. "I never promised to stop completely."

Next to me, Wynonna's petite body started to shake. I reached for her, about to ask if she was okay, when she unleashed a primal scream and then threw herself at Wes. Her body collided with his, knocking him off of the exam table. Scrambling over the table, I found Wynonna straddling Wes on the floor. She'd already landed one solid blow to his injured shoulder. She was drawing back for another one when I grabbed her arm and yanked her to her feet. Pulling Wynonna away from her brothers, I shoved her into a chair and told her to calm down.

Murph and Waylon moved to help up the sniffling Wes. They'd just helped him back to his feet when I walked up and slapped him across the face. Just so Waylon didn't feel left out, I gave him a smack as well.

"Where are you selling it at this time?" I asked. "And don't you dare lie to me!"

"Carrie, leave the boys alone," Murph said.

"What? You know about this, don't you? You know where they're selling at?"

"And I've got it handled," Murph said.

"You mean you're covering it up and protecting them?"

"I said it's handled!" Murph guided the brothers back to the exam table and instructed them to sit down. "Does the stabbing have anything to do with ... you know?"

"Yes and no," Wes said. "We weren't at ... you know. And it didn't involve ... the green stuff. But product was being exchanged."

"You're running moonshine, too? Since when?" I asked.

"Since Cousin Randy went to jail. But we ain't gonna make his mistake. We aren't running it across state lines," Waylon said. "We won't even take it across county lines."

Wynonna tried to launch herself at her brothers a second time, but I caught her midair and hugged her tightly to my side.

"Let me at them!" Wynonna screamed. "After I'm done with them, they're going to be coming right back here. This just saves everyone a trip."

"Cool it, sweetheart. If they want to ruin their lives, let them. Just take care of your own," I said.

"You're one to talk." Wynonna jammed her elbow into my side, forcing me to let go. Instead of going after her brothers, she placed her hands over their knees and whispered, "I'm done with both of you."

"Good choice," I said to Wynonna. "Now, boys, what happened tonight?"

"We were ... making a personal delivery," Wes said. "We've done it a bunch of times before without problem. Everything was going fine at ... the location ... until the nutcase with the knife wandered out the back door of the ... building. He saw us and came at us with the hunting knife."

"Pocket knife," Waylon said.

"It was a knife! Does it really matter what kind of knife?"

"Yes," Murph and I said in unison.

"Okay, officially it was a pocket knife. But I'm going to tell everyone it was a hunting knife," Wes said.

"I don't care what fictional story you tell people. All I ask is that you tell me the truth. Who stabbed you?" I asked.

"Nate Palmer. He came at us like a madman; screaming at us about avenging Kyle's death. He stuck the knife in Wes's shoulder before we even had time to react," Waylon said.

"And it freaking hurt," Wes said, tenderly rubbing his injured shoulder. "We got the rest of the cuts trying to wrestle the knife away from him. Luckily our customers were there to help us out. Once they got Nate away from us, we jumped in the car, and Waylon drove us here."

After forcing them to give us some more details, Murph and I left Wynonna to further chastise her brothers. Meanwhile, we slipped out a side door and headed down the sidewalk to Murph's car.

"Which one is Nate Palmer?" Murph asked.

"He's the one who got busted for drug possession last month. He's out on bond awaiting trial," I said. "He's also one of the Palmers that was at the club and then crashed our party."

Nate was one of Omar Palmer's grandchildren. Omar was Oscar's younger brother. He was heavily involved in the Palmer's crimes, and wound up going to jail for one of them. Omar died in prison a few years ago. As for Nate, he was a year ahead of me in high school. While I coexisted alongside other Palmers, Nate was the one who I went out of my way to avoid. Most of the student body tried to avoid him unless they were buying drugs off him. Nate was constantly starting fights and beating up other kids. After getting suspended at least a dozen times, the school finally expelled him. He then had a brief stint at a military school, before he wound up getting sent to a juvenile detention center. He has been in and out of prison since then.

Murph put the cruiser in drive and pulled off of the sidewalk. "Let's go find the little bastard and see what he has to say for himself."

With the help of our night dispatcher, we were able to locate Nate Palmer's current address in a neighborhood on the southern side of Holler. Without informing the Holler Police Department that we were invading their territory, we rolled up to Nate's small house.

"I'll take the front." Murph handed me his backup piece. "You get the back."

"I hate covering the back door. Why can't you do it?"

"Because I have the front door."

"Fine." As I picked my way around to the back of the house, I heard sounds coming from inside that indicated Nate was still awake and that he was not alone.

I'd only gotten to the back door when I heard Murph pound on the front door and demand that Nate come outside.

Seconds later, a naked Nate Palmer barreled out the back door. In the dark, Nate didn't see me standing just outside the door. Before he blew past me, I stuck my arm out and caught him across the chest. It was a move that pro wrestlers call a clothesline. My friend, Red Devereux, taught me the move many years ago, and I'd used it on multiple occasions while apprehending suspects. The clothesline didn't take Nate down, but it slowed him down enough for me to jump on his back and tackle him to the ground. Plopping down on Nate's back, I pressed the gun to his head.

"I don't appreciate that you stabbed two of my cousins," I said.

"They deserved it."

"And you deserve this." Murph walked up to Nate and kicked him in the ribs. "Let's flip him over and get him cuffed."

Murph had just gotten the handcuffs on Nate when Nate's half-dressed female companion stomped out the back door and threw a pair of sweatpants at me.

"Hi, Sparkles," I said.

"Screw you!" Sparkles hurled a pair of sneakers at my head and retreated back into the house, slamming the door behind her.

"Your girlfriend?" I asked Nate.

"No! She's just a piece of ass," Nate said.

"Aren't you charming?" I asked.

After helping Nate into the sweatpants and sneakers, Murph and I hustled him around to the front of the house and into the cruiser. We had to get out of the area before Sparkles had a chance to let the Palmers or the Holler police know what was going on.

On the drive north towards the center of Holler, Nate kept up a verbal barrage of insults and threats directed towards me, Murph, and the entire Shatner family. I wanted to pull over to gag Nate, but Murph didn't want to waste the time.

"Uh, Uncle Murph, you passed the department." Squirming around, I watched the sheriff's department slowly shrink as we sped away from it.

"I know," Murph said.

"Where are you taking me?" Nate asked. "This is a kidnapping."

"No, it's not. He came willingly, didn't he, Carrie?" Murph asked me.

"We were never going to the department, were we?" I asked.

"Nope," Murph said.

"Let me out of the car. I don't know what you think you're doing, but I don't want any part of it," I said.

"I want out, too!" Nate yelled in my ear. "Take me with you."

"You're not going anywhere, Nate," Murph said.

"Pull over up there," I said, pointing at the Roadhouse Motel's dimly lit parking lot. "I'll use the office phone to call Andrew. He can come pick me up."

"Sorry, Carrie, but I can't do that. You're too far in this now," Murph said.

"I don't want to be part of this!" I yelled. "Let me out of the car!"

Since there weren't any other cars on the road, I reached over and grabbed the steering wheel. I jerked the wheel to the right, and the cruiser veered off the road. The tires on the right side of the cruiser spun on the damp grass and Murph fought to get the car under control.

"All right, all right. Just don't do that again," Murph said as he pulled into the Roadhouse Motel's parking lot. As he spun the cruiser around in the parking lot, the headlights flashed over Hardy's black truck. Murph slammed on the brakes. "That's Sergeant Hardy's truck. Did you know he was staying here?"

"How would I know what Sergeant Hardy is doing? You know he doesn't want anything to do with me after what I did earlier," I said.

I mentally cursed Hardy for leaving his truck parked under an overhead light in the middle of the nearly empty lot. Had he parked in the shadows, Murph might not have seen the truck and realized that Hardy was at the motel. Now that Murph knew Hardy was at the motel, there was no chance he would willingly leave me there. I grabbed the door handle just as Murph gunned the engine and tore out of the lot.

"Damn it, Uncle Murph! Let me out! I don't know what you're doing, but I don't want any part of it!"

"Whether you knew Sergeant Hardy was there or not, I can't leave you at the motel. I can't risk you ratting me out for this," Murph snapped. "Face it, Carrie, you're part of this now."

That far north of town, there was no question that we were headed to somewhere on the Shatner land. Over the years, I'd heard bits and pieces of stories concerning some of the things that Granddaddy, Dad, and Uncle Murph did to unfortunate people out on the more isolated parts of the property. They never put anyone into a shallow grave, but what they did was nothing to be proud of. Arriving at the Shatner's Alpaca Farm and Wild West Town, Murph rattled over the cattle guards and entered the pasture land.

The Alpaca Farm was home to a small herd of longhorn cattle, two zebras, three camels, a few emus and llamas, and close to a hundred alpacas. As Murph drove through the pasture, the alpacas mistook Murph's car for the feed truck and rushed out of the darkness. They ran alongside the car as Murph drove down the dirt road. He tried blowing the horn to scare them off, but that only seemed to attract more of them. Don't get me wrong, I loved the alpacas and thought they were adorable, but there was something sinister about them surrounding the car like that. And I didn't like the looks some of them were giving us.

By the time we made it to the other side of the pasture, the alpacas lost interest in us and went off to do whatever it was alpacas did in the middle of the night.

Murph pulled up next to an old, rundown shack almost hidden by a small group of trees. During the Halloween season, when the ranch was turned into a massive haunted attraction, the hayride passed by the shack. For the last few years, the shack had been used as the cannibalistic hillbilly family's cabin. As the hayride approached, the hillbillies barreled out waving their shotguns and yelling incoherently. There were hacked up dummies lying around to portray their earlier victims. I'd heard from visitors that it was the scariest part of the ride.

I almost screamed with the shack's door swung open and Houston stepped outside. At least he wasn't waving around a shotgun.

"Uncle Murph, what are we doing here?" I asked.

"You, me, and Uncle Houston are going to have a chat with our new friend, Nate."

"I ain't got nothing to say to you psychos." Nate slammed both of his feet into the back of my seat. "I want a lawyer!"

Houston and Murph dragged Nate out of the back of the car and hauled him into the shack. The shack was lit up by a couple lanterns that hung on the walls. I scurried into the shack, trying to come up with a plan to get Nate out of there before things went downhill. He needed to be punished for stabbing Wes and Waylon, but this was not the punishment I had in mind.

"Come on, Uncle Murph, we can't do this. Let's take Nate back to the department and talk to him about the stabbing," I said.

"I'm with her. Go ahead and charge me with assault. I'll admit to stabbing both of those idiots," Nate said.

"We're not the kind of people who press charges." Houston picked up a bag off the floor and pulled out a set of jumper cables. "We take care of things our own way."

"We'd also like to talk to you about New Year's Eve. You look like the kind of man who would lie to the police. I bet you know something you didn't tell them. But I can make you tell me," Murph said before he took one end of the jumper cables and left the shack.

"All right, Uncle Houston, you boys have had your fun," I said, trying to hide the fact that I was terrified over what Houston and Murph were about to do. Houston and Murph did not have a simple chat with Nate in mind—had they wanted that, Murph and I could have done that at the sheriff's department. They were going to cross the line in getting answers out of Nate. And I was not about to stand back and watch. "Put the jumper cables down, and let Nate go."

"Shut your mouth." Houston gave me a warning look over his shoulder before turning to face Nate. "Are we going to do this the easy way or the hard way?"

"I'm not telling you anything," Nate said.

Houston shrugged and stuck a ball gag in Nate's mouth. He then pulled on a pair of rubber gloves and yelled at Murph to get ready.

"You can't do this," I said, trying to step between Houston and Nate. Houston pushed me out of the way. I stumbled and tripped over a rut in the wood floor that sent me sprawling. I hit the ground with a thud. "You could kill him!"

A twelve-volt car battery didn't have the power to kill a person, but it could give them a very nasty shock. Even with the truck running, the voltage could only get up to about fourteen volts. Still not enough to electrocute a man, but it could disrupt Nate's heart rhythm and kill him that way. Or Nate could choke on the ball gag.

"This ain't my first rodeo," Houston said. "And I ain't killed anyone yet."

"That's hardly reassuring," I snapped. I pushed myself up off the ground and dove at Houston. Colliding with my great-uncle, I tackled him and knocked him to the ground. The jumper cables flew out of Houston's hands and he braced for impact. "When I said you can't do this, I meant you are not doing it!"

"God damn it, Carrie! Uncle Houston is almost eighty-six. You could have broke his hip or something." Murph grabbed the back of my coat and pulled me off of Houston. He then helped Houston to his feet and dusted him off. "You all right, Uncle Houston?"

"I'm fine. But get Carrie out of here. If she won't help us, I don't want her here," Houston said.

"I don't want to be here either." I still had the handgun that Uncle Murph gave me at Nate's house. I pulled it out of my coat pocket and pointed it at Houston and Murph. "But the only people leaving are you two."

"Put the gun down, Carrie," Houston said. "We all know you ain't gonna pull the trigger."

I pulled the trigger, firing a bullet into the floorboards between Houston's feet. "You want answers? I'll get your answers. But we're doing it my way. And my way doesn't involve shocking people with car batteries or any other form of torture."

"You've got five minutes, Carrie. If you can't get Nate to talk in that time, then Uncle Houston and I get to do things our way," Murph said as he helped Houston limp out of the shack.

"Now that Nate knows what you two are capable of, I'm sure he'll tell me everything I want to know." I kicked the shack's flimsy wooden door shut and then turned to face Nate. After removing the ball gag from his mouth, I worked at the knot that bound his arms behind the chair. "I should probably apologize for my uncles, but you really shouldn't have stabbed my cousins."

"I wouldn't have stabbed them if your family hadn't made a sacrifice of Kyle."

I couldn't help myself; I started to laugh. "Yes, that's exactly what happened. We sacrificed Kyle to appease our god. His life bought us another year of getting away with all of our crimes."

"I don't think any god would put that much value on Kyle's worthless life."

"You weren't one of Kyle's fans?" I asked.

"I hated him."

"Nate, this might be your lucky day. If you tell me about what really happened on New Year's Eve, I'll forget that you stabbed my cousins."

"How do you know we haven't been telling you the truth?" Nate asked.

"Because y'all are a bunch of liars." Freeing Nate from the ropes that bound him to the chair, I helped him stand up. "And something just isn't adding up. No one in my family claims to have seen Kyle at the fairgrounds. But twenty-one of your relatives swear that Kyle was there. You're one of those twenty-one. How about you be the one that tells the truth?"

"You'll let me go? Free and clear?"

"Like it never happened."

"I'll take the deal." Nate leaned closer, his nose almost touching mine. "I don't know how Kyle wound up at the fairgrounds, but he didn't go there with us. The truth is that Kyle was never at our party."

Chapter Twenty-Two

———◆———

"**W**hat's going on over there, Juan?" I asked Chief Deputy Quaranta when I found him standing at the edge of the parking lot behind the sheriff's department. Across the street, the Holler police had the entire block around You Wreck 'Em, We Fix 'Em Paint and Body Shop roped off with caution tape. There was a garbage truck parked in the nearly empty back parking lot, and the front parking lot was full of the cars and trucks that the mechanics were working on. A handful of the Holler police were crowded around the auto repair shop's dumpster, and there were another half dozen officers running in and out of the building. Chief Yates was standing in the middle of the parking lot, shouting instructions at his officers. "I haven't seen Chief Yates work this hard in … well, ever. I mean, aside from when he's coming after my family."

"I only just got here a few minutes ago," Quaranta said as he stroked his Fu Manchu mustache. "But one of the deputies working the night shift told me that the garbage men found a body in the dumpster behind the shop about three hours ago. The Holler police have been processing the scene all morning."

"Another dead body in a dumpster? You think there's a serial killer in the area?" I asked. On average there were only two or three homicides per year in Wyatt County. Two homicides within the first week of the year was disconcerting. It was also a bad omen for the rest of the year. "Or is this just a coincidence?"

"I don't believe in coincidences. And as for a serial killer … I would need more information about what's going on over there before I can make any assumptions about there being a serial killer," Quaranta said.

"Then let's go get some information." I glanced both ways and then stepped out into the street. The Holler police had the streets on all four sides of the You Wreck 'Em, We Fix 'Em cordoned off, and the officers were directing traffic away from the crime scene. Instead of acting as a deterrent, the officers and the crime scene tape were attracting rubberneckers—both in cars and on foot.

"What are you doing, Carrie?" Quaranta asked as he hustled across the street after me. "You can't just go barging into the Holler police's crime scene."

"Why not? They crashed my crime scene on New Year's Eve. And Chief Yates tried to take over. All I'm looking for is some information about what's going on one block over from our department. I think we have a right to know." I stepped up onto the sidewalk and then smiled at the Holler officer guarding the crime scene tape. He frowned in response. "What's going on over here?"

"None of your business is what's going on, Detective Shatner," snapped the officer. "Why don't you head back across the street and leave us alone?"

Ignoring the officer, I glanced around the auto repair shop's parking lot. I spotted a man in a familiar white Stetson walk out of the building through one of the open garage bays. Waving my arms around to get his attention, I shouted, "Sergeant Hardy!"

Hardy jogged over. "I was just about to call and ask you to get over here."

"What's going on?" I asked.

Hardy held up the crime scene tape and gestured for me and Quaranta to step under it. He then yanked the crime scene log out of the Holler officer's hands. While Quaranta wrote our names down in the crime scene log, Hardy drew me aside.

"The garbage men came by just after five this morning. They were hooking the truck up to the dumpster when one of them spotted an arm sticking out from under one of the lids," Hardy said. "The victim has been IDed as Amanda Booker. She's your cousin Dale's ex-girlfriend."

"You mean the woman who dumped him on New Year's Eve?" I whispered back.

Hardy nodded. "It looks like she's been dead for a few days."

And her body was in the dumpster behind where Dale worked. "Did you tell Chief Yates about the victim's connection to Dale?"

"Nope. I haven't officially been brought into the investigation so it's Chief Yate's job to investigate and figure things out."

"Yeah, except as soon as he finds out that Dale was dating his victim, he's going to decide Dale killed her and stuffed her body in the dumpster, and that will be it."

"You don't find it suspicious that Dale's ex-girlfriend's body is in the dumpster behind where he works?" Hardy asked.

"I find it extremely suspicious."

"There are a few things about the crime scene that just seem off. Starting with the victim's body being found on top of the garbage bags. According to the shop's owner, he and one of the mechanics finished filling up the dumpster last night before they closed up. Considering the victim has been dead for a couple days, that means her body was dumped sometime between five o'clock last night and five o'clock this morning. Just in time for the garbage men to collect the trash and haul it away," Hardy said as he led me and Quaranta over to the crime scene. The body had been removed from the dumpster, and a couple officers were working on the garbage bags. The victim's body was currently lying on a sheet in the parking lot while two of the officers processed her for evidence. "I'd really like your opinion on this, Carrie. I want to see if the same things jump out at you."

"What are they doing here?" Chief Yates shouted when he saw me and Quaranta invading his crime scene. "Get out of my crime scene!"

"I asked Detective Shatner and Chief Deputy Quaranta to come over and take a look at the crime scene," Hardy said.

"What? Why would you do that?" Yates asked.

"Because I would like their opinions. Detective Shatner has far more experience with crime scenes than any of your officers. And Chief Deputy Quaranta has worked on more murder cases than almost everyone in your department," Hardy said.

Yates sucked in a deep breath and then blew it out. "Fine, but they ain't allowed to touch anything. It's still my crime scene."

"Nice of you, Chief Yates. Especially considering the way you tried to overrun my crime scene the other night," I said.

Ignoring me, Yates reached into his coat pocket and dug out a fresh pinch of chewing tobacco. He stuffed it into one of his jowly cheeks.

"We're just about finished processing the body," Officer Ethan Yates said as he handed me the laptop on which he'd uploaded the crime scene photos. "Unless you see something we missed."

I clicked through the pictures. The first few were of the victim's arm sticking out of the dumpster. The next set were of her lying face-down on top of the garbage bags. The rest of the pictures were close-ups of the body—both in the dumpster and on the ground—as well as pictures of each garbage bag. Almost immediately I spotted a couple things that seemed off.

"Was she killed in the shop?" I asked.

"Don't know yet," Chief Yates snapped. "My officers are still processing the inside of the building. So far we haven't found anything, but that's not to say we won't."

"Are there any security cameras around here?" Quaranta asked.

"We're still working at getting the footage," Ethan Yates said.

"So, what do you know?" I asked.

"The victim's name is Amanda Booker," Chief Yates mumbled around the wad of chewing tobacco. "Twenty-three years old. Just moved to Wyatt County about six months ago."

"She live around here?" I asked even though I remembered Dale saying something about his ex-girlfriend living in the Whispering Pines trailer park that was on the northwest side of Wyatt Lake. The trailer park was about fifteen miles away from the center of town.

Whispering Pines got its start about twenty years ago when two of my uncles bought a few single-wide trailers and put them up near the northwest side of Wyatt Lake. They planned to rent them out to people as vacation homes. The plan really didn't work out too well for my uncles. Tourists didn't seem overly interested in staying in the trailers. And the locals all lived within forty-five minutes of the lake, so they didn't have much use for the trailers either.

When my uncles realized that they couldn't rent the trailers out as vacation homes, they sold them to people who wanted to live in them year-round. Then, like rabbits, the trailers multiplied.

When Chief Yates confirmed that the victim lived in the trailer park, I asked where she worked. There were a number of businesses and restaurants in the area. If Amanda worked at any of them, it was possible she was killed while at work. She also could have been snatched up by a predator while arriving at or leaving work.

"The victim worked at the Dancing Cowgirl," Officer Ethan Yates said. "Last night, as I was leaving the club, a couple of the girls pulled me aside and told me they haven't seen or heard from Amanda in a few days. I stopped by her trailer before I went home. I knocked a few times, but no one answered. So I gave up. I guess she was already dead."

Dale's ex-girlfriend had worked at the Dancing Cowgirl? Did he know what she did for a living? How had he met her? What was he thinking?

"Is the victim's car here?" Quaranta asked.

"Nope. It was at her trailer," Ethan said.

"Let's see what we've got." I waited until the Holler officers packed up the evidence and their crime scene kits before I knelt on the ground next to the body. The thick layer of foundation and smoky eye makeup weren't enough to hide the early stages of decomposition. Amanda's face was bloated and discolored. Her tongue protruded from her mouth, and her eyes were sunken in the sockets. The rest of her body was also showing signs of decomposition. "Poor girl is too far gone to have an open casket."

"Amanda was a lot prettier when she was alive. Obviously," Ethan said.

"She was probably the prettiest dancer at the club."

Amanda's bleached blonde hair was pulled back into a sloppy ponytail, and she wore a hot pink tracksuit. The front of Amanda's tracksuit was damp and covered in what appeared to be grease or oil. I tugged up the jacket to get a look at Amanda's side. Underneath the jacket, Amanda wore a lacy, lilac babydoll lingerie top. Perhaps it was one of the outfits she wore at the club. She also had a colorful butterfly tattoo covering her left ribcage.

"Could someone help me roll her onto her side?" I asked. Two of the Holler officers rolled Amanda onto her right side and held her there while I looked at the dark purple discoloration on the victim's back. Lividity, or livor mortis, takes place after a person dies. The discoloration was caused by the blood settling in the lowest portion of the body. "She was lying on her back for a while after she died."

"We know," Chief Yates snapped. "The victim was stuffed in the dumpster last night. We don't know where she was before that."

"She's also not wearing any underwear," I said after I tugged down Amanda's pink pants to reveal a large, floral tattoo on her lower back. The tattoo also covered part of her right butt cheek. "You can lay her back down, officers."

"Are we supposed to be shocked that she ain't wearing panties?" Chief Yates asked. "The victim got paid to take her clothes off after all."

"I just think it's weird. Not to mention that she's wearing sandals in winter," I said, pointing at Amanda's hot pink espadrille sandals that had a four-inch heel. "They don't seem like the most appropriate footwear for winter."

"Again. She's a stripper. She probably wears those on stage," Chief Yates said.

"I've never seen her in pink sandals. They don't match her usual outfits," Ethan said. "Normally she wears white or silver heels. But she's been changing things up ever since she dyed her hair blonde."

"Well, Detective Shatner, what's your expert opinion?" Yates asked. "What killed her?"

"The proper question would be how did she die?" I grabbed a section of the victim's over-the-top fake eyelashes and pulled her eyelid back. Amanda's blue eyes were clouded over, but I could still make out red dots and streaks in the whites of her eyes. "I'm not a doctor or anything, but that looks like petechial hemorrhaging to me."

"Are those bruises around her throat?" Hardy asked as he leaned over my shoulder.

"Yes, they are. I think she was strangled." I examined the faint, purple colored bruises around the front and sides of her neck. I picked up the victim's arm and examined her hands. There was dried blood under each hot pink acrylic nail. There was a good possibility that the killer still bore Amanda's claw marks. "There's blood and tissue under her nails."

"How long do you think she's been dead?" Ethan asked.

"Rigor has come and gone, so she's been dead over forty-eight hours," I said.

The five of us stood over the victim's body in silent vigil.

Yates let a minute or so pass before he turned to me and asked, "You done looking yet, Detective Shatner? 'Cause I think you've seen enough."

"Yeah. I think I've seen enough. Good luck solving this one." I wasn't sure if I'd seen enough, but I had seen plenty. I backed up a few steps, preparing to flee the scene. "Now, if you'll excuse me, I've got my own murder to solve."

"More like cover up," Yates shouted at my retreating back.

Trying to appear nonchalant, I hustled back across the street to the sheriff's department and found Uncle Murph standing in the parking lot with a pair of binoculars. Last night, after I got Nate Palmer to confess that Kyle was never at the Palmer's New Year's Eve party, Murph and I took Nate home. After once more vowing not to press charges against Nate for stabbing Wesley and Waylon, Murph made Nate swear that he would never tell anyone that Murph kidnapped him and planned to torture him along with Uncle Houston. I hadn't spoken to Murph since he dropped me off at my house. I wasn't planning to speak with him until I was over being furious at him. It didn't look like I was going to have much of a choice at the moment.

"If you want to see what's going on, why don't you just walk over there and ask," I said.

"I can see just fine from here." Murph lowered the binoculars. "Should we be concerned about what's going on over there?"

"Nope. Nothing for us to worry about," I lied. I didn't want to tell Murph that the victim was Dale's ex-girlfriend. At least not yet. I wanted to handle this by myself for the time being. If Murph found out that Dale's ex-girlfriend's body was found in the dumpster behind where Dale worked, he would ship his son off with the Peace Corps to a country that didn't have extradition. It would be years before any of us saw or heard from Dale again. And I just couldn't let Murph do that until I figured out if Dale killed Amanda. There was no reason to send him away if he didn't kill her. And, if he did killer Amanda, the only place Dale would be sent was jail. "I've, uh, I've got a few things to check out. I'll be back in a while."

"Call me if you need me." Murph shuffled down the sidewalk as he peered through the binoculars. "I know how much you hate getting your hands dirty."

"It's your idiot son that's giving me no choice," I mumbled to myself. I jumped in my Jeep and pulled out of the lot. As I drove away from the sheriff's department, I debated on whether I should find Dale or drive down to Amanda's trailer. I pulled my cell phone out of my coat pocket and called Dale. "Where are you at?"

"I'm at Grandpa's house. His truck is leaking oil," Dale said. "My boss called and said the shop is closed for the day. He didn't say why, but I don't really care."

"Stay at your grandpa's house. And don't answer your phone for anyone other than me. Not even for your dad."

"Why? What's going on?" Dale asked.

"I'll tell you later." Hanging up on Dale, I headed south towards Wyatt Lake. I'd just take a quick look at Amanda's trailer before I went to pick up Dale. It took about fifteen minutes to drive to the Whispering Pines trailer park. I spent every single minute questioning what I was doing. If Dale killed Amanda, I couldn't cover it up. I wouldn't cover it up. But I needed to look into it. If Dale didn't kill her, I needed to be able to prove it. "I really need to quit my job."

When I entered the Whispering Pines Trailer Park, I remembered Dale saying that Amanda lived on Cedar Drive. I had no idea where Cedar Drive was. The main road that cut through the trailer park ran in a straight line. The other roads snaked off of it into loops and dead ends. One could easily get lost driving through the streets.

As I drove around, I came across a half dozen teenagers loitering on a street corner. For ten bucks, they not only directed me to Cedar Drive, but also told me which trailer was Amanda's. It seemed that having a bona fide stripper in the neighborhood was the most exciting thing that had happened in their young lives.

Cedar Drive was a short, dead end street just off the main drag. Oak Lane looped around it, starting and ending on either side of Cedar Drive. There were six single-wide trailers on the narrow cul-de-sac. One was in total disrepair and clearly had been abandoned. The other five were in passable condition.

I studied the single-wide trailer that the teenagers claimed Amanda Booker was renting. It was small and nondescript—just like all the other single-wide trailers I passed while driving through Whispering Pines. A couple newspapers lay scattered about Amanda's postage-stamp size front lawn, and the mailbox was overflowing. One would think the homeowner was away for a few days, except a car was still parked in the jerry-rigged carport.

I parked down the street from the trailer. I then walked over to Amanda's front yard and picked through the newspapers.

"What're you doing, missy?"

"Who's there?" I looked around, trying to figure out where the nasally voice had come from. I spotted a little old lady sitting outside the trailer that was across the street from Amanda's. I held up my badge and said, "Official business, ma'am."

The woman harrumphed, as she pushed herself out of her lawn chair. After yanking her plaid muumuu out of her crotch, she ambled across the street. As she got closer, I noticed that she was wearing a pair of beat up bunny slippers. She was also smoking a lumpy joint.

"Name's Ethel." She held out her hand, so I dropped the newspaper and shook it. "Been living here 'bout fifteen years now. I know just about everything that happens on Cedar Drive."

I didn't doubt that. Ethel seemed like the kind of woman who didn't miss much. I bet she would get along with my neighbors, Floyd and Margie.

"What do you know about your neighbor?" I pointed at Amanda's trailer.

Ethel peered over my shoulder at the trailer before shifting her gaze to me. "Hey, ain't you one of those Shatners?"

Over the years, I'd learned that there were times when denying a shared ancestry was more beneficial than admitting to it. This didn't seem like one of those times though. "I'm Carrie Shatner. One of Crockett's grandkids."

"Your family grows some good pot." Ethel held up the joint. "Rivals anything I had in the sixties. I was at Woodstock, you know."

"Oh yeah?" I pushed Ethel's hand away from my face. "Where are my relatives selling at these days?"

"Giovanni's Pizzeria. All you gotta do is call up, order a pizza with mushrooms, anchovies, pineapple, extra cheese, and no sauce." Ethel held up the joint again. "This is what gets delivered."

"Uh huh." I was going to wind up getting charged with assault by the time I was done with Uncle Houston. Giovanni's Pizzeria was within the Holler city limits, putting it in Chief Yates's jurisdiction. Until I could confront Uncle Houston, I had other things to take care of. "So, what do you know about Amanda Booker?"

"That her name? I only know her as the tramp." Ethel spat on the ground near my shoe. "You know what she did for a living? She got paid to take her clothes off. Disgusting. As a good, Christian woman, I'm morally offended by her."

I tried to keep a straight face. "Yeah, I heard that she was a stripper."

"So what did the tramp do this time?"

"This time?"

"Yes, this time. You think this is the first time the po-po's been out here because of her? This used to be the best street in the community. That tramp ruined that."

"Oh yeah?" Considering what I saw earlier, Cedar Drive looked like it was the worst street in Whispering Pines. I didn't think Amanda Booker was the sole cause of that. It seemed to me that Ethel and her collection of gnome statuary might have played a contributing role. "Why was the sheriff's department called out the other times?"

"Well, let me see, the tramp's only been here a few months ... " Ethel sucked on the joint, held her breath for a few seconds, and then blew the smoke in my face. I tried not to breathe it in. "Po-po been out here a few times because the tramp was blasting her rap music all day and night. And there was that time she was having it out with some man in the street. We got kids in the neighborhood, they don't need to be seeing that."

I had the feeling that Ethel was the one calling the Wyatt County Sheriff's Department on Amanda. I also suspected that Ethel was exaggerating her stories.

"The tramp also had men coming and going at all hours." Ethel poked me in the side with a talon-like finger. "I think she was a prostitute."

"Have you seen Amanda recently?" I asked, hoping to speed up the conversation.

"No. What kind of woman do you think I am? I got better things to do than spy on my neighbors."

"Oh, yeah, I bet you do. But certainly you notice things about them."

"Well, it's been a few days since I saw her, I guess." Ethel scratched at her greasy hair. "So, what did she do?"

"She hasn't been in to work the past few nights and her coworkers were worried. I'm checking up on her."

"Sure. Sure. Well, I ain't seen nothing."

"All right, then, thanks for all your help."

Ethel nodded a few times, told me to thank Uncle Houston for the top quality pot, and then shuffled back across the street.

I went back to checking out the newspapers. The oldest was from New Year's Day, meaning Amanda probably wasn't killed before that. I wasn't sure when the newspapers get delivered in Whispering Pines, but I assumed it was early in the morning.

All I could think about was how Dale saw Amanda on New Year's Eve. Could he have been so upset when she broke up with him that he snapped and strangled her? While possible, I couldn't picture it. If Dale killed her, he would have called his dad to help him clean it up. Murph would have done a better job of getting rid of the body. I also couldn't fathom Dale telling us he'd been with her, and even providing her contact information, if he knew we couldn't possibly contact her. Dale was dumb, but he wasn't that dumb.

Knowing Ethel was watching me, I marched up to Amanda's house and pounded on the door. Letting a believable amount of time go by, I tried peeking in the window by the front door. The curtains were drawn.

Taking a lap around the trailer, I found that the curtains were drawn over all of the windows. Just my luck, I couldn't even get a glimpse inside. When I got back to the front of the trailer, Ethel was waiting for me.

"What are you really doing here?" Ethel asked.

"Like I said, I'm trying to find Amanda."

"Oh … You want to check inside?" Ethel held up a house key. "Unless the tramp changed the locks, this should still work."

Ethel refused to leave until I tried the key, which worked. I sent Ethel back to her side of the street before I opened the door and went inside.

I had an extra pair of latex gloves in my coat pocket, but I didn't have any cloth booties. Leaving my shoes by the front door, I stepped into the small living room. The room was sparsely furnished with mismatched furniture that looked like it came from someone else's curb. While the living room was a tad messy, nothing in the room seemed to be disturbed.

I found a handful of framed photos of an attractive, young woman with auburn hair hanging on the living room walls.

"If this is the victim, she was too pretty to be dating Dale." Amanda was well-endowed and gorgeous. While Dale wasn't ugly, he was nothing great to look at either. "Maybe she was dating him for something other than his looks."

Using the camera on my cell phone, I snapped a few pictures of the living room before I moved into the combined kitchen and dining room. On the dining room table I found a bouquet of dead flowers next to a stack of overdue bills. In the sink was a tower of dirty dishes.

I was about to continue down the hallway to the bedroom when I noticed that there were a bunch of pictures of the victim tacked to the front of the refrigerator. One of the pictures was of a bleached blonde Amanda hanging on Kyle Vance's back.

"Oh … my … God … " I was reaching for the picture of Amanda and Kyle when I heard someone rattling the knob on the front door. I hadn't bothered to lock the front door after I let myself in. Assuming that it was Ethel checking up on me, I scurried around the half wall separating the kitchen and living room, hoping to intercept her. I was almost to the door when it swung open. "Oh, hey there, what are you doing here?"

"The better question is what are you doing here?" Hardy asked.

"Oh, you know, nothing."

"Sure … " Hardy looked around the living room. "This is what you do, isn't it? You break into houses. You break the law. Cover up a few crimes. Has anyone ever told you that you're unbelievable?"

"Yeah, but most of them don't mean it as an insult." I dug Ethel's key out of my pocket. "Besides, I didn't break in. The neighbor lady gave me a key."

"Great, now I can arrest her for aiding and abetting." Hardy snatched the key out of my hand. He then gave me a gentle push towards the door. "I should arrest you, but I don't think it would make any difference. There's no stopping you, is there?"

"No. Now let go of me." I pounded at Hardy's hand until he released my arm. "There's something I need to show you."

"No. Absolutely not. You're done here."

"Jerrod, seriously, you need to see this. Trust me."

"Trust you? That's what got me into this mess in the first place." Hardy sighed. "Fine. I'm going to humor you. You have one minute to show me whatever it is you feel you need to show me. Then we are out of here."

Since Hardy refused to move away from the door, I ran back into the kitchen, snagged two of the pictures off of the refrigerator, and rushed back to him. I handed him a selfie of Amanda with the bleached blonde hair. "Look familiar?"

"So this is the victim … Officer Ethan Yates is right, she was very attractive. But, no, I can't say she looks familiar."

"How about now?" I handed Hardy the picture of Amanda and Kyle.

"Is Amanda the bleached blonde woman in that one picture we found on Kyle's computer?" Hardy asked as he handed the picture back to me. "So she knew him. And probably had sex with him. That doesn't necessarily mean anything."

Sighing in exasperation, I pulled Hardy into the living room and pointed at one of the framed photos of Amanda hanging on the wall. "Jerrod, Amanda had natural red hair. She probably had red pubes. Amanda might be the redheaded woman that Kyle was having sex with before he died."

"Before they both were killed. She's been dead for a few days," Hardy said. "Damn it. I knew I should never have passed off the job of tracking down Dale's girlfriend to confirm his alibi. I actually believed he didn't kill Kyle, so I left it up to one of the deputies to find the girlfriend. He said he called, but she didn't answer the phone. It's my own fault for forgetting to follow up. For not doing it myself. Had I tried tracking down Amanda in the first place, I would have realized that Dale's girlfriend and Kyle's mystery caller were the same woman … "

"Don't beat yourself up so much. Chances are Amanda was already dead by the time you interviewed Dale." Moving away from Hardy, I returned to the kitchen and hung the picture of Amanda on the refrigerator. "I'm looking around some more."

"No. You can't," Hardy said. "I'm not, well, I'm just not."

"Not what? Sinking to my level? Look, Jerrod, you can leave. Or you can stand here by the door if you want to. But I'm looking around. If Chief Yates or one of the Holler officers shows up, just tell them you caught me breaking in, came in after me, and was in the process of arresting me."

"No ... All right, fine. Fine. Just don't ... I was going to say don't touch anything, but I know you will." Hardy ran his hands over his face and groaned. "What's wrong with me? I can't believe I'm letting you do this. This is your fault."

"How's it my fault?" I asked as I hurried back the hallway to Amanda's bedroom.

"I'm talking to myself." Hardy started grumbling to himself. I only picked up a few words including 'sexy', 'criminal', and 'ridiculous'.

"Why are you letting me do this?" I asked.

"Because I can't do it myself. Now, is there anything interesting about the bedroom?"

"Well, I like Amanda's decorating in here." The walls were painted hot pink, the furniture was black, and the bedspread, curtains, and rug were all pink and black zebra print. "Otherwise, well, there's nothing glaringly wrong about it. But something doesn't feel right."

The bed was made, but the bedspread was hanging crooked. And the throw pillows were just tossed randomly all over the bed. Since I didn't personally know Amanda, I had no way of knowing if this was how she usually made her bed or not.

"I found Amanda's panties," I said, taking a picture of the lacy, lilac thong hanging from a ceiling fan blade. "Something fishy is going on here. Amanda was wearing a lingerie top under her tracksuit. The bottom half of the set is still in her bedroom. And she was wearing high heeled sandals in January."

The large mirror above Amanda's vanity table was cracked, but I had no way of knowing when it was broken. On the vanity, Amanda's perfume and lotion bottles, makeup compacts and tubes, hair accessories, and costume jewelry lay jumbled around. I found a cell phone with a hot pink, rhinestone-studded cover stuck under a discarded bra. The battery was dead.

"How did you know I was here?" I asked.

"I saw you drive off. At first, I assumed you were running off to talk to Dale," Hardy said. "But then I got this horrible gut feeling that you were headed down here to snoop around."

"Your gut seems to be at war over how to feel about me," I said.

"Yeah, my gut and certain other body parts."

Across from the foot of Amanda's bed was a wheeled TV stand, but no TV. Hardy suggested that maybe Amanda pawned it. It was possible, but, if I was her, I would have pawned the larger flat-screen in the living room.

Next to the TV stand was a dresser so old that it had to be an antique. I noticed that the drawers weren't pushed in all the way and that most of the keepsakes and picture frames on top of the dresser were knocked over. I gave the items a cursory glance before I moved on to the drawers. The first three drawers I opened were packed full of lingerie. The fourth was full of socks and what I assumed were the victim's day-to-day underwear. The bottom drawer was full of shorts and yoga pants.

"Now who puts a heavy dresser in front of a door?" I peered into the six-inch-wide space between the side of the dresser and the wall. There was a narrow door set into the wall.

"Maybe it's the only place she could put it," Hardy suggested after I explained the situation to him. "Can you get the door open?"

"I can try." I stuck my arm in the narrow space and grabbed the door handle. I managed to get the door open just enough to peek inside. "Hot water heater."

"Like I said, maybe that's the only place she could put the dresser," Hardy said.

Losing interest in the victim's questionable furniture arrangement, I moved on to her closet. I grabbed the one closet door and tried to swing it open. The door opened about two feet before catching on the ratty area rug that lay perpendicular to the dresser.

"And who lays a rug in front of their closet? Especially when the closet door gets caught on it," I said.

"Maybe not everyone has your expert interior decorating skills," Hardy said. "Now, would you hurry it up in there? We've got to get out of here."

After glancing over the contents of the closet, I slid the doors closed. I then turned my attention to Amanda's solitary nightstand. I found her birth control pills, along with a surplus of sex toys and a tangled mess of chargers and cords.

I peeked under the bed and found a bunch of shoeboxes. I also found a shard of glass and another cell phone. Upon closer inspection, I realized that the piece of glass was really a piece of shattered television screen. The cell phone had a camouflage cover. The battery was dead, so I had no way of confirming whose phone it was.

On my way back to the living room, I stuck my head in Amanda's bathroom. Hanging on a towel rack were two dark purple hand towels. There was also a dark purple bath towel and washcloth sitting on top of the toilet tank. They were the same shade of purple as the towels we found in the dumpster behind the Dancing Cowgirl.

"Jerrod, there's no shower curtain."

"What?"

"There's no shower curtain. There's a shower curtain rod and there are shower curtain hooks, but there is no shower curtain." Except for a ragged piece of leopard print vinyl hanging from one of the hooks. "Oh, shit."

I trudged down the hall to the living room. Hardy was standing by the front window, peeking out at the street.

"I think this is our crime scene." I told Hardy about the purple towels and the missing shower curtain.

"You do know that makes Dale the number one suspect again, right?" Hardy said. "Maybe he came back later that night, found Amanda and Kyle together, and just snapped."

"And then what? He beat Kyle to death while Amanda watched? Or did he strangle Amanda while Kyle watched? Besides, I told you, if Dale had killed Kyle, he wouldn't have dumped Kyle's body at the fairgrounds. He also wouldn't have dumped Amanda's body in the dumpster where he works. And, to be perfectly honest, if Dale had killed them, Uncle Murph would have made both bodies disappear."

Chapter Twenty-Three

———◆———

Hardy and I found Dale in the two car garage that was attached to Uncle Bowie's house. Bowie's house was a short walk through the woods from Uncle Houston's house. Dale was under his grandpa's old truck, searching for the source of the oil leak. Hardy and I each grabbed one of Dale's legs and hauled him out from under the truck.

"What are y'all doing?" Dale sat up, and just missed whacking his head on the car's bumper. "This is harassment."

"We have some more questions," Hardy said.

"Oh no, I already told you everything I know about Kyle." Dale laid back down on his little mechanic's creeper and prepared to pull himself under the car. "I've got to get Grandpa's truck fixed. I'm sick of him coming out here and asking what's taking me so long."

"This isn't about Kyle," I said.

"Then leave me alone." Dale disappeared under the truck.

"I'm going to give you a choice, Dale." Hardy dragged Dale out from under the truck a second time. He then grabbed Dale by the arm and yanked him to his feet. "You can either talk to me and your cousin now, or you can talk to Chief Yates later."

"Whatever. Just give me a minute to clean up," Dale said. Hardy and I waited in the garage while Dale went into the house to wash his hands. A few minutes passed, and then Dale returned. He'd washed off some of the grime and grease, and changed into shabby street clothes. "I don't know what you two think I did. But I didn't do it."

I would have preferred to talk to Dale at Uncle Bowie's house, but Hardy insisted we take him in to the sheriff's department. Dale took a nap during the short drive back to town.

A handful of deputies and the receptionists were the only people in the sheriff's department when we got there. Before going to get Dale, I bribed Quaranta into taking Uncle Murph out for a lengthy lunch. I knew that if Murph found out that Hardy was questioning Dale again, he would try to interfere and refuse to let Dale talk without a lawyer. I didn't know how long it would take Chief Yates to realize that Dale was connected to Amanda Booker, but I didn't want to waste any of the time we had until Yates came looking for Dale.

When Hardy and I escorted Dale into the interrogation room, Dale immediately went to the one-way mirror and began to fix his hair. Hardy gave me a wide-eyed look before he took Dale by the arm and escorted him around the metal table and forced him down into the steel folding chair.

"What is all this about?" Dale said.

Hardy and I had a seat across the table from Dale. I laid a handful of papers face-down on the table. Before Hardy and I went to get Dale, I hooked my cell phone up to my office computer. I then printed out a bunch of the pictures I had taken inside Amanda's trailer. The pictures were a little grainy, but they were good enough. I wanted Dale to take a look at them. My gut was telling me that something was off about her bedroom. Dale would be able to tell me what that was.

"We brought you in to talk about Amanda Booker," Hardy said.

"Amanda? What does she have to do with anything?" Dale scooted forward in his chair and propped his elbows on the edge of the table. "She's not claiming I'm harassing her, is she? 'Cause I'm not. I mean, I called her a couple times, but that's not harassment. If we're not getting back together, then I want my stuff back. She can't just keep it, can she?"

"No, Dale, Amanda isn't pressing any harassment charges against you."

"Then what is this about? Why are you asking me about her?"

"We'll get to that, Dale. First we need you to answer some questions," Hardy said.

Dale sank back into the chair. "Ask away."

"When was the last time you saw Amanda?" I asked.

"New Year's Eve. When she dumped me."

"Have you talked to her since then?"

Dale shook his head. "I called her a few times. And texted. She never answered. I thought about going by her house or visiting her at work, but I didn't want her to think I was stalking her, you know."

"So you have had absolutely no contact with Miss Booker since Monday night?" Hardy asked. "You haven't seen or spoken to her in nearly four days?"

"That's what I just said." Dale pounded his fist on the table.

"What can you tell us about Miss Booker?" Hardy asked.

"What do you already know?"

"We know she's a stripper and that she worked at the Dancing Cowgirl," I said. "So, how did you meet her?"

Dale looked past me and Hardy and focused on the one-way mirror behind us. "Is my dad back there? I don't want him to hear this. He'll tell Mom and she will probably disown me."

Dale's mom was a deeply religious woman. While she turned a blind eye to the antics of her in-laws, I couldn't fathom her being receptive of Amanda's profession. No, Aunt Lydia would have given the poor woman a lecture on her moral shortcomings, and then badgered Dale into breaking up with her.

"No, Dale, your dad is not back there. And even if he was, I don't think he would care where or how you met this woman," Hardy said.

"I'm serious; I don't want anyone to know about this," Dale said.

I stood up and slammed my hands down on the table. I then leaned over, placing my face inches from Dale's. "Dale Earnhardt Shatner tell us where and how you met Amanda."

Dale sighed. He then whispered something too quietly for either Hardy or me to hear. We had to ask Dale to repeat himself. The second time, Dale spoke louder, but he mumbled the words and was too incoherent to understand. We had to ask Dale to repeat himself a third time.

"The Dancing Cowgirl!" Dale's face flushed a hot pink shade, and beads of sweat dampened his face. "Are you happy? I met Amanda at the Dancing Cowgirl!"

"Do you hang out at the Dancing Cowgirl a lot?" I asked, imagining how disgusted and betrayed the rest of the family would feel knowing that Dale had been frequenting a strip club owned and operated by the Palmer family. Stuff like that simply wasn't done.

Dale nodded. "The Palmers don't care as long as I pay my tab each night."

"Each night?" Hardy leaned across the table and stared Dale in the eye. "How often do you go?"

"Couple times a week." Dale shrugged. "Come on, Ranger, you know what I'm talking 'bout. Women taking their clothes of till they're mostly naked. Nothing better than that."

"I don't frequent strip clubs, Dale, so no, I don't know what you're talking about."

"For real? Are you gay or something?" Dale leaned across the table and whispered, "I think you're betting on the wrong horse, Carrie. I don't think the Ranger is into women."

I reached across the table and smacked Dale on the side of the head.

"Dale, I am just as interested in women as you are. I just don't enjoy watching them exploit themselves for money," Hardy said.

"Would you rather they did it for free? Because they would be pretty sweet."

Hardy sighed. "I just find something ethically and morally wrong with paying women to take their clothes off, all right?"

Dale rolled his eyes. "Is this for real or are you just trying to impress Carrie?"

Hardy cleared his throat. "This isn't about me, Dale. This is about you and Miss Booker. Tell us how you two met."

"I already told you, I met her at the club. Her performer name is Chas-Titty. Get it?" Dale laughed. When he realized that Hardy and I weren't laughing, he continued with his narrative. "She would come out in this all white, lacy thing. Sexy, but real chaste looking, you know. I liked that. She would start out dancing to 'Like A Virgin.' She did this whole innocent act at the beginning, like she had no idea what she was doing up there. Then she would start getting into it and taking the white lace stuff off. By the end of the song, she would be wearing nothing but a thong. That's when the real show got started."

"Dale, we don't need all these details," I said. "And I personally don't need to hear a play-by-play of her act."

"You sure?" Dale looked over at Hardy. "Thought the Ranger might like to know what he's missing out on. Some of the other girls down there are pretty hot, too."

"I'll take your word on it, Dale. I wasn't too impressed with what I saw while there."

"Your loss, man. So if you don't want to know about Amanda's act, what do you want to know about?"

"About how two met exactly," I said. "And what your relationship was like."

"Oh. I paid her for a private lap dance the third or fourth time I saw her. She took me into the back room, and I had the most erotic experience of my life. Well, up to that point, at least."

"Dale ... " I didn't bother to hide my disgust.

"Sorry." With the stupid grin on his face, Dale looked anything but sorry. "I was, like, obsessed with her, you know. Her performances were hypnotizing. I couldn't get enough. I kept paying her for lap dance after lap dance. Then, about a month after she started working there, Amanda invited me back to her house for something a little more private and personal."

Due to Amanda's vast collection of lingerie in every color and style known to mankind, and the plethora of sex toys, I had a good idea of what kind of "private and personal" interactions went on between them.

"Did you pay her for that, too?" Hardy asked.

"No, I didn't pay her. Amanda wasn't a hooker. She just liked me. She thought I was cute and nice. I wasn't a perv like some of those men at the club."

"Was she inviting other men back to her place?" Hardy asked.

"Not that I knew of."

"How would you describe your relationship then?" Hardy asked.

"Very physical." Dale held his hand up to Hardy for a high-five. Hardy left him hanging. "Oh come on, Ranger. Don't be such a prude."

"I'm not a prude," Hardy said. "We're not asking these questions because we're curious about your personal life, Dale. We're continuing our questioning from earlier this week."

"Oh come on. Do you even know what Amanda looks like? Here, I'll show you." Dale dug his cell phone out of the pocket of his jeans. He messed around with it for a few seconds before sliding it across the table. "Check that out."

The picture—which could only be described as pornographic—was of Amanda lying on what appeared to be her bed. She was completely naked if one didn't count the whip cream. When the picture was taken, Amanda still had red hair.

"See what I mean, Ranger. Totally banging, right?" Dale held up his hand, still hoping for that high-five.

"Dale, we're not here to celebrate your sexual exploits," Hardy said.

"Are we done then? Because I have no idea how any of this is going to help you find Kyle's killer."

"Just a few more questions, Dale. Then we'll be done," Hardy said.

"We want to know why Amanda broke up with you," I said.

Dale screwed up his face. "She dumped me for another guy."

"Did she say who the other guy was?" Hardy asked.

"No, she didn't say who the other guy was. And I didn't want to know. It was bad enough to find out she was cheating on me. I didn't want to know who it was with. Why, do you know who the other guy was?"

I opened my mouth to say something, but Hardy grabbed my leg and cut me off.

"No, Dale, but we may have an idea," Hardy said.

"Who is it? Tell me. I gotta know."

"We can't tell you that Dale," Hardy said. He continued to dig his fingers into my thigh.

"Why not? Come on, Ranger, I've answered all of your questions. Least you can do is tell me who my girl was screwing behind my back."

Hardy let go of my leg and gestured that I should be the one to break the news to Dale.

I took a deep breath and blurted it out. "Dale, we've got some bad news. Amanda Booker is dead."

"Dead?" Dale slumped back in his seat. He ran his hands over his face and then back through his blonde hair. Tears welled up in his blue eyes. "You're joking, right?"

"I'm sorry, Dale. But I saw her myself. So did Sergeant Hardy and Chief Deputy Quaranta."

"She can't be dead. I just saw her the other day." The tears ran unchecked down Dale's face. "What happened to her? How did she die?"

"We can't tell you that," Hardy said.

"Why not?"

"It's part of an ongoing investigation."

"Investigation?" Dale turned to me and leaned across the table. "Was she murdered? Did someone kill my Amanda?"

"That's what it looks like," I said.

"So someone killed Amanda." Dale jumped out of his chair and paced back-and-forth across the room. "Someone killed Amanda, and you think it was me."

"We don't think anything, Dale," I said.

"I swear to you that I didn't kill her," Dale said. "You've got to find the other guy. Maybe he killed her."

"Maybe he killed her." The bright light at the end of the tunnel was getting closer. The medical examiner found scratches on Kyle's forearms. We thought the scratches were one more set of wounds inflicted on Kyle while he was fighting for his life. Instead, it was possible he got the scratches while taking a life. Up until then, I'd assumed the same person killed both Amanda and Kyle. Thanks to Dale, I was beginning to think there were multiple killers. I turned to Hardy and screamed, "Maybe he killed her!"

I sprinted down the hall to my office and dug through the file folders that Hardy had piled up on my desk. Finding the folder containing autopsy photos, I flipped through them until I came to the close-ups of Kyle's forearms. From his elbows to his wrists were bloody scratch marks.

"Now what is going on?" Hardy asked.

I shoved the picture in Hardy's face. "Look! Look! Look!"

"I'm looking." Hardy said as he bent his head over the photo. "It might have been an accident. Zeke said he'd heard some of the dancers talking about Kyle getting rough with them."

"Back when Kyle was pursuing me, he told me all his weird little sex fantasies. One of them was choking."

"Jesus Christ." Hardy and Dale said it together. Hardy was reacting to my statement. Dale, who'd just wandered into the room, was reacting to the grisly pictures of Kyle that were scattered all over my desk.

"I thought I told you to stay in the interrogation room," Hardy said.

"You did. But I just thought of something." Dale held up a few sheets of paper. He then spread them out across my desk. "These pictures of Amanda's bedroom? They're not right. The furniture has been moved around."

"I knew it!" I rushed around the desk to stand beside Dale. "What's wrong with them?"

"The dresser was across from the foot of the bed. And the rug was on the floor between the bed and the dresser," Dale said. "And she had the TV stand beside the vanity. She would move it out when she wanted to watch TV."

"Then either she had just moved the furniture around or K–"

Hardy cut me off before I said Kyle's name. "Why would the killer move the furniture around?"

"Maybe he was looking for something," I said. "Or trying to hide something."

"Hey, is this Amanda's stripper pole?" Dale picked up a picture of the rod that we thought was the murder weapon. "Because it sure looks like it."

"Stripper pole?" Hardy and I asked.

"Yeah. She had one of these in her bedroom. In the corner where the dresser now was. Man, I had so much fun watching her swing around on this."

"Stripper pole?" I asked. "We thought it was a shower rod."

"Holy shit," Hardy whispered.

Kyle Vance had been beaten to death with a stripper pole.

"He killed her," I said.

"Yeah, but who killed him?"

Chapter Twenty-Four

———— ◆ ————

"That was my lieutenant." Hardy tossed his cell phone onto my desk. "He wants me to take over Chief Yates's investigation. Two homicides in Wyatt County in less than a week is suspicious. My lieutenant wants me to find out what is going on around here."

"He's not the only one," I said, setting down the crime scene pictures from the fairgrounds. "So, when you take over for Chief Yates, are you going to tell him that the two deaths are connected?"

"We might know that the two are connected, but the only evidence we have was illegally and unofficially obtained." Hardy gave me a very pointed look.

"You'll just have to act surprised later."

Hardy rolled his eyes. "Look, I have to go find Chief Yates and take over. I think it would be a bad idea to take you with me. The second body wasn't found in your jurisdiction, and I think Yates will throw a fit if I let you help out."

"I understand. Besides, I've got to get Dale somewhere safe before Yates finds out that he was dating the victim. Like I said, Yates will come after Dale. And it'll be ugly."

"I know. But what are you going to do after you take Dale somewhere safe?"

"Oh, you know, obtain some information," I said. "Illegally and unofficially."

Hardy came over, planted his hands on my shoulders, and leaned in closer to my face. For a second, I thought he was going to kiss me.

"Carrie, promise me you won't do anything stupid. Please? Just leave this to me. I know Dale didn't kill anybody, and I'll find out who the real killer is.

There is no need for you to be running around, risking your life just because your family expects you to."

"All right, I promise I won't do anything stupid."

EVEN BEFORE HARDY LEFT THE Wyatt County Sheriff's Department, I knew I was going to do something stupid. But, in the grand scheme of things, it really didn't seem all that stupid at the time.

After dropping Dale off at Uncle Bowie's place, I headed back to Holler to talk to Oscar Palmer. After mulling it over for a while, I thought I had a pretty good idea about what happened on New Year's Eve. It all started when Kyle choked Amanda to death. It was probably an accident, but, even if it was on purpose, Kyle would have panicked once he had a dead body on his hands. He most likely would have called someone for help. His own family lived out of state and he didn't seem to have that many friends. The only people he really had to call were his in-laws.

The Shatners called me and Uncle Murph when they were in trouble. I didn't know who the Palmers called when they were in trouble, but I assumed it was probably Oscar.

Oscar lived on a four-acre property on the north side of Holler. I parked down the street and then snuck through the trees to Oscar's house. Oscar's car was in the driveway, and the front door of the house was hanging open.

I pulled my gun out of my holster and crept up the front walk and into the house. I'd only ever been in Oscar's house once, and that was at least twelve years earlier. While Oscar and his late wife were on vacation, some of my cousins and I broke into the house and rearranged all the furniture. It was a harmless, teenage prank. Except Oscar almost had a heart attack when he came home and found his favorite recliner jammed into the tiny downstairs bathroom.

Poking my head around the doorjamb, I found Toby pacing back and forth in the living room while talking to someone on his cell phone. I waited until he had his back to me and then snuck up behind him, whacking him across the back of the head with my gun.

Toby collapsed, crashing through the cheap coffee table on his way down.

From the other room, Russell yelled, "What you doing out there, Toby?"

A few seconds later, Russell stomped into the room. I jumped out from behind the couch and hit him with my stun gun.

With both brothers down, I rolled them onto their stomachs and handcuffed them behind their backs. I then wrestled them into a sitting position and propped them against the couch.

Keeping my eyes peeled for Oscar and other Palmers, I crept into the kitchen and filled up two glasses of water. Back in the living room, I dumped the water over Toby's and Russell's heads.

"What the hell, Carrie?" Russell mumbled around the drool running out of his mouth.

"Where's Oscar?" I asked.

"We don't know," Toby said. "We're looking for him, too."

"His truck is parked in the driveway," I said.

"Yeah, well, he ain't here. We were trying to find him when you attacked us," Toby said.

I wasn't too concerned about Oscar. He was probably off hassling my relatives or some other type of nonsense. I was just worried about him coming back and catching me interrogating his grandsons in his living room.

I had a seat on the floor across from the boys. "You guys know who Amanda Booker is? You might know her better as Chas-Titty."

Toby nodded. "Yeah, she's a fine piece of ass."

"Well, now she's a dead piece of ass. Her body was found this morning."

"No kidding," Russell said. "Where at?"

"In the dumpster behind You Wreck Em', We Fix 'Em. She was strangled."

"That's too bad," Toby said. Russell echoed his brother's sentiments.

"Yeah, it is too bad. But, you know what's interesting?" I leaned closer to the boys. "She wasn't killed at the garage. She was murdered in her trailer and then the killer cleaned it up."

"We wouldn't know anything about that," Toby said.

"No? Well how about this? It also looks like Kyle killed her." I waited a few seconds to let that sink in. "And then someone came along and beat him to death with Amanda's stripper pole. You boys wouldn't know anything about that, would you?"

"Heck no," Russell said. "We was at the strip club on New Year's Eve. We never left until we went to crash your family's crappy party."

"Uh huh, so you're going to stick to that story?" I looked back and forth between Toby and Russell, waiting for one of them to crack. Neither of them blinked. Maybe I was wrong in thinking that they knew about, or were even involved in, Kyle's death. "What about your story that Kyle was with you all night and that he went with you to the fairgrounds? We know that's a lie. Kyle was dead for a couple hours before that happened."

"Who says?" Russell asked.

"The evidence says. And I think a jury is going to believe the evidence over your little story."

Toby and Russell exchanged a look. They grunted at each other and made some faces. It was a very primitive way of communicating, but it seemed to work for them. After a few seconds, Russell raised his leg and slammed it down on Toby's knee. Toby yelped in pain.

"What did you do that for?" I asked Russell.

"We ain't talking to you. You're crazy, you know that? Why can't you just accept that your family killed Kyle?"

"Because we didn't. Now, I don't appreciate your attitude." I leaned over and jabbed the stun gun into Russell's chest. "Someone needs to teach you some manners."

While Russell flopped around on the floor, I grabbed a lamp off the nearby end table, ripped the cord out of the base, and then used the cord to tie Russell's legs together at the ankle. I then ran into the kitchen and grabbed a roll of duct tape that I had spotted on the counter earlier. I ripped off a piece of tape and slapped it over Russell's mouth.

Sitting down beside Toby, I said, "Seems to me, you want to talk and Russell doesn't, right? I always knew you were the smart one."

"I got nothing to say to you."

"Well, that's too bad. Because I'm not going anywhere. And you're not going anywhere. So, we can just sit here and exchange insults. Or you can tell me about what really happened on New Year's Eve."

"I already told Chief Groves about what happened on New Year's Eve. I ain't changing my story just because you asked nicely."

"I'm not asking nicely," I said, holding up the stun gun. I didn't want to use the stun gun on Toby. I didn't even want to use it on Russell. But I had to do what I had to do if I was going to get to the bottom of what happened to Kyle and Amanda. Unfortunately, it made me no better than Uncle Houston and Uncle Murph. Except I stopped them before they used the jumper cables on Nate Palmer. No one was there to stop me from using the stun gun on Russell. "I'm just going to let you know that, sooner or later, Sergeant Hardy is going to come by to question you. We've got Kyle's body and the murder weapon. Now we've got Amanda's body. We know where both of them were killed. It's only a matter of time until we find evidence linking you two, or some of your other fine relatives, to Kyle's death. Y'all might have done a pretty good job at cleaning up Amanda's trailer, but we'll find some evidence."

Behind the duct tape, Russell attempted to say something.

Toby groaned. "All right, since you already know Kyle wasn't at the strip club, I'll admit that he wasn't at our party. He said he had another party to go to, which was fine with us. Most of the family hated him. But Whitney insisted she loved him, so we put up with him."

"Did you know where Kyle was?"

Toby shook his head. "Not until Pop-Pop said we had to do something for him. He told us that Kyle had gotten into some trouble, and that we needed to go help him take care of it."

"Some trouble?" I asked. "That's how Oscar phrased it?"

Russell rolled over onto his side and attempted to kick out at Toby. I grabbed his bound legs and spun him around so that his head was next to Toby's hip.

"I'm not sure I want to tell you this," Toby said.

"Why not? We're just having a friendly conversation is all. It's not like it's on the record or anything."

"Oh, yeah, sure. Like I'm going to fall for that."

"You think I'm lying? Because I'm not. It won't be long until Sergeant Hardy gets here. You can just take your chances with him, but I can guarantee that he isn't going to do anything to help you."

"And you are?" Toby asked,

"I could help you." When Russell started rolling away from me, I had a seat on his stomach. I was glad Hardy wasn't here to see me do that. It would kill whatever notions he had of me being a good person. In my defense, I did feel horrible about what I was doing. "Or I could call my Uncle Murph. He won't be nearly as nice to you as Sergeant Hardy."

"You think the Ranger won't arrest you when he finds out what you've done?" Toby craned his neck to look at Russell. "This has got to be illegal."

I grinned at Toby and said, "Oh, it is. But I have ways to convince Sergeant Hardy to let me go. Now, get to talking or I'm calling Uncle Murph."

"You really are crazy … Fine, you want to know what happened that night, I'll tell you. Just don't use that stun gun on me," Toby said. "I asked Pop-Pop what Kyle had done, but all he said was that Kyle had done something stupid, and we needed to help him clean it up. It's not like this was the first time Kyle made a mess and someone had to help him clean it up. It's just that the other times were nowhere near as bad as this. We didn't know Kyle had killed Chas-Titty until we got to her trailer and Kyle showed us her body."

"Did Oscar know that Kyle had killed Chas—Amanda?" I didn't want to use Amanda's stripper name. "Her name was Amanda."

Toby slowly nodded. "Later, Russell and I asked Pop-Pop why he didn't tell us Kyle had killed her, but Pop-Pop swore that he had. He's been getting senile lately. He's supposed to be taking these pills, but most days he forgets to take them."

Great. Oscar was crazy enough as it was. I couldn't imagine how much worse he could get once the senility started to kick in.

"So what happened after you realized that Kyle had killed Amanda?" I asked.

Toby let out a long-suffering sigh. "I started yelling at Kyle, and Kyle kept insisting that it was an accident. You can shoot someone by accident, but I don't understand how you strangle someone by accident."

I wondered the same thing. Amanda had dried blood under her fingernails, and Kyle had those deep scratches on his forearms. Had Kyle thought that Amanda's scratching was her way of showing she enjoyed it. And wouldn't she have been thrashing around and making choking sounds.

"Kyle said it was her fault because she asked him to choke her," Toby said. "Kyle just wouldn't shut up about how kinky Chas ... Amanda was, and how she was into choking and bondage. He even bragged about how good the sex was while he was choking her. He claimed that's why he didn't realize he was choking her to death. Then he said he was going to miss her because she was into the same stuff as him. He said Whitney wouldn't do that sort of stuff, which was why he was cheating on her with Amanda and all those other women. All Russ and I could think about was how Amanda could have been Whitney. That Whitney could have been the one he choked to death. And that next time it could be. That's when I snapped."

"Shut up, Toby," Russell said through a hole he had gnawed through the duct tape. "I ain't going back to prison over that son of a bitch."

I ripped another piece of tape off the roll and slapped it over Russell's mouth. "Go ahead, keep chewing."

"He's right, Carrie. I'm done talking," Toby said

"Why, did you kill Kyle?"

"No."

"So Russ killed him."

"Yes ... NO! ... No, neither of us killed Kyle."

"So, what did you do? Help Kyle clean up Amanda's trailer, and then dump her body behind You Wreck 'Em, We Fix 'Em last night?" I asked. Toby shook his head. "No? Then one or both of you must have killed him. You know, I bet Sergeant Hardy will make a deal with you guys. Whichever one confesses will get some charges dropped. How's that sound, Toby?"

"Sounds like you're trying to get me to confess to something I didn't do."

"Then who did it? Who killed Kyle?"

"I did!" Russell chewed another hole through the tape. "I killed the bastard and I would do it again. You happy now, you whacked out bitch?"

"Eh, I could be happier." I ripped the tape off Russell's face, taking some skin and hair with it. "Tell me what happened."

"I hit him," Russell said. "And then I kept hitting him."

"What were you doing, Toby?" I asked.

"Kyle was screaming at us and begging up to stop," Toby said. "I grabbed something and shoved it in his mouth to shut him up."

It must have been Dale's work shirt. If Toby shoved it in Kyle's mouth to gag him, it would explain how part of it was still in Kyle's mouth when I found him. "Then what?"

"I started hitting him," Toby said. "Look, Carrie, what happened on New

Year's Eve was a long time coming. When Whitney married that scumbag, Russ was in prison and I was in Iraq. Neither of us met Kyle until about a year ago."

"We didn't like Kyle too much," Russell said. "But we were both caught up in our own problems to pay attention to Whitney's marriage."

"Yeah, Russ and I had no idea Kyle was cheating on our sister until this past fall. We were at the strip club and we walked in on him sticking it to one of the dancers. Kyle tried to tell us it was a mistake and that was the only time he cheated. It was Zeke who told us that Kyle was constantly screwing the dancers."

"We wanted to chase Kyle off, but Whitney wouldn't let us. She said she loved him and that they were going to work it out."

"So we left it alone," Toby said. "We did beat him up back in early December. That's when we found out he was smacking Whitney around. She freaked out on us about it afterwards. Told us to leave Kyle alone and to stay out of their lives."

"Did you?" When Russell and Toby both nodded, I asked, "So you were hitting him? Then what happened?"

"We were also kicking him," Toby said.

"Who hit Kyle with the stripper pole?" I asked.

"He did," Toby and Russell said at the same time.

"So, what, you took turns or something?"

"Yes," Russell said.

"No," Toby said.

"Then which is it?"

Toby and Russell glared at each other. Russell finally admitted he was the one who beat Kyle with the stripper pole.

"I just ripped it out of the floor and beat him with it. I guess it was the second blow to the head that killed him. I just hit him a third time to make sure he was dead," Russell said.

"It was over in minutes." Toby leaned over and looked me in the eye. "We didn't mean to kill him. We just snapped."

"Understandable." I jumped up from the floor and paced around the living room. "You need to turn yourselves in. Make a deal and confess."

"I told you, I don't want to go back to jail," Russell said. "Can't we just pretend this never happened and move on with our lives?"

"Nope, sorry." I grabbed my cell phone and called Hardy.

"Where are you?" Hardy asked. "Please tell me you're not doing something stupid."

"Fine, I won't tell you that. But I have good news, I caught the killers." I told Hardy to come to Oscar Palmer's house, and to bring the cavalry with him. After hanging up on Hardy, I turned to Russell and Toby, and said, "Now, boys, while we've still got some time together, why don't you tell me about what happened after you killed … .after Kyle was dead."

"We called Pop-Pop," Russell said. "He told us to clean it up."

"So we wrapped Kyle in the shower curtain and tossed him in the back of his truck," Toby said. "We used some of Amanda's towels to clean up the blood. Then we took Kyle and left. I drove my car, and Russell drove Kyle's truck with the body in the back. We went back to the strip club and asked Pop-Pop what we should do with him."

"Then what? Did you stuff Kyle in the dumpster at the fairgrounds while our two families were fighting?"

Toby shook his head while Russell said, "Pop-Pop said someone else would take care of getting rid of Kyle's body."

"So you have no idea how Kyle's body wound up in the dumpster at the fairgrounds?" I asked. I believed Toby and Russell when they claimed they hadn't dumped the body. They'd already confessed to killing Kyle, why would they deny the body dump? "What about Amanda?"

"We left her where she was. We have no idea who cleaned up her place or moved her body." Toby said.

"Ask Pop-Pop. He knows who dumped both of the bodies," Russell said.

"I plan to. Once I find him." It was possible Oscar sent some of his other relatives to clean up the crime scene and get rid of Amanda's body. If Zeke and some other Palmers knew that Dale spent multiple nights a week at the Dancing Cowgirl, it was probable that they also knew Dale was having a relationship with Amanda. The Palmers must have been framing my family from the beginning.

While we waited for Hardy to arrive, I told Toby and Russell about my brother-in-law who was a defense lawyer. Out of the goodness of my heart, I was going to help the boys out and make sure that they had the best legal representation available. I didn't condone what they did, but I understood why they killed Kyle.

Before long we heard sirens in the distance.

"This is it, isn't it?" Toby asked.

Hardy ran in Oscar's house with Uncle Murph, Chief Deputy Quaranta, and about a dozen deputies on his heels. After assessing the situation, he came over to me. "Do I even want to know?"

"Toby and Russell confessed to killing Kyle, but you don't need to know how I got them to do that," I said.

"But it was off the record," Toby said. "Right? You said it was off the record."

"That's fine. Later we can go on the record and you can tell me everything," Hardy said. While Uncle Murph and Quaranta handcuff Toby and Russell,

Hardy drew me over by the window and asked, "What were you thinking? You could have gotten yourself killed. You could have ruined the entire case."

"But I didn't."

"That has yet to be seen," Hardy said. "Seriously, what is wrong with you? Why couldn't you just let me take care of it?"

"I don't know." I really didn't know what possessed me to go looking for Oscar Palmer. I just felt I had to do it, so I did. As for Russell and Toby, deep down I knew I shouldn't have forced them into confessing. "I just wanted to help catch the bad guy."

"Well, at least you managed to accomplish that," Hardy said. Through the window, we watched as Toby and Russell were loaded into the sheriff's department's cruisers. "Where's Oscar Palmer? Or do you have him tied up in the bathroom?"

"He's not here. The boys were here looking for him. That's how I found them."

"Well, I'm sure he'll turn up. So what did they tell you?"

I repeated Russell's and Toby's story for Hardy, leaving out the part where I used the stun gun on Russell multiple times.

"You know, I can't say I really blame them for killing Kyle. He'd already killed one woman—whether accidently or on purpose—and Whitney could have been next. In a way, it almost seems justified," I said.

"But that still doesn't make it right. They should have just called the police and reported that Kyle had killed Amanda," Hardy said.

Outside, Murph and Quaranta finished loading Toby and Russell in the backseats of two of our cruisers. The deputies climbed into the cruisers, and, one by one, they fired the engines, flipped on the sirens, and then drove off down Oscar's street.

"I guess we better go find Oscar and figure out what exactly happened on New Year's Eve," I said.

"I'm sorry, but I can't let you do that," said a familiar voice.

I slowly pushed away from the window, and turned around to find Chief Isaac Yates standing behind me. Yates should still be at the crime scene in the You Wreck 'Em, We Fix 'Em parking lot. What was he doing as Oscar's house?

Before I had a chance to ask, Yates grabbed one of Oscar Palmer's wooden canes and swung it at my head.

I DIDN'T KNOW HOW LONG I was out, but it couldn't have been too long. When I came to, I was lying on the floor in Oscar Palmer's living room. My whole head hurt, but it felt like the pain was radiating out of my left temple. At least that was the general area where the blood that was running down my face and into my hair was coming from.

"She's got a backup piece," Hardy said as he tugged my right pant leg up to my knee. Hardy, whose face was pale and drawn, was kneeling beside me. But, since I was seeing double, there were actually two Hardys. And both of them had an arm wrapped around their midsections. "I think you broke my ribs."

"Don't worry, in a few minutes a couple broken ribs will be the least of your problems," Chief Yates said. "Now throw her gun over here."

Hardy slipped the gun out of my ankle holster and then slide it across the floor. Pain shot through my head when I twisted my neck to get a better look at Chief Yates. He was standing about five feet away from us. In one hand he clutched a wooden cane, and he used the other to point a gun at us. Piled up on the ground at his feet were Hardy's and my handguns, as well as our cell phones, my stun gun, and all the other things I had brought along to confront Oscar.

There had to be a reason Chief Yates was doing this. He may have been harassing me since the day I started working at the sheriff's department, but he had never been this sadistic about it. He'd never assaulted me before.

"Are you all right, Carrie?" Hardy swiped his sleeve down the side of my face, and it came back red with blood. "How many fingers am I holding up?"

Two Hardys and six fingers hovered before my eyes. I moaned in response.

"I think you might have a concussion, Carrie." Hardy turned my head to the side and inspected the damage.

"Stop playing doctor and cuff her." Yates threw a pair of handcuffs on the ground near my head.

Hardy cradled the back of my head in one hand and slipped his other arm under my shoulders, and gently raised me into a sitting position. I think I might have blacked out again. Hardy pulled my arms together behind my back and handcuffed me. He then propped me up against the couch.

"Now you." Yates swung the wooden cane at Hardy, catching him on the side of the head. While Hardy was unconscious, Yates handcuffed him behind the back and then sat him up next to me.

Closing one eye so that there was only one Yates standing before me, I asked, "Why?"

"Why?" Yates asked. "Why what?"

"Why did you help the Palmers get rid of Kyle's body?" I asked, now knowing that he had to have done it. Why else would he attack me and Hardy? There was also the fact that Yates was the only person, aside from the Palmers, who hated my family enough to try to frame us for murder.

"Because Oscar Palmer has me by the short hairs." Yates paced back and forth across the living room. He continued to keep his gun pointed at me and Hardy. "Years ago, I made a big mistake. I had a body I needed to get rid of. Oscar helped me do that. He's helped me out with a few other things over the years. Thanks to that, I wound up in serious debt to Oscar. Getting rid of Kyle's body, and making it all go away was supposed to make us even. Now I'm only deeper in the hole. I should just kill that son of a bitch and been done with it."

"Why my family?" I asked. The words rang in my head, and I wasn't sure how coherent I sounded. The blood from my head wound dribbled down my neck and soaked into my jacket and shirt. "Why the dumpster?"

"That was my idea. Oscar had just gotten off the phone with Houston when Toby and Russ showed up with Kyle's body in the bed of his truck. Oscar was upset about Houston opening a rival strip club—"

"Adult store," I said, interrupting.

"Whatever. Oscar was mad, and he decided he'd round up his family and head over to crash your family's party at the fairgrounds. I realized it was the perfect way to get rid of Kyle's body." Yates stopped pacing and crept closer. He hunkered down so he could look me in the eye. "Framing your family for killing Kyle was too good to pass up. I waited until after the Palmers left and your family went back inside that building. Once the music started, I unlocked the side gate closest to the dumpster and then hauled Kyle's body back to the dumpster. I found a tire iron in the back of Kyle's truck, so I threw that in hoping someone would mistake it for the murder weapon. It was the perfect plan."

"Except your plan failed," I said.

"That's because you found the body." Yates waved his gun under my nose. "You weren't supposed to do that, Detective Shatner. I didn't want him found until the weekend."

"Sorry I ruined your plan." If Kyle's body hadn't been found until the weekend, it only would have affected the state of his body and the medical examiner's estimated time of death. Regardless of when he was found, Kyle would have last been seen on New Year's Eve.

Yates attempted to backhand me across the face, but Hardy, who had come to while Yates and I were talking, threw himself in front of me and deflected the blow with his shoulder. Angered that he'd been thwarted, Yates grabbed Hardy by the hair. He then pressed the barrel of his gun against Hardy's forehead.

Hardy continued to glare at Yates. Had it been me, I would have been crying and begging for my life. I had a dog to take care of, and pro wrestling would be on in a few hours. I didn't want to miss my hot, sweaty men in speedos. Hardy twisted around and managed to grab hold of my hands. If it wasn't for the death grip he has on my fingers, I might not have thought he was scared.

"Don't try that again," Yates said. "You don't get to play hero anymore."

Yates let Hardy go, and the two men leaned back and eyed each other. Hardy continued to squeeze my hand. I could feel his body shaking.

"You also ruined my plan, Mr. Hot Shot Ranger," Yates said. "The fairgrounds may not be in my jurisdiction, but you were supposed to let me help you investigate."

"I could have," Hardy said. His body may be shaking, but his voice was strong. "But you couldn't have been impartial. Not when the Shatners were involved."

"But she was impartial?" Yates laughed. "Tell me something, Hardy. Was she on her knees first, or did she go straight to her back?"

"Hey!" I kicked out at Yates. I aimed for his midsection, but, with my vision still messed up, I wound up striking him in his fleshy thigh.

Yates grabbed my leg and twisted it to the right, wrenching my knee.

"Ouch!"

Hardy squeezed my hand as a warning. "No, Detective Shatner wasn't impartial. But her family is innocent. There was no evidence they had been involved. Therefore, she was more determined to find the actual guilty party than you would have been. Of course, you already knew what had happened."

"No, I didn't know everything." Yates stood up. It took some effort considering his girth. "At the time, I didn't know who killed Kyle. All Oscar told me was that Kyle was dead and that I needed to make it go away."

"What about Amanda?" I asked.

"I had no idea about the dead woman until the next day when Oscar called me and told me to get rid of her, too. I went over and cleaned up her place that night. I only stuck her body in the dumpster early this morning. I found out she'd been dating your cousin, Dale, so I decided to dump her body where he works. I figured I could frame him for her murder and maybe for Kyle's, too." Yates resumed pacing. "My career is gonna be over. And my life's work is nowhere near complete."

"Life's work?" Hardy and I both asked.

"To bring down the Shatners." Yates took on a condescending tone. "I have to stop them, Sergeant Hardy. I've been trying for over twenty years, but I just can't do it alone. They're too good at covering up their crimes. You don't know Detective Shatner like I do. You have no idea what she does to keep her family out of trouble. To keep me from finding evidence against them. Or maybe you do have an idea of what lengths she'll go to. What were you two doing at the motel last night?"

"We weren't doing anything," Hardy said.

"Sure … I wasn't looking or nothing, but I noticed you had an erection last night. I bet Detective Shatner would have been blowing your brains out if I hadn't showed up."

"Fuck you," Hardy and I both said.

"Shut up!" Yates fired a shot over my head, striking the wall behind us. I screamed, and Hardy shifted his body so that he was between me and Yates. "Just shut up, Detective Shatner! You're a criminal. Every single one of you Shatners is a criminal. And you have to be stopped. I'm going to stop you!"

"Calm down, Chief Yates," Hardy said. "There are better ways to do this."

Hardy tugged at my handcuffs. As he did so, I realized that they were loose around one of my wrists. I glanced up at Hardy who mouthed 'get out of here' at me. I shook my head. It would be easy to slip off the handcuffs and make a run for it, but, in my condition, I didn't think I would make it too far. And, even if I did, I wouldn't be able to live with myself knowing I ran away and left Hardy behind. But maybe, just maybe, I could get to Yates before he had a chance to fire the gun. I'd rather go down fighting than get shot in the back running away.

"There are no easy ways when it comes to the Shatners. I think they made a deal with the devil," Yates screamed. "The body should have been enough. It should have been enough to get the Rangers to finally look at the Shatners. I thought you would help me, Sergeant Hardy. I thought you would help me bring down the Shatners. Instead you failed me."

As I tried to slip out of the handcuffs without Yates noticing, my hand bumped into something under the couch. I closed my fingers around it and slid it out from under the couch.

It was a sawed-off shotgun.

Years ago, when my cousins and I broke into Oscar's house and moved around the furniture, we found a dozen guns hidden around the house. Luckily for me, Oscar was still doing it. If I ever saw that wrinkled, semi-senile man again, I would kiss him.

"I didn't fail you, Chief Yates. I listened to your stories, but they seemed too far-fetched even if they were true. And your evidence was crap. Some blurry, long-distance photos were not enough. You had no real, solid evidence," Hardy said. "What did you want me to do? Did you want me to open an investigation just because you asked?"

I couldn't help but wonder why Hardy was being so antagonistic. We were the ones handcuffed while Yates was free to pace around and wave his gun.

I nudged Hardy with my shoulder and used my eyes to direct him to the shotgun lying on the floor between us. Hardy looked back up at me and mouthed, "Do it."

"You would have made a great Ranger, Sergeant Hardy. But then you met Detective Shatner." Yates waved his gun around and cursed. "I've got to stop you, Sergeant Hardy. Stop you before it's too late and you make the same mistakes I did. I can't just stand back and watch you be in debt to a family of criminals. That's no way to live, son. I didn't used to be like this. I used to have a soul, but Oscar Palmer took that from me. I used to have a lot of things, but the Palmers and the Shatners took everything. I just wanted to stop the Shatners, Hardy. That was it. I just wanted to stop them."

Yates stomped across the room, still yelling about how he was a failure. With his back to me, I grabbed the gun and raised it to my shoulder. I could only hope that Oscar had loaded it before stashing it under the couch.

"Hey, Yates," I said.

When Isaac Yates turned around, I let go with both barrels.

Chapter Twenty-Five

———◆———

"How's your head, Carrie?"

"It looks worse than it is." I reached up to touch the golf ball-sized lump on my left temple, but Hardy stopped me. It took seven stitches to close the gash. There was still blood in my hair, but the headache was down to a dull throb. Roughly forty-eight hours after the attack, I was feeling somewhat better. Physically, at least. "But I have a concussion."

Hardy and I were outside Holler's VFW Hall. My family was gathered inside, waiting to give Hardy a hero's welcome. I'd opted to meet him in the parking lot since I hadn't had a chance to talk to him since our near death experience. Chief Isaac Yates was dead. The sawed-off shotgun had been loaded, and I hit Yates right in the face and neck with it. I felt bad that I killed him, but it was a kill-or-be-killed type of situation.

"Are you okay?" I asked. Hardy had a cracked rib and a couple other ribs were bruised. He also had a gash on his head from where Yates hit him with Oscar's wooden cane.

"It's not too bad." Hardy opened his jacket and then tugged up his shirt to reveal a purple and black bruise that spread across his midsection. "I'm sorry I couldn't check on you sooner. The doctors wouldn't let me in to see you, and then, as soon as my lieutenant knew I wasn't going to drop over dead on him, he hustled me back to Tyler."

"It's okay. I had plenty of other well-wishers." Every single Shatner had filed through the hospital room at least once. My mother had even driven over from Dallas to see me. I also had just about every high-ranking official stationed in East Texas stop by to question me about the case. My brother-in-law, who was acting as my legal counsel, kept most of the jackals at bay. But I still wound up answering the same questions for a number of different people.

Much to my embarrassment, I began to cry.

Hardy drew me against his uninjured side and rocked me back and forth. "Don't cry, Carrie. It's all right."

Hardy and I stood there with our arms wrapped around each other. Two days earlier, I was afraid that we were going to die together. It was nice to be alive.

"There he is!"

Grandma ran out of the VFW, followed by the rest of the Shatners, cutting off my alone time with Hardy. I yelled out a warning that Hardy was injured, saving him from being crushed. Grandma planted a kiss on each of Hardy's cheeks. Granddaddy pumped his hand and thanked him at least fifteen times for saving me. Hardy tried to explain that he hadn't actually saved my life at any point, but no one was listening.

After the rest of the family went through their own unique ways of thanking Hardy, the two of us were ushered inside and shoved up onto the small stage. The family wanted to hear all about what happened to us. Neither of us wanted to share our story. Besides, Hardy had an announcement to make. He'd invited the Palmers to the Shatner get-together.

My family didn't have much to say after that. They just stood around grumbling until the Palmers walked in a few minutes later. Oscar, Russell, and Toby were not with them. Russell and Toby were still in jail. My brother-in-law was doing his best, but it was clear that the Palmer brothers were going to be charged for killing Kyle. Oscar, who was found at the strip club, was still maintaining his innocence. He was telling everyone who would listen that he had no idea Kyle killed Amanda. He also denied that he sent two of his grandsons to help Kyle take care of the situation. He even swore up and down that he had no idea Toby and Russell killed Kyle or that he told Isaac Yates to get rid of the bodies. The good news was that no one believed Oscar.

"Y'all need to put the past in the past," Hardy announced once both families were packed into the VFW. "I'm not saying y'all need to be best friends. I'm sure I can speak for every law enforcement agency in the area when I say that we would prefer if you didn't combine your talents. But this feud has to stop. You've got to stop pranking each other and getting into fights."

Soon both families were mingling—tentatively, swapping fishing stories and recipes. The little kids all started playing together, setting a good example for the adults.

I wandered around the room, pleased to see that the Shatners and Palmers seemed to be getting along for the time being. But Hardy was right. A truce with some civility between the two families was a good thing. Becoming best friends was in no one's best interests.

It wasn't long before Whitney cornered me. If I thought she had looked haggard a few days ago, she looked ready for the grave today. Of course, knowing her younger brothers killed her husband couldn't be easy to live with.

"I just wanted to say I'm sorry for the way I acted," Whitney said. "I knew you and Kyle weren't really having an affair, but I was just so angry and upset with him."

"Why didn't you just leave him, Whitney?"

"Because I loved him. I really did."

"Did you know about your brothers?"

Whitney shook her head. "I knew something was up, but I didn't want to believe it. I'm not sure if I should thank them for saving me or hate them for what they did."

"Maybe a little of both." I patted Whitney on the arm and walked away.

As I wandered around the room, I ran into Hardy, who had been mingling with both families. He took me by the hand and guided me outside.

"There's something I need to tell you." Hardy leaned against the side of his truck and crossed his arms over his chest.

"Bad news?"

"I've been put on desk duty," Hardy said. "Indefinitely."

"Why?"

"I'm being investigated. My superiors don't think I followed protocol. But what has them really upset is this." Hardy opened the driver's side door of his truck and grabbed something off the front seat. He then handed me an envelope of photos. "One of the crime scene technicians found these on Chief Yates's computer. Seems he was following us."

I flipped through the photos that Yates had taken of me and Hardy at various points during the last few days. Taken out of context, I could see how they might be misconstrued. There were photos of Hardy and me sitting in the town square and at Baby Doll's Tavern. The one of Hardy pressing me against his truck and all-but kissing me was going to be hard to explain, but probably not as hard to explain as the ones of me outside Hardy's motel room. I hoped the photos didn't fall into the wrong hands. A scandal like that could easily kill Hardy's career as a Texas Ranger.

I shoved the photos back in the envelope and handed them to Hardy. "I can see why these would upset some people. But we're two consenting adults. And we didn't even do anything."

"At this point, I don't think that matters." Hardy chucked the envelope across the cab and onto the passenger seat. "I shouldn't be telling you this, but Chief Yates's house was full of evidence against your family. He had boxes full of information. It seems that he was holding back on the good stuff. I haven't seen any of it, but I've heard it's pretty damning. My lieutenant is talking about passing it on to the DEA and ATF."

Ever since I was a kid, I always knew this day would come. I'd really been dreading it since I joined the sheriff's department. "How much longer do you think my family has?"

Hardy shrugged and looked over my shoulder. "Hard to say. If anyone comes after y'all, it probably won't be for a while. They'd have to build a case and obtain more evidence first. That's if anyone takes Chief Yates's evidence seriously. As far as I'm concerned, everything he had in his possession is tainted since he tried to frame y'all for murder."

"I'm just glad the investigation is over and everything can go back to normal for now. I just want to forget this whole thing ever happened."

"Hold on there, Carrie." Hardy pulled me closer. "I'd like to think there's at least one thing you want to remember."

"What would that be?" I had a good idea what he was going to say.

"I'd like to think you'd want to remember me at least." Hardy tightened his grip. "You interested in going on a date?"

"You'd want to date me after all this? After what I did? What I put you through?" I'd hampered his investigation, annoyed him to no end, and I could have gotten him killed if I hadn't found the shotgun. Yates was right—Hardy was going to be a great Texas Ranger. He didn't need me or my family getting in the way of that.

"I'm either crazy about you, or just plain crazy." Hardy smiled, but it didn't quite reach his eyes. "Just give me an answer."

"Maybe it's not such a good idea. I don't want to cost you your job or anything." For the first time in a long time a man I was interested in was asking me out and I had to say no. Life could be so unfair at times.

I pulled away, spun around, and headed for the VFW. Let Hardy think what he wanted. At the door, I ran into Bubba, who came barreling out of the VFW.

"Whoa, there. I think you're headed in the wrong direction. The Ranger's back there."

"I know what I'm doing Bubba." I tried to push past him, but he sidestepped in front of me and refused to let me pass. "It's the right thing."

"Right for who? You? Him? The family?" Bubba put his hands on my shoulders and lowered his head until we were eye-to-eye. "Listen, Carrie, you did the one thing that everyone else in this family is afraid to do. You stood up to Grandpa Houston. If you hadn't done that, I never would have found the balls to tell him to go screw himself."

"You did what?" Bubba stood up to Houston? Why hadn't I heard of it yet? I'd have paid good money to see it.

I heard a car door slam and glanced over my shoulder towards the parking lot. Hardy was still leaning against his truck. Veda was parked a few spaces over from him. Bubba and I both waved at her.

"The right person only comes along once in our lives, Carrie. And that's if we get lucky. You can't just keep standing on the cliff. There comes a time when you have to jump."

"But when you jump, you fall."

"Oh, Carrie." Bubba pulled me into his arms and hugged me. "You don't always fall. Sometimes you fly."

I'd never heard Bubba speak so poetically before. Either Veda's love or standing up to Houston had a good influence on him.

"You took your life back, Carrie. Don't let my grandpa have it again."

Bubba took a few steps towards Veda before he broke into a run. She met him halfway and launched herself into his arms. After a nearly X-rated groping session, they jumped into Veda's car and sped off. I had a good feeling that those two were going to be all right.

Taking Bubba's advice, I shuffled back down the sidewalk. When I got closer to Hardy, he pushed away from his truck and took a step towards me.

"You said something about a date?"

Hardy slipped his arm around my waist and pulled me up against him. The kiss started off soft and tender, but quickly grew intense. Before I knew it, Hardy had me pressed against the side of his truck. I didn't think we were quite as explicit as Bubba and Veda, but I was sure we were close.

"Let's go back to your house."

I pulled back from Hardy. "I'm not that kind of woman."

"I know you're not." Hardy kissed me. "And that's not what I meant. I don't think either of us is up for an actual date, but we can sit around and talk."

"Oh. Then yeah, let's go back to my place."

Hardy was just about to kiss me again when his phone rang. "It's my lieutenant. I've got to take this."

The call was short, and the person on the other end did the majority of the talking. Hardy made a disgusted face when he hung up.

"They want me back in Tyler." Hardy shoved his phone back in his jacket pocket. "They told me to stay away from you—all of you—but that's not going to happen. I guess we'll have to wait until Saturday for our date. I've got the whole day planned out."

"Is that so?"

"Yep." Hardy pulled a set of faux fur-lined handcuffs out of his coat pocket and winked. "And, Carrie, next time you get it in your head to handcuff me to something ... make it worthwhile."

Randee Green's passion for reading began in grade school with *Little House in the Big Woods* by Laura Ingalls Wilder. She has a bachelor's degree in English Literature, as well as a Master's and an MFA in Creative Writing. When not writing, she's usually reading, indulging in her passion for Texas country music, traveling, or hanging out with her favorite feline friend, Mr. Snookums G. Cat.

For more information, go to www.randeegreen.com.

www.ingramcontent.com/pod-product-compliance
Lightning Source LLC
Chambersburg PA
CBHW010302100726
47904CB00011B/2711